Indiscreet

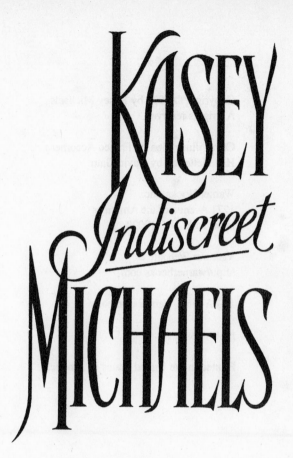

KASEY
Indiscreet
MICHAELS

WARNER BOOKS

A Time Warner Company

Cover illustration by Franco Accornero
Hand lettering by David Gatti

Warner Books, Inc.
1271 Avenue of the Americas
New York, NY 10020

Visit our Web site at
http://warnerbooks.com

Ⓦ A Time Warner Company

ISBN 1-56865-994-6

Printed in the United States of America

To Maggie Osborne, who lifts my heart;
to Jill Churchill, who teaches me how to be
grown-up;
to Jasmine Cresswell, who knows what
real life is;
and to Marianne Shock, who seeks my dreams
and takes them higher.

If we believe our logicians, man is distinguished from all other creatures by the faculty of laughter.
—Joseph Addison

Prologue

Once upon a time . . .

An apology for the Devil:
It must be remembered
that we have only heard
one side of the case.
God has written all the books.

—Samuel Butler

Nearer, my God, to thee,
Nearer to thee!
        —Sarah F. Adams

If there existed anything more stultifyingly dull than one of Lady Buxley's house parties, that gloomy event had not yet been invented. Being herded through drafty portrait halls to admire some deservedly deceased Buxley relatives, being forced to participate in pantomimes, and tame-stakes card parties drove Lady Buxley's guests to inventiveness. And the inventiveness of her guests, meant to alleviate their nearly mortal pain of boredom, was anything but ordinary.

Sir Harry had commandeered a prodigious collection of slim wooden toothpicks with high hopes of building a miniature Saint Paul's. He eventually settled on a less lofty aspiration, the finished project much more closely resembling the new King's stables at Brighton. Everyone admired the creation mightily anyway—so great was their boredom—until one of Lord Buxley's dratted hounds bounded into the morning room, batted his tail about like

Joshua's trumpet, and brought the toothpick walls tumbling down.

Lady Beechum had begun writing a wildly romantic novel peopled with beautiful maidens in dire peril and the handsome knights who rescued them. She spent a full afternoon scribbling notes for a tome that had a lot to do with her wishes and dreams, and very little to do with either her reflection in her mirror or the estimable, and quite abdominally expanded Lord Beechum.

Baron Bader had ferreted out a hidey-hole on the third floor, just behind the family chapel. He'd proceeded to outfit the small, windowless room with a table and chairs, candles, several decks of cards, and a goodly supply of port and cigars. He had then cleverly peopled this snug den with three fellow guests whose pockets were sufficiently deep as to be interested in playing for five times the tame stakes Lady Buxley insisted upon. Once all of this was done, the baron clapped a green-leather visor on his head, and announced around the cigar clamped in his teeth: "Stakes, gentlemen?"

Mr. Reginald Stokes had retired to his chamber on only the second day of the party, locked the door behind him, and fallen headfirst into a bottle. There he steadfastly remained for three days running. But then, Reggie had never possessed much of an imagination.

It fell to Lady Buxley's most esteemed guest—the coup her sister-in-law, the much hated Isobel, could not possibly hope to top—to His Grace himself, Cecil, Eighth Duke of Selbourne, to find his own amusement until the curst rain stopped and he could flee the house party.

His Grace also was not without invention. Oh my, no. And he had a particularly wonderful "invention" in mind.

Her name was Constance Winstead. The Widow Winstead. A small, beautifully rounded (especially in the heels) creature possessed of the brightest smile, the greatest wit, the most delicious disposition—and the most incredibly perfect pair of lush, fully rounded, rose-tipped breasts England had ever been privileged to see. And, if Dame Rumor could be believed, a whacking great lot of England had enjoyed that privilege.

As Constance had been heard to say, widowhood did not, in her opinion, constitute a sentence of celibacy. With a love for her fellowman that, in some quarters, might be considered taken to extremes, Constance had been wooed by and bedded by a great variety of gentlemen. Indeed, her lovers had ranged from scions of the great houses to the powerful in His Royal Majesty's government—and everyone in between.

These gentlemen all shared two things in common: their attraction to Constance and healthy fortunes. The former was a given—every man with eyes in his head and a beating heart was attracted to Constance. The latter was of importance to Constance, who had found that amassing jewels, houses, fine furniture, and a comfortable income from the Exchange were the most potent aphrodisiac of them all.

That is not to say that Constance Winstead's liaisons were motivated by greed. Oh, no. She had a warm, giving, possibly too-trusting heart, and had genuinely adored every last one of her lovers. But, of them all, Cecil had most invaded her heart; so much so that she had been steadfast to him for three long years, their association now having outlasted that of Constance's with her late husband, Godfrey. The pair had become as close to inseparable as Society allowed, which meant that they were often seen together at Covent Garden and Vauxhall. It also meant that Lady Buxley would have no more included the Widow Winstead in her list of houseguests than she would have clutched a canary feather in each bejeweled paw and attempted to fly from the parapets.

Which brings us back to Lady Buxley's ongoing house party and His Grace's inventive turn of mind. . . .

Leaving his wife behind in the music room while Lord Buxley sang off-key and the resurfaced but still three-parts castaway Mr. Reginald Stokes whimpered in a corner, His Grace bounded light-footedly up the two flights of stairs that took him to his bedchamber.

"Rain's stopped, has it, Reese?" His Grace asked his valet jovially, already stripping off his cravat as he peered hopefully toward the pair of French doors that led onto the narrow balcony outside his chamber. "Good. Good. Now take yourself off, and don't come back." He winked, sure his man understood. "I'll fend for m'self, if you take my meaning?"

Reese moved to assist his master in removing his jacket. "Muggy night, Your Grace," he said. "I should imagine you'll want the doors opened, as is your custom? I can return later and take care of all the particulars. You have the headache, Your Grace? Is that why you're retiring so early? I can mix you up some laudanum, Your Grace, if that's—"

The duke turned and heavily laid his hands on the conscientious valet's shoulders. "Reese," he intoned solemnly, "you're a good man. You're even a fine man. A veritable treasure. I'm blessed to have you, truly I am. But if you don't go away right now, and much as it would pain me, I'm going to have to strangle you where you stand."

His eyes wide in his head, Reese backed halfway out of the room, turned, and ran like a rabbit.

His Grace checked the time on the mantel clock against that of his pocket watch, then stripped out of his shirt and slipped his arms into a maroon silk banyan, tying the robe tightly at his still trim waist. He paused in front of a cheval glass to inspect his appearance, satisfied to see that he still looked quite dashing, even as he yearly nudged closer to sixty than he cared to remember.

And then he smiled, and smartly saluted his reflection. It was time.

Going to the burled cabinet in the corner, he withdrew a most fantastic invention he'd paid a stable hand handsomely to fashion for him—a compilation of two tremendous lengths of stout rope with a wide, leather strip tied midway between the two ends. When these rope ends were secured to the stone balcony and the contraption lowered over the balcony railing, it hung nearly down to the ground, greatly resembling a country swing.

Which was exactly Constance's observation when she came creeping out of the bushes. Sitting her diminutive, perfect, pocket-Venus body on the wide leather strap, she declared, "Oh, Cesse, a swing! How very clever of you! How very much I adore you!"

"Yes, it is clever, my little dove, and I adore you as well," he responded, groaning a bit as Constance's slight weight tugged at his arms. "But softly, my dove, softly. It wouldn't do to have the whole household down on us."

She peered up at him from a distance of thirty or more feet. At the moment, it looked to be closer to sixty feet to His Grace, who had once thought this such a jolly, smashing idea but who was now having second thoughts. Her smiling face was caught by moonlight, and he watched in dismay as she gave her legs a small kick, setting the rope to swinging. "Lift me up, my sweet knight, and I will whisper most discreetly in your ear. Amongst other pleasantries I've been contemplating whilst cowering in yon bushes. None of them at all discreet, may I add."

"For the love of Heaven, Connie," he warned in a whispered shout—not an easy accomplishment, especially when one was doing one's best to conserve one's breath. "This ain't a country fair and I ain't a twenty-year-old buck. Have a care with that swinging or we'll both be in the basket."

"La, Sir Knight, do not say you are not up to the adventure," Constance chided. Smiling at him, she lay back until she was nearly horizontal, her hands tight on the rope as he slowly, jerkily, began reeling her in like a prize fish. "You who are always *up* to any adventure."

If Constance insisted upon acting the silly miss on a swing hanging from a mighty oak branch, she was bound to be in for a major disappointment. Although he had securely tied both ends of the rope to the balcony, it was now left to His Grace to do the actual *tugging* on the rope so that his lady love could be hoisted to the balcony. His plan was to grab on to each rope a foot or two below the knots, and yank on them as he walked backward, sliding his sweet Connie closer to the balcony with each step he took away from it—that's what he would do.

Which was a fine idea. In theory. In practice, the maneuver was bringing a sheen of perspiration to the duke's brow and a burning pain in his shoulders and arms.

"I'm warning you, Connie—" he said as her musical giggles reached him. Finally, she seemed to understand the seriousness of the affair and sat up, sat very still, awaiting his next move. The duke breathed a silent sigh of relief, then took another deep breath and began walking backward, the ropes wrapped twice around his forearms and held tight in his fists. He staggered across the balcony and into the bedchamber. He backed, slower and slower, across the Aubusson carpet, twice nearly losing his footing.

He pulled and he cursed, and he cursed and he pulled until, at last, just as the back of his knees made contact with the edge of the bed, the dragging weight on the other end of the rope vanished and he went flying backward onto the mattress.

"We did it, we did it, we *did* it!" Constance trilled a moment later, landing on top of him on the bed. "Oh, Cesse! I love you so much! And I'm so proud of you! Of course, I was also quite wonderful—climbing over the balcony rail all by myself, to become Lady Buxley's most unexpected guest."

She pushed at the lapels of his banyan, raining down kisses on his bare, and still wildly heaving chest. "How long may I stay? Will you keep me in a cupboard, dear Cesse? Will you feed me scraps you've pilfered from the dinner table? I've brought no clothing, thinking it difficult enough for my dear knight to heft this shameless baggage to the balcony without bringing a stuffed hatbox along on the trip. But it is of no concern to me. I shall wear your banyan over my nakedness, rolling up the sleeves a thousand times, and look most adorable as I sit in my corner, nibbling stale crusts. Oh, Cesse!" she exclaimed, rubbing herself against him. "Let's make love on that adorable balcony! *Our* balcony. We haven't done anything silly in far too long. The stars are bright, and the moon is full—shining down on the wet flagstones after this horrible day of rain."

"Make—make love on the balcony?" His Grace gasped out, for what air that had remained in his lungs after his exertions had been crushed from his body by Constance's enthusiastic greeting. His ears were ringing, a few stars were circling just above his head, and he had the nagging suspicion he was no longer quite as young and hearty as he believed himself to be. "But, Connie—sweet love, little princess—just think about it a moment. We're already in bed. So much more convenient this way, don't you agree?"

"Oh, *pooh* on this silly bed!" she exclaimed, pushing the banyan off his shoulders and then swiftly going to work on the buttons of his breeches. "I want to make love in the moonlight, Cesse. Do you remember the night we frolicked outside that lovely inn near Epson? We rolled over and over in the grass like children—"

"We damn near rolled into a curst cesspit, the pair of us, mad fools that we are," His Grace put in, wincing at the memory. Then he brightened, smiling up at the canopy over the bed. "Although I will admit I enjoyed sneaking about in the Tower last spring while m'wife wandered off to admire some stupid statuary. I backed you up against the cold stone walls almost under one of the Guard's noses and hoisted up your skirts, remember? And you wrapped your legs around me, and then I . . ." He gave a small shiver as the last button of his breeches released and Constance freed him. "What was that you were saying about the balcony?"

She slipped from the bed and untied the strings at the throat of her black silk evening cloak. "Look, my darling!" she commanded, throwing open the cloak to reveal her perfectly nude, perfectly perfect body. Those more than perfect breasts. The woman hadn't an ounce of shame in her, Lord love her, and no reason for any, now that Cecil considered the thing.

He lifted his head a little higher off the mattress and looked down the length of his body at her, even as his traitorous body remained prone, his legs draped over the edge of the bed, feeling numb from their exertion. But, saints be praised, one part of his anatomy had not been rendered exhausted by his small adventure, and immediately sprang to attention. He wasn't sixty *yet*, by God!

"Oh, Cesse, how I do love you!" Constance giggled. "I knew you were *up* for anything!" She bent and gave his lower belly a quick, nipping kiss, then bounded for the narrow balcony, her bare buttocks catching the glow from the moon as she turned to drape her cloak over the wide stone railing.

"I'm going to Hell for what I'm thinking, what I'm doing, what I've done," His Grace muttered under his breath as he pushed himself up onto his elbows. "But I don't regret a moment of it either, by damn!"

"Come, come, my darling," Constance called to him as she daringly seated herself on the cloak and opened her legs to him, twining her lower legs behind two of the fat stone balustrades. She braced her palms against the railing on each side of her as she sat, looking as if suspended in air above the black as night cloak.

Her head was thrown back in an expression of freedom, her perfect breasts glowing alabaster white in the moonlight, like twin beacons guiding him into harbor. "Let us be free and wild, Cesse, like mad creatures of the night!" She lifted her arms for a moment, daring the laws of balance, of gravity. *Sir Isaac Newton*, the duke thought randomly, *would have been amazed, dumbfounded.* Why, the learned fellow would have taken a single look at Constance and promptly forgotten to write down his stupid theories (and been a happier man for it).

"Connie! Be careful!"

"Careful? Oh, *that's* no fun, darling! Look! Look at me, Cesse—I'm all but flying!"

Now, Cecil might have been tired. He might have thought a small nap in order, or at least a few minutes spent chatting over glasses of wine before they moved on to more carnal pursuits. But Cecil was also a man. A man with wants, a man with needs. A man very seriously in love for the first time in his life. A man who had been without his woman for five long and lonely nights.

His Grace's evening slippers went flying—one hither, one yon. His feet hit the floor. The banyan followed. He let out a long, low growl. With his breeches dragging at his ankles until he could kick free of them, Cecil Seaton, Eighth Duke of Selbourne, went to his woman. Tall. Strong. Proud.

And randy as hell.

He slammed the balcony doors behind him as he stepped out onto the narrow span, sealing the pair of them off from the world, and, as an old army man, spared himself a moment to consider the logistics of the thing. The cold stone against his stockinged feet had brought him back to sanity—or as close as he could come to that state with Constance perched straight in front of him, naked as a jaybird. "God's teeth, Connie. It's too narrow out here for any real sport. If I take more than two steps backward, I'll be hitting my rump against those damn doors. Can't we go inside?"

"What? My knight stumbles just as he brings himself to the *sticking* point?" Constance pouted prettily. "It was such fun being hoisted up here in my swing, Cesse," she said. "Just like those acrobats I've seen flying through the air. Why, I feel quite young again. You will, too, darling, I'm sure of it. Please don't make us go inside to anything so mundane as a *bed.*"

"You render a man insane, Connie," he said, sighing as she slowly rolled her head from side to side, the tip of her small pink tongue drawing a moist circle along her lips.

She laughed low in her throat as she reached out her arms to him, balancing precariously above the ground. "Come and get me, darling. Let us fly free as the birds."

He came and got her.

Five minutes later Reese—the Compleat Valet, who knew his master preferred to sleep with the night air blowing across his body, no matter what the man might say to the contrary—tippy-toed into the duke's darkened bedchamber. Still moving quietly, so as not to wake His Grace, he crossed the floor and pushed open the doors to the balcony, giving them an extra shove when his action unexpectedly met with resistance.

Lady Buxley had never given such a famous, talked-about house party. Her sister-in-law, Isobel, was later rumored to have been quite crushed by the woman's coup.

In fact, in the end, Lady Buxley's house party was acknowledged by one and all as the most exciting of the season.

Book One

Oh, no!
Never say twice!

I am past thirty,
and three parts iced over.

—Matthew Arnold

Oh! no! we never mention her,
Her name is never heard;
My lips are now forbid to speak
That once familiar word.
      —Thomas Haynes Bayly

Chapter One

"Don't say her name, Nephew," Lady Gwendolyn Seaton declared with some heat, clapping her hands over her ears as she sat in the drawing room of the Portland Square mansion. "Don't ever say her name!" She then lowered her hands and looked at her nephew owlishly. "You did say Constance Winstead, didn't you? Oh, you did. You *did*! Oh, the horror!"

Bramwell Seaton, Ninth Duke of Selbourne, crossed one elegantly clad leg over the other as he sat back in his chair and looked at his aunt. "Now I remember why I chose not to tell you about any of this until this morning, when I could put it off no longer. Please don't fly up into the boughs, Aunt, for it will get us nowhere."

The duke watched in some sympathy as the old woman visibly attempted to rein in her overset emotions. He loved his Aunt Gwendolyn dearly, which was a good thing, as he had inherited his father's spinster sister along with his title and fortune.

Although he really did rather wish she'd stop "admiring" things. That was Lady Gwendolyn's word for what less generous persons might call stealing, the habit she had of picking up anything that took her interest—and carrying it home with her. It had taken the duke a while to realize what was happening, to understand it. But he now found himself dutifully spending the morning after any party visiting his hostess of the previous evening and surreptitiously putting back decorative seashells and crystal paperweights and—just the once—a half dozen silver teaspoons discovered in his aunt's reticule.

The duke knew little of any of his family, when you got right down to it. He had spent his youth in the country while his parents spent their time in town. Upon reaching adulthood, he went off to sea—mostly to pique his father, who had chosen the more prestigious Horse Guards in his salad days. In fact, Bramwell had only met his aunt a single time before leaving his commission in the Royal Navy to come home and claim his title after his father had done his damnedest to tarnish the family name straight into the next century.

While his aunt sniffled and shivered, obviously still somewhat overcome by what he'd been saying to her, His Grace glanced up at the portrait over the mantelpiece, looking, as it were, straight into his own eyes. His father also had been a tall man, his eyes the same piercing blue as Bramwell's, his hair the same warm brown. In fact, except for the changing fashions since the portrait had been commissioned, and the lack of a similarly mischievous glint around Bramwell's eyes, the two men could have been cut from the very same bolt of cloth.

It was almost spooky, that's what it was.

The current duke thanked his lucky stars he was *not* like his father. He thanked God that he was more sober, much more serious, conscientious, and never so scandalous. Only occasionally did he admit to himself that just once— just once—it might be fun to feel some of the same love and lust for life his father had enjoyed up until, and probably including, his last moments on earth.

"Bramwell?" his aunt inquired, tilting her head as she looked at him in some agitation. "You're being unusually quiet. Does that mean we've finished talking, or just that you hate speaking about this as much as I?"

He looked at his father's portrait once more, then shook his head, clearing it. "Forgive me, Aunt. I was only considering your plea, and searching my brain for some alternative. Unfortunately, I have found none. We probably have to air our dirty linen just this one last time, and just between ourselves, before we face the day. Now, what shall we call her? I can think of several names, none of which I believe proper for delicate female ears. Would you care to pick one?"

Lady Gwendolyn took a deep breath and blew it out through her faintly pudgy nostrils. "Well, I'm sure I most certainly wouldn't know any of *those*, Nephew. To make my lips form *the late Widow Winstead* makes my flesh crawl. And to call her Constance? Oh, no, no, no! That means *constant*, you know, which just goes to prove that there are more misnamed people in this world than one might suppose."

His Grace shrugged, not really much caring what they called the woman, as long as they could discuss her, then forget her forever. "I'm not so sure the creature was misnamed. After all, she was *constantly* in trouble. *Constantly* in the way, *constantly* at my father's side. Right up until the end, as it were."

"Bramwell! It's not like you to be facetious." Lady Gwendolyn rolled her eyes. "Oh, the shame of it. I remember the whole thing as if it were yesterday, and not three years past. The loud thump outside the music-room doors as they tumbled off the balcony while in a state of, a state of—Bram? What is that called?"

"I believe the term you're searching for, Aunt, is *in flagrante delicto*, or caught in the act." A rare smile played about the duke's mouth. "United in death might be a nicer term, until one remembers that they were both jaybird naked at the time."

"Don't remind me! I can still see myself seated beside Lady Buxley, never knowing tragedy was about to strike. I can still hear the terrified shout from Reese as he opened the doors to the balcony and mistakenly sent the pair of them tumbling over the railing. The poor man has never been the same since; it was so good of you to keep him on as your own valet. And then there was that drunken Mr. Reginald Stokes throwing open the doors to the patio and all but falling on the bodies. Our first sight of that tangle of black silk and arms and legs. *Bare* arms and legs. Your mother's truly bizarre reaction—I still cannot believe that dear, quiet woman actually walked up to my poor brother's body and *kicked* him. *Twice!*"

Bramwell suppressed another small smile that was rising, unbidden, to his lips. He must be an unnatural son, to be rather enjoying all of this rehashing of what had come to be commonly spoken of as "His Grace's Tumble from Grace"—the word *tumble* always being given extra emphasis, of course.

Because the ninth duke was a sober man, past thirty, and not easily amused. The farces at Covent Garden rarely brought so much as the ghost of a smile to his lips. Unlike his father (or because of him), he was known for his calm and steady disposition. He was respected, admired, and would never think to do anything foolhardy or impulsive just for the lark of it. He kept his wit for his closest, most trusted friends, and it was a dry wit, one that did not lend itself to open displays of hilarity.

And he certainly never would have made love to his mistress on the balcony of Lady Buxley's country house while the remainder of the guests were just below them, in the music room.

Oh, no. There was not the faintest hint of recklessness or buffoonery—or, Heaven forbid, scandal—about the ninth duke of Selbourne.

And yet now, all of his carefully nurtured sobriety to one side, this talk of the eighth duke and the Widow Winstead was all but threatening to reduce him to a round of hearty knee-slapping and embarrassing guffaws.

"Yes, Aunt," Bramwell said now, his tongue smarting where he had bitten it to hold back a chuckle. "I can't imagine why my mother did that. After all, her husband only had been all but openly living with the lady we cannot mention by name for years, with not a care for her feelings in the matter. And then, to get on with the story, once my mother had decided to faint, Mr. Stokes, or so I've heard it told, swayed drunkenly where he stood, looked down at the lady we cannot name and said, 'Damme if those ain't the best-looking breasts in all of England, just like good old Cecil always said,' " His Grace ended for his aunt, who had lifted her handkerchief to wipe at her eyes, obviously too distraught to go on.

"*Yes!* Yes, that's precisely how it happened!" Lady Gwendolyn fairly leapt to her feet, frantically waving her hands as if to erase her nephew's words from the air. He quickly stood as well, being a polite sort, a gentleman raised by the very best of nurses and tutors. But he wished the woman would stop flitting from place to place. He'd had a late night, most of it spent in his study, drinking away his sorrows, and his head wasn't quite on straight this morning.

"Oh, the humiliation!" his aunt exclaimed, now wringing her hands. At least she was keeping them where he could see them, which he should consider a blessing. "Thank goodness we had to retire to the country and go into mourning, for I knew I couldn't show my face in Society again. Not after that! Well, it killed your mother, Bramwell. Simply killed her."

His Grace lifted one finely sculpted eyebrow as his aunt went to stand in front of a small table weighed down with *objets d'art* he'd been told had been his mother's pride and joy. "Mother died after eating bad fish while on holiday in Hampshire with *her* lover, Aunt. I scarcely see how the deaths are related. Unless, of course, you think the nameless hussy managed to come back to life as a spoiled carp, and with the express purpose of murdering her paramour's widow."

"Oh, this isn't getting us anywhere!" Lady Gwendolyn exclaimed, turning around quickly, but not before the duke saw her slip a small china shepherdess into the pocket of her gown. He'd have to remind himself to have Peggy retrieve it later. "I just don't see why you should have to bring that woman's child *Out*. It's inhuman, that's what it is. And it will bring back all the old gossip. I shan't be able to show my face."

"I'll explain it again, Aunt," Bramwell offered wearily, motioning for her to retake her seat, then gratefully sitting himself down again as well. "The woman whose name we cannot mention and my father were lovers for almost four years, whether we like it or not. The Wid—the *Woman*—was far from a penniless widow. Far from it. But she put a great deal of dependence on my father's financial advice. And, while she didn't see fit to name him as her daughter's guardian—a blessing for which I go down on my knees nightly, as that duty would have fallen to me upon his death—she did make him promise to bring the girl Out, present her at Court if possible, get her a voucher for Almack's, etc."

Aunt Gwendolyn sniffed rather indelicately. "She could have done those things herself, had she lived. After all, the child is legitimate enough." She leaned forward, her cheeks pale. "Dear Lord! She is legitimate, Nephew, isn't she?"

"Oh, there's no doubt of that. The child is Godfrey Winstead's, and her lineage quite impeccable if not overly impressive. Her mother's reputation, however, was and is not the sort that would do her daughter any good, no matter how much of a dowry there might be—and I understand it is considerable. Mistressing, if done right, seems to pay very well, in case you ever decide to take up the trade."

"Nephew, please!"

"I'm sorry. I believe I'm still a little overcome, even though my solicitor first showed me the papers more than a fortnight ago, and apprised me of my responsibilities in the matter. Now, to continue. Her mother being either alive or quite dead, the daughter needed a suitable sponsor. Someone unimpeachable, someone with a great deal of social power even if he was a bit of a loose screw. In short, a person like my father."

"Hrruumph!" Lady Gwendolyn snorted, obviously not feeling quite in charity with her late brother at the moment.

"Yes, well," Bramwell said, liking his aunt very much. "So, while this woman, this Edith Farraday, is the child's guardian, it is left to me, as my father's heir, to live up to his agreement—his *written*, legally witnessed agreement, I might add—to sponsor the daughter for the Season. The woman may have had round heels, but she was crafty. She knew a duke would give her daughter an *entrée* into Society that she and her sorry reputation never could. Also, as my solicitor has reminded me, it would be an insult to my father's memory to renege on his written promise."

"No one could insult Cecil's memory more than he did by rolling off Lady Buxley's balcony while stuck to that horrid woman," Lady Gwendolyn said with another sniff. But she then straightened her shoulders like a good soldier, obviously remembering that she was a lady. "Well, I suppose there is nothing else for it then, is there? The die is cast, the deed is done, and we shall have to pay the consequences. The girl arrives this afternoon, is that right?"

"Just after luncheon, if I've calculated the drive in from Wimbledon correctly. I've already ordered bedchambers prepared for both the girl and Mrs. Farraday."

"Do you think she's much like her mother? You never saw the woman, did you—being away at sea while your father was running amuck. What if she resembles the mother, in face, in manner? What will we do then? Perhaps you know of some armorer who can fashion a chastity belt for the chit? Unless she's fat as a house, of course, or homely as a stump, or has one of those strange gaps between her front teeth and whistles when she speaks. You silly gentlemen look only for outer beauty, you know, never caring a whit about what's *inside*. However, that being the case, if she is anything like the mother, Nephew, I fear we are in for a siege. Have you prepared dear Isadora?"

"Isadora? Why, of course I have, Aunt," Bramwell said, noticing that his neckcloth had grown rather annoyingly tight at the mention of his fiancée's name. "She's being the best of good sports about the whole unpleasant situation, and even offered to help me outfit the child and prepare her for the Season. Her name is Sophie, by the way. Sophie Winstead."

"Sophie," Aunt Gwendolyn repeated, rolling the name around her mouth, over her tongue. "I rather like that. But I won't like her, Nephew. Not one little bit. I've already made up my mind to that!"

The girl entered the foyer just as Bramwell was passing through on his way to—well, he had to have been going somewhere, undoubtedly to do something at least vaguely important. Not that he could remember his destination now, as he stood stock still and stared at her, his brain turned to jelly.

Her nose was small, pert.

Her eyes, below well-defined, arched brows, were a winsome brown, childlike in their innocence, engaging in their brightness, intriguing in their tip-tilted outer corners and lush, thick black lashes. And enchantingly, bewitchingly wicked when she smiled.

She was smiling now.

There was a single, small brown mole, a beauty mark many would say, perched just at the upper curve of her right cheekbone. A man could spend a week worshiping that beauty mark—a lifetime.

Bramwell sucked in a breath and realized that the girl was enveloped in the mingled, tantalizing scents of spring, and sunshine, and fresh air, and, faintly, of freshly sliced lemons. His gut involuntarily tightened as he silently called himself several extraordinarily unflattering kinds of a fool.

But he didn't stop looking, making his inventory. He couldn't. No more than he could will himself not to breathe in yet another sweet, tantalizing wave of spring and fresh lemons.

She wore her amazingly abundant golden brown hair simply, in a center part, and it hung to her shoulders in a soft fall of row after row, layer after layer of silky corkscrew waves only Mother Nature could have created. Lush. Barely tamed. Innocent and yet decadent. Eminently touchable.

Oh, Christ, sweet Christ. To touch that hair! To touch it, feel its warmth between one's fingers, bury one's face in it, to beg for any small favor, and be damned!

Bramwell swallowed down hard on what had to be his mounting madness, then watched as she raised a hand to her face, to push a long, errant ringlet away from her eye. Her cuff fell back to reveal a delightfully molded forearm below an artistically small-boned hand and long, slim fingers topped by strong, white-tipped nails.

No flaw. No flaw. The woman was perfect. But how? Nobody was perfect. And surely not this woman of all women.

A footman stepped forward sprightly, grinning from ear to ear, and relieved her of her cloak, revealing the rest of her.

Bramwell gave a small cough, sure something had lodged in his throat.

He'd been right, if mad, to believe his own eyes, his instincts. There *was* no flaw. Everything about her was perfect, if somewhat in miniature. Rounded, but not running to fat. Lush, while never coming within a thousand miles of overblown. From the top of her naturally curling hair to the slim span of her waist, to the soft flare of her hips and all the way to the tips of her small shoes, she stood not much higher than five feet. Five feet and approximately two inches of glorious perfection.

All this Bramwell could see.

One could only imagine the perfection of her breasts, then weep.

Or take refuge in icy disdain, a smidgen of arrogance, and perhaps even a dollop of stiff-backed pride.

The ninth duke of Selbourne, at last locating whatever tattered shreds remained of his senses, opted for the latter, and remained poker-straight and silent. Although one also could, if one were of a delicious bent of humor and of a mind to contradict the man, say Bramwell Seaton had been rendered dumbstruck.

If there was a God, and Bramwell sincerely prayed there was, the apparition standing in front of him, clad in a dark blue traveling gown—and carrying some large something covered with a paisley shawl—would open her mouth to speak and croak like a frog. Or screech like an owl. Or drop her H's. Or do something, *anything*, to make him stop thinking that he'd just had his first glimpse of Heaven when he knew full well he'd just been dropped headfirst into Hell.

"Well, hello there," the apparition said, just as he was about to say something hopefully crushing. Her voice came to him with the sweetness of honey, the lilt of a song-bird, and the faint, confusing, and quite annoyingly adorable trace of a French accent. "You must be the duke, mustn't you? Yes, of course you are. You look very much like Uncle Cesse, or will, when you grow older and less sober. I suppose I should curtsy to you now, yes? Will you please hold Ignatius for me? I'm not quite so polished in my curtsies as dear Mrs. Farraday would like, and would hate to make a cake of myself so early in our acquaintance. I'm Sophie, by the way. Although I suppose you already know that."

All right. So he hadn't gotten the first words in; she had beaten him to it. But surely there were a lot of things the worldly, urbane ninth duke of Selbourne could say now in answer to this breathless, entirely enchanting little speech.

He'd be damned if he could think of a single one.

Maybe later, when he could get his tongue unstuck from the roof of his mouth.

He settled now for a single, strangled, "Ignatius?"

Sophie Winstead smiled again. Her nose, Bramwell noticed, crinkled up rather adorably when she smiled. Did it have to do that? "Yes, Ignatius. My parrot, of course. Oh, dear. You don't mind, do you? Mrs. Farraday said I should leave him behind in Wimbledon, but I just couldn't. We're very close, you understand. Ignatius and I, I mean—although I'm also quite devoted to dear Mrs. Farraday, who is still snoring most soundly in our coach. She's rather deaf, you understand, poor dear, and it will take Desiree— she's my maid—a few more shouts and nudges to rouse her."

She smiled again, tipping her head to one side. "You don't say much, do you? As I remember it, Uncle Cesse could talk the limb off a tree. Perhaps you're not feeling well, yes? Shall we dispense with curtsies and the like and just go upstairs to the drawing room? I'll pour you a drink, find you a nice footstool, and you can rest. Yes, that's what we'll do. Mrs. Farraday can just follow after as best she can. Now, come along. Sophie will fix everything. You'll see."

Pour him a drink? Fetch him a footstool? What on earth was she talking about? The duke's stomach dropped to his toes. Good God! There was no other explanation—the chit obviously had been raised to be a gentleman's *mistress*! Before Bramwell could unstick that startling thought from his brain and form an answer, Sophie had lifted the hem of her traveling gown a bare inch and, still clutching the shawl-covered birdcage, gone lightly tripping up the curving staircase.

Bramwell glared at the footman, who quickly slid his gaze from Sophie's derriere and lost his admiring leer. The duke then found himself following along after his father's mistress's daughter, muttering under his breath: "Uncle *Ces-ee?* Oh, Father, how *could* you!"

Secret thoughts and open countenance . . .
—Scipione Alberti

Chapter Two

Sophie gritted her teeth, smiled prettily, and turned from the drinks table, a glass of Madeira in her hand. "There you are, Your Grace! See? I've found the wine, just as I was sure I would. Now, you just sit down right over there, rest your feet on that footstool, and I'll see to Ignatius for a moment, if you don't mind. He's a most sociable creature, and isn't accustomed to being shuttered during the day."

The duke took the glass she offered—had she left him any choice?—but remained standing. Obviously he was doing his best to pretend that she was a lady, and not the daughter of the notorious Constance Winstead. Sophie shrugged and didn't insist. If he wanted to stand until she had seated herself, it was his prerogative. However, if he wanted to stand until Hell froze over and the Devil went ice-skating, well, then she'd just have to make him see the error of his ways. As long as he ended by sitting down, and believing that taking his seat had been his own idea.

She would do whatever made the man happy, or made him think he was happy. That's what her mama had always said. And her mother had always made it a point to keep her men happy. All of her men. So many, many men. For years, Sophie had thought herself to be the luckiest of children—having so many doting uncles.

Until she realized that, although her uncles numbered in the dozens, she strangely had never met any aunts or cousins.

That's when Desiree had taken her aside and explained the ways of the world to her—something her mama never would have done, preferring her daughter to be innocent of such things. But Desiree had "lived the life," as she called it, before fleeing Paris in 1804 with her latest protector, who had made the mistake of backing the hapless duc d'Enghien in his plot against Napoleon. When that man had tossed her over a few years later for no other than Constance Winstead, Desiree had come to Wimbledon bent on a hair-pulling match, and ended by becoming Constance's sometimes lady's maid and boon companion, an arrangement that had suited them both.

The gentleman in question, however happy at first, had not found this arrangement quite so pleasing when he learned Desiree was now officially *out* of the life (Lord only knew what naughty ideas that man had harbored in his head!). He soon dejectedly departed for friendlier climes with both an English and Gallic flea in his ear, leaving behind him two giggling ladies much in charity with each other.

Desiree had immediately thrown off her stays, indulged

her love of French pastry, and taken the then still-quite-young Sophie under her motherly wing.

Firstly, lastly, and probably eternally—it was Desiree who had tried and failed, and tried and failed again, to break Sophie of her one seemingly insurmountable fault: her rather volatile temper. If the maid had not succeeded in banishing that temper over the years, she had at least brought Sophie to the point of recognizing her failing, and for the most part successfully curbing it, twisting it, turning it, using it to her advantage.

Which was not the same as saying that the grown Sophie now had the disposition of a cute, cuddly kitten. Unless one was speaking of cute, cuddly young *tigers*, who could just as easily lick your hand or nip off your nose, depending on their mood. As Desiree had been heard to mutter more than once as she tried to console herself, if the little tiger had not changed her stripes, at least she had over the years learned how better to hide them from view.

It also had been Desiree who had carefully explained a man's needs when Constance had done with her lessons on a man's wants. It had been Desiree who had helped school the young Sophie in her lessons, which explained the young woman's hint of a French accent. It had been Desiree who had hidden Sophie from the worst of her mother's life, and allowed her a peek or two at the best of it.

And it had been Desiree who had held a sobbing Sophie when the heartbreaking news came that her beloved, scatterbrained mother and her dear, sweet Uncle Cesse had unexpectedly perished in a tragic carriage accident.

It had been the resourceful Desiree who had so cleverly written the letter concerning Sophie's come-out, forged the various signatures that made it all look so wonderfully important and legal. A highly enjoyable round of slap and tickle with the local solicitor—coming out of retirement for the sake of her beloved Sophie, and just to see if she could still do it—had secured all the proper stamps and seals that cemented the legitimacy of the letter then forwarded to the ninth duke.

It had been the endlessly enterprising Desiree who had hired the nearly stone-deaf and perfectly oblivious Mrs. Edith Farraday. She had proclaimed the woman to be Sophie's legal guardian, then cast herself in the role of Sophie's maid.

And then, with all of this so neatly accomplished, she had proceeded just today to set them on the path that led to the front door of Uncle Cesse's son. Sophie sneaked another peek at the ninth duke, the insufferably priggish man just now standing in front of the mantel, an untouched glass of Madeira in his hand. Did he think she had slipped a love potion into it, one meant to have him at her feet in an instant, her willing slave?

Men were so silly. And so transparent. But lovable enough just the same. Rather like puppies, her mother had told Sophie; friendly, and eager to please, willing to play fetch and carry, even to roll over and do tricks to amuse you. Except that pug dogs, according to Desiree, didn't lie to you to get what they wanted, use you, and then toss you over without a blink.

And so this was how Sophie Winstead had grown to young womanhood, filled to the brim with her mother's romantic notions, well schooled in what it took to woo and win a man, but also firmly grounded in her practical French friend's caveats. And with a temper that kept her interesting.

With her anger on simmer and her smile still firmly fixed, Sophie crossed to the table where she had set the birdcage—knowing the duke's gaze was riveted to her every graceful, gliding step. She whipped the paisley shawl from the cage with a flourish, awakening the sleeping Ignatius.

"Good afternoon, Ignatius," she cooed, bending forward slightly, putting her face close to the cage. "I trust you've had a pleasant nap. Did you enjoy your trip in the coach, or was the ride too bumpy for you?"

The bird lifted its yellow head from beneath one bright green wing and blinked. It then fanned out its blue, green, and scarlet tail feathers, swiveled its head about to quickly inspect its new surroundings, and protested in deep, guttural tones, "Demmed coachie! *Squawk!* Quick! My flask! Secrets to tell! *Squawk! Squawk!* Demned coachie! Secrets to sell! Quick, my flask! *Squawk!*"

Sophie bit her tongue to keep from laughing, knowing the word *coach* was always followed by this particular answer from Ignatius. "Oh, naughty bird! Sophie's very angry with you," she exclaimed, wagging a finger at Ignatius so that his head bobbed and weaved, following her every movement.

"Sophie loves you! Sophie loves you!" Ignatius shrilled in a higher voice, much like Sophie's own, pushing his head against the bars until she reached in two fingers and stroked his feathery head. "Sophie loves you! *Squawk!*"

"No, no, no, Ignatius," she corrected. "It's Sophie loves *me*. Sweet, silly, *literal* bird!" She turned her back on the parrot and smiled sunnily at the duke. "You'll have to excuse Ignatius, Your Grace. He is quite the mimic, and repeats nearly everything. Why, just now he sounded just like Uncle Tye, didn't he—and then just like me. Isn't that precious? He's *such* a clever bird."

"Uncle Tye?" the ninth duke repeated, looking past her, at the birdcage.

"Yes," Sophie said, pleased but not surprised that he'd taken the bait she had so carefully offered. "Sir Tyler Shipley. Do you know him?"

"Sir Tyler is your *uncle*? Sir Tyler Shipley, of His Majesty's government?"

Sophie knew her smile wrinkled up her nose. Desiree had told her so. She'd also told her that such small, endearing quirks could cause many a man to tumble into malleable insensibility, if not into believing himself to be in love. "One and the same, although I haven't seen him in ever so long. I doubt he'll remember me now as the rather pudgy child I was then. But I shall remind him."

"One most sincerely hopes not," the duke muttered, finally falling into the chair Sophie had pointed out to him five minutes earlier. "Dear God, I hadn't thought about this. Mayfair must be shin-deep in your mother's discarded lovers." He absently lifted his booted legs onto the footstool Sophie hastened to place closer in front of him. "This isn't going to work. I don't care what my solicitor said. There must be some other way. This isn't going to work at all."

Sophie sat down on the small bit of footstool left to her and patted His Grace's knee, wishing she could "pat" it with an anvil. "There, there. It's not to worry. Only think about it, Your Grace. So many important men, and all of them so collectively eager to see me happily wed and out of London, yes? Out of London and stuck in Hampshire, or Sussex, raising babies and watching my husband go off to the city to bed his mistress. Just as they wed their wives and went off, in their turn, to bed my mother. Why, I imagine they will all prove most eager to assist you in settling me as quickly as possible—once they realize how very *discreet* I can be, of course."

The duke looked at her fully, his blue eyes so like dearest Uncle Cesse's. Intelligent, all-seeing—yet without a trace of humor in them. How had any son of Uncle Cesse's come to be such a prig? "I see. You've figured this all out, madam, haven't you? And you rather delight in the notion of strong men quavering in their boots as you walk into any gathering, fearing that their liaisons with the notorious Widow Winstead are about to be served up at the supper table."

The notorious Widow Winstead, indeed! Sophie longed to slap his face for such an insult. It was enough that her mother had been who she had been; it was too much to hear His Grace say the words, hear the tone of his voice when he said them. But she tamped down her temper yet again, and doggedly, determinedly, assumed a hurt expression, her full bottom lip pushing forward in a pout. "Oh, no, Your Grace! It's nothing of the kind. I just thought you should know that, grateful as I am for your kindness in sponsoring me for the Season, I am not without resources of my own. I shouldn't wish to be a *burden* on you, you see. And I'm quite confident my uncles will be of great assistance to both of us."

"If one of them doesn't decide to strangle you in order to protect himself from scandal," His Grace muttered, then drained his glass and looked up as Edith Farraday tippy-toed into the room and took up a chair in the furthermost corner. "Who's that?"

Sophie, grateful for the interruption, turned and waved to her make-believe guardian, waggling two fingers at her, and then explained the woman's presence. "I would introduce you, but I'm quite convinced Mrs. Farraday will be snoring again within the minute. Travel is anathema to her—a delicate stomach, you understand—so that Desiree prudently dosed her with laudanum before we set out. Frankly, I'm surprised she has been able to toddle up the stairs without assistance."

The duke looked at the tall, rail-thin woman for another moment, until Edith Farraday's chin once more made contact with her bony breast. Then he turned to Sophie. "Shouldn't she be in her bed?" he asked, then quickly swept his legs off the footstool and glared at her as if only belatedly realizing that his left boot had been resting most intimately against her hip, her hand on his knee. "Miss Winstead, please get up. This is highly unsuitable."

Don't rush your fences, Sophie, she warned herself as she obediently rose, holding her breath so that her cheeks blushed a becoming peach. "I'm prodigiously sorry, Your Grace," she apologized, smoothing down her skirts. "Uncle Cesse so liked it when I sat at his feet. He called me his little girl, and told me the most marvelous stories. He was always making me laugh, and teasing me back into a good humor whenever I complained to him about my studies. I particularly disliked sums." She frowned, looking down at him in real sympathy. "You must miss him very much."

The duke abruptly stood up, turning away from her, but not before she caught the fleeting flash of anger—of pain?—in his blue eyes. "You must have your *uncles* confused, Miss Winstead. I never knew the man you've just described. And now, as my aunt has taken to her bed—that is, as my aunt is resting this afternoon, I suggest you rouse Mrs. Farraday, and I'll have someone show you both to your rooms. We'll meet again at dinner."

"You don't like me, do you?" Sophie called after him as he made to quit the room. "I didn't think you would, but I had hoped we could cry friends. After all, our parents were quite fond of each other."

He slowly pivoted on his heels, his eyes boring into her, causing her to take a deep breath rather than let him see her flinch. "Our parents, Miss Winstead, behaved like alley cats for nearly four years, scandalizing all of Society and making total fools of themselves. I have spent these last years raising the Selbourne reputation up and out of the muck, only to have my father's whore's daughter thrust on me. Do I *like* you, Miss Winstead? To be frank, no."

Sophie relaxed, smiling at him. She needed the duke's cooperation, if hers was to be a successful Season. Her task, getting him to like her, would be difficult, but not impossible. Especially if he felt as much emotion as *that* about her to begin with.

"Well, it's early days yet, Your Grace," she said sunnily. "You'll like me well enough in time. I'm convinced of it, and shall work very hard to bring you round my thumb.

Men are so much more *convenable* when they are dazzled, you see, and Mama taught me just how to be dazzling."

"Is that right? Then I have nothing to fear, Miss Winstead, as I do not *dazzle*," the duke gritted out from between clenched teeth.

"Oh, of course you do, Your Grace. But it's not to worry. I'm simply grateful for your kindness in launching me. Because I should marry at least once, as Mama did, so that I can be marginally respectable, yes? A fairly elderly, titled gentleman, I believe, who shouldn't stay above ground long enough to prove inconvenient."

The duke braced a hand against the back of a side chair, shaking his head as he looked at her. "I'm not sure if I should admire your candor or toss you out of here on your ear. Why are you telling me all this, Miss Winstead?"

Sophie shrugged. It was an artlessly deceptive movement taught to her by Desiree, and perfected by dint of practicing for years in front of her mirror until the gesture had become quite natural to her—and yet another weapon in her feminine arsenal. "I suppose because of your father's involvement with my mother, yes? I shouldn't want you to think I have similar designs on you. I cannot help being charming, you see. I've been taught too well, and have no notion of how to be unlovable or disagreeable. And I also shouldn't want you chasing after me, or believing yourself to have fallen in love with me. That wouldn't do at all, because I adored Uncle Cesse, and have no intention of breaking his beloved son's heart. I am simply here to be launched, as it were. That's all. Other than that, you really should ignore me."

She watched as the duke pressed a hand to his forehead,

squeezing his brows together as if in real, physical pain. "I see," he said, dropping his hand to his side and looking at her levelly. "You have been raised to be irresistible and have therefore warned me against the inevitable in order to keep me from the unthinkable. Is that about it?"

Sophie considered this for a moment, then laughed aloud, a pleasant, tinkling sort of laugh that also had been practiced to perfection. "Why, yes, Your Grace. I think that just about says it all. So, are we agreed?"

He spread his arms wide, shaking his head. "Agreed? Agreed to *what*, Miss Winstead? I still don't have the faintest idea what you're talking about! You don't sound in the least interested in finding yourself a suitable husband. Just one titled enough and old enough and infatuated enough to wed you and then cock up his toes."

"Exactly!" Sophie exclaimed, clapping her hands together. "I don't want to marry, not really. I don't *need* to marry—I'm nearly odiously wealthy, you know. You do know that, yes? But it was *Maman*'s wish that I enter Society, and that I marry, at least the once. And I should like to have a child or two or three. I must think of them, yes? The daughter of a kept woman is difficult enough to launch, but bastards, I know, are never in season."

He was rubbing at his eyebrows again. "Refined young ladies do *not* say bastard, Miss Winstead."

"Well, of course they don't! They don't swear, they don't play cards—well, not the way I was taught, I'm sure. They don't drink port, they don't enjoy the aroma of a good cigar circling in the air over dessert and male conversation. They usually don't shoot better than most men, and they don't, frankly, know their way around a man. But then, Your Grace, most young ladies were not raised by an assortment of uncles who taught them everything from thieves' cant, to sailors' chants, to some of the more delicious scandals of government service and the *ton*. They were not privileged to watch as the most beautiful, alluring, wondrously *alive* woman in all of England entertained her equally entertaining gentlemen. I miss the company of my uncles, Your Grace, and long to be among them again. I long for the dash and intrigue and excitement of Society. But, as I said, I must marry at least the once in order to be totally accepted, to remain in Society, where I wish to be. I cannot prevail upon your kindness forever, now can I?"

"I should hope not!"

She closed her eyes and gave herself up to a single, honest moment. "Oh, it will be so good to be out and about, having fun. I already can see why *Maman* enjoyed Society so much for, at the heart of it, it's all just one mad, delicious game in which everyone wins, yes?"

"I do not, Miss Winstead," Bramwell said frostily, "believe I can in good conscience allow you to—to *flirt*, to hoodwink anyone into marriage."

"Oh, pooh!" she responded, still all light and sunny and really quite pleased with herself. "Everyone does it—flirt, that is. All of us females. I just believe I probably will do it *better* than most. You'll see. And what's the harm? As long as everyone knows the rules, of course. According to *Maman*, most do, and you must simply avoid the rest—or warn them away if you don't intend to play the game to the end, whatever that end may be." She opened her eyes once more, to see that the duke was once again in the process of removing himself from the room. "Where are you going, Your Grace? Never say I've frightened you away."

"You haven't frightened me away, Miss Winstead," he tossed over his shoulder, never slackening his pace toward the doors. "I'm simply off to inquire if any of my servants knows the whereabouts of a discreet armorer." And with that he was gone.

"Armorer?" Sophie mouthed quietly, then shook her head, tossing back her curls, and crossed to where Ignatius sat preening himself. "That went well, Ignatius," she said, sticking her fingers through the bars to ruffle the bird's feathers. "And to think it was only my first go at dazzling a man. The silly duke of Selbourne doesn't know if he's on his head or on his heels. Outraged over my plans. And yet interested. Confused. Confounded. *More* interested. Precisely where a man should be, in the gospel according to Constance Winstead."

"Kiss me, Connie!" the clever Ignatius shrilled as he heard Constance's name, his voice now sounding much like Uncle Cesse's. "Pucker up! *Squawk!* Pucker up!"

Sophie sat cross-legged in the middle of the high, wide bed, fresh from her bath, dressed in new undergarments and wrapped in a warm dressing gown. She watched as Desiree busied herself loading clothing into cupboards. The Frenchwoman moved more slowly now, much more slowly than when she had been younger, and less devoted to her pastries. But she was still all bustle and business, her graying blond hair pulled back tightly in a bun and covered by a mobcap she'd considered to be "maidlike," her expensive yet simple silk gown covered by a massive white apron she'd commandeered from the cook left behind in Wimbledon.

Sophie had offered to help settle them in, but Desiree had declined. She was happy to be occupied and definitely did not believe Sophie could so much as place a night rail in a drawer without wrinkling it beyond hope of rescue.

"He's nothing like Uncle Cesse except in his looks," Sophie said now in answer to Desiree's questions concerning the ninth duke. "So sober. So staid. But more than passably pretty on the eyes, if that is what you're wondering." She grabbed on to her crossed ankles and began slowly rocking on the bed. "I believe he thinks me to be the Devil incarnate. In fact, he all but said so."

Desiree eyed her carefully. "You didn't lose your temper with him, did you, *chérie*? Conk him on the head with something heavy?"

"I was everything you wanted me to be, Desiree, a patterncard of propriety. Polite to a fault, and overwhelmingly ingratiating. Although there were a few moments when I did wonder how much the compleat gentleman His Grace would look with a flowerpot dumped over his head."

"I see. But you did as I instructed? You remembered to tell him not to fall in love with you, *oui*? You warned him that you were raised to be irresistible? You explained why we are here? Left nothing out?"

"Yes, Desiree, I did everything we'd decided, everything we've discussed—except for our deceit in writing the letter, of course. He took it all quite well, considering. I shouldn't want to hurt Uncle Cesse's son, even as I have not caviled at using the man so shamelessly in order to enter Society. At least now he has been warned, and I shall be spared any declarations of undying love from that quarter. But, oh my, how he did *look*! He was interested, even if he refuses to admit it to himself, even if he believes he detests me. He's fortunate he's off-limits."

"Ha! There is no reason to set your sights lower than a duke. Your *maman* got herself a duke, *n'est-ce pas?*"

Sophie sighed, pushing back a curl that had fallen forward onto her cheek. "I know, Desiree, I know. But there are other dukes, surely. Besides, first I want to enjoy myself. Because that's what this is all about, *n'est-ce pas?*" she ended, grinning.

"*Oui*, my pet, life it is to be enjoyed, as you say. And love is a cheat."

"I know, Desiree," Sophie said, suddenly serious. "I know. Never fear. I'm my mother's child, but I am also your student. I won't make *that* mistake! Now, where is Giuseppe?"

Desiree stopped in the act of picking up a pair of half boots and turned in a full circle, peering into every corner of the large bedchamber. "Giuseppe? He is not here?"

Sophie bit her bottom lip. "No, Desiree," she said, dragging out the two words, "Giuseppe is not here. I had charge of Ignatius, remember? And you had charge of Giuseppe."

"No, *chérie*, I had charge of the drowsy Mrs. Farraday," Desiree countered, dropping the half boots onto the chest at the bottom of the bed and jamming her fists against her hips. "Now where do you suppose—"

Both women looked to the door to the hallway as a female shriek sliced through the air. "Giuseppe!" they both exclaimed, racing toward the door, pulling it open, and

turning to their left, to head in the direction of the contin-
uing shrieks.

They were met by the duke just outside the last door before the hallway widened. Stepping back, Sophie watched
as Bramwell Seaton pounded a single time on the door,
calling out, "Aunt Gwendolyn! What is it?" before throwing open the door and racing inside.

"We should follow him, yes?" Sophie asked her friend,
dread filling her heart.

"You should follow him, *oui*." Desiree shrugged, much
more eloquently than Sophie ever could. "I am but the
maid, *mademoiselle*," she said, grinning from ear to ear.
"The maid who warned her headstrong mistress to leave
the so-mischievous Giuseppe in Wimbledon. Now, I have
the unpacking to finish. You can just go be charming."

"Wretch!" Sophie aimed the word at Desiree's swiftly
departing back as a mobcapped maid ran shrieking from
the room. Sophie squared her shoulders and entered the
bedchamber just as its occupant—Lady Gwendolyn was
it?—let out yet another ear-piercing shriek.

"Yours, I imagine," the duke said calmly, pointing to the
bundle of brown fur dancing about on the chandelier in the
center of the room.

Sophie sighed and smiled as she passed by him, then
lifted a finger to scold her pet. "Giuseppe, shame on you!
How many times must I tell you—no chandeliers! One of
these days you'll burn down the house."

"Get it out! Get it out! Get it *out*!"

Looking to her right, Sophie spied the elderly lady just
now plastered against the heavy mahogany headboard, her
bare toes poking out beneath the hem of her rather lovely

pink dressing gown. "Lady Gwendolyn?" she inquired, dropping into a flawless curtsy. "How delighted I am to make your acquaintance. I'm Sophie."

The lady looked to Sophie and then to her nephew, her eyes still as wide, her expression remaining one of abject horror. "Get her out! Get her out! Get her *out!*"

Oh, dear. This wasn't going well, now was it? Obviously the woman had made Constance's acquaintance.

Deciding to deal with Giuseppe first, Sophie gave a single clap of her hands and held out her arms, knowing the monkey would leap into them, which he did. "Naughty baby," she crooned, as the monkey wrapped its long arms around her throat, threatening to choke off her air. "And where's your hat? You lost it again, didn't you? Now you can't tip it to the nice Lady Gwendolyn and show her just how sorry you are to have frightened her. Give her a smile, Giuseppe, and prove to her that you're nothing but a big, bad baby. Perhaps then she will forgive you, yes?"

The monkey did as he was bid, pulling back his pale monkey lips and exposing two rows of very large, somewhat yellow teeth.

Lady Gwendolyn shrieked again, covering her eyes with her hands. "Bramwell!"

"No more party tricks, if you please, Miss Winstead," the duke ordered from somewhere behind her. "Just take the animal and leave."

"Yes, Your Grace," Sophie said, dropping into another curtsy, one equally as charming, even with Giuseppe clinging to her neck. She looked, in fact, very much like a Gypsy child, clad in her white, heavy cotton dressing gown, her corkscrew curls full and faintly wild.

Although, if truth be told, she had given no thought as to what impression she might be giving the gentleman just now scowling down at her. Sophie's mind was fully concentrated on Lady Gwendolyn, and on finding a way to that woman's heart. "But if I might first apologize to your aunt? You see, I had Ignatius, and Desiree had Mrs. Farraday and, well, that left no one for Giuseppe. You can see how it happened, yes?"

"I can see my aunt cowering in her own bed, Miss Winstead, while a jungle creature swings from a very expensive chandelier. I can see, Miss Winstead, that my aunt, already overset by this intrusion into her bedchamber, has been further agitated by the sight of your face. What I can *see*, Miss Winstead, is that if you do not remove that animal and yourself from this same bedchamber in the next three seconds I shall be forced to remove you myself. Do you see *that*, Miss Winstead?"

Sophie's hopeful smile faded. Her slim shoulders slumped. Her winsome eyes grew round and moist. Her full bottom lip began to tremble, then parted slightly, to let out the pitiful, soft, shuddering moan of a badly used child. She looked small, much younger than her actual years, and vulnerable. Definitely vulnerable, and easily crushed by the vehemence of the big, bad ogre who had so unjustly attacked her.

At least that's how she hoped she appeared, and Lady Gwendolyn's reaction proved her right. "Bramwell! How unaccustomedly severe you sound," the dear lady exclaimed, sliding from the edge of the mattress, her feet unerringly landing inside a pair of pink-satin slippers as she made her way across the room. "Shame on you,

Nephew. Can't you see the girl is sorry? What else do you want from her? Next you'll be calling for boiling pitch and thumbscrews, I suppose? You should be ashamed of yourself."

"*What?*" The duke's head all but swiveled in a full circle on his shoulders as he whipped about to glare at his aunt. "Aunt, do you have any idea what you're—oh, my God!"

He turned to stare daggers at Sophie, dropping into a low, fierce whisper, "I wouldn't believe it if I hadn't seen it, hadn't been warned—and out of your own mouth! You're being *dazzling*, Miss Winstead, aren't you? Those tears are no more real than our new King's tales of how he rode at the head of the troops at Waterloo!"

His upper lip curled into a most unlovely sneer. "You disgust me," he ground out, then looked to his aunt, who was tipping her head as Giuseppe tipped his, the two of them eyeing each other up. "And you, too, Aunt!" he exploded before stomping out of the room.

"Well, that was certainly uncalled-for, and most ill-mannered," Lady Gwendolyn said, watching her nephew go. "Please accept his apologies via me, and my own as well. It isn't as if I've never before seen a monkey, or a Winstead for that matter. Why, as a matter of fact, I do believe Lord Upchurch once brought a monkey to Lady Sefton's, years ago. Yes, I'm sure it was he. The cutest little thing, with a red cap perched on his—oh, look!" she exclaimed as Giuseppe jumped down from Sophie's arms, dug under a skirted table, and came out with a bright red cap he quickly perched on his head.

"Yes, ma'am," Sophie said, winking broadly at the now-congenial-looking old lady. "Giuseppe was given to me by Uncle Dickie. Lord Upchurch, that is."

Lady Gwendolyn frowned for a moment, then her face lit in what only could be termed unholy glee. "Uncle Dickie? Oh, never say Lord Upchurch was one of your mama's—well! If *that* isn't delicious." She took Sophie by the hand and led her to a small couch in front of the windows. "You know, my dear, I wasn't very much for this arrangement when Bramwell told me of it this morning. But I now begin to see its advantages. And you're just as beautiful as your mother. Mayhap even more so, and altogether more charming—probably because you don't have your claws dug into my only brother. Oh, I believe this is going to be a most *interesting* Season. Yes, yes. Indeed I do!"

"Yes, ma'am," Sophie said, waiting for the older woman to sit down, then seating herself on the floor at her feet, the better to smile up at her. "Now, how shall we go about getting ourselves better acquainted? Perhaps if I told you of the time Uncle Dickie came to Wimbledon with the notion that *Mama* should ride up beside him, bare-breasted, on his way to the races at Ascot?"

"Bare-breasted! She never did!"

"Oh, madam, but she did!" Sophie replied, giggling. "And suffered the most painful burns from both the wind and sun for her folly. They never did make Ascot, which was a good thing, for Lady Upchurch had decided, last moment, to join her husband. Well, you can just *imagine* what a to-do that would have caused!"

Lady Gwendolyn rolled her eyes heavenward. "Julia

seeing her husband roll into town with a bare-breasted Constance beside him? Yes, my dear, I most certainly *can* imagine it. Never met a woman so full of starch as Lady Upchurch, or one more deserving of any come*upp*ance, as it were. Next time I see her, all regal and condescending in her plumes and purple, why I imagine I shall secretly simply *dissolve* in mirth."

Sophie leaned her cheek comfortably against Lady Gwendolyn's knee, happy to forget her short, sharp flare of hastily concealed anger at the duke of Selbourne for behaving so badly a few moments ago, and over so silly a thing as a harmlessly mischievous Giuseppe. The man really wasn't worth such an exertion of emotion on her part, she decided, although he certainly was handsome. Why, even when angry and frustrated, he was quite the most handsome man she'd ever seen. "Yes, my lady. We will have fun, won't we?" she said, sighing as a strange, new contentment floated through her body, mingled with an even stranger excitement. "And isn't that what it's all about?"

A young Woman her name was Dull.
　　　　—John Bunyan

Chapter Three

Nephew, be warned. I expect considerably more civil behavior from you at table this evening.

Bramwell crushed the unsigned note in his fist and threw it into the drawing-room fireplace, but not before noticing that his aunt had made use of his own personal stationery to pen her warning. Considering that he kept this stationery in a locked desk drawer in his study, he spared a moment to wonder if his favorite paperweight, a Spanish doubloon encased in a sphere of glass, remained where he'd seen it that morning.

But that wasn't really important.

Had he actually risen this morning believing that Sophie Winstead could come into his house, and that his life would remain unchanged, the hard-won calm tenor of his days undisturbed? No. Certainly not. Otherwise, why would he have spent the previous evening sulking in that same private study, downing more than his usually quite prudent ration of brandy?

He had known there could be problems—*would* be problems connected with having Constance Winstead's daughter under his roof. But he certainly had not counted on also housing a profane parrot or a chandelier-swinging monkey. He really should have put his foot down about that, said the animals had to go. There was a reason why he hadn't, he was quite sure of that. He just didn't know what it was.

Bramwell also had not counted on the girl being so blatantly conniving, so frank with her conclusion that she was about to set London on its head.

He most certainly of all had not counted on the girl being so damnably beautiful.

And to warn him not to believe himself to be falling in love with her? What cheek! As if he would ever be so foolish as his father, who had spent nearly the last four years of his life running amuck through a second childhood that had been the talk of the *ton*.

Oh no. He was not his father. He, Bramwell Seaton, Ninth Duke of Selbourne, wasn't anything like his father. He was sober. Mature. Levelheaded. Well grounded.

Betrothed.

He downed the last of his Madeira, wincing slightly as he thought of Miss Isadora Waverley and the evening that stretched—open wide like a pit, actually—in front of him. Isadora had been so kind, so understanding, so serene and unruffled, as was her custom. Sophie Winstead was to be their shared project, her successful launch the removal of the only impediment standing between them and a June wedding.

But Isadora had confidently spoken of shopping trips to Bond Street, lessons in deportment given to a docile, faintly backward little country miss, a few small social gatherings, perhaps a visit or two to the theater, followed by marriage to some half-pay officer and a swift removal back to the country. Or to America, if it could be arranged. That would be very nice, very nice, indeed.

Bramwell could no longer even fantasize that hopeful scenario unfolding before his still-shocked eyes. He'd have more reason to suppose his Aunt Gwendolyn might take it into her head to dance on a table at Carlton House for the amusement and edification of their new King and his aging cronies.

If only Sophie weren't so damnably beautiful. He could no more hide her in a crowd of simpering debutantes at Almack's than he could hope the world would overlook a peacock in a cage of wrens.

Because Sophie Winstead was full of color, brilliant with life. She shone, She glowed. She *dazzled*.

And, damn it all to hell, she knew it!

What he most resented, the duke decided for the third time in as many minutes, pouring himself an unusual second glass of Madeira, was that she had warned him of her irresistible charms, telling him that she was terribly sorry, but she had no control over them. She had warned him that everyone found her lovable—just as if it were a foregone conclusion that he would soon be drooling at her shoe tops, begging for her favor.

"The Devil I will!" the duke declared out loud, jamming the stopper back into the decanter and picking up his glass.

"Miss Isadora Waverley, Your Grace," Bobbit announced from the doorway. The duke put down his Madeira untouched and turned to see his betrothed sweep past the butler. Her abigail was probably already on her way to the servant's parlor, to sit prim and proper, waiting for her summons to accompany her mistress back to Mount Street.

Isadora held her gloved arms out to Bramwell as he moved to welcome her as a shipwrecked man greets rescue, taking her hands in his and lifting one of them to within an inch of his lips. When she spoke, it was with the very proper, rather clipped accents favored by the most stringently proper of the *ton*. "My dear Selbourne, how goes the evening? Has your little charge arrived as yet? I do so long to make her acquaintance, certain that we shall be the very best of good friends during her sojourn here in Mayfair."

The duke closed his eyes for a moment, gratified by the serenity Isadora radiated, some of his admittedly foolish fears calmed by her cool presence, her even demeanor, her practical outlook. She had all the makings of a perfect duchess. Tall, graceful, she held her chin high above her long neck and wore her black-as-night hair simply yet elegantly drawn back from her face. Her blue eyes were cool, controlled, her gown of the first stare, eminently elegant, not in the least overdone.

There was nothing flamboyant about Isadora Waverley. Nothing to cause unwanted attention. She was admired by all, perhaps envied by some, but there was no whiff of scandal about her. No whispers followed after her, no one had a bad word to say of her—or a bawdy joke to tell about her.

She was nearly three and twenty, past the age of silliness, but never considered to be on the shelf. Her contemplated marriage to Lord Coulbeg had sadly ended with His Lordship's demise in a hunting accident, and she had only come out of black gloves the previous Season. With the beauty, the breeding, the parental wealth, and the good sense to pick and choose where she gave her hand, Isadora had returned to the London scene as one of its brightest if not its most original lights. Bramwell knew himself to be one very fortunate man in that she had chosen him from among so many, that she had seen what he had seen—that she would make a most admirable duchess.

"Good evening, my dear," he said now, "so good of you to ask. I'm loath to tell you this, but Miss Winstead's arrival has, unfortunately, not been without incident." Bramwell led Isadora to a satin-striped sofa and sat down beside her once she had arranged her skirts. She sat as regally as she stood, with her spine ramrod straight, her hands neatly folded in her lap as she slowly turned her head and looked into his eyes.

"There are complications?" she asked, not quite frowning, not quite smiling. "Lud! Nothing that can't be overcome, I'm sure."

Bramwell visualized Sophie Winstead as he had last seen her as he'd passed by his aunt's open doorway on his way downstairs. The two of them had been giggling like children as Sophie held out her skirts and pirouetted in front of his delighted aunt, showing off her gown for the evening as his aunt's maid, Peggy, had clapped her hands in approval.

"My aunt has kindly seen fit to take Miss Winstead in hand," he hedged, wondering if he had always harbored this heretofore unnoticed knack for twisting the truth to suit his hopes.

"That's good, then," Isadora pronounced, nodding her head a single time. "Lady Gwendolyn is unimpeachable. Lud, the child could do worse than to emulate her."

While the unimpeachable Lady Gwendolyn pilfers her host's snuffboxes? Oh, yes, Bramwell thought fatalistically, that could only be a help.

"Papa has written that he hopes he'll be coming to town in time to watch the Season wind down with us," he heard Isadora say, obviously believing the matter of Sophie Winstead settled. "He regrets that his gout has kept him confined to the estate, but promises he shall be up to walking me down the aisle. Isn't that sweet of him?"

"Your father is too kind," Bramwell answered politely and automatically. This was a role he knew, a role he slipped into easily and played well, that of the urbane gentleman carrying on a safe, polite conversation with the woman he had chosen as his hostess, his wife, the mother of his correct, upright, and unexceptional children. He was playing a role? Damn! Did the whole world play at life, rather than just live it?

"Yes, he is," Isadora agreed. "I immediately posted back to him, assuring him that we had no objection to postponing the nuptials until the fall if his health should not prove robust. You agree, of course."

"Of course," Bramwell assured her. June. In the autumn. Next spring. It didn't matter. There was, after all, no great rush. "Your father's health must be our first consideration. Would you care for a glass of ratafia, my dear?" he then asked after finding himself shocked onto his feet by the sudden realization that he didn't give a tinker's dam if the marriage was delayed another six months.

He crossed to the drinks table, his hand shaking ever so slightly as he pulled the stopper from a crystal decanter and poured Isadora's ratafia. Shouldn't he be outraged at this possible delay? Shouldn't he be panting to wed his be-trothed? Panting to *bed* her? No! No, he shouldn't be. He was a gentleman. A sober, refined, upstanding gentleman. A duke. Not a randy goat who ran stark, staring naked through his hostess's guest bedchambers and dived head-first off balconies.

"Lud, but I so admire your consideration, Selbourne," Isadora told him as she accepted the glass. "It is your good-heartedness and consideration that first drew me to you. That, and your calm, even ways and lack of heated pas-sions. Lud, I so dislike any hint of upheaval, of discord. And, which follows most naturally, I abhor even the faintest whiff of scandal, your late father's indiscretion to one side and thankfully forgotten, naturally. One cannot be held entirely responsible for another's foolhardiness, now can one? Especially once that other person is most bless-edly deceased. But, la, if your father were still alive? Well, I daresay I would not be here now. You do understand, don't you? Oh, of course you do. As I've said, dearest Sel-bourne, you're so eminently reasonable."

"Thank you, Isadora," he said, doing his best not to

flinch under her compliments, all of which made him sound the most dashed dull fellow in Nature. He hadn't always been so sober, he recalled with a slight straightening of his own shoulders. He'd cut quite a dash while in the Royal Navy, narrowly escaped more than a few scandalous but quite satisfying skirmishes, and all with the odd romantic peccadillo thrown in for good measure. But that, of course, was all before his father's inglorious and very public demise. "I do my best to bring only honor to the family name and station."

The dinner gong sounded again just at that moment and Bramwell was saved from a further detailing of himself as an utter bore and stodgy stick in the mud. And if something deep inside of him rebelled at being thought of as a man who would not defend his own dead father? Well, he'd think about that later. He had a lot to think about later . . .

As the gong died, his Aunt Gwendolyn appeared in the doorway to the drawing room, her smile wide and beaming as she tripped toward the sofa, a greeting to Isadora already dribbling from her lips.

Her faintly painted lips.

"Aunt Gwendolyn?" Bramwell inquired, as if not quite sure he knew this woman who had somehow left off her turban this evening, showing her graying curls to the world. Yes, her lips were rather pink, as were her cheeks. Not unnaturally so, but just enough for him to notice. And where had he seen that highly colorful paisley shawl before? Surely it wasn't the same one he'd last glimpsed draped over a gilded parrot cage?

The lady sat herself down beside Isadora, patted at her graying curls, and smiled up at her nephew. "Yes,

Bramwell? Oh—you're probably wondering where dear Sophie is that she's not with me. She'll be along in a moment. Giuseppe was being naughty and hid one of her earbobs under my bed and—last I saw her—the dear girl was down on her hands and knees, attempting to locate the thing. I told her Peggy could do it, but she wouldn't hear of it. Her monkey, she said, her mess. Such a lovely girl. Just grand. Good evening, Miss Waverley. You look very nice, as usual. Fine night, isn't it?"

"Exceptionally fine, my lady," Isadora answered, looking to Bramwell, who could do nothing more than shrug his shoulders, for he certainly had no explanation for his aunt's faintly bizarre, if rather attractive appearance, or her ramblings about Sophie Winstead, an earbob, and monkeys. "Congratulations are in order, or so Selbourne tells me."

Lady Gwendolyn frowned. "Congratulations? Whatever for? Have I done something wonderful? I have no recollection of it, in any case."

"Lud, why, for taking Miss Winstead in hand, my lady, of course," Isadora explained, patting Lady Gwendolyn's knee as if to assure her that it was all right, one did understand the mental lapses of the elderly. "Although you must feel nothing but antipathy for anyone even vaguely connected with the Winstead name, you are generous enough, charitable enough, not to blame the child for the sins of the mother."

Bramwell busied himself in inspecting the cuff of his jacket, thus avoiding his aunt's flashing eyes. He certainly wasn't about to remind Lady Gwendolyn that she had, in fact, been more than ready to condemn Sophie—before she had fallen under the dratted girl's spell, that is.

"Stuff and nonsense!" Lady Gwendolyn declared heatedly, proving that Bramwell had been correct, and his aunt had already conveniently forgotten her earlier reluctance to sponsor her brother's mistress's daughter. "I should be poor-spirited indeed to lay any of the blame for that horrible interlude at the door of such a sweet, loving, *innocent* child as our own dear Sophie."

"Innocent? I should certainly hope so, Aunt," Bramwell broke in reasonably, unable to resist a sudden impulse to make his aunt as uncomfortable as he was himself. "But you must remember, we hardly know the girl."

Lady Gwendolyn straightened her spine, indignation in every line of her body. "Are you suggesting, Nephew, that your aunt is too old, or too—*blockheaded*, to be able to see what's directly in front of her own nose? I've met the girl. I've spoken with her. And I approve of her most thoroughly. Besides," she ended quietly, adjusting the folds of her colorful shawl, "she tells the most delicious stories."

Knowing his aunt to be a dedicated lover of gossip, Bramwell only nodded, certain that the enterprising Miss Winstead had quickly taken the old lady's measure that afternoon. Then, as is the way of conniving women, she had honed in on her most vulnerable weakness—and waltzed straight into his aunt's sympathy.

In short, Sophie Winstead had *dazzled* his aunt. Dazzled her into liking her, accepting her, becoming not only her friend but her ally. They had most probably spent the afternoon giggling, and sharing secrets, and brushing each other's hair, and doing all sort of mysterious things to their faces and nails that women do that confound a man. And what purpose did the girl have for such a dedicated assault on his aunt's tenderhearted emotions? Heaven only knew. Heaven, and Sophie Winstead.

Bramwell longed to wring the girl's neck. That lovely, lovely, bound to be glorious to touch neck. He closed his eyes and gritted his teeth, mentally slapping himself back to his usual sanity.

"Good evening, all!" came the faintly breathless greeting as the young woman he wanted to throttle floated into the room. Her smile was wide, her countenance open, her eyes shining as brightly as new copper pennies, her curls flying away from her face as if she were lightheartedly running into a soft, fragrant summer breeze. Indeed, the heady smells of summer drifted into the room with her, as well as thoughts of the innocence of a carefree youth long gone and sadly lamented. "I'm late in coming down, yes? Oh, of course I am. How terribly rude of me. Please, I beg your forgiveness."

She stopped in front of Bramwell and dropped into a low curtsy, her head held high so that, looking down at her, the duke found himself staring at her partially exposed breasts rising above the demure yet somehow daring cut of her ivory-silk gown. Her rounded, creamy, undoubtedly perfect breasts. Perfect to look upon, surely equally perfect to touch, to kiss, to bury one's head against and know, at last, the full measure of what Heaven promises.

Bramwell felt suddenly light-headed, his balance shaky, and only Sophie's delighted grin brought him back to his senses. *Dazzling*, he reminded himself. *She is being pur-*

posely dazzling, damn her eyes. And damn mine as well, for looking.

"And you must be Miss Waverley, yes?" Sophie said, turning to Isadora and dropping another curtsy, not quite so low, but equally as graceful and deferential as her first. "Aunt Gwendolyn has told me about you—everything lovely, to be sure. I'm Sophie. How very pleased and honored I am to make your acquaintance."

Aunt Gwendolyn? Bramwell turned on his heels and went to rescue his glass of Madeira, which he had forgotten on the drinks table, leaving behind his fiancée, his traitorous, gullible aunt, and that Devil's spawn, Sophie Winstead.

If he could, he would have left the room as well, left the city, left the country, departed the hemisphere. Because, as sure as rain fell when one was first wearing a new hat, Sophie, with one conquest already under her belt, was about to set out to dazzle his levelheaded Isadora, and he really didn't think he wanted to watch.

"Oh, yes, Miss Waverley, all my gowns come to me directly from France, as did my mother's, even during the war, I'm ashamed to say. Desiree—my maid, you understand, and a fine friend as well—well, Desiree and I had such fun taking measurements and the like for the form we then packed up and shipped off to Paris. Now my gowns are made to fit the other me, you see, so that I must be very careful not to gain so much as an ounce, for fear we should have to do all of that measuring again. But that is so much more than you asked, yes? Please forgive me."

"That's quite all right, Miss Winstead," Isadora said, her blue eyes raking over Sophie's figure as they sat in the drawing room once more with Aunt Gwendolyn after dinner. The duke had forgone blowing a cloud in manly solitude in order to join them. He had done this not because of any dislike for his own company, Sophie was convinced, but in order to be on hand to step in at any moment, to rescue either of the ladies if she had mischief on her mind. Smart fellow. Of course she had mischief on her mind. Didn't she always?

"And I will say it again," Isadora went on as Sophie beamed at her. "Your gown is quite lovely, if a trifle more *French*, shall I say, than is popular in town this Season. And quite flattering to your fuller figure."

Sophie's smile remained bright, just as if she were so redbrick stupid as to not know she'd just been the victim of a backhanded insult. Fuller figure, indeed! The woman sitting in front of her was narrow as a whittled stick. There was nothing there for a man to admire, no hint of a comfortable cushion for his head, no hope of soft curves or dimples.

Sophie felt a clever set-down very naturally climb to her lips, and just as easily fought it down. Why waste time fighting an enemy when it was so much easier to make a friend? She actually felt rather sorry for Miss Isadora Waverley, poor thing, for she probably couldn't help being such a stick, both physically and in her narrow brain. Besides, with the opening the duke's fiancée had so nicely given her, she now could put her plan into action.

Sophie had taken her measure of the oh-so-proper Miss Waverley during dinner, and already knew what it would take to make the self-important young woman happy. Happy enough that she would be no problem, prove to be no impediment to Sophie's own happiness. And it was all so simple. If Miss Waverley wanted insecure and malleable, Sophie was more than willing give her insecure and malleable. In spades.

"La, yes, Miss Waverley," Sophie trilled. "You are *so* right. I am not nearly so aristocratically lean as, say, yourself. I am much like my mother, I'm afraid, built along more earthy lines. And inches too short into the bargain. Why, I believe I rise no higher than His Grace's cravat, yes?" She then frowned, leaning forward to show a measure of her unease, of her uncertainty—of her perfect breasts (after all, His Grace was watching). "But pray tell me I am not entirely out of style. I should so hate to be termed an Antidote, not worthy of any attention, which would reflect badly on my sponsor and dear Aunt Gwendolyn."

Isadora set down her teacup before answering and delicately patted at her lips with the serviette that had been reposing in her lap. Only when she had arranged the linen square over her knees once more did she speak, and she did it with the air of authority of one who is reading from stone tablets just carried down the mountainside. "I admit it will be a struggle, my dear Miss Winstead, as you are unfortunately short, and darker hair is more in vogue this year. But, lud, I'm quite sure we will contrive. Certainly there are one or two gentlemen whose interest might be aroused, then cultivated. Isn't that right, Lady Gwendolyn?"

"Hrruumph!" that lady replied shortly. "Where are your eyes, Miss Waverley? The chit's all but perfect, very nearly the eighth great wonder of the world. We'll be beating eager gentlemen away with sticks, that's what we'll be doing."

Sophie hid a smile behind her own serviette as the duke choked on his drink, then coughed, then excused himself and made his way to the drinks table in search of something more bracing than tea. Her smile faded, however, when Isadora responded, "Lud, yes, dear lady, I do know that, although I dislike pointing out the obvious. Miss Winstead will attract all manner of men. But none to suit our purposes, I fear. Not if *marriage* is the prize we hope to secure."

Silly woman. Why was she still fighting the inevitable? Was she that thick? If Sophie were to leap onto Miss Waverley, climb her like the tree she was, and rip loose that neat figure-eight coil of coal black hair that sat so primly at the nape of her neck—would the woman even flinch? And, more importantly, what would such an assault, no matter how justified, serve? It was so much easier to be nice. Sophie considered this, and much more, as she took another sip of tea, looking through her lowered lashes at the duke, to gauge his reaction to his fiancée's insult.

"I believe that might have been a bit strong, Isadora," Bramwell said, seating himself once more, crossing one leg over the other as he balanced a wineglass on his knee.

Well, now. This was interesting. The duke might not like her overmuch, Sophie decided, might thoroughly detest her, in fact. But he was gentleman enough to defend her. She longed to kiss him, thought about shedding a tear or two to gain even more of his sympathy, then dismissed both possible responses as being much too transparent for the forewarned duke. Besides, he wasn't her target.

Still and all, she decided, it *was* nice of him.

"No, no," Sophie protested instead, looking to Bramwell, then to Isadora. "Brutal frankness is just what's needed here, yes? I was not so sheltered, am not such a sad nodcock, that I'm unaware my mother's reputation precedes me into any social gathering His Grace might allow me to attend. I'm fully cognizant of the great sacrifice he is undertaking—that *all* of you are undertaking—in hopes of making my dream to be just another debutante a reality. Just, please, dear Miss Waverley, continue to be frank. I am your willing student, and you shall be my mentor, yes?"

The duke choked again and put down his glass. Which was probably wise of him, Sophie concluded. Who knew how deeply she'd have to dig, how high her pile of compliments would have to grow, before Miss Waverley was won over.

"Lud, such a pretty speech, Miss Winstead, and so wisely spoken!" Isadora said, smiling most benevolently, and Sophie mentally laid down her shovel, her job done much more quickly and easily than even she could have imagined. "I am above all things flattered, and grateful that you see the need for guidance. Why, just the way you all but *bounded* into the room earlier this evening gave me, I must admit, more than a qualm as to how we should ever launch you successfully. I will be more than happy to show you how to go on, Miss Winstead, how to converse with gentlemen, how to walk, how to talk, how to stand. Shall we begin our lessons tomorrow? Selbourne, surely you can bludgeon either Sir Wallace or Baron Lorimar into accompanying us on a morning drive through the park?"

"Lord Lorimar has already expressed an interest in making Miss Winstead's acquaintance," the duke answered—his lips barely moving as he spoke, Sophie noticed. "Shall we say at eleven, Isadora?"

He looked to Sophie then, glared at her actually, and she smiled back at him as she wriggled very slightly in her seat, content with this night's work. She gave in to impulse and lifted her hand, just a little, so that only he could see, winked at him, then held up two fingers, just in case he had forgotten to keep count of her conquests.

"Miss Winstead, I've just now remembered something," he said, abruptly rising to his feet and holding out his arm to her. "I've quite forgotten to show you a letter that has arrived for you late this afternoon, forwarded from Wimbledon, I'm sure. It's from Paris, I believe. Would you care to accompany me now for a moment, please, while I retrieve it from my study?"

Sophie wrinkled up her nose at him as she smiled. Did he really think she harbored some terrible death wish, that she'd go off with him now, when he was so angry—not that she hadn't given him good reason? She'd rather walk barefoot over broken glass. "A letter, you say? Probably just another bill, alas, as I'm quite the spendthrift. Surely it can wait, Your Grace, thank you just the same. We were all just having a most comfortable coze. Weren't we, ladies?"

His jaw was set, making him look quite manly. Appealing, in a strange, definitely to be avoided way. "But I'd really rather you came with me now, just for a few moments," he said. "Otherwise, I might forget the letter, and it could be lost."

"Really, Nephew," Lady Gwendolyn scolded, "if the gel don't want to go, she don't want to go."

Sophie smiled demurely at Gwendolyn but the duke kept his arm held out, so that she longed to slap it away with her serviette.

Isadora clapped her hands together like a schoolmistress calling her students to order. "Now do you see, Lady Gwendolyn? Miss Winstead is proving to us right now that she has no real grasp of proper social behavior." She turned to Sophie and explained. "Lud, my dear, His Grace is your social superior as well as your sponsor while you are here in Town with us. He has very politely asked your accompaniment on a small errand. You, as his inferior as well as his guest, must be amenable to such requests, eager to please, and polite at all times. Isn't that right, Selbourne?"

The duke turned and bowed in his betrothed's direction. "I couldn't have conveyed that conclusion better myself, my dear lady. Thank you so much for leaping into the breach and saying it for me."

Sophie damped down the impulse to roll her eyes in disbelief at both Isadora Waverley's blind stupidity and His Grace's veiled sarcasm—which obviously had flown straight over his fiancée's head. Instead, she merely got to her feet, took Bramwell's arm, and left the room with all the cheer one might show walking the plank.

"We'll have to work on that," Sophie heard Isadora informing Lady Gwendolyn consideringly as the duke's long strides had her all but skipping along beside him in order to keep up. "From sunny to sullen in a heartbeat, my lady.

Lud, that's so like young girls today, poor thing! But she'll learn. I have every confidence in my own abilities—oh, and in yours as well, of course."

Once they were out of the drawing room and headed down the stairs to his grace's ground-floor study, Sophie looked up at the duke, saying, "That was very neat, Your Grace."

"Hardly. But effective enough, for all it was clumsy."

"I meant your veiled insult to Miss Waverley, not the cowhanded way you all but ordered me out of the room," she pointed out, made slightly breathless by trying to match his pace on the stairs. "Tell me, please. How uncomfortable is it, being led around by the nose?"

"If that question means that you've belatedly become concerned for my poor, gullible aunt, I suggest you ask her yourself. And Miss Waverley as well, now that you've got her believing you're nothing more than a brainless ninny eager to sit at her feet and drink in all her great knowledge."

He stopped for a moment at the bottom of the stairs and glared down at her. He was really quite good at glaring, as if he'd had considerable practice. And there were those interesting lines around the outside corners of his eyes, crinkles as it were, as if he'd spent a lot of time squinting into the sun. Hadn't Uncle Cesse said something about his only son trying to disgrace him by going off to the Royal Navy? Yes, that was it. Bramwell Seaton had spent years looking out over the ocean, his eyes on distant horizons. Strange how he couldn't see clearly now.

Sophie deliberately teased him again as they turned toward the back of the house, pouting as best she could as she skipped along beside him. "You're really quite angry, aren't you?" she asked, knowing she was only pointing out the obvious. "But it's not to worry. I doubt Miss Waverley has the slightest idea that yours was only a hastily made-up fib meant to get me alone with you. And I find it all quite flattering, if unnecessary. After all, we're living under the same roof. Getting me alone, day or night—anytime at all—could hardly be more convenient, yes?"

He put his hand at the small of her back and all but pushed her into the study ahead of him before closing the door on the hallway and the interested footmen milling about in the foyer. "I did not want to get you *alone*, as you term it, for any romantic notion you might have taken into your head."

Sophie spied out a decanter of brandy warming on a small table near the fire and went straight to it, pouring His Grace a snifter and returning to hand it to him. "Why, did I say anything about *romantic* notions, Your Grace?" she asked, smiling up at him as she insinuated herself between Bramwell and the desk. "No, I'm quite sure I didn't. I'd rather assumed you'd brought me down here to read my incorrigible self a stern lecture, yes?"

He took the drink from her without so much as a word of thanks, brought it almost to his lips, then leaned forward and slammed the snifter down on the desk, its contents untouched. "Oh, no, you don't! You're not going to do that again."

"Do what again, Your Grace?" Sophie asked, bracing her palms against the desktop and gracefully lifting herself onto the surface so that her slippered feet swung freely, only the faintest glimpse of well-turned ankle visible below her hemline. "I'm sure I haven't the faintest notion what you're talking about." She turned her head, inspecting the wide, clean expanse of desk, then looked up at him again, her expression one of absolute innocence and confused inquiry. "I don't seem to see my letter here."

Bramwell made a growling sound low in his throat as he ran a hand through his warm brown locks, effecting great inroads on its sleekly combed style and making himself look much younger, much more approachable. Not, she was sure, that he knew it or, if he did, that he would ever do such a thing again. She couldn't remember when last she'd seen such an unhappy man—or a man so woefully unaware of his unhappiness.

"You're enough to drive a man out of his mind," he said at last. "You do know that, don't you? Hell and damnation—why am I even asking? Of course you know that. You do it on purpose. You do *everything* on purpose. You don't make a single move, a single gesture, without a purpose. You wheedled yourself into my aunt's good graces with woebegone expressions, some lip rouge, and promises of lurid gossip. And then you turned yourself around and played the eager, feather-headed ninny so that my fiancée sees you as no more dangerous than a lump of clay that she, in her goodness, will mold into her own image—as if *that* were possible."

"You're absolutely right, Your Grace. Of course I did— I do! And you've seen through it all. Even the lip rouge." Sophie sighed and shook her head. "But, all that being said, I don't see why you're flying so into the treetops, Your Grace. It isn't as if I didn't warn you, yes? I was raised to please, raised to see a need, then accommodate it—until it has become second nature for me. I simply can't help myself. I warned you of that as well. Besides, it's much nicer all round when people like you, yes? You're happier, the people around you are happier." She spread her arms wide. "The whole *world* is happier."

He raised his own arms from his sides, then brought his hands close together in front of him, as if trying to hold on to something he could not quite see, found impossible to completely grasp. "But—but that isn't *honest!*"

Now Sophie did roll her eyes, beginning to feel the first flush of what Desiree had once called her "fire-flash" of anger. She took a deep breath, letting it out slowly, hoping to remain calm, in control—thus retaining the upper hand over this man, this unexpected and unexpectedly attractive adversary. "Honest? What isn't honest, Your Grace? I very *honestly* enjoy both the ladies who are sitting upstairs in the drawing room, planning ways to make me a success. Truly I do. Lady Gwendolyn is happy to have a companion, someone to laugh with, to make her feel young again. Miss Waverley is happy to have found a project that will elevate her already fine opinion of herself and further ingratiate her into your affections. In their own way, they're both quite delicious. I do no harm, Your Grace. I just see what is needed, and I do it; find a lack, and fill it. Which makes it easier for *me* to be happy, for *my* life to be easier. Does sincerity—or honesty, as you call it—matter all that much, when everyone is happy? And that's why we're here, isn't it, Your Grace? To be happy? Certainly we aren't here to be sad."

He opened his mouth to speak, raised his hands as if to gesture once more—and ended by saying nothing, doing nothing. He just stood there, staring at her for a very long time, his expression growing increasingly solemn. "You don't like your fellow creatures very much, do you, Miss Winstead," he pronounced at last.

"What nonsense!" Sophie hopped down from her perch, avoiding the duke's eyes. "It's a good thing you didn't drink that brandy, Your Grace. You're already two parts drunk for you to think such a thing of me. Now we'd best go back to the drawing room, or else they'll send someone after us," she said, trying to brush past him and out the door before she exploded in rage and ruined everything she and Desiree had planned for so long.

But he grabbed her arm just above the elbow and almost roughly turned her around to face him. She felt the tips of her breasts brush against the fabric of his coat, could feel his warm breath on her cheek. Confusion covered her anger, then the anger fought through once more. She attempted to move away, to protect herself from an enemy she could not recognize, because the enemy seemed to be inside her, a just-discovered part of her that was in danger of betraying her in some unknown way.

"Now where have all your smiles so suddenly disappeared to, do you suppose? Your playful winks, your practiced shrugs? Your impossible-to-control wiles meant to drive a man out of his mind? What's the matter, Miss Sophie Winstead? Have I stumbled onto the truth all that easily? Is it true? Do you really hate us, hate all of us men in particular?"

Sophie took another moment to compose herself, to remember who she was, how she was raised, what she had observed, the lessons she had learned. And she decided to be honest with His Grace—just this one more time—so that she wouldn't have to be honest again. She refused to listen to the small, niggling voice that whispered that she had not really *chosen* to do anything, that she had no choice, that the duke had left her no other choice.

But he'd pay for what he'd done to her, the truth he was drawing from her. He'd pay dearly.

Deliberately lifting a hand to Bramwell's smooth cheek, then drawing her fingers lightly down to his chin, Sophie summoned her most winning smile, and said, "Since I've already warned you against me, out of my affection for Uncle Cesse, I suppose I owe you all of the truth, yes? Very well. You're wrong, and you're right. I *am* very fond of my fellow creatures, Your Grace. In my own way."

"In your own way? I dread thinking what *that* might mean, Miss Winstead," Bramwell interrupted, and Sophie gave out a soft gurgle of laughter. He disapproved of her. That was obvious. But he did not step away from her, or ask her to remove her hand from his face. Of course he didn't. She hadn't expected him to. He was a man, wasn't he? Her touch didn't repel him. It fired something base and entirely male within him, as Desiree had explained, robbing him of everything but his own wants, his own needs. In fact, he stepped even closer to her now, their bodies touching even more intimately.

He disgusted her. Her reaction to him disgusted her.

"I find other women quite genuinely likable," Sophie said, beginning her explanation. "But," she continued quickly, sensing that he was in her power now, "I am fond of gentlemen most of all, because they are heartless little boys and can't be hurt—not really. I'm also fond of laughter, of gaiety, of lighthearted days and exciting nights. I fully intend, Your Grace, to dance and laugh and enjoy myself to the top of my bent for as long as I live. Without any regrets, without any sorrows. Without," she ended, dropping her hand to her side, "any real attachments to anyone save the children I hope to have one day. Uncle Cesse would have left my mother in the end, you know. They all leave, they all left. But I won't care when anyone leaves me, because I will be happy when they are near, happy when they go—happy all by myself. No one, you see, will ever make *me* cry."

Sophie then shut her mouth quickly, calling herself ten times the fool, for she had said too much, gone on a sentence or two too long. The veiled insult about men being heartless little boys was to have been enough. Why had she said so much? Perhaps it was because the ninth duke so resembled his father? It had always been so easy to talk to Uncle Cesse, confide all her girlish secrets in him. Uncle Cesse had promised her a Season, promised to dance with her at her very own ball, promised to be the father she'd always longed for and never had. And then he'd died, and her mother along with him, and Sophie had been left alone, to mourn.

"Well, that's that, isn't it?" she said brightly, putting her hand on Bramwell's as he stood staring down at her, silently hinting that he release her arm, end this suffocating closeness that had so muddled her mind. "Shall we rejoin the ladies?"

"My father made you cry, didn't he?" Bramwell asked quietly, still holding tight to her arm, keeping her where she did not want to be. "All those men who came into and out of your life—all your *uncles* who played with you as a child, gave you gifts, and petted you, and then left you. They all made you cry. So I'm at least partly right, as you said, at least when it comes to men. For all your charms, all your smiles, all your protestations that you only want to live a life of happiness, you're out to hurt as many of us as you can, without ever letting your own heart be touched in any way."

Sophie wanted to hit him, he was that infuriating. How could he think so poorly of her? Because she couldn't hurt anyone—not ever. She knew, all too well, how much the pain of rejection hurt. Didn't he understand anything? "You dolt!" she cried out, spinning out of his arms and picking up the brandy snifter, sending it to shatter against the wall, somewhere depressingly left of the fireplace. "Now look what you made me do! You thick, stupid, infuriating, *dolt*! I would never put it before myself to hurt anybody—*never*. I couldn't!"

Bramwell looked to the rapidly spreading stain on the wall, then to Sophie, who couldn't believe she had been so foolish, so revealing of the one thing Desiree had most admonished she hide. Her abominable temper.

"Well, now, Miss Winstead," the duke said silkily, wiping one hand against the other as if he'd just done something wonderful. "Perhaps you're not so perfect after all. Although I must say, I somehow find this side of you more than passing *dazzling*, in its own odd way."

He stepped closer as her feet refused to move. Her body betrayed her by leaning forward slightly, making it easier for him to capture her in his arms. She watched, all wonder and confusion, as he lowered his smiling mouth, sealing his warm lips over hers as his arms came around her back, pressing her against him.

She felt the shock down to her toes. Her first kiss. Begun in amusement and, as he pulled away from her, ended in much the same way. "Why—why did you do that?" she asked, her head spinning.

"Why, Miss Winstead?" he asked in return, a frown now marring his smooth forehead. "Why not?"

She shot a look at him, deliberately wiping the back of her hand across her mouth. "Just as I've always suspected, already known in my heart. You're a fickle lot, the whole of you men. With a fiancée upstairs while you paw another woman all but under her nose. Lustful, rutting, unfaithful dogs. That's what you are, to a man. But not, Your Grace, to *me*. Not now, not ever."

"Oh, God, Miss Winstead, I'm sorry," Bramwell said, taking hold of her arm, trying to guide her to a chair. "The smiles, the hand to the cheek, the knowing glances. You play the game so well. You seem to know the steps, each deliberate move. I thought you had been offering to have me join you in the game. Obviously I was wrong. You were only practicing, weren't you? It's just as you'd warned me. I'm off-limits, was never meant to be one of the players. Forgive me."

Did she have any choice? Not if she were to remain under his roof, go into Society, have the Season her mama had craved for her, the Season she craved for herself. She had to forgive this man, this typical man, this lustful, taking, rutting boar of a man who was like every other man in creation. Much as she realized, with a pain that tore straight through her, that she'd hoped Uncle Cesse's son might be different.

"We won't mention this again, Your Grace," she said at last, lifting her chin and smiling her most practiced, natural smile. "We've both learned a lesson that will stand us in good stead over the next weeks. I won't dazzle you again, and you won't kiss me again. For neither action serves any good purpose, yes?"

He bowed over her hand, pressing his lips against her skin. "You're too kind."

"Probably," Sophie said with a lilting giggle that cost her more than he would ever know. Then she escaped to the hallway, stopping just outside the doorway to compose herself. She walked toward the stairs, her head held high, her smile bright. Determinedly bright, so that no shadows could be seen.

Chapter Four

The comfort of one's oldest and dearest friends during times of trial is one of life's blessings, or so the ninth duke had always believed. Which did nothing to explain his current hope that Sir Wallace Merritt and Baron Marshall Lorimar would disappear into the hole His Grace was wishing would appear at their feet.

However, as the duke of Selbourne did have more than a modicum of fondness for his two friends, the fact that no hole appeared in the study floor could only be termed a good thing. Even if it made for a damned uncomfortable morning, although not as uncomfortable as the interlude he had spent in this same room the previous evening. He had been most especially unnerved when Sophie had asked why mankind was here, if not to be happy. When he'd nearly answered, "We are here to be *earnest*," he'd realized that perhaps, just perhaps, Sophie Winstead wasn't all fluff and nonsense. And that he, Bramwell Seaton, might just be turning into a bit of a "stick."

Which was why he'd kissed her. That had to be why he'd kissed her. To prove to himself that blood still flowed through his veins. Hot blood. Hotter, and much more uncomfortable than he'd expected.

But not, it appeared, as hot as Sophie Winstead's quick, unexpected temper. He bit back a smile as he remembered the brandy snifter suddenly taking flight, smashing against the wall. He looked at the stain now, still fairly damp where one of the housemaids had done her best to sponge it from the Chinese wallpaper.

Had her mother taught her that? To appear the perfect woman, biddable, eager to please—then with this other, darker, most surprising, intriguing side? Not that it mattered. Because he wasn't interested. Even if her lips had tasted of honey and promise. Even if her body, those perfect breasts, had all but branded him, marked him as both vulnerable and pathetic, a man who could be turned from his most rational thoughts and decisions and thrown into turmoil without the first notion of how he had come to be so unbalanced.

God, but he wished he'd never heard of Sophie Winstead. He didn't need this complication in his life. His well-ordered, well-thought-out life with his suddenly not quite so clear plans for the future.

"So? Out with it, man?" Sir Wallace commanded, holding tightly to the arms of the straight-back, leather-bottomed chair, the better to keep his relaxed, brandy-greased body from gracefully sliding to the floor in a heap. "Is she or ain't she?"

"Bram's not going to answer you, Wally," the baron pointed out, watching the trio of smoke rings he'd just puffed through his pursed lips as they ascended toward the ceiling. "He's a gentleman. Ain't you, Bram?"

"A gentleman? I suppose so. But he wasn't always," Sir Wallace responded before Bramwell could answer, then slapped his knee. "No, he was not! Why, I remember the time we were on leave in Dover. You remember that, Bram?" He turned to the Baron. "There we were, Lorrie, stuck in port until the tide turned, and bored to flinders. And drinking a bit. I won't lie and say we weren't. So Bram here takes it into his head to steal us a pig. Oh, not a big one. Just a little one, he says. Our own private, seagoing pig. We'll hide the thing away until we're sick of the garbage they feed us aboard ship and are ready for a feast. Think of it, Lorrie—heading out to sea for God only knew how long, to face all sorts of dangers, to maybe get blown to Hell and beyond—and Bram here is worrying about our bellies. Well, it seems a fine enough plan to me anyway— o'course I'm drunk as a wheelbarrow at the time—until he tells me he wants to take the pig aboard *alive!*"

Bramwell bent his head and bit on the inside of his cheek, wishing his friend silent.

"He tells me the pig we find is too little to make much of a meal. We'll have to take him with us, Bram says, hide him well, and then fatten him up once he's on board. So I say to him, 'I say Bram, how're we to do that?' And he doesn't even blink. He says, he says to me, we'll call him Ensign Porker. And we do! Give him space in our own damn cabin! Feed that damn pig, fatten him up, clean up after it—and that's no fun, let me tell you. And then Bram here decides he loves the thing, and won't kill it. Two months of feeding and mopping up after that damnable pig, hiding it from everyone, and now he won't eat it." He turned to his friend accusingly. "You still have the thing somewhere, don't you, Bram?"

Bramwell rubbed at his forehead, embarrassed, then reluctantly smiled. "Ensign Porker resides most happily at Selbourne Hall, yes. But you didn't want to slaughter the animal either, Wally, in the end. I believe you even went so far as to say it was fratricide."

"Yes, well," Sir Wallace explained, puffing out his rosy cheeks, "I was also fairly deep in my cups at the time, celebrating the end of the war, as I remember, and feeling overly sentimental."

"You're always fairly deep in your cups, Wally," the Baron broke in kindly enough, handing his friends what would be their first glasses of wine for the day—well, his and Bramwell's that was. Sir Wallace was already at least a half bottle of wine and several snifters of cherry brandy ahead of them. "That's why your nose is so red. By the bye, it looks like you forgot to powder it again this morning. I believe, if I sat close enough, I could read by the shine on the thing."

"Don't deny a man his only pleasure," Sir Wallace said gruffly, then downed the contents of his glass in a single long swallow. "Ah, that's better. Now, where were we?"

"We were asking Bram here to tell us about his new ward," the Baron supplied helpfully, earning himself a quick, withering glance from the ninth duke.

"She's not my ward, Lorrie, and well you know it," Bramwell corrected, wondering how he was going to warn his friends that they were about to go out for a morning drive with a young woman bent on breaking their hearts. Bent on breaking the heart of every gentleman she met.

The baron smiled, exposing two rows of very even white teeth. "Yes, Bram, I well know it. But that doesn't mean I don't delight in watching you wince every time I prod at you with that particular pointy stick. Now, tell us the whole of it. I saw the Widow Winstead once, remember, when I was home on leave. Oh, she was older than me, but I was still young and faintly fuzzy, and would have given up my hope of Heaven to have her smile at me. So— what's the daughter like? Give us a hint."

"Dangerous," the duke heard himself saying before he could monitor his thoughts.

"Ah! Well, I like that!" Sir Wallace fairly shouted. "Dangerous, is it?" He turned to the Baron. "Either she walks about with a sword between her teeth, Lorrie, or we've got us another Constance Winstead. And, from the look on Bram's face, I'd say it was the latter, wouldn't you?" He sat up straight, rubbing his palms together. "Lead me to her, lads, and then make yourselves scarce."

The duke would have told them then, told them the whole of it; everything he'd learned, everything he'd supposed. But that would have been betraying secrets Sophie had told him in confidence, secrets she had purposely told just to him, just to infuriate him. Confuse him. Confound him. Keep him awake half the night, not knowing whether he should toss her out on her fairly provocative rear, or try to comfort her for all the times the child in her had been hurt, been betrayed.

But there was something else, something that still bothered him. What if she hadn't been so artless in her truths after all? Perhaps she had simply found a new way to dazzle him, a new way to charm herself into his sympathy and good graces, the way she had discovered his aunt's weaknesses, Isadora's weaknesses—and then used them to her own advantage.

After all, if he felt compassion for her, she could count on him to go out of his way to see that she wasn't snubbed by anyone in society.

He just didn't know, couldn't be sure. When she told the truth he wasn't sure. When she lied, he was even less sure. And when she smiled? When he'd kissed her?

He really didn't want to think about that.

"Bram? I say, Bram—you're not answering me."

The duke blinked away his thoughts and looked at Sir Wallace inquiringly, hoping the man would repeat his question. "Forgive me, Wally. I was woolgathering, I suppose."

"Yes, Bram, we know. That's what I just said. Woolgathering. Actually, I said you look sunk in a funk. Don't tell me Miss Winstead frightens you? Not the same man who climbed into the riggings, cutting loose a mangled sail in the midst of a Channel storm."

Lord Lorimar held up his hands, motioning for Sir Wallace to be silent. "What is it, Bram?" he asked, cocking his head to one side. "There's something you're not telling us. What's the matter? Is the girl a complete loss? Is she so fat she needs to be rolled into a room? Pick at her teeth at table? Or is it something else? Perhaps she's the beauty her mother was before her, and Miss Waverley wants her shot at dawn?"

Bram's head shot up. "Isadora is *not* a jealous sort!"

"Ah-hah!" Lord Lorimar exclaimed. "And there you have it, Wally. The chit's beautiful. Probably gorgeous. Well, there's nothing wrong with that, now is there?"

"That would depend on how she plans to go on," Bramwell pointed out, doing his best to say what he meant without really saying anything. "If it's marriage she's after in coming to London, as she says, then her beauty can only be considered a help—along with her very impressive personal wealth."

Sir Wallace shook his head as if trying to rattle his brains into action. "Wait a moment! As she says, Bram? You don't *believe* her? Why else would she be here? Why else are we bombarded with young misses and conniving mamas every Season, all powdered and primped and dressed to the nines—if not for the purpose of leading any number of us happy, carefree bachelors into marriage?"

"Just remember that when you meet her, Wally," Bramwell answered warningly. "And you, too, Lorrie. Because the girl is out for marriage. As my aunt has already said, I believe we're in for a siege. I wouldn't want either of you trampled in the rush of gentlemen callers breaking down my front doors once Miss Winstead is presented. She's going to break dozens of hearts, and I don't want two of them to be yours."

He knew he wasn't being entirely honest with his friends, but what else could he say? He couldn't say that he worried Sophie's aim might be to go into Society in order to seek out some of her "uncles" and then embarrass them, even blackmail them—not because she needed the money, certainly, but just because she wanted to hurt them. He couldn't say that she might be entering Society in order to purposely break hearts, to lead on as many men as she could, just to give back some of the pain she'd felt each time she watched another man leave her mother—leave her. He couldn't say that she was here, in London, to play her own little game, run her own small rig on Society, then pick a titled gentleman to act as stud for her legitimate children—an older, titled peer who would then conveniently expire, leaving her to return to Society and wreak havoc with even more gullible gentlemen.

He couldn't say any of that because, in his heart of hearts, he couldn't really bring himself to believe any of it. He could only think about everything Sophie had said, about the way she had said it, about the way she had vehemently denied his accusations.

But what else was he supposed to think of a woman who had the body of a courtesan, the face of an angel, the deviousness of a court intriguer, and the most infuriating, chameleon-like way of making everyone she met believe that she was precisely who they needed her to be?

"Break our hearts, is it?" Lord Lorimar slapped his knees and rose to his feet, looking tall and blond and extremely handsome, the secret wish of many a debutante in Seasons past. "I think we've been insulted, Wally. Damme me if I don't. As if we're green-as-grass young bucks, about to succumb to the first pretty face we've ever seen. Tell you what, Bram—let's have us a wager. Wally, you up for a wager?"

"What sort of wager?" Sir Wallace asked carefully. "None of this business where the loser has to stand up at Covent Garden at the intermission and pull down his trousers before making a backward bow toward the box across the way."

"But you were splendid, Wally," Bramwell said, smiling at the long-ago memory. So long ago. Perhaps a lifetime ago? No, not really. Only a half dozen or more years ago— before he had gone off to sea, before his father had run so publicly mad with the Widow Winstead. "It was only poor luck that Lady Radford had taken that moment to raise her lorgnette and do an inventory of that night's attendance."

"If it's very, very quiet," Lord Lorimar put in face- tiously, "I believe I can still hear her shrieks. Oh, very well, Wally, if you're going to be a spoilsport otherwise, we'll make it something simpler. We won't even call it a wager. We'll call it a challenge—with a forfeit to be paid by any or all of us who fail to meet that challenge."

"Something less embarrassing, that's what," Sir Wallace corrected, looking into the bottom of his empty glass. "But first, Lorrie—what are we wagering—um, *challenging*— about?"

"About Miss Winstead, of course," the baron explained reasonably. "We're to make a pact among the three of us— or a challenge, or a wager, whatever we want to call it. I'm including you, Bram, as you're betrothed, not dead, and just in case Miss Winstead is as beautiful and desirable as you seem to be afraid she is. And now, this is the challenge. We three will agree here and now that we will not have our hearts broken by Bram's ward. In fact, we three cannot, will not, become in any way infatuated with, fall in love with, or even very much *like* Bram's ward. Maybe some- one should be writing all of this down?"

"Not my ward," Bramwell slid in, automatically contradicting his friend who undoubtedly knew he would, for the Baron's smile grew even wider.

"And if we do?" Sir Wallace asked, shifting uncomfortably in his chair. "What is the forfeit? And shouldn't we at least meet the chit first? What if she isn't anything out of the ordinary? We might be able to resist her with no effort at all. Where's the sport in that?"

Lord Lorimar looked to Bramwell, who was now biting the insides of both cheeks in an attempt to keep any betraying expression from his face. "I've seen the mother. And our friend here called the daughter *dangerous*, Wally, remember? That's definitely out of the ordinary. Now, to the forfeit," he continued, beginning to pace the carpet in front of the duke's desk. "It has to be something sufficiently sobering, so that we really, really don't want to do it."

"Rescue Ensign Porker from Bram's estate and ride him bareback through the Park?" Sir Wallace offered, looking hopefully to Bramwell.

"Don't punish an innocent pig," the duke said, giving in to a small smile. He really should put a stop to this, tell his friends *no*. But, then again, when was the last time he'd had himself a spot of fun?

"Point well taken," Lord Lorimar agreed. "This must remain private, just among ourselves." He walked behind the desk and drew a sheet of paper from the center drawer as the duke held a pen out to him. "Thank you, Bram," he said, dipping the pen into the inkwell and beginning to scratch across the paper. "We shall work out an ascending series of forfeits. And we must be honest, with ourselves, and with each other. This is to be a test of honor as well, gentlemen. Now let's get down to it. If, for instance, any of us was to find ourselves *admiring* Miss Winstead, the offending party will . . . will—I've got it! The offending party will be forced to attend Almack's three weeks running."

"Three weeks?" Sir Wallace dropped his chin into his cravat. "I never attend but the once, and that's only because m'mother expects it, her being such great chums with Lady Jersey and all. Make it two, Lorrie. Any more than that and Mama will be having expectations of her own. I have enough on my plate without that."

The baron scratched out the line he had just written and began again. "All right. That's *two* weeks for admiring Miss Winstead. You don't have to confess to your admiration, but you must be honest within yourself. Within *ourselves*, as I naturally am included. What else?"

There was a slight scratching at the door, and Bobbit entered, carrying a tray of small cakes.

"I have it!" Sir Wallace exclaimed, snagging one of the iced confections before the butler could place the silver tray on the desk and retire. "For everything else after the first infraction—from feeling in charity with the girl for a moment, to asking her to dance more than once of an evening, to entertaining the notion of taking her out for the Promenade or to the theater—for everything up to proposing marriage—we have to give Bobbit here five pounds. Every time, every infraction. We don't have to shame ourselves by confessing anything to each other that way. We just have to pay Bobbit. Agreed?"

"Five pounds? Each and every time? I say, Wally, ain't that a bit steep?"

"What's the matter, Lorrie?" Sir Wallace quipped, grinning. "You that unsure of yourself?"

"Your Grace?" Bobbit asked, turning to his employer in some confusion.

"It's not to worry, old fellow," Bram said comfortingly, winking at Lord Lorimar. "You're about to become independently wealthy."

"Yes, Your Grace. Very good, Your Grace," the butler said, bowing—and looking toward Sir Wallace hopefully. "Anything else, Your Grace?"

"Not really, no. Unless you know when the ladies will be ready for their drive?"

"Miss Waverley has just now arrived, Your Grace, and Lady Gwendolyn and Miss Winstead are with her in the drawing room. Shall I have the equipage and your mounts brought round, Your Grace?"

Bramwell nodded, and the butler withdrew, but not before taking one last, quizzical look at Sir Wallace. "Well, that's it then, gentlemen," the duke said, ready to have this unnerving conversation behind him as he motioned for his friends to depart the room ahead of him.

"Not quite," Lord Lorimar said, holding up the pen. "There's one more thing. Marriage."

"*Marriage?*" Sir Wallace stumbled to the drinks table to fortify himself. "It would take a bit more than a pretty face to lead me to proposing marriage, let me tell you. A whacking great lot more. Besides," he added, turning to point at Bramwell, "Bram here is already all but bracketed. That leaves only you and me, Lorrie."

"True and true, Wally, but the list isn't complete unless we include the forfeit if one of us actually loses our head sufficiently to think about proposing marriage. A large forfeit, so that we'll think twice, perhaps three times, before allowing this *dangerous* woman to snare us in any parson's mousetrap."

"I don't believe I'm actually listening to this conversation, let alone being a part of it," Bramwell said, sighing.

Sir Wallace wagged a finger in his direction. "Now, now, Bram, Lorrie's got a point. I came within a whisker of offering for Miss Keller last Season, if you remember. What a lucky escape that was, let me tell you. But I never would have fallen to that point if there had been a heavy forfeit to pay. Think of all the trouble a forfeit would save us."

Bramwell crossed to his friend and laid an arm across his shoulders. "Wally, Miss Keller went to an earl before you so much as got up your courage to ask if you could accompany her down to dinner. I don't think she even knew your name."

Sir Wallace flushed to the roots of his dark blond hair. "I was about to declare myself, Bram, but Wakefield stole a march on me, that's all. And thank the good Lord he did."

"This is getting us nowhere, gentlemen, and the ladies mustn't be kept waiting," Lord Lorimar declared, sanding the paper and then leaving it on the desk to dry. "Done and done. I've made up the forfeit myself. Any man among us who finds himself thinking about proposing marriage to Miss Winstead," he said, looking down at what he had just written, "must make Samuel Seaton his bosom chum for a month."

Bramwell dropped his arm from Sir Wallace's shoulder and glared at the man he had been so foolish as to believe was one of his best friends. "That isn't funny."

"It isn't?" Lord Lorimar's gray eyes twinkled with barely concealed merriment. "I think it's jolly amusing myself. He might be your heir, Bram, until you and Miss Waverley reproduce yourselves, but he's also the most pathetic person in all the world. There have been, or so I'm told, those who have leapt in front of charging carriages on Bond Street, rather than have to meet up with him as he approaches along the flagway. Strong men who have cowered behind potted palms or small, innocent children, simply to avoid him. Whole battalions of people who have emigrated to America, just to assure themselves they won't be seated next to him at some dinner party."

"Don't tease, Lorrie." Sir Wallace slid his arm around the duke's shoulder, first giving him an encouraging slap on the back. "Oh, come on, Bram," he said bracingly. "Lorrie's only funning with you. Your cousin isn't that terrible. No, never mind. He is. Sad Samuel Seaton." He shivered. "I'd rather listen to my Uncle Winston go on and on yet again about the purulent carbuncle he had on his backside last year."

He shivered once more, mumbling half under his breath as he dropped his arm and turned to walk toward the hallway. "Sad Samuel's even worse than a purulent carbuncle, I swear he is. Well, that settles it. I'm ready to meet Miss Winstead now, forewarned and forearmed, knowing full well I'd never think of proposing marriage to her. Every time I look at her, all I'm going to see is a month of Sad Samuel."

As Baron Lorimar moved to follow after Sir Wallace, the duke took hold of his sleeve, pulling him to a halt.

"You're a bad and woefully twisted man, Lorrie, do you know that?"

"Yes, Bram, I know. I've always considered it to be a large part of my charm," Lord Lorimar replied, patting Bramwell's cheek. "But you yourself have nothing to worry about, right? You and Miss Waverley will soon be married, and Miss Winstead—the *dangerous* Miss Winstead—will be long gone. Or so you say."

"What's that supposed to mean?" the duke asked, following after the Baron and stepping in front of him.

Lord Lorimar stopped at the bottom of the stairs now that his friend had blocked them. "It means just this, Bram. I've never before heard a woman described as dangerous. And that makes me wonder. Clearly you're not totally unmoved by the girl. It might be nice, frankly, to see you do something, well, something at least vaguely stupid, even foolhardy. You've been so dedicatedly upright since your father and the Widow Winstead flew off that balcony. Not that I'm saying you don't have good reason to be as unlike the man as you wish, for the sake of the family name and all of that. But we used to laugh more, Bram, I'm sure of it." He shook his head. "Never mind, Bram. I think we're just getting old, that's all. We'll never see thirty again, none of us. It's damned depressing, that's what it is. Well, *hul-lo!*"

Bram didn't have to peek behind him to the head of the staircase, to where Lord Lorimar and Sir Wallace were now staring. "She's up there, isn't she?" he asked quietly, hoping to shake his friends out of their stunned immobility.

"Oh, yes. Oh, yes, Bram, she most certainly is up there." Lord Lorimar put his hand on the duke's arm and unceremoniously pushed him out of the way so that he could mount the stairs. "And so am I!"

The duke stood back, waiting until Sir Wallace had also begun climbing the stairs, then finally turned and looked to where Sophie Winstead was standing, peering down over the curving sweep of banister that ran along the first floor of the mansion. She was cloaked and ready for her drive through the still-cool morning, dressed all in cherry red, accents of ermine on her ridiculously adorable hat, her wide collar, and making up the outrageously large muff she carried.

A small riot of warm brown ringlets escaped the ridiculous hat, framing her face. A wide smile lit her gamine-like features, and her throaty laugh as Lord Lorimar bent over her hand filled the air like a heavenly chorus. She looked like Christmas morning. A long-hoped-for present just waited to be unwrapped. A succulent pudding, bursting with sweetness. A bright, luscious, delicious cherry set atop the season's first dish of iced cream. A faintly rumpled, touchable Gypsy. Eager. Alive. Part innocent, part temptress. A gift. A curse.

She looked, Bram decided, *dangerous*.

And then Isadora Waverley appeared behind Sophie. Taller, slimmer, straighter. Her outer garments were a sedate slate blue, cut along more severe, sophisticated lines. That was his betrothed. Icily beautiful, composed, regal, quietly elegant, without a single sleek black hair out of place. She was the epitome of good breeding, excellent taste, refinement. Bram attached his gaze to her—as a drowning man would cling to a bit of driftwood.

There is, however, a limit at which
forbearance ceases to be a virtue.
          —Edmund Burke

Chapter Five

Lady Gwendolyn's shiny black landau, its divided roof folded back to open it up to the sun, comfortably seated four persons. Uncomfortably, it sat six, if one did not balk at being stuck cheek by jowl with two other persons. Lord Lorimar and Sir Wallace, whose mounts remained behind at the Portland Square mansion, seemed not to mind at all—clambering up into the landau like drooling, near-to-blithering idiots directly after Sophie, then seating themselves on either side of her.

The duke, however, had graciously chosen not to discommode his aunt and fiancée, or—as Sophie thought—to make such a cake of himself over her saucy smile and outlandishly overdone ensemble. After handing the other two ladies up into the laudau, he had mounted a handsome-looking bay gelding and followed along behind as the party was driven to the Park. To see. To be seen.

And Mrs. Farraday, the dear, oblivious Mrs. Farraday,

was left behind on the flagway, forgotten by everyone and still frowning at a footman who was all but screaming in her ear, telling her she was being allowed a morning free of the responsibility of her ward.

Sophie was delighted, both with the day and with her company. The sun was bright, even though the air still had more than a bit of a nip in it. She laughed out loud as an unexpected breeze caught them as the landau moved away from the protection of buildings and into the park, nearly costing Sophie her wonderful new hat.

"Oh, this is lovely!" she exclaimed, sitting up very straight and looking around her at all the nurserymaids and their charges walking the paths, at the gentlemen, on horseback or strolling about, swinging their canes and acting very much like young colts just turned out into the fields for the first time. There was color everywhere. In the bright green new leaves, the flowers lining the paths, the ladies' gowns, the gentlemen's canary yellow waistcoats, the brightly colored carriages and curricles and high-perch phaetons.

And the air smelled so good. Delicious. Whenever the wind shifted Sophie smelled something else new and exciting. The aroma of hot meat pies and currant pastries. The heady fragrance of pollen-rich flowers. The smell of horse, of freshly turned dirt, of chimney smoke; the odd attraction of Sir Wallace's wine-sweet breath, even the tangy scent of tobacco that lingered on Lord Lorimar's clothing.

How she had missed the company of gentlemen!

"Lud, Miss Winstead," Isadora Waverley prompted from the facing seat—she and Lady Gwendolyn were, of course, ensconced on the front-facing seat, so that Sophie had to content herself with seeing where she had been rather than where she was going, "a word of advice, if I might? You're not to gawk, my dear. It smacks of the country miss, you understand."

Sophie dragged her gaze from the rows of distant rooftops and the comical sight of the dozens of variously shaped chimney pots that poked against the sky. "Oh, Miss Waverley, you are *so* right!" she exclaimed, taking her gloved hands from her muff and spreading them wide— nearly clipping the grinning Sir Wallace on his shiny red nose. "I'm such a silly goose. Why, my jaw has been at half cock ever since we started out from Wimbledon, Desiree and I, so that I shouldn't be surprised if I end up with a sparrow flying into my open mouth. I have never seen the city, you understand—and find it all so exciting, so beautiful. To have seen London is to have seen the world, yes?"

Lord Lorimar bent forward to retrieve Sophie's muff from the floor of the landau, handing it back to her with a flourish even as she thanked him as if he had just presented her with a diamond the size of Sir Wallace's nose. "You have seen but a small part of our fair metropolis, Miss Winstead," he told her. "However, I would consider it an honor and a privilege to show you more of it."

Sophie was about to agree, then bit her lip, looking to Miss Waverley. "Would—would that be all right?"

Isadora smiled her usual cool, gracious smile. "I should think that Lord Lorimar might have better presented his invitation to Lady Gwendolyn, my dear, and asked her permission before approaching you, but I see no reason to withhold such an innocent treat. Lady Gwendolyn?"

"Me? You're asking me?" Lady Gwendolyn frowned.

"Shouldn't he be asking Bramwell? She's *his* ward. That's a lovely brooch you're wearing, Miss Waverley. I do so admire garnets. May I have it?"

Isadora looked at her ladyship in some shock. "May you have it? Lud, my lady, I think not. It was a gift from my father." She looked at the now crestfallen Lady Gwendolyn queerly, then seemed to remember that the woman was her betrothed's aunt. "But I do thank you for the compliment, my lady. Truly."

"You like garnets, Aunt Gwendolyn?" Sophie interposed quickly, seeing her ladyship's distress. "I have dozens— more than any one person could wear in a month of Seasons. Brooches, necklaces, bracelets, rings. When we return to Portland Square we shall perch ourselves on your bed, munch sugarplums, and paw through the pile of stones together. And you shall have your pick of the lot to keep—as my gift to you for being so wonderfully kind to this undeserving stranger. All right?"

"Such a nice girl," Lady Gwendolyn cooed, still staring at Miss Waverley's brooch. "Bramwell is fortunate in his ward."

Miss Waverley's head moved a fraction, as if she were trying not to react to having been slapped, even as she protectively closed her fingers around the coveted piece of jewelry. "Not his ward, Lady Gwendolyn," she corrected kindly but firmly as Sophie watched from beneath lowered lashes. "But only Miss Winstead's sponsor for the length of the Season. Nothing more permanent than that."

"Oh, heavens, no, nothing more permanent than that," Sophie agreed, giggling. "I shouldn't wish to be a burden to the dear duke."

"I can envision the sun tumbling from the sky, Miss Winstead," Lord Lorimar broke in feelingly. "I can imagine the birds mute, the stars falling dark, the grass at our feet turning purple. But I cannot, Miss Winstead, ever imagine you being any sort of burden."

"Oh-ho—there he goes!" Sir Wallace exclaimed, and Sophie turned to him in time to see him rolling his eyes heavenward. "Can you swim, Miss Winstead? It's getting to be dashed deep water in here."

"Stubble it, Wally," Lord Lorimar spat from between clenched teeth, so that Sophie smiled brightly at the ladies sitting across from her, then shrugged, as if she had no idea why gentlemen acted the way they did, silly things.

"Do you know what I should like?" she chirped as the landau stopped, for the curricle in front of them had come to a halt on the pathway, one of its wheels obviously having worked loose. "I should like to get down and walk for a while, that's what I should like. Is that permissible? Miss Waverley, would you care to take a small stroll?"

"Walk?" Miss Waverley repeated hollowly, as if Sophie had asked her accompaniment on a journey to the moon. "Lud, just the thought! But the dew—your hem? No, I shouldn't think I'd like to do that."

Sir Wallace had already flung open the low door. "I'll accompany you, Miss Winstead," he offered eagerly, holding up his hand to her. "They can just catch us up on their next circuit around the Park."

Before Lord Lorimar could do more than whisk himself across the seat as Sophie jumped down, Sir Wallace had slammed the door shut once more and called to the driver to move off around the disabled equipage as they were holding up the coach behind them. Sophie watched as the duke glared down at Sir Wallace, then followed off after the landau, leaving her and the shiny-nosed schemer alone together beside the pathway.

"My congratulations, Sir Wallace," Sophie told him as he offered her his arm and she slipped hers around it, leaning against him as they made their way across the grass. "I fear I would never have been able to convince the ladies that it is much more fun to be walking on such a lovely day as this instead of sitting all prim and proper and being driven about like melons in the back of a wagon."

"And twice the fun to be walking rather than to be stuck listening to the drivel that pours out of Lorrie's mouth," Sir Wallace grumbled, then brightened. "Would you like to pick some flowers, Miss Winstead? It isn't strictly allowed, but the Park is fairly thin of company, and I saw some posies back there a while ago that would look very fetching tucked into your, um, into your . . ."

"Buttonhole?" Sophie suggested helpfully, raising her muff-covered arm to indicate the top button of her cherry red ensemble.

She watched as bright color ran into Sir Wallace's cheeks, staining them nearly as deeply as his shiny nose. *"Harrumph!"* he said, coughing into his fist. "Buttonhole, Miss Winstead. That would be it. Precisely that. Buttonhole. Yes, yes. Buttonhole."

"Some buttercups for the buttonhole," Sophie recommended as she tugged on his arm, leading him toward an area of the fairly ragged spring grass where the wildflowers had not yet fallen to the scythe. "That way we will not fall afoul of the law, if the flowers are considered the property of the Crown, yes? I should like to see as much of London as I can, Sir Wallace, but I don't believe I would find the inside of the local guardhouse at all edifying. You drink, Sir Wallace, don't you, poor dear?"

She danced away from him then, leaving him to stand openmouthed and dazed at her last words. By the time he had caught up with her she was sitting on her skirts in the dewy grass, busily filling her lap with creamy yellow buttercups. "Forgive me. I can't have heard you aright, Miss Winstead. What—what did you say?" he asked, dropping to his knees beside her, which put paid to his pantaloons, not that he seemed to notice.

"Oh, but you did hear me aright, Sir Wallace." Sophie picked up a half dozen blooms and threaded them into the top buttonhole of Sir Wallace's waistcoat. "I smelled wine on your breath," she explained, looking steadily into his sad, puppy brown eyes. "And, I believe, just the hint of cherry brandy, yes? I have always enjoyed the sweetness of cherry brandy when I was allowed the occasional sip. It makes the insides all warm and comfortable and cosseted. Rather as if everything in the world was rosy and wonderful. But to have imbibed so much this early in the day? That can't be good, now can it? There," she said, patting his waistcoat before resting back on her heels, admiring her handiwork. "Now, don't you look handsome?"

"Ladies ain't supposed to drink cherry brandy," Sir Wallace said, then winced, as if he had spoken before he could think. But, as she had already supposed he would, he opened his mouth yet again, and went on to dig himself deeper into a pit of unfortunate wonderings. "I suppose your mother drank cherry brandy, and fed it to you as well.

She did lots of things ladies ain't supposed to do. And had a lot of fun doing them, I've no doubt. But you really shouldn't drink it anymore, Miss Winstead. Ratafia. That's the way to go. Ratafia, the occasional glass of wine, I suppose, if someone offers it and the other ladies are drinking it. And lemonade. You can't go wrong with lemonade."

"I'll try to remember that, thank you. Why do you drink, Sir Wallace?" Sophie asked him as she tucked a small nosegay of buttercups into her own buttonhole. "Uncle Horace drank because his wife was a shrew. That's what *Maman* said, and she must have been, because the woman finally came at Uncle Horace one night with his own campaign sword."

She grinned up at him. "They locked her away for a bit after that, *Maman* told me, where she couldn't hurt anyone. But Uncle Horace was much happier even after they let her out again, and didn't drink half so much. Although I must say he still liked his cherry brandy. We were always careful to keep some on hand for when he called."

Sir Wallace sat back on his heels as if trying to distance himself from Sophie, wagging one finger back and forth in front of his nose. "Oh, no," he said on a nervous chuckle. "Oh, no, no, no! You're not talking about Horace Autley, are you now, Miss Winstead, him who's been dead since Waterloo? My *uncle*, Horace Autley?"

Sophie opened her eyes very wide, then blinked several times, just as if she didn't already know everything she was about to ask. She really didn't remember Uncle Horace very well, but *Maman*'s journals had been very detailed, very precise on the man and his family—complete to a shade as a matter of fact. "Uncle Horace was *your* uncle, too? Not that he was *really* my uncle, but I called him Uncle Horace, you understand. Oh, but that's famous, Sir Wallace. He would have been your mother's brother?"

He shook his head, dismissing that notion. "Uncle Horace was married to the shrew. Um, that is, I mean to say that Uncle Horace was married to my mother's sister. Her twin, actually. Alike as two peas in a pod they are in every way, now that I think on it." He shivered in the bright sunshine. "Except that m'mother wasn't ever locked up. And you're right. She's not anymore, you know. Locked up, that is. My aunt, you understand. Lives with m'mother."

"Oh, dear." Sophie pushed out her bottom lip as she laid a hand on Sir Wallace's forearm, looking at him tenderly. And then she believed herself to have a blazing moment of insight. "Just as you still live with her, don't you?"

She thought the man would break down and cry. "Yes! Yes, I do!" he exclaimed, laying his own hand over hers. "I'm her only family now besides Aunt Millicent, what with my papa turning up his toes nearly a dozen years ago. They neither of them feels safe nor comfortable living in an all-female domicile, so I stay on. She still hasn't forgiven Bonaparte for taking me off to war, you understand."

"What a dear, good son you are, Sir Wallace," Sophie soothed, allowing him to help her to her feet, a shower of buttercups spilling to the ground as she shook out her skirts. "Although I'm sure the arrangement is pleasing to your mother and aunt, it's not one free of difficulties, yes? I imagine cherry brandy, among other spirits, helps to make you feel all warm and comfortable and cosseted."

"Difficulties? They're enough to grind a man straight into the ground, the pair of them. I could drink gallons—

and that's just at breakfast!" Sir Wallace exploded, then clapped a hand over his mouth and stared at Sophie. Slowly, he drew his hand away and smiled at her. "My God, Miss Winstead. Aren't you the downy one."

Sophie smiled in genuine happiness. The world was so simple, if one just took the time to listen, to learn, to look. "Do you know, Sir Wallace, that Uncle Horace found that a stout, strong butler and a few strapping footmen can make even the most nervous woman feel more secure in her surroundings? Handsome footmen, of a certain age, shall we say, can even be a comfort to fragile ladies fearful of being alone through the dark and lonely nights. So comforting, in fact, that one could think, couldn't one, that they might not even miss the presence of a devoted son and nephew—or require it, for that matter?"

Sir Wallace narrowed his eyes thoughtfully. "Uncle Horace died nearly penniless, so that Aunt Millicent was forced to move in with us. She's always going about, lamenting the loss of her butler, whom she had to let go. Goes on and on about it, when she's not kicking poor old Peterson, the family majordomo, and calling him useless as a third thumb. Miss Winstead, you're never saying that . . . and that m'aunt . . . that my uncle *arranged—my God*, what a thought! And my *mother*? That she might . . . that she might be interested in . . . that she'd even *think* to . . . But that's, that's—"

"A simple solution? And so, *so* much healthier than too much cherry brandy. At least that's what my dear mother told Uncle Horace when she suggested just that solution to him. You might want to think about that, yes?" Sophie offered, then danced away, waving gaily as the duke approached, his face dark as any storm cloud.

"Where are you headed, Wally?" his Grace called out as he stopped in front of Sophie, looking over her head at Sir Wallace, who was moving away from them rather than joining them.

Sir Wallace waved his hands in front of him as he backed toward the path, as if to say he had no time to dawdle, no time to answer questions. "Miss Winstead—farewell, and thank you. Thank you so much! Give my farewells to the other ladies, won't you, Bram? I've just remembered something I have to do, that's all. Then I'm off for home. Tomorrow is Wednesday, remember? I have to make sure my man knows to get my knee breeches ready for Almack's."

"Posies, Your Grace?" Sophie pulled a sadly crumpled bunch of buttercups from inside her muff, offering them to the frowning duke. "All the best-dressed gentlemen are wearing them this Season, you know. Or at least I hope they are, or Sir Wallace is going to feel extremely silly when he finally realizes that he's running about London with a clutch of them stuck in his buttonhole."

The duke looked down at her accusingly, his eyes steely, his jaw firmly set. "What did you do to him? What did you do to Wally—to Sir Wallace?"

Sophie sighed, shrugging her shoulders. He really should smile more. It would bring out those lovely crinkles around his eyes. But, then, he was probably suffering the tortures of the damned this morning, which fairly well served him right. Not that she'd let him see how much *she'd* suffered last night, reliving his unexpected kiss, her impossible-to-describe reaction to that kiss. "*Do* to him, Your Grace?" she now asked innocently. "I don't think I like what you're implying. I don't *do* anything to anybody."

Bramwell pushed his palm against his mouth, squeezing his cheeks as he turned his head to one side, as if he couldn't bear to look at her any longer, then dropped his hand and glared at her once more. "I knew better, you know. I knew better than to leave the two of you alone."

"Is that why you've come back, Your Grace? To effect a rescue?" Sophie asked, longing to slap him until his eyes rolled in his head. Goodness! She had to do no more than come within ten feet of the man for her temper to flare to life, for her fingers to itch to throw something. With every amount of will she could command, she suppressed the red wall of anger surging within her and returned to their verbal battle. Because she really did enjoy teasing the duke. She enjoyed it very much. "Because you're *afraid* of what I might do, yes?" she went on with a smile, prodding her dimple into evidence. "How many times must I tell you? I've not set out to harm anyone; I only want to make people happy. I *do* make people happy. Sir Wallace looked happy to you, didn't he? Surely you can't say he looked unhappy?"

Now His Grace looked as if he could slap *her*. "You dazzled him, didn't you?" he ground out accusingly as they began to walk back toward the pathway. "*How*, Miss Winstead? Wally never walks when he can ride. And he most certainly doesn't run. But you? You've got the fool *skipping*! Just tell me how. How did you do it?"

Sophie's smile widened, and she knew that smile to be

nearer an unholy grin. She could even feel her nose crinkling up. Should she tell him? Should she tell him that she
had known who Sir Wallace was all along, thanks to her
mother's marvelously detailed journals, and known of his
family, of his problems—even of her mother's positively
brilliant solution to those problems? Should she tell him that
she had only done what she had been taught to do—tried to
make those around her happy? Or should she fib, make up
some farradiddle about giving Sir Wallace a sad, depressing
sermon on the evils of drink and the joys of sobriety?

She saw that the landau had stopped ahead of them on
the pathway. The door was open, Lord Lorimar standing
on the ground, awaiting her pleasure, offering her sanctu-
ary. "Very well," she said at last, deciding on a half-truth,
an explanation that fell somewhere between fact and an
outright fib. "I'll tell you."

"You will?" Bramwell said, sounding more surprised
than angry now—which would change the moment she
opened her mouth.

"Yes, I will," she said as she judged the narrowing distance between herself and Lord Lorimar, and decided it
was safe to speak. "I simply suggested a way to make Sir
Wallace's mother and aunt happy. I pointed out to him that
if they were happy, he could also be happy—so much so
that he might not need such copious amounts of cherry
brandy to put a rosy haze around his life."

"And what would that *way* be?" the duke prodded, as
Lord Lorimar removed his curly-brimmed beaver and executed an elegant leg in Sophie's direction.

Sophie measured the distance between herself and the
landau once more, just to be certain. "I am nothing if not a

student of my mother, Your Grace. So, as would quite naturally follow, I simply told Sir Wallace to find his unhappy mother and aunt lovers. Once *they're* happy, Sir Wallace will find his own life much less oppressive."

"You—you did *what*?" Bramwell shot another look over his shoulder, to where Sir Wallace had been but was no longer, and then glared, narrow-eyed at Sophie once more. "I don't believe you."

"Oh, don't fib, Your Grace. Of course you believe me. It's just what you expect of me," Sophie answered with a quick giggle, then ran ahead to launch herself onto the steps of the landau and lightly vault onto the cushioned seat, the baron close behind her. "Have I kept you waiting? Oh, what a lovely parasol you've just opened, Miss Waverley," she said breathlessly, feeling Bramwell's eyes boring into her even as he stomped off to remount his horse. "Yes, it is quite the prettiest parasol I've ever seen. I must have one, I simply must. A dozen couldn't be too many. Do you think you could arrange an outing to Bond Street, Aunt Gwendolyn?"

"I imagine so," Lady Gwendolyn murmured absently, turning on the seat to look back over her shoulder, watching her nephew. "Now, what do you suppose is the matter with Bramwell? I vow I've never seen his face quite so red."

Sophie lifted the ermine muff to her face and buried a smile in the soft white fur. Kiss her, would he? Confuse her, befuddle her, break down her carefully built defenses and release the temper she had done so well to hide beneath her happiness—her hopes for a lifetime of happiness.

Silly, silly man. He couldn't win against her. No man

could win against her. Not if she did as Desiree said, as Desiree had taught. Not if she remembered that all men were ruled by their lusts, their desires, their *needs*.

All she had to do was to hold on to her heart, keep it safe. That's all she had to do, and her life would be wonderful. And, unlike her *maman* before her, she would never, ever cry.

Bramwell glanced at the small clock on his desk, then slipped the gold watch from his pocket and consulted it as well. He straightened the blotter on the desktop, aligned the ornate silver inkwell and sanding set an eyeball-measured five inches from the right edge of the desk, moved the humidor a fraction, and carefully, precisely, folded his hands on the blotter.

He would have occupied himself in turning his favorite paperweight over and over in his hands, but Aunt Gwendolyn's larceny had saved him from that bit of fidgeting.

Still, something else was wrong. He couldn't quite put his finger on it, but something else was wrong. Out of place. Or missing.

Missing? He jerked his hands away from the desktop as if the surface had turned into a hot stove. He pulled open the center drawer of the desk and began a careful search that soon evolved into a frantic shuffling of papers.

Missing. It was missing. It had been written out, sanded, and left lying on the desk. Right here. On the desk. On *this* desk. And now it was missing.

"Damn Lorrie all to hell and back!" the duke exclaimed, opening and closing the remaining drawers, knowing it was an exercise in futility. The list was gone.

"Aunt Gwendolyn," the duke growled just as there was a rather cheerful, loud rapping at the study door, and Sophie Winstead entered, as ordered. Bramwell quickly pulled his chair and himself forward to reassume his practiced pose, then just as rapidly shoved himself back from the desk again as he shot to his feet, remembering—only fleetingly—that he was a gentleman. "I said seven o'clock, Miss Winstead. You're early," he said accusingly as Sophie took up a chair directly in front of the desk, allowing her skirts to billow and fall where they might as she broke into a sunny smile.

"I am? I hadn't thought so, Your Grace." She laid her hands on the arms of the chair, obviously preparing to rise. "I could go out and come back, yes?"

The small clock on the desktop began chiming out the hour, striking seven times as Sophie breathed a small "Ah," then folded her hands in her lap and continued to smile. Innocent. Happy in her innocence. Not reproachful at all in the face of his accusation, his clumsy, bumbling incivility—making him feel ten times the fool he already knew himself to be.

It wasn't fair, that's what it wasn't. Even the damn clocks had turned on him.

And look at her. Dressed all in China blue silk, a wide fall of ivory lace foaming along the neckline of her low bodice, a triple-strand choker of perfect ivory pearls accenting her long, slender throat, disappearing beneath her artlessly tumbling curls that were so out of fashion. Or they would be, until she entered Society, at which time every lady's maid in Mayfair would be wielding hot curling sticks under the direction of a small battalion of frantic, clucking mamas.

Her gown wasn't the usual debutante's gown, although it was not so old-fashioned or so obvious or so *outré* as to cause her to be shunned. It was simply different, as all of Sophie's ensembles were different. A little "more" here, a little "less" there. The richest fabrics, the finest laces, the most clever arrangement of bows and ribbons.

Her jewels were also her own. Pearls were, of course, one of the few acceptable means of adornment for a debutante, and Sophie was wearing pearls. Only, on her, they looked like precious diamonds. How did she do that? How did she do any of what she was doing? How did she always manage to look like she was standing in a benevolent shower of sunlight, casting everything and everybody around her into the shade?

She was so different. So curiously unique. So completely Sophie.

Bramwell felt a sudden, insane urge to flee for his life.

He took refuge in anger instead—and he'd had ample time to build up a goodly store of it since they had last spoken that morning in the Park. Indeed, he'd already summoned up enough anger to construct a concealing wall between his conscience and his reprehensible behavior of the previous evening. Why, in another day or so, he'd probably find a way of convincing himself that kissing Sophie Winstead had been all her fault. Especially when he considered that she was acting as if that kiss had meant nothing, less than nothing . . . as if dukes kissed her all the time, and the exercise had been just too boring to speak about.

Which, of course, a small, hopeful voice inside him prompted, didn't explain the brandy stain on the wall. . . .

He remained standing and looked down his aristocratic nose at her. "I asked you here this evening to discuss your behavior this morning in the Park, Miss Winstead. It was, as you must know, reprehensible."

"I shouldn't have left the landau, yes? I shouldn't have sat on the grass? I shouldn't have picked the buttercups?"

Oh, he could murder the chit. Cheerfully. "You know damn well what I'm talking about, Sophie!" he exclaimed before he could think. Then he all but fell into his chair, wondering if a few more days of Sophie Winstead in his house would send him all the way around the bend. He certainly had lost half his wits already, and she'd only been in Portland Square for two days and one night. Had he just so slipped as to have addressed her as Sophie? Dear God, he had.

She nodded her head, smiling. "Ah, I think I know what it is. It's what I said to Sir Wallace, isn't it?" She tipped her head to one side, so that her curls tickled at her throat, slid forward slightly over one perfect cheek. "I'm sorry. I simply couldn't help myself, seeing as I'd fairly well decided what was troubling him. All that cherry brandy, Your Grace—it can't be good for one's spleen, yes?"

"He could have sent them on an edifying visit to Italy!" Bramwell exploded. "A leisurely tour of the Lake District would have gotten the pair of old biddies out from underfoot for a time. Or he could have done any of the other things I've suggested over the years, beginning with straightening his spine and simply moving out, setting up his own household."

"But he didn't, did he? Listen to you, that is," Sophie pointed out reasonably, leaning forward to slant the silver inkwell a fraction, making the entire desktop look—damn her—much more attractive, less rigidly proper. She then pulled the top from the humidor and took a deep breath of the aroma of fine cigar tobacco. "Would you care for one, Your Grace? I would very much enjoy watching you smoke."

"You all but told Sir Wallace to *pimp* for his mother and aunt," Bramwell persisted, but with waning anger, for he'd already realized that Sophie Winstead had no real notion of what she had done. Or, if she did, that she cared a jot for any of it. She had made Wally *happy*. It could only be considered a stroke of the greatest good fortune that she hadn't decided that killing the two oppressive old ladies and burying their bodies in the Park at midnight would serve to make Wally even happier.

"That sounds like such a nasty word, Your Grace, even if I don't fully know its meaning. I really don't think you should use it, yes?" Sophie drew out a single cigar and passed it just beneath her nose, drawing in more of the aroma. A look of near ecstasy flitted across her features before she offered the cigar to him. "Would you like me to light it for you? I used to clip off the end for Uncle Cesse, then light it for him. He taught me how to do it just right, I promise. I won't bungle it."

Bram gave up the fight. He took the cigar. He watched as Sophie located the small kit containing the cigar scissors and sulfur-tipped matches. After she'd snipped off the end, he stuck the cigar between his teeth before she could offer to do that for him as well, and puffed until the end was glowing, then followed Sophie with his eyes as she returned to her chair.

She looked so damn pleased. Pleased with him, pleased with herself, pleased to be alive. Not at all deceitful, or as if she had done anything that was the least artificial, the least out of the ordinary or against her own best wishes. He doubted she ever did anything she didn't truly want to do. She had lit his cigar because she *liked* lighting a man's cigar. She *liked* the aroma of a good cigar. She *liked* watching a man smoke. It made her—God help him—*happy*.

"Thank you," Bram said as the tobacco mellowed him slightly, took away the sharp edges that had been sticking inside his brain, inside his gut. "What do you plan for Lord Lorimar?" he heard himself ask. "I would only consider it a kindness if you'll agree to warn me."

"Lord Lorimar?" Sophie repeated, her nose crinkling up most delightfully, so that Bramwell found himself looking away, gazing toward the window and the growing dusk outside. "Why, nothing, Your Grace. He seems a very pleasant man, and more than marginally happy with himself."

"Cocky as a rooster clearing his gullet a minute before dawn," Bramwell agreed, feeling the corners of his mouth turning up in a smile around the cigar still stuck in his teeth. Sophie was nothing if not astute. He pulled open a drawer, extracted a crystal glass dish, and laid the cigar in it before pushing back his chair and rising to his feet. The cigar would extinguish itself, and he could smoke the rest of it later.

Walking around to the front of the desk as Sophie also stood up, he perched himself on the edge and smiled at her. She returned his smile, then reached past him, the side of her breast brushing up against his sleeve as she laid the spent match beside the still-smoking cigar.

Bramwell's brain became clogged with her sweet perfume, with the unexpected nearness of her, her total unawareness of what he was thinking. Lord help him—what he was thinking! He swallowed down hard over the sudden lump in his throat.

"I don't profess to understand you today any more than I did yesterday, Miss Winstead," he said, gazing down at the top of her head—she was such a tiny thing, for all her seeming voluptuousness. "But I'm beginning to think you might be more harmless than I at first thought."

"Oh, I'm entirely harmless, Your Grace. But this is wonderful, to hear you say so. Then you are beginning to like me, yes?"

Bramwell didn't know what to say. Telling this wide-eyed, winsome, amenable Sophie Winstead he didn't like her would be like beating a puppy for bringing him his slippers. One moment a child, the next a woman, and always a female. Winsome, yes. That was Sophie Winstead. But she was also wanton, wicked, winning, and wonderful. And, Lord, how he wanted her, even as he knew he couldn't, shouldn't, even think of such madness. "Yes, Miss Winstead. I'll admit to it. I *am* beginning to like you."

"Sophie," she said quietly as she stood back once more.

His Grace stiffened visibly, a niggle of apprehension taking hold somewhere inside his brain. *Forget the perfume, Selbourne*, he told himself, *and pay attention! Something's going on here; something you don't yet understand. A game; a strategy. Something. And none of it benefiting you! So forget the smile, the hair, that damn, luring, bewitching mouth.* "I beg your pardon?"

"I said, *Sophie*. You called me Sophie earlier, Your Grace, when you were scolding me. I rather liked it, even if I was not quite so enamored of the scolding. But, to call me Sophie? It's so much more friendly, yes?"

There wasn't any safe response to that question, so Bramwell didn't answer. "I'll be leaving for my club now," he said, straightening, standing rather rigidly in front of her even as the heady smell of wildflowers and fresh lemon intensified the curious feeling that was growing in his belly. If it *grew* much more, in fact, he'd have to sit himself back down and not move again until Sophie left the room.

"Of course," Sophie said, preceding him to the door, then stopping just at the archway, so that he couldn't move past her. "I'll miss you tomorrow, as I already have plans for the day, but you will be going to Almack's with us tomorrow night, Your Grace, yes?"

What? The devil he would. Was that all her game had been; all this business of lighting his cigar and the rest? Had it all been done in the hope of luring him to Almack's tomorrow evening? Silly girl. As if there were any way to get him to set foot inside those depressing walls. He relaxed visibly. "No, Sophie," he answered kindly but firmly, as he would have denied a child's request to remain downstairs past her bedtime, "I have no intention of attending Almack's. I never do. My aunt will accompany you and Mrs. Farraday. And Miss Waverley, of course."

Sophie pouted, just a little bit, her full bottom lip coming forward only slightly—enough to tease, to madden—to remind him that he had kissed those same sweet lips just twenty-four hours ago. And then, as he had stood there, relaxing, smugly congratulating himself, vowing to himself that the kiss had meant nothing, less than nothing, she applied *le coup de grâce*.

"Then you *lied* just now?" she asked, wide-eyed. "You really *don't* like me? Even though you kissed me? I don't understand; really I don't. Perhaps if I were to apply to Aunt Gwendolyn for an explanation—tell her how you kissed me, how you—well, you know what you did, yes?" she ended with a smile that told him she'd won, he'd lost. Game, Set, Match—and he'd barely even known he'd been playing! He'd might as well admit it. He and Almack's were going to meet tomorrow night, Heaven help them both!

And not, he also felt sure, merely because of the kiss, the threat of telling his aunt about the kiss. Oh no, Sophie wasn't that simple. If he'd learned one thing this day, it was that Sophie Winstead was about as "simple" as a Gordian knot.

"I see no need to involve Lady Gwendolyn in this," Bramwell said stiffly, wondering where Sophie had the paper Lord Lorimar had written, how she'd gotten hold of it. "I've kissed you, I agree. I also agree that you could possibly construe that to mean I might, in some way, at some level, like you. Liking you, I am honorbound to attend Almack's tomorrow evening, and next week as well. You know that. I know that. Now, can we just get on with it? Will you please say anything else you want to say on the matter now—or are you of a mind to strip my hide a single inch at a time?"

"Don't tempt me, Your Grace," Sophie purred, and he

watched, bemused, as she reached into the bodice of her gown. Extracting a piece of paper—*the* piece of paper— she unfolded it right in front of him even as he found his traitorous gaze concentrating on as much as he could see of what had to be the most perfect, creamy breasts in all of England. Just as she wanted him to do, damn her!

Had he actually begun to think Sophie Winstead to be relatively harmless? Had he truly begun to tell himself that he'd been wrong to term her "dangerous"? Did he also be- lieve black-and-white cows routinely somersaulted over the moon?

Sophie smiled up at him, then began reading. " 'We three, His Grace, the duke of Selbourne, Sir Wallace Mer- ritt, and myself, Baron Marshall Lorimar, cannot, will not, become in any way infatuated with, fall in love with, or even very much *like* one Miss Sophie Winstead. Infraction is punished by two successive weeks' attendance at Al- mack's, beginning with the next planned Assembly.' "

"I remember the words, Miss Winstead," Bramwell said. "I can only wonder how you came to possess something that is my property, something that belongs to me."

"Belongs to you, yes—but which concerns me." She folded the paper once more and replaced it in her bodice. "Giuseppe has one very small failing, Your Grace—be- yond chandeliers, of course. He brings me things, and ex- pects a treat in return. He received a very lovely treat this afternoon, as you can imagine. Sir Wallace has already mentioned his intention to attend Almack's tomorrow night. You can arrive with him, if you like, if you don't want to be seen entering the Assembly in the company of the Widow Winstead's daughter."

Bramwell stopped himself before he could make a potentially fatal lunge for the incriminating list. "That was all Lorrie's idea—I mean, Baron Lorimar's idea." He winced as Sophie blinked at him, knowing he wasn't being fair to his friend. There was nothing else for it. Either he cried craven, hid behind Lorrie, or he stood up and behaved like a gentleman. So thinking, he took a deep breath, straightened his shoulders, and intoned formally, "Be that as it may, we did go along with it. The whole business smacks of the juvenile and the absurd. It is also unfortunate, embarrassing to me, insulting to you, and I hereby apologize for all three of us."

"Nonsense!" Sophie countered happily. "I'm enjoying all of this very much, and am not in the least insulted. As I think Bobbit a good sort, I also shall enjoy watching as he amasses his unexpected fortune, if that doesn't make me sound too much the shameless braggart. And I most certainly look forward to meeting this person, this Sad Samuel Seaton, who must be a relative of yours, yes? Poor fellow, to be so unhappy as he must be to have earned himself that horrible name. I'll have to make it a point to see him happy, too. Yes, I will most definitely do that. Oh, and one thing more, I think. You, Your Grace, won't tell Sir Wallace and Baron Lorimar a word of what I know, yes? Because *that*, Your Grace, would most certainly not be fair."

Bramwell hadn't felt so chastised, or so threatened with dire consequences, since he'd been called in front of the headmaster and read a lecture on the folly of flying a kite into the bell tower when he should have been at vespers—the kite tail having tangled in the bell ropes, thereby putting a very large crimp in the evening's religious services.

As he had been caught out then, he had been caught out now. And the only thing left was to take his punishment like a man.

"I would be honored to be one of your party tomorrow night, madam," Bramwell said at last, each syllable he uttered cutting at his tongue like shards of sharp glass. "And now, if you'll excuse me?"

"I never meant to keep you, Your Grace." Sophie dropped into a curtsy, then moved to one side, to allow him to depart the room before he was left with only the memory of his former dignity.

He was inside his coach and on his way to his club before Sophie's words repeated themselves inside his weary brain. Over and over again. *I never meant to keep you, Your Grace.* He began to think the coach wheels were singing out the words with every turn over the cobblestones. *I never meant to keep you, Your Grace.*

No, she never meant to keep him. Bramwell knew that was true. "She's been honest enough about that at least, from the very outset. She's in London to enjoy herself, her mother's child: to dance, to flirt, to do God knows what with God knows whom. But she doesn't mean to keep anyone, most certainly of all Uncle *Ces-ee*'s son," he said, muttering the words into his cravat as he slumped against the squabs, wondering why this thought cheered him not at all.

Veni, vidi, vici.
    —Julius Caesar

Chapter Six

"*Alors!* If you are not soon for sitting, I shall never get this right."

Sophie leaned to her right once more, trying to catch another glimpse of herself in the long mirror, then backed up until she felt the edge of the dressing-table bench against her legs. She sat down, careful not to crease her gown, and bowed her head so that Desiree could clasp the near-to-waist-long string of perfect pearls around her throat.

She looked into the mirror over the dressing table—how she had begun to *adore* mirrors these past few days—and grinned at her friend's reflection. "I am pretty, yes?"

"You are *ravissante,* my little love," Desiree responded, giving the clasp a pat and stepping back to admire her handiwork. "*Ravissante!* Your mother's daughter, with your mother's beauty, your mother's genius, your mother's wit and admiration for the ridiculous, and—we thank the good Lord—none of her silly, sentimental heart. We

French know, Sophie. Women are made to break hearts, not to have them broken. There will be no tears for you, not while I am here. Only laughter and a heart to call your own. You've read your *maman*'s journals, you know what I say is true. Now, stand up and turn about, and let me see to this bodice. It will not do to be *too* charming at this Almack's, *oui?*"

Sophie happily complied, knowing herself wise to put her appearance in Desiree's capable hands. It had, after all, been Desiree who had chosen the fashion plate from those sent across the Channel from Madame Lisette in Paris. Desiree had also chosen the material for this gown, a brilliant, watermarked white taffeta that rustled when Sophie walked.

The gown was cunning in its simplicity. Where there should have been velvet ribbons, there were none. Where there should have been flounces kicking at the hem, there was no adornment. There was no embroidery on the puffed, cap sleeves.

The beauty of the gown lay in its utter lack of fripperies. It was almost plain, in fact—until one noticed the artful curve and sweep of the seams that ran just beneath the bodice, the large "diamonds" of carefully seamed cloth that made up the softly draping skirt and demitrain.

The bodice, the very plain, unadorned bodice, also was much, much more than a single piece of cloth. It had been, in fact, fashioned out of no less than two dozen cleverly cut pieces; diamonds upon diamonds sewn to accent the breasts, flatter the shoulders, mold against the upper back.

The result was so simple, so clever. Sophie's every movement, every breath she took, set the gown to glowing, sparkling, shimmering with light.

White kid gloves encased her hands and arms to above her elbows. White kid slippers skimmed her small, narrow feet. The rope of perfect pearls caressed her perfect neck, kissed the creamy, perfect skin exposed by the low bodice, tumbled over her perfect breasts, then fell to a good eight inches below her perfect waist. Like a magnet, the pearls drew a man's eye to all he could see—then down to all he could wish for, all in life he would ever long to possess.

Perfection.

Sophie's hair, as always, was allowed to riot where it willed, curling from her center part to her shoulders, a mass of touchable, barely tamed ringlets that formed a halo around her, yes, perfect features. No rouge pot was necessary to lend color to her cheeks or lips, and her eyes sparkled with an inner life, a private humor that would draw anyone not already mesmerized by her gown or her long rope of pearls.

"That fool Bonaparte would never have left Paris, had you had been there, *ma petite,* knowing that you were the only world worth conquering," Desiree cooed, looking exceptionally pleased with both herself and her charge. "Of course, Josephine would have had your head sliced off," she ended, shrugging. *"C'est la vie."*

"The good duke would also like to slice off my head, Desiree," Sophie said, fingering the small pearl that held the glove snug to her skin at the inside of her wrist. "Unless he has an apoplexy first. You should have seen his face when I waved that nasty little wagering list under his nose. He was caught between wishing to melt into the floor in embarrassment and wanting to strangle me. He's very handsome, yes?"

Desiree shook her head as she handed Sophie her reticule, a cunning little diamond-shaped piece that matched her gown, slung from a long, thin satin rope and edged with a three-inch-long fringe. "You shouldn't have told him what Giuseppe found. Now he'll be watching you twice as hard."

"Yes, I know," Sophie said, taking the reticule and playing with the fringe, allowing it to slide across her fingers like river water would cascade over a smooth rock. She hadn't told Desiree about the kiss; she wasn't so foolish as that, even as she loved the woman. But the kiss was her secret, her dilemma, her puzzle to solve. "I like when he watches me. He looks so hungry."

"Hungry, is it? I could call it something else." Desiree rolled her eyes and muttered something short and Gallic— and probably obscene—beneath her breath. "For all I try, for all my lessons, she remains at heart her mother's child. Next she'll be telling me she loses herself in his eyes. Lord help us all!" She gave Sophie a gentle shove toward the door. "Now get yourself downstairs, *ma petite,* before they leave without you."

"I'm not my mother, Desiree," Sophie said firmly, accepting the fringed shawl the woman handed her. "As you said, I've read her journals. I can remember listening to her weep behind the closed door of her bedchamber when yet another uncle gave her her *congé.* Always, she believed she loved them. And always, they left her. Take and give, give and take—but keep your heart to yourself, yes? I'm your student, Desiree. I've listened to you, and learned everything you've taught me. Men speak of love, but only to get what they want. In truth, there is no such thing as love. Only desire."

Desiree laid her hands on Sophie's shoulders. "Desire, yes, *ma petite,* and it is a lovely thing. Very enjoyable, for both the man and the woman, if it is done right. But never love, *chérie.* Love will leave you alone." She kissed her young charge on both cheeks. "And frowns will give you the wrinkles, *oui?* Now go, have fun, be dazzling. Be the innocent you are. Find yourself a husband, for this respectability you must have. Only after that, *chérie,* will we speak again of desire."

Some perverted trickster had poured molasses in all the clocks. There could be no other explanation as to why time was passing so slowly. How long had Bramwell been here, watching Sophie dazzle the *ton?* Two hours? Three days? How could it only be just past eleven, with half the evening still to be survived without running stark, staring mad?

Warm lemonade, warmer rooms, stale cakes, tame-stakes gambling, marriage-minded mamas, simpering debutantes—*that* was the Almack's the duke remembered. Or it had been, until his friends Wally and Lorrie had made the rounds of their clubs, tripped up and down Bond Street, telling anyone who would listen that the Widow Winstead's daughter would be attending Almack's. Her beautiful daughter. Her very rich daughter.

Between the curious and the fortune hunter, the ambitious and the randy—some of them (God only knew how many) possibly once the recipient of her mother's favor— Almack's was packed to the rafters this evening with eligible and not so eligible but still eager gentlemen.

All of them waiting for Sophie's arrival.

All of them struck damn near dumb when she'd walked into the room—except for Robbie Sykes, who'd been drunk enough to loudly call out to Bramwell to step aside, so that he could get a better look.

As Bramwell had watched, Sophie had smiled as if she knew this "party" was being held expressly for her. She had then succeeded in that first, unbelievable moment, and without so much as lifting a finger on her own account, to dazzle every last man jack of them.

Either that, or some mischief-making witch had sprinkled looby dust over every gentleman present. A sane person could think none of them had seen a women in a dozen years, for the way they'd stamped, herdlike, to Sophie's side the moment she'd opened her dance card and gifted the company with a knee-melting, hopeful smile.

It was pitiful. They were pitiful. His male friends. His acquaintances. High and low and in between. All of them. Why, the earl of Watton had actually offered Bramwell one hundred pounds if he'd scratch himself from leading Sophie out for her first, patronesses-approved waltz—just as if he were a racehorse who had suddenly turned up lame before the opening race.

Yes, it was embarrassing. Lowering. An insult to his own species. And Bramwell was disgusted with the lot of them.

How would they all feel if they knew what he knew? That she was deliberately flirting with them all. That she was on a determined husband hunt. That she wanted only a name, preferably a title, and a stud service. That the young and strong need not apply, but only the old, with one

foot already in the grave—soon to be followed by the remaining foot and the entire, worn-out body. That, as he had
thought late last night while unable to sleep, she might be
wanting that title and that old man—but that she also might
be simultaneously inspecting the younger gentlemen, who
would become the actual fathers of her desired children,
while her husband played the foil, the fool. That, in reality,
she either hated men, or just plain despised them.

No, she didn't hate men. He knew that wasn't true. But it
was easier to believe badly of her than it was to think badly
of himself. Of what *he* might want from Sophie Winstead.

He closed his eyes as his brain teased him yet again. *I
never meant to keep you, Your Grace.*

She didn't mean to "keep" him. She didn't mean to
"keep" any one of them. Ha! How would all these fawning
gentlemen feel if they knew all of that?

And would any of the idiots—from the ambitious, to the
curious, to the randy—even care? Probably not.

Probably not. . . .

Bramwell drained the last of his drink, scowled at the
empty glass, and remembered the waltz he had danced
with Sophie.

She'd been so demure, curtsying her thanks to the
sweetly accommodating Lady Cowper as that patroness
had given her permission to waltz. And then she'd walked
into his arms, her body lighter than any feather, more
graceful than a swan, her right hand burning into his left.
With her left hand, she held up the train of her impossibly
flattering gown as they dipped and swirled, instantly re-
sponsive to each touch of his fingers against the small of
her back.

She'd floated around the floor, chattering nineteen to the dozen to him about how happy she was, how lovely everything looked, how lucky they all were to be alive in such a wonderful time. All without missing a step, as if they'd waltzed together a thousand times and she knew his every move a full second before he'd even thought to make it.

And he'd danced as if he was marching guard in front of the palace. Stiff-backed, his spine rigid, his eyes looking straight ahead, steadfastly staring above the enchanting mass of curls, the creamy sweep of shoulder, that cursed rope of pearls that all but screamed at him to drop his gaze, to send it lower, lower.

He'd made himself no friends among the ladies gathered here tonight, their hopes raised for this first Assembly of the Season, then dashed the moment Sophie had entered the shabby rooms, turning them to gold. In fact, except for his aunt and his fiancée, not a single woman had spoken to him all evening, as if he had deliberately set out to ruin their lives.

Bramwell consulted his pocket watch once more. Was it only a little past eleven? How long *was* the last day, before the earth exploded?

Isadora approached, a single vertical line creasing her flawless forehead just between her eyebrows, advertising her concern, and quite possibly a hint of distaste. "She's out on the balcony," she said flatly, motioning toward the doors open to the evening air.

Bramwell didn't have to ask her whom she meant, but he did anyway. *"Who* is out on the balcony, Isadora?"

His fiancée rolled her eyes heavenward. "Lud, Selbourne. Your ward, of course. You must rescue her. Viscount Eglinton—you *know* what a loose screw he is—all but dragged her off the floor at the end of the last set, and took her out there. They're drinking lemonade."

"How very scandalous," Bramwell said, wishing his fiancée wouldn't be quite so protective of the young woman who was tearing his once-well-ordered life to shreds. "It's hot as blazes in here, Isadora. Half the company is swilling lemonade on the balconies and praying for a breeze. And she's not my ward," he added, feeling as if that particular sentence should possibly be tattooed onto his forehead.

"Lud, Selbourne, I know that," Isadora whispered fiercely, drawing him into a corner even as she nodded and smiled to the Countess Lieven, one of Almack's most formidable patronesses. "The thing is, nobody *else* seems to know it. If she had been presented at Court with her true guardian in tow, perhaps we wouldn't be facing this embarrassment. But she wasn't—lud, she couldn't possibly be, could she?—and now everyone is whispering and gossiping, retelling that terrible old gossip. I'm sure now that it was only Lady Jersey's love of a juicy scandal that secured you the voucher for Almack's in the first place. The dowagers are furious, and poor Lady Shipley had to be escorted home, saying she feared she was about to suffer a spell, she was that shocked by the laxity of the patronesses in allowing Miss Winstead a voucher."

"Lady Shipley?" Bramwell remembered Sir Tyler Shipley, and Ignatius, and barely suppressed a flinch. If the dieaway Lady Shipley could meet Ignatius, hear her husband's voice coming out of the parrot's mouth—well, she would be bound to suffer much more than a simple "spell." She'd probably kill her husband, who depended on his wife's private fortune to sustain his rather voracious appetite for gaming at high stakes.

"Yes, but that's neither here nor there. Lud, that woman, dear as she is, goes into a taking over most anything. The thing is, Selbourne, you shouldn't have come with us. You're *never* at Almack's. You used poor judgment being here this evening, lending Miss Winstead entirely too much consequence for a mere acquaintance—much as I dislike railing at you. Although, in a way, she *is* in your charge, isn't she?"

"There is that, yes. But what's to do?" Bramwell felt his spine going stiff. "I suppose I could always storm out onto the balconies, yell for the chit to heel, toss her over my shoulder, and then carry her out of here?" he suggested, immediately hating himself for being sarcastic with his affianced. "I'm sorry, Isadora," he said quickly. "I'm no happier about the gossip than you are. But my attendance here was unavoidable, I'm afraid."

Isadora nodded sagely. "Lady Gwendolyn demanded it," she said, obviously assuming that Bramwell was led around on ropes by his aunt—a conclusion His Grace was happy to embrace.

"She's an exemplary woman, a charitable woman," he said, sighing the sigh of the good, loyal, beleaguered nephew, and knowing himself, yet again, to be a coward. "I could not gainsay her. But now that I've attended the once, I won't be required to return." *Until next week,* he added mentally, remembering the terms of the forfeits Lorrie had devised, damn the man.

"Well, that's good, then, I suppose," Isadora said, breathing out a sigh of relief. But then the crease was back, and Bramwell looked about for an avenue of escape, feeling sure he wasn't going to like what she said next.

He was right.

"I don't know how to phrase this," she began, and he pinned a polite smile on his face, knowing full well she'd probably rehearsed whatever she was about to say, until she had committed every word to memory. "But, lud, Selbourne, I'd never dreamt, never supposed—"

"The gossip?" he put in helpfully, trying to see his fiancée in a good light. He *needed* to see her in a good light. "You hadn't counted on it all being dug up again for another airing, had you? That's because you're a good soul, Isadora, and not small-minded, like so many of this scandal-mad company we call Society."

"Exactly! Lud, Selbourne, you're so astute. It all seemed so simple when first you approached me with your dilemma. Your title, your consequence—your fine, sober reputation. You should have been above such gossip. But I must confess to having some small reservations on the thing now. I hadn't thought Miss Winstead's presence here in London would bring the whole sordid business to everyone's attention again. Frankly, I hadn't heard much of the details, as I was only a girl then, and not privy to such, such—"

"Titillating scandal?" Bramwell put in, wondering why he was being so damnably helpful.

"All right," Isadora said, quickly agreeing with him. "It's embarrassing for me—for *you,* I mean. That's what it is. And with Papa coming to town in less than six weeks? Well, we must have her gone by then, Selbourne. Married and gone. There's no other way. She doesn't *blend,* you un-

derstand. There's no hiding her, even here at Almack's."
She sighed again. "She's a sweet little thing. If only she
weren't so *singular.* Margaret Simmons tells me that her
mama told her that she very much resembles the mother.
That, Selbourne, worries me more than I can say."

"Why, my dear?" he asked, watching as Sophie appeared
on Lord Lorimar's arm just as another set was forming. She
was smiling up at him, one of those wide, unaffected, crin-
kled-nose smiles, and Lorrie was looking thoroughly infatuated. Bobbit should be a happy man, next time Lorrie
stopped by Portland Square. "Are you afraid it's true,
Isadora, what they say? Like mother, like daughter?"

Isadora took out an ivory-backed fan, unfurled it, and
began beating at the still, humid air. "Lud, you could wrap
it up in clean linen before saying such a thing—but yes. I
am afraid it could be like mother, like daughter. Aren't
you?"

He looked at her levelly, at last saying what was on his
mind. What had kept him awake most of the past two
nights. "That would depend, Isadora, on whether you also
believed the saying could expand to include *like father, like
son.* Or haven't you thought about that, my dear? No, I
suppose not. Shall we join the set?"

Isadora closed her fan with a snap, then held her hand
out to her betrothed, her stare deep and unblinking, as if
seeing her future husband through new, rather startled
eyes. "Lud, Selbourne," she said, her lips barely moving,
"I'd never quite thought of that."

Another hour and it would be over. The opening salvo in
Miss Sophie Winstead's war to conquer the *ton,* one

gullible, grinning man at a time—or so it seemed to Bramwell.

She'd danced every dance, except for those she spent out on the balcony with her partner, sipping lemonade and holding court to a dozen or more gangling youths, gout-ridden old lechers, gaily dressed half-pay officers—and more than a few married men who should have known better than to be seen with the Widow Winstead's daughter.

Meanwhile, Bramwell knew he'd had enough daggers sunk into his back by glaring mamas and disappointed debutantes to slay a battalion of Caesars.

But when he saw Miss Ann Sturbridge put a handkerchief to her mouth and run for the anteroom, sobbing, and turned to see the girl's fiancé kneeling at Sophie's feet, making a great business out of reciting some drivel as he held a hand to his heart? Well, that's when the duke of Selbourne had decided that enough was enough!

"You're coming with me," he said, grabbing Sophie's forearm as she stood talking to three young gentlemen and the kneeling fiancé—three fools and an outright baboon, Bramwell decided—and hauling her toward the balcony.

"I say, Selbourne!" the baboon called after him. "That ain't sporting!"

Bramwell turned on the man, all but baring his teeth at him, so that the baboon subsided.

Unfortunately, the baboon's outcry, coupled with Bramwell's rather florid face and pained expression, had brought the attention of several other gentlemen in the area.

"Oh-ho, Selbourne, what's forward?" one of them called out jovially, as Bramwell and Sophie whizzed by, Sophie smiling just as if the duke was taking her to see some amusing jugglers at a country fair. "Never say another balcony scene. Watch your balance, old fellow. How many *tumbles* from grace can the Selbourne name take, even for a willing Winstead?"

"Stubble it, Farnsworthy," Bramwell gritted out, giving Sophie's arm another tug as she stopped, looking curiously at the grinning gentleman who'd just spoken. He saluted her, then gifted her with an elegant leg, flourishing a lace-edged handkerchief and bowing nearly to the floor.

"What's he talking about, Your Grace?" she asked, still looking back at Farnsworthy as Bramwell pulled her out onto the balcony, then unerringly directed her toward the bench that waited in the shadows at the far end of it. The fact that he'd had to growl at the young couple already ensconced on the bench, so that they had immediately taken themselves off to friendlier climes, did not bother him a jot.

"You know damn full well what he's talking about, Sophie," Bramwell accused as he all but pushed Sophie onto the bench, wincing as he realized he'd done it again. He'd called her Sophie. *Sophie, Sophie, Sophie.* That's what he called her at night, when he couldn't sleep, when she invaded his dreams, when she left him tossing and turning and calling himself every kind of fool imaginable.

"Well, no. I don't, actually, *Bramwell,*" she answered, patting the space beside her on the bench, indicating that he should sit down, just as if they were bosom chums or some such ridiculousness. "Does it mean something in that sporting cant gentlemen use when they want to say something the ladies shouldn't understand? Something none of my uncles told me about? Does *balcony* serve as another word for liaison? For keeping a mistress?"

She shrugged her perfect shoulders, then sighed. "Balcony. It seems a queer sort of word, the way that man said it. And perhaps insulting to my mother's memory? All the gentlemen I've met have been so nice, so that I hadn't thought anyone would be *mean*. Perhaps I should have, yes?"

Well, that stopped Bramwell, just as he was about to read her a lecture on circumspection, on proper behavior, on not reducing every man she met to a puddle of frustrated desire—at least not the betrothed ones.

"You don't know how—" he shook his head, attempting to rearrange his thoughts. "No. No, of course you don't. You couldn't, and still ask such a question."

He sat down.

Sophie leaned toward him, the flowery yet lemony scent of her drifting to his nostrils, infiltrating his brain. "Please, Bram," she said, laying a hand on his arm. "Tell me. What is it I don't know? Now that I think on it, that wasn't the first time tonight someone has made references to a balcony in my presence. And they're always *smiling* when they do. Why is that? I thought perhaps there was some joke I didn't understand. So I just smiled, and they soon were talking about my eyes, or how lovely my hair looks in the moonlight, so that I let it go. I'm a great success this evening, yes? But now I must know, please. *What* is a balcony?"

Bramwell was dumbstruck, a part of him pleased beyond his wildest imaginings, another, saner part of him, totally aghast. Well, God damn! Who would have thought it, who would believe it? Sophie Winstead was an innocent. A totally exasperating, maddening, horribly complex, woefully simple *innocent*. Gentlemen admired her eyes, her hair, and she thought that was all they admired? All they wanted from the Widow Winstead's daughter? For all the duke knew of the mother, for all he'd thought of the daughter, Sophie was an innocent. Playing at woman, playing in her mother's world, believing she knew the game, the rules—and woefully ignorant of both.

She hadn't known the word *pimp*. Oh, yes, she'd most certainly sent Wally on a quest for servants cum lovers for his mother and aunt. But had she really known what she was about, what she really had been suggesting when she'd sent Wally off on his merry way, to pimp for his freedom? Bramwell had thought so at the time, but he didn't think so now. She was only playing the games learned at her mother's knee. Smiling, flirting, giving out come-hither glances, and warning that she could not help but be irresistible.

Yes, that was it. She thought she knew the game.

But her mother obviously had not told her *all* of the ins and outs of that game. All the consequences. Sophie saw the dash and flair of romance, not a tawdry sexual arrangement. She probably saw her mother's liaisons with her many "uncles" as marvelously romantic—full of happy times, pet monkeys, lively discussions and the aroma of cigars—and was without a notion as to how her mother actually had sold herself, her body, her good name, over and over again.

And she most certainly didn't know how his father and her mother had died, how their deaths had rocked London

Society with one of its most shocking, titillating scandals. If she did, she'd probably not be in London at all, giving the *ton* another opportunity to giggle over her mother, his father, the scandal—over Sophie herself.

Poor little girl. Poor little Sophie.

By God, what a shock! Bramwell Seaton, Ninth Duke of Selbourne, was shocked. Shocked to his toes. He cursed Sophie's mother for a dangerous, romantic fool, cursed the men here tonight, leering and laughing and hoping for a hurried tumble in the shrubberies, a quick peek under Sophie's skirts. He cursed himself for all he had thought of her, imagined of her, wanted of her.

"Well? Are you going to tell me?" Sophie asked, frowning up at him. "It's bad, isn't it? I'm not going to like what you say, yes?" He looked down at her, looked down on a beautiful woman-child, no more sophisticated than any of the debutantes at Almack's this night, and just as virtuous—maybe more so, because at least she was honest about her reasons for being here.

Bramwell took a deep breath, steadying himself, cursing himself again, cursing his fellow man for the randy goats they all were—and started in to lie for all he was worth.

"You danced every dance? And everyone was kind to you, *chérie?*"

Sophie smiled into the mirror, shaking her head at the concern she could see in her friend's reflection. "Everyone was *wonderful* to me, Desiree," she said, waiting impatiently until the row of buttons was opened and she could step out of the last of her undergarments, turn around, and throw herself into the woman's loving arms. "I am the Sensation of the Season, just as you said I would be!"

"And the duke?" Desiree persisted, giving Sophie's cheek a kiss before her charge skipped off to the other side of the room to seek out her night rail. "He did not spend the evening glowering and growling?"

Sophie dived into the night rail, hiding her face from the all-too-observant Frenchwoman. "Bramwell was very solicitous of me, actually. But we decided together that we will not be returning to Almack's."

"Never say that! The duke made a wager; he must pay the forfeit. He is already committed to another week at Almack's. Don't tell me you're going to allow him to squirm out of it, Sophie. Don't be your *maman,* and let your soft heart rule your hard head."

Sophie took a deep breath, letting it out slowly. "Desiree," she said earnestly, walking over to the bed the woman had turned down for her, "I will tell you the truth now, yes? For you'll get it out of me one way or the other. Almack's is not for me. I must be more discreet, less visible now that I have made my so brilliant entrance as we both wished."

"Who hurt you?" Desiree asked coldly, looking ready to do murder. "Who dared to hurt my baby?"

Sophie climbed onto the high bed, unsurprised that her good friend had seen straight to the heart of the matter, without need for a long explanation. "I'm not hurt, Desiree. Not really. But there were whispers, you understand. I tried to ignore them, but they were there. Gentlemen—ha! are there any gentlemen?—making some sort of sly references to *Maman.* Bramwell knew, but he tried to pro-

tect me, shield me from the truth with some farradiddle
about balconies being the perfect spot for marriage pro-
posals. It was a gentle fib, I suppose, as I'd already pretty
much decided that balconies are more for liaisons, yes?"

Then she smiled. "But I'm too harsh, Desiree. For there
were very many nice gentlemen as well. Sir Wallace,
Baron Lorimar, and several others. And Bram, of course.
He was kindest of all."

"*Mon Dieu!* Bramwell, is it? *Bram?* Not the duke; not
his grace? And *balconies?*" Desiree began energetically
tucking the covers around her charge, clucking over Sophie like a hen with her only chick. "*Bâtards!* How cruel
the English are! I do not like the sound of this, of any of
this. This is my fault, all of it! I am stupid, *stupid*! I hadn't
thought! All I could see was your beauty, *chérie,* your great
heart. I only wanted what was best for you; a safe man, a
reasonable marriage, some babies for us both to love. Perhaps we should go home now, *oui*? Or, better yet, to Paris!
They will adore you in Paris, my sweet child. In Paris, no
one is cruel."

Sophie reached up to hug her friend, dislodging the
neatly tucked-in covers. "No, no, Desiree! You're wrong. I
adore London. I couldn't leave now. I just couldn't."

"You couldn't leave London, *chérie?*" Desiree asked
quietly. "Or the duke? The very much disapproving if polite duke. The duke we tricked into presenting you. The
betrothed duke."

Sophie subsided against the pillows, eyeing the Frenchwoman anxiously, glad once more that she'd not told
Desiree of Bramwell's kiss that first night. Of her longing, ever since, to have him kiss her again, of her

strange excitement each time she watched him walk into a room. "You're talking about how besotted *Maman* became over all the uncles, yes? How she fell so top over heels for Uncle Cesse—and how much the duke is like him. But I'm not my mother, Desiree. I am not so foolhardy as to give my heart to *any* man, pretending, if only for a moment, that there really is such a thing as love."

Desiree looked at her penetratingly. "Love, no. You don't believe in that nonsense. But we probably should soon speak more of desire, *oui?* For that is all love is, *chérie,* desire in masquerade. Lust, dressed up in lace and ribbons, but none the less base for all its fine outward trappings. The fluttering pulse, the flushed cheek, the wish to melt softness against strength, plumb the unknown. All this, and more, were your *maman*'s downfall."

"Oh, stop, Desiree! I'm a long way from desire, eons from even beginning to think of doing what *Maman* did. I'm even farther than that from believing that such a loss of one's own senses could be worth the delights *Maman* wrote about so glowingly. I simply believe that Bramwell is a very nice gentleman, that's all. I'm not just another silly romantic racing headlong into disaster, Desiree. I promise you that." She bit her full bottom lip, refusing to acknowledge the tears that had begun to sting at her eyes as she thought of the whispers she'd heard at Almack's, remembered how protective Bramwell was of her, how kind. "Am I?"

Johnson: Well, we had a good talk.
Boswell: Yes, Sir; you tossed and gored several persons.
—James Boswell, *Life of Johnson*

Chapter Seven

"Tell me again, Bram—*why* was it I just got to watch you beat Geoffrey Farnsworthy into a jelly?"

Bramwell rubbed at the rather satisfying soreness of his knuckles as he and his friend descended the stairs from Gentleman Jackson's Boxing Saloon. "And I'll tell you again, Lorrie. I don't know what you're talking about. Farnsworthy wanted an opponent. I merely obliged him."

"Wrong. Allow me to correct you, if I may. You *merely* haunted every place in Mayfair you could haunt for the past few days, hunting for him, then found him here—and immediately *merely* half killed him," Baron Lorimar countered as they dodged raindrops and quickly climbed into Bramwell's coach. They were on their way to their club, and an arranged meeting with Sir Wallace Merritt, who had been conspicuous by his absence these past three days. "Toyed with him first, of course, teased with him, let him know you could take him out of the game at any time you chose, and then—wham!—you annihilated him. I think the poor fool was almost relieved to feel himself going down that last time. What a wisty castor, a fine punch! I've always known you to be handy with your fives, Bram, but that was a brilliant display of cross-and-jostle work. Simply brilliant."

Lorrie lounged back against the velvet squabs, looking at his friend levelly as the coach moved off into the street. "And I'm sure Farnsworthy deserved every punch, Bram, and then some."

"You nag worse than an old woman, Lorrie, you know that?" Bram wiped raindrops from the top of his curly-brimmed beaver before sitting it on the cushion beside him, then sighed. "You're more clever about it, more subtle, but you're not going to let this go until I tell you everything, are you?"

"You know me so well," the Baron purred, rubbing at his chin as he stretched his neck, still looking at his friend, a hint of danger in his usually laughing gray eyes. "As we'll be at the club in less than ten minutes, the only question that remains would be whether or not you want Wally to hear the whole of it as well."

"God, no," Bramwell said, groaning. "He's already so besotted he'd want to call Farnsworthy out, for all the mess that would make of everything."

"Ah-ha! Then it *is* about Miss Winstead," the Baron said, nodding as if in agreement with his own thoughts. "I've thought our dearest Sophie to be a bit downpin these past days, although she does her best to be sunny, the dear little thing, as she entertains half the men of the *ton* in your drawing room. Can't take more than two steps in any direction without tumbling over some fool clutching posies to his breast. What did Farnsworthy do—at Almack's I'll assume? Offer her *carte blanche?*"

Bramwell's hands drew up into fists. "Use your head, if you please, Lorrie. If Farnsworthy had offered to set her up as his mistress, you'd be attending my trial for murder today, not watching while I merely rearranged the idiot's face."

"True enough. You are her guardian, after all, and she your ward. So, what did he say?"

"He made what he thought was a brilliant reference to my father's death," Bramwell explained, then stopped, realizing that he had been stung by that as well as the insult to Sophie. It hadn't occurred to him until this very moment that he had, in part, also been avenging his father's good name. Well, that was a singular event, wasn't it, as he'd been spending the past three years doing his best to blank his father from both his memory and that of Society. "That is, he made a fairly snide reference to the fact that I was leading Sophie out onto the *balcony.* You can, I'm sure, imagine what he said. It doesn't bear repeating."

The baron remained slouched on the seat as he looked at Bramwell from beneath heavily shuttered eyes. "Have your man turn the coach, Bram, if you please," he said quietly. "I suddenly find that I'd like a poke or two at the fellow myself."

Bramwell shook his head. "Let it go. I've dealt with Farnsworthy in my own way, Lorrie. And I believe I've delivered a message to anyone else who might think it jolly good fun to utter veiled remarks in Sophie's presence. But that's not the problem. Not really."

"Then what is? Does Sophie want a piece of him, too? That's no shy and retiring miss, you know. She told me one of her uncles taught her how to shoot."

Bramwell chuckled deep in his throat, then sobered. "She doesn't know, Lorrie," he said rather sadly. "Oh, she knows that her mother was mistress to more than one man, to my father. She knows that a certain hint of scandal must surround her own entrance into Society. But she has no idea how her mother and my father died. None."

"None?" the Baron repeated, sitting forward.

"None. She believes I resent her because of the scandal of Constance Winstead's liaison with my father and, for my sins, she's probably fairly close to the mark on that one. But she had no conception of the depth of the scandal that rocked the family name to its very foundations."

"And turned you into the boring pillar of society you've become, much to my distress, and Wally's as well," the Baron continued for him as Bramwell subsided into a corner of the coach, to rub at his aching head. Farnsworthy had gotten in at least one good shot before the duke had taken command. "But, now that I think on it, we should have known that, Bram. Sophie is *not* a stupid girl. She has her father's name, and several pockets full of money, so that nobody could bar her from making her debut, making a successful match. She had your father's written promise to lend her his power, his consequence."

"True. That has to be how she saw the thing. A bit of gossip, a bit of giggling, but nothing she couldn't overcome. She's dazzling, you know," Bram said with a ghost of a smile. "She believed herself up to winning everyone over to her. Lord knows she made short work of my aunt, even of Isadora. Not to mention you and that other looby, Wally. She saw nothing ahead of her but one success tumbling on top of another."

"Yes, Bram. But if she had known how the late duke and her mother died? No, Sophie would still be in Wimbledon, had she known that, had she realized just how deep your humiliation would be at having to present her. And then there's her own mother's memory. She wouldn't want to have her mother tarnished all over again, not to that extent. Ah, Bram, we all of us should have known. I'm thoroughly ashamed of myself. But Hell and damnation, man, it's not enough to go about milling down idiots like Farnsworthy. There are too many of them, for one thing. You have to tell her, Bram. Tell her now, today, before somebody else does."

"I'll kill the man who tells her!" Bramwell bit out, glaring at his friend.

"Yes, I believe that, having just seen Farnsworthy. But it won't work, Bram. I'm fond of her too, very fond. Just ask Bobbit, if you don't believe me. He'll soon be listing to one side, for all my coins now in his pocket. But we have to be commonsensical about the thing. Some day, some way, someone is going to let it slip. Or tell her on purpose. She has to know, know it all, before that happens. This is an understandably sore subject with you, as your father was involved. Do you want me to do it?"

Bramwell was tempted, sorely tempted. But he shook his head, knowing he couldn't take the coward's way out. Not on this one. The coach pulled to a halt at the curb in front of their club, and the two men got out, pausing on the flagway as the duke assured his friend that he would tell Sophie the truth. The whole truth. Tonight.

"Just don't let her put her tail between her legs and run away from London, Bram," the Baron warned as they entered the club. "She's got to stay, got to see this through now that she's started it. You must make her understand that. For Sophie's sake. For you, for me, for all of us. She'd take all the sunshine with her if she left, this rainy day notwithstanding."

"You're in love with her?" Bramwell asked, something tightening painfully, deep in his chest.

"No, Bram. But I could have been," the baron answered, waving to Wally, who was sitting across the room, a drink already in his hand. "Unfortunately, that's not how I see all of this falling out. But I'm her friend, Bram. Her very good friend. And I'll not see her hurt. Not by the *ton*, not by anyone, if you take my meaning. Now, shall we see how Wally's doing, pimping for his mother and aunt? From that frown, I'd say it's not going well, poor silly old sot."

Bram followed his friend through the maze of tables and chairs. "Then you know what Wally's been about these past few days?" he asked, hoping Lorrie didn't also know who had put their mutual friend up to the ridiculous stunt, then realizing that the Baron had to know. Wally couldn't keep his mouth shut if all their lives depended upon it.

"When he stood in my foyer yesterday, eyeing my footman like a racetrack tout? I thought he was going to ask one fellow to strip, to show him his muscles. How could I not know, Bram? And yes, before you ask, I do know *all* of it, and I think Sophie's plan brilliant. Wally's already added two footmen to his mama's staff, and a second majordomo, one his aunt once employed, although why they'd need two in that small household I couldn't know. Oh, and a cook. The cook is fat, and bald, and French into the bargain, but Wally does enjoy a fine *crêpe,* so he figured it couldn't hurt."

Bramwell threw back his head and laughed aloud, the first bit of good humor he'd experienced since that terrible evening at Almack's. "That's Wally for you, Lorrie. If he can't make the females of his household happy, he'll at least find a bit of pleasure for himself. Now, not a word to Wally about Sophie, all right?"

The baron gave a single, nearly imperceptible nod, then they crossed the room and joined Sir Wallace at the table. "How goes the hunt, my man?" he asked as a waiter rushed up, eager to take their order for wine.

Bramwell told the servant what they wanted, then settled back in his chair to listen to Sir Wallace's story of his exploits of that morning, banishing thoughts of what lay ahead of him that evening, when he would have to tell Sophie what she needed to know.

"My aunt was smiling this morning," Sir Wallace was already informing an attentive Baron Lorimar. *"Smiling!* Can you picture it, Lorrie? Don't, if you don't want to. It's not a pretty image, I assure you. But she was. Smiling, that is. Not pretty. Never been pretty."

"She resembles your mother to a great degree, Wally, as I recall. Twins, ain't they?" the Baron pointed out, so that Bramwell found himself coughing into his hand to cover a laugh.

Sir Wallace spread his arms wide as if inviting his friends to inspect his less-than-imposing appearance. "Yes,

Lorrie, twins. And I look like the both of them. Is that enough for you?"

"I think your mother's nose might be a trifle less florid," Bramwell put in as the servant set two bottles and as many glasses in front of them, then withdrew once more. "What say you, Lorrie?"

Sir Wallace dismissed any answer the Baron might give with a wave of his hands. "It's working, gentlemen. I had only faint hopes at first, but it's *working*. And the *crêpes* are wonderful. Had six just this morning. I think I'll take Noé with me when I go. I'm already hunting up a place, you understand. Nothing too fine, but with a full kitchen, and room for Noé. I'd be a fool to give him up." He picked up his wineglass, then set it back down without taking a sip—or draining the glass, as was his custom. "Lord love Sophie. I know I do. How is she, by the bye? I haven't been by to see her since Almack's."

Bramwell was saved from answering when he heard his name being called from halfway across the room. He turned in time to see Sir Tyler Shipley advancing toward him, two other gentlemen in tow. Bram decided he'd rather not have been rescued from answering Sir Wallace, for Uncle Tye was looking extremely agitated. As were the other two gentlemen.

Rising to his feet, Bramwell bowed slightly to each of the men in turn. "Lord Upchurch, Lord Buxley, Sir Tyler. How good to see you all." He was lying through his teeth, of course, as Lord Upchurch was a loose screw of the first water, Lord Buxley had been host to the most infamous house party in recent memory, and Sir Tyler was, plain and simple, a very unlovable man.

"Good to see you, Selbourne, good to see you!" Lord Upchurch responded heartily, reaching out to take Bramwell's hand in both of his, then pumping it up and down as if trying to wrench it from his wrist. "I just got in from Surrey, you know, leaving Lady Upchurch there nursing one of the granddaughters. Measles, you know. Poor sprite, our Annabella, but anything that keeps Julia in Surrey and away from the shops has my vote, you know. Heard my little Sophie is in Town, and just had to tell you how happy I am to hear you bear her no ill will over that business, well"—he lowered his voice and leaned in close—"over the *balcony*, you know."

Bramwell extracted his hand from his lordship's two-fisted clutches and, barely suppressing a smile, answered, "Yes, my lord. *I know.*" Behind him, he heard Baron Lorimar choking slightly as it was that man's turn to disguise a laugh in a cough.

"Did she bring Giuseppe with her? The little rascal's still above ground and making mischief, ain't he? Miss that flea-bitten monkey, you know, but it took such a shine to Sophie I just couldn't bear to separate them when Buxley here came on the scene and Constance and I—well, enough of old history. Julia never could abide Giuseppe anyway, you know. Made me sleep in the dressing room until I agreed to get rid of it, as Julia was going through one of those woman things, you know, and was always finding something to complain about. Best reason to keep the thing about, I thought, what with Julia always either too hot, or too cold, or just finding fault with the whole world. But Sophie loved the monkey, you know, and I loved little Sophie. So it all worked out."

Lord Upchurch shrugged his sawdust-stuffed shoulders, which probably matched his sawdust-stuffed hose, for his lordship was a tall, too-thin man with illusions of putting himself forth as a well-put-together Corinthian. "What was a man to do? But no matter. I soon found reason enough to return to the dressing room. I'm a bad man. I am, you know, and happy enough for it, much as I love my Julia, especially now that she's through that bad patch. No chance of more kiddies, either, which suits the pair of us just fine," he ended with a nudge and a wink, so that Bramwell smiled politely, wishing the man would simply shut up.

"Stubble it, Dickie," Lord Buxley broke in, pushing his rather paunchy body forward in between his companions, leading with his belly where another man would lead with his chin. A rather coarse man, and an avid hunter, His Lordship would never see another ride across a fallow field if it weren't for the winch that hoisted him onto his horse for the hunt. "Selbourne here don't give a tinker's dam about your talk of measles and women's vapors and the like. Now look here, Selbourne, we've got us a problem here, although Dickie, half-wit that he is, don't see it that way. Sees it all as a lark, the fool. We need to talk, the three of us." He looked hopefully about the room, as if seeking out a hidey-hole now that the trio had made themselves the center of all attention by confronting the duke publicly. *"Alone."*

"Is that so, Your Lordship?" Bramwell asked, for once not going out of his way to be proper, to be polite. And why should he? After all, he wasn't having a really good day. "You had little enough to say to me three years ago, when I came to your estate to gather up a few of my father's possessions that had been left behind in the rush to get the man buried and forgotten. And even less to say to me since, now that I think on it. No, Your Lordship. Either you and these two bookends of yours join my friends and me," he ended, pointing to Lord Upchurch and the curiously silent Sir Tyler, "or you can all be on your way." He then wrinkled up his nose, rather the way Sophie did, he realized, then added, "You know."

Lord Buxley began to bluster, his jowls quivering as he built up a full measure of outrage. "Now see here, Selbourne—"

"Did Sophie call you Uncle Billy?" Bramwell asked, cutting him off even as he pulled out a chair and motioned for the man to seat himself before he fell down. "Or, perhaps, Uncle Willy? Oh, and I imagine you're the one who taught her to shoot?"

Lord Buxley subsided into the chair, pulling out a large, none-too-white handkerchief and mopping at his moist brow. "Uncle Willy," he admitted, then glared at Sir Tyler. "Oh, for God's sake, man, sit down. He knows, he knows. I told you he wouldn't believe we were just trying to be nice."

And Bramwell did know. Baron Lorimar knew. Only Sir Wallace, who was wearing a most confused expression, did not know. Constance Winstead had been mistress to Lord Upchurch, as the man had already admitted. But she had also been mistress to Sir Tyler. And to Lord Buxley— which was rather interesting, seeing as how she had come to her lurid, unexpected end while in the midst of an assignation at His Lordship's estate, but not with His Lordship.

Cheeky woman, Constance Winstead. Bramwell was beginning to admire the lady, for her dash, her flair, her obvious love of whimsy and the ridiculous.

While the baron, who had moved his chair closer to Sir Wallace, whispered into that man's ear, and while Sir Wallace's eyes grew round and large as chestnuts, Sir Tyler laid his elbows, and his cards, on the table.

"Here's how we see it, Selbourne," Sir Tyler said, looking much the most handsome of the three, and twice as bright into the bargain. He was older than Bramwell by more than twenty years, but he had aged well. He didn't have to be as sharp as a tack to be in His Majesty's government—brilliance in that quarter was almost always a handicap if one had little patience with incompetence—but he was not a stupid man. "We can't have Connie's daughter traipsing all over London, you can see that, can't you? I almost had an apoplexy when my wife came home early from Almack's the other night, wailing and swooning. And that's without knowing that Connie and I once had, well, had an arrangement."

Lord Buxley soundly clapped Sir Tyler on the back, laughing. "And without knowing that you were probably in her very own bed as she was racing up the stairs to collapse in her chamber, and in the midst of tipping over her very own lady's maid, I'll wager. You always was the randy one, Tye. Connie told me why she tossed you over. Chasing after that Frenchie maid she had, weren't you, hoping for a tumble? Nearly broke Connie's tender heart, you did. Not that I wasn't grateful to be there to mend it again after Dickie here stomped on it in his turn, throwing her over for his own wife, which is just about the silliest thing I've ever heard. And not that I lasted above a year m'self, not once Cecil showed up to spoil m'fun. Now *there* was a love match!"

Bramwell couldn't help himself, although he knew he'd probably also hate himself once he'd had time to refine, to reflect. He leaned forward, pointing from one to the other of Constance Winstead's lovers. "Let's see if I have the order correct, all right, gentlemen? Sir Tyler, you were first, I suppose. Then Lord Upchurch, then Buxley here, then my father. Do I have the right of it?"

"Not nice to keep score," Sir Wallace broke in weakly, looking to Baron Lorimar. "Is it?"

Bramwell raised his hands, warning Sir Wallace to be quiet. "No, no. This is interesting. Sir Tyler, followed by a viscount, then an earl, then a duke. My God, the mind begins to boggle. Had she lived, one of the royal dukes might have been next, then the King himself!" He sat back in his chair and laughed until tears ran down his cheeks.

"I had thought you more mature, more sober, Your Grace," Sir Tyler said coldly. "But, laugh as you might, we three see Miss Winstead's appearance in Society as much less than amusing. Almack's was a disaster that cannot be repeated. Young Sophie was old enough to remember us, remember us all, though I'm sure there were a half dozen before us, when she was still in leading strings. She cannot be allowed to run amuck in Society, even you must see that now. If she is to remain in London, discretion must rule— and, yes, for our sake as much as hers. Now, as we're already fairly sure we cannot buy her off, or make her believe she must leave London before she is completely and publicly disgraced, and as you obviously refuse to do

anything even vaguely helpful—I hadn't noticed before
how very much you resemble your father in manner, Selbourne—we've decided that we must step into the breach,
as it were, and take care of young Sophie."

Bramwell was suddenly all attention, even as a part of
him found it difficult to believe just how much he was enjoying himself. Even the reference to resembling his father, not just physically, but in his manner, brought him a
bit of joy, rather than his usual disdain. "Take care of
her?" he repeated in some real confusion, tipping his chair
forward once more. "How? I don't think I can allow you
to tie a large stone to her ankles and toss her into the
Thames, gentlemen."

"No, no. Nothing like that! We mean to find her a husband, of course," Lord Buxley said, wiping at his cheeks,
at the beads of perspiration that had collected just above
his upper lip. "And not the way you've been going about
it, boy. Dragging her scent in front of a pack of hounds,
then setting them loose. That works well enough for the
Quorn, but not in Mayfair, as anyone can tell you. Match
her up, get her bracketed, get her gone—out of sight, out
of mind. One, two, three."

"Any Americans in port?" Lord Upchurch asked, looking hopeful. "The war's over forever now, you know, so
there could be one or two of the fellows about. Can't have
her marrying into Society, you know. Have to get her
gone." He shivered beneath his padded shoulders. "Calls
me Uncle Dickie just the once and I'm as good as a dead
man, you know. Julia will murder me."

"We need to meet with her," Sir Tyler slid in as Lord
Buxley began pounding on Lord Upchurch's back this

time, telling him to buck up, to be a man. "Sit down with her, talk to her, explain our problem to her. She's a good little thing; biddable, like the mother. She'll understand. And in return, we'll—the three of us—do our utmost to see her happily wed. And gone," he said, looking to his two companions. "Definitely gone."

"That's right. Good enough sort, Sophie, as I remember, but there's never been the woman yet who could keep her mouth shut for long," Lord Buxley pointed out. "Witness the way m'wife had it all over England in a trice, about your father and Connie, I mean. Bodies had barely hit the flagstones before she was off, scribbling notes to all corners of the kingdom."

Bramwell looked to Baron Lorimar, who had his brow furrowed in thought. He knew what his friend was thinking. Tonight Sophie had to be told the truth about her mother's death. That news would all but crush her. But if he could leaven the sad news with the information that three of her dear "uncles" wanted to visit with her? Well, that might help soften the blow. "Tomorrow afternoon at two in Portland Square, gentlemen," he said, watching as the Baron nodded his agreement.

"And your aunt?" Lord Upchurch inquired, pulling a face. "Woman, you know. Talk, talk talk."

"I'll send her off shopping with my fiancée," Bramwell said, agreeing with his lordship. "You can rest assured, gentlemen, that your meeting with Miss Winstead will be entirely confidential. I'm equally sure Miss Winstead will be overjoyed to see her *uncles* again."

"Mayhap I'll bring her a doll," Lord Upchurch said,

thinking out loud. "Sophie liked dolls well enough, you know, as I remember."

Baron Lorimar leaned forward, smiling. "A doll, Your Lordship? Then you haven't seen Miss Winstead since she came to London?" He looked from one man to the next, then the next, and repeated his question. "Lord Buxley? Sir Tyler? Have either of you seen Miss Winstead since she was a child?"

Lord Upchurch shook his head. "Of course, Lorimar. You're right. We remember her as a child, you know. My goodness, it's been at least eight or nine years since I saw her last, hasn't it? A doll is ridiculous, you know, if the child is now old enough for Almack's. Should have thought of that. How does she look? I remember her as rather short, you know. And rather plump, too, now that I think on it. Buxley, you were after me. How did she look to you?"

Lord Buxley began to bite on his bottom lip. "Oh, dear," he breathed quietly, his anxious gaze flying to Bramwell's face. "She looked like the mother," he said, swallowing down hard as he ran a finger beneath his neckcloth. "Plump, as you said, Dickie, and still very much the child. About ten years old, or mayhap eleven, I'd say. I remember curls. Lots of curls. But smart, and with the look of Connie to her. And she'd be more like nineteen now, I believe." His florid face suddenly gone white, he picked up the Baron's half-empty glass of wine and drained it. "Oh dear."

Bramwell looked to Lord Upchurch, to see him smiling wistfully, obviously still remembering the child Sophie had been when he had been a part of her life. He'd probably spent more time dandling Sophie on his knee and feeding her sugarplums than he ever had in bedding her mother.

And then he looked to Sir Tyler Shipley. He, too, was smiling. Not at all wistfully.

The stem of Bramwell's wineglass unexpectedly snapped as he held it tightly in his fingers.

Once the trio of "uncles" was gone, scuttling back to their own table, Bramwell swore his two friends to secrecy and called for two new glasses and another bottle of wine.

"I want to be there," Baron Lorimar said. "But I don't suppose you'll allow it."

"I'd sell tickets if I could," Bramwell answered honestly, knowing he was going to be privileged to watch as Sophie went about dazzling her "uncles" all over again, as she obviously had done as a lovable, eager-to-please child. "But, no. I think not, Lorrie. Although I'd like your opinion now, if you don't mind."

"Upchurch is a sentimental fool," the baron supplied willingly. "So is Buxley, although Upchurch has more to lose if word of his liaison with the Widow Winstead comes out. Sleeping in the dressing room, *you know.*"

Bramwell laughed. He'd actually found himself counting the number of times Upchurch had slipped another "you know" into his sentences. "I agree. But Buxley has everything to gain. Who would have thought he could capture the lovely Constance, even for a short time?"

"That's true enough," Sir Wallace put in, patting his own fairly expanded belly. "Gives me all sorts of hope, it does."

"But Sir Tyler is another matter," Bramwell said, remembering the avaricious look on the man's face when he'd considered the notion that Sophie could resemble her beautiful mother. "I think he'd delight in bedding the daughter as well as the mother. Ambition, as someone once said, can crawl as well as it can climb."

"Yes, I'd watch him. He's deeper than the others, Bram," Baron Lorimar agreed solemnly. "And with more to lose, I think, as his wife controls the purse strings. "I don't think he wants to bed Sophie as much as he wants to be rid of her."

Bramwell threw back the last of his wine and stood up. "Well, it's been quite an afternoon, hasn't it, gentlemen? And a conversation to remember, although I'd ask you both to forget it. But I hope you'll excuse me now. I've got some thinking to do."

"Fine enough, Bram," Sir Wallace said, waving him away. "I want Lorrie here to myself for a while anyway. There's this footman of his I've been considering."

"Told you," the Baron said, smiling at Bramwell. Then he propped his elbows on the table and his chin in his hands, and turned to Sir Wallace. "I'd never suspected this of you, Wally," he drawled, sparing a moment to wink up at Bramwell. "Tell me, how long have you been admiring men's calves?"

Bramwell smiled until he was back in his coach and on his way home to Portland Square, upon which time his countenance became decidedly more solemn. Then, mentally, he began preparing his speech to Sophie Winstead, already dreading the evening.

. . . has told enough white lies to ice a cake.
                              —Margot Asquith

Chapter Eight

It was three in the afternoon, and there had to have been less commotion in the Roman Coliseum when the lions were set loose and tasty Christians were in Season.

As it had been since the morning after the opening night of Almack's, the mansion in Portland Square was crammed to the rafters with a seemingly never-ending parade of eager young men, optimistic old men, middle-aged men with empty pockets—men with an eye to beauty, with posies clutched in their fists, poetry at the ready, and the burning hope that Miss Sophie Winstead would deign to smile in their direction.

Instead, Sophie gave them Giuseppe, who hopped about the drawing room tipping his red hat and baring his teeth while collecting flowers and optimistic love letters. He then dutifully delivered everything to his mistress, who sat in court with Lady Gwendolyn to her right, Miss Isadora Waverley to her left.

Mrs. Edith Farraday, who had hidden her ear horn and steadfastly refused to retrieve it, sat in a chair quite apart from the rest, tending to her knitting.

As each bouquet or Ode to the Beauty Mark Caressing Milady's Fair Cheek was delivered, the gentleman responsible for either the posies or the poems stepped forward for his treasured five minutes of conversation with The Winstead, as Sophie had already found out she was now referred to in gentlemen's circles.

"You smiled much too broadly at that one," Miss Waverley whispered to Sophie as Baron Somebody-Or-Other backed from the drawing room as if leaving the presence of the Queen, nearly tripping over the earl of Somewhere-Or-Other as he went.

"Oh, but how could I not, Miss Waverley?" Sophie whispered back, already smiling encouragingly at the red-faced young man now advancing toward her, looking as if he might suffer an apoplexy at any moment. "He promised to die for me, should I wish it. What nonsense! As if I would ever ask anyone to die for me. I should have been much more impressed if he had said he would fetch me a glass of lemonade. Unfortunately, all that many of these sweet, foolish creatures want to do is promise me the impossible—the stars, the sun, the moon. As my dear Desiree says, a woman could perish of thirst, Miss Waverley, waiting for the moon, yes?"

"Ah, she's got you there, Miss Waverley," Lady Gwendolyn said, leaning across Sophie to wink at her nephew's fiancée. "I waited for the moon, you know, and all it got me was splinters in my backside from sitting on the spinster's shelf." She winked at Sophie, then sat back as the younger woman dealt with the red-faced young swain who wouldn't know what to do with a Sophie Winstead if one dropped ripe and ready into his lap.

Today, as she had done since Sophie's arrival in Portland Square, Lady Gwendolyn had once more left off her turban, choosing instead to consider herself as definitely removed from the spinsterly shelf she'd been on these past thirty years and more, and back in the hunt.

After all, there had been more than a few contemporaries of hers, gouty widowers now for the most part (as well as a few octogenarians who should have known better and been ashamed of themselves), traipsing through the house. The dear lady, thanks to Sophie's careful suggestion, thought it couldn't be but prudent to let the gentlemen know that she, too, was available for courting.

So far, she'd gotten herself two winks, one pat on the cheek, and an invitation to go out driving tomorrow afternoon with Sir Wilford Kingsley, who had been one of her beaus back in her salad days. His wife had been underground for more than five years, he was childless, and he had the most endearing way of calling her Gwenny. Yes, Sir Wilford was definitely a possibility.

It was the rouge pot, Lady Gwendolyn had confided to Sophie just that morning. The rouge pot, and taking off those dratted turbans, burning those dashed caps. She had thought herself old, had acted old, and everyone had seen her as old. Until Sophie had come into her life. Now, Lady Gwendolyn was feeling decidedly younger. Happier. Even, as she'd confided to Desiree—never to an innocent child such as Sophie—a bit frisky, like a young colt just released into the pasture. And if Sir Wilford wanted her? Well, she just might give that notion some thought, that's what!

Sophie kept smiling, even after it had become an effort, until the last of her gentleman callers had departed. She then, as Bobbit brought the ladies a fresh round of cakes and tea, obediently turned to Miss Waverley for that young woman's critique of the afternoon.

She listened with only half an ear as Isadora recounted the names, titles, and fortunes of the small army of eager gentlemen, sorting them out by rank, by social importance, and discarding those who were impecunious second sons or half-pay officers on the hunt for a fortune. Isadora was really rather good at this type of thing, her store of information seemingly boundless, her enthusiasm, although carefully contained, forever at a high, civilized pitch.

Isadora liked to organize, Sophie had observed, and delighted in planning out strategies, fitting person to person, rank to rank, interest to interest. A born manager, that was Miss Isadora Waverley.

She'd probably "manage" Bramwell into either a bottle or his grave within a decade.

"I particularly favor Lord Anston's suit, Miss Winstead, disa—er, *surprised* as I was to see him here," Isadora said, carefully patting at her lips with a corner of her serviette. "A widower, not without considerable funds of his own, and with four daughters to marry off. Four, Miss Winstead! Lud, such an interesting challenge, don't you agree? Yes, you'd be confined to the country on and off for some years yet, as the oldest is no more than ten and five, I believe, and you'd want to be setting up your own nursery. But the country does have its charms, especially Surrey, where

Lord Anston is situated. I adore the country. And you'd be back in Town soon enough, an established matron, your mother's past forgotten as you go about setting up the girls for their come-outs. Lud, the shopping, the presentations at Court, the balls, finding just the right gentleman for each of them." She pressed her clasped hands to her breasts. "And no male heirs in sight, so that your offspring would one day have the earldom. I cannot think of anything more perfect."

"Except to have your son be the tenth duke of Selbourne," Lady Gwendolyn put in, her elbow jabbing sharp and quick into Sophie's side.

"Lud, my lady, as if that signifies a scrap." Miss Waverley rolled her eyes, gaining Sophie's admiration as she did so, for today was the first time she'd seen real emotion in the woman. "Lord Anston's title, although not as high as Selbourne's, is every bit as honorable, dating back as far as anyone can remember. And without a whiff of scandal attached to it," she added thoughtfully, and Sophie looked at her quickly, her admiration now tempered with the realization that Miss Waverley put great store by such things as untarnished reputations. Why, of course she did. What a blow it must have been to her to have the Widow Winstead's daughter thrust on her, and how noble Miss Waverley was to be bearing up so well under the strain. Yes, Sophie really did like Isadora Waverley.

She just didn't like the idea of Isadora Waverley married to Bramwell Seaton.

She didn't like it at all.

"Lord Anston does seem a very nice gentleman, Miss Waverley, and rather handsome into the bargain. And all those daughters to be herded, taught, organized and successfully launched? What delicious fun!" Sophie said now, as if truly considering the man as a possible husband. "Would you please be so kind as to tell me more about him?"

Miss Waverley would be pleased, and went on at some length, until, in fact, Lady Gwendolyn began yawning into her fist. But Sophie paid very close attention to the woman's every word. . . .

"There were a pair of them here today, you know," Sophie told Lady Gwendolyn as the two lounged in that lady's bedchamber before dinner. They were sitting at their ease, clad in their dressing gowns, their bare toes wiggling against the carpet, both of them sipping wine Bobbit had sneaked upstairs to them and enjoying a few peaceful moments together out of the sight of the bound to be disapproving but now thankfully departed Isadora Waverley.

"Only two of them? Oh, pooh. There were three yesterday. But never say Sir Wilford was one of them, because I don't want to hear that, Sophie. Truly I don't."

Sophie shook her head in the negative, then watched as Lady Gwendolyn breathed a sigh of deep relief. She'd noticed her ladyship eyeing Sir Wilford as that man departed the drawing room. There had been a certain spring in his step that hadn't been in it as he'd entered looking much like a man come to see an oddity he'd been told not to miss, but not sure he wasn't about to be brought into the presence of some fascinating Medusa, snakes waving in her hair. "Never Sir Wilford, Aunt Gwen," she assured the woman. "He's not to be found anywhere in *Maman's* journals."

Her ladyship's aristocratic nose actually seemed to quiver as she sat up very straight, gaping at Sophie. "Journals? Did you say *journals?* Good God, Sophie—the woman took *notes?"*

Sophie became busy with pleating the skirt of her dressing gown as it lay over her knees. "Did I say that?" she asked sweetly, then giggled. "My goodness, Aunt Gwen, you look ready to fly up to the chandelier, like Giuseppe. And that's exactly what I meant. *Maman* did keep a journal. Several of them, as a matter of fact. She had a full life, yes?"

"Yes. Fair to bursting, I'd say," Lady Gwendolyn murmured in some distraction, hopping to her bare feet and beginning to pace. "If those journals were to fall into the wrong hands . . ." She stopped, a finger stuck between her teeth, and turned to Sophie. "You wouldn't think to *publish* them, would you, Sophie? Harriette Wilson has thoughts along those lines, or so I've heard it said, charging her former paramours to keep them *out* of her memoirs. But, no. You don't need the money, for one thing. And you would never be so tasteless." Her eyes began to twinkle. "But that doesn't mean that you and *I*—"

"You don't really mean to beg me to allow you to read them, do you, Aunt Gwen?" Sophie asked quickly, to save the old woman embarrassment. "Oh, no, of course not! How silly of me to even think such a thing. You'd never ask such a question, not my dear Aunt Gwendolyn."

Lady Gwendolyn cleared her tight throat, gave herself a shake, and sat down once more. "Me? La, of course not, my dear. I shouldn't think any lady would wish to read another lady's private journals. Oh, no. Not a lady. Not me.

Oh, no. Never." She took a deep breath, letting it out slowly, wistfully, almost painfully. "Never . . . never . . . never . . . nev—"

"The two were Colonel Blythe, and his lordship, the earl of Strood," Sophie supplied quickly, as it appeared Her Ladyship might go into a sad decline, caught between a nearly overpowering curiosity and the need to set a good example to her young charge. "I don't remember either of them, of course, any more than the gentlemen who came to call before them," she went on as Lady Gwendolyn's expression cleared. "I was still in the baby nursery, as *Maman* termed it, and not allowed into the drawing room until I had become a very precocious ten-year-old."

"And that's when you began meeting the *uncles?"*

Sophie nodded. "Yes. And *Maman* began keeping the journals only a few years before that. I met Uncle Tye first, just as another gentleman was departing—I barely saw him at all. He's dead now, so that doesn't matter. Then came Uncle Dickie, Uncle Willy, and, lastly, and for nearly four years, Uncle Cesse."

She became quiet for a moment, reflective. "I liked them all, but I adored Uncle Cesse. He was so lively, so full of fun and mischief. I cried for weeks and weeks when he and *Maman* died. At times, Aunt Gwendolyn," she said, blinking back tears that stung her eyes, "I was hard-pressed to say which of them I missed most."

Lady Gwendolyn had already pulled her handkerchief from the pocket of her dressing gown, and was dabbing at her own watery eyes. "Cecil *was* wonderful, wasn't he? Always up for any rig, ripe for any adventure. I tend to forget sometimes, when I'm angry at what he did. But he was a good brother. A terrible father, but a good brother."

Sophie eyed her companion in purposeful confusion. "A terrible father? But how could that be? He was all that was good to me." She bit at her bottom lip, remembering how Bramwell had reacted when she had praised his late father, remembering her mother's journal concerning the ninth duke. It was all so sad. "They didn't get on—Bramwell and Uncle Cesse?"

Lady Gwendolyn shrugged. "Who could tell if they ever would have been friends? Cecil and his wife were social animals. Lord knows my sister-in-law didn't want any babies hanging on her skirts, spoiling her fun. The only thing she cared about was producing an heir on the first go, which she did. After that? Well, my nephew was pretty much on his own then, especially when Cecil was off playing at war. Yes, Bramwell was stuck in the country until he could be shoveled off to school, while Cecil was always running about somewhere, warring, hunting, fishing, dancing, drinking—wenching. I think he was waiting for Bramwell to grow up, so that they could meet each other man to man. But Bramwell took it upon himself to go into the Royal Navy, just to spite his father, I'm sure, and the two were never more than civil to each other after that the few times they did meet."

She sighed, downing the last of her wine. "And then Cecil died and—well, that was that, then, wasn't it?"

"So they never did get together, get to know each other? I think I understand now," Sophie said, her mind full of memories of her Uncle Cesse, of the times she'd spent sitting on the floor at his feet, her chin propped on her folded hands as they rested on his knee. For hours on end she had listened to him talk about his life, his happiness, his regrets, his hopes for the future. And, she had read the journals. "I suppose I should have understood. Bramwell did seem to dislike his father, the one time I spoke of him. Oh, dear. He doesn't know. Poor Uncle Cesse. Poor Bram. Well, I'll just have to fix that somehow, won't I? But how?"

"Fix what, my dear?" Lady Gwendolyn asked, blowing her nose.

"Oh, never mind," Sophie said quickly, jumping up from her chair and going over to Lady Gwendolyn's large jewelry chest, pulling open the top drawer before turning to look at her dear friend. "Shall I help select your jewelry for this evening, Aunt Gwendolyn? We're to go to the theater, remember. I can barely contain myself, having never been to the theater. Pearls, I think, as you're to wear the burgundy taffeta, yes?"

Lady Gwendolyn, fully occupied in trying to rein in her tender, slightly wine-befogged emotions, merely nodded her agreement. Sophie happily turned back to the jewelry box, intending to locate the triple strand of pearls she remembered her ladyship wearing the other evening, to Almack's.

And there it was.

Not the necklace, although it was in the drawer, pushed to the back in the haphazard way Lady Gwendolyn had about her jewelry.

Sophie put out her hand and lifted Isadora Waverley's garnet brooch from the deep blue velvet, turning toward the windows while presenting her back to Lady Gwendolyn, the better to inspect the piece of jewelry, the better to think.

She'd seen other strange things in Lady Gwendolyn's chamber over the past days. A paperweight fashioned of thick glass, with a gold coin suspended inside. A lovely thing. Odd that it had been stuck in Aunt Gwen's shoe cupboard rather than displayed on a table.

There had also been that small, carved, jade elephant she'd seen in the curio cabinet in the drawing room her first day in Portland Square, seen the next day on Lady Gwendolyn's night table, and the third day back downstairs, on display inside the curio cabinet once more.

And then there was the snuffbox, the one with the initials Q.R.T. engraved on its lid. Sophie had passed that off as a gift from a long-ago admirer, or something her ladyship had admired and picked up in some secondhand shop.

Which didn't explain the snuffbox's disappearance the very next day, or the fact that Peggy, her ladyship's maid, seemed to make a fairly thorough inspection of her mistress's chamber each morning, as if looking to locate something that had been mislaid and needed to be found.

"Oh, dear," Sophie breathed quietly, recognizing the signs. After all, she had Giuseppe, who also had a way of seeing things that caught his fancy, and then picking them up.

She turned the brooch in her fingers, the stone hot and all but throbbing brightly, guiltily against her skin. How had Her Ladyship said it the other day, when they'd all gone for their drive in the Park? Oh, yes, she remembered now. *That's a lovely brooch you're wearing, Miss Waverley. I do so adore garnets. May I have it?*

"Oh dear, oh dear," Sophie whispered again, tucking the brooch into the pocket of her dressing gown, then turning about to smile brightly at the darling old lady she'd already come to adore. Quickly snatching up the pearls, she made a great business of opening and closing the many drawers of the jewelry cabinet. She pretended to be having trouble locating the earbobs that went with the necklace, but all the time she was hoping against hope she wouldn't discover other bits of admired property.

At the same time, she was already planning just how she would return the brooch to Bramwell's fiancée without Isadora, not a stupid woman, taking it into her head that the duke of Selbourne's aunt was a common thief.

Or worse.

After all, Isadora could, and without censure, believe that Lady Gwendolyn was mad. Dotty. Insane. She could prevail on her husband to have the woman sent to the country, away from the London Society she so loved. Perhaps even have her incarcerated in one of those asylums people found to house inconvenient, embarrassing relations.

Because, obviously, Lady Gwendolyn's penchant for admiring, then taking things, did not begin and end with rearranging the contents of Portland Square. There was the snuffbox, for one. And now Isadora's garnet brooch. Lord only knew what else was secreted here, in the lady's bedchamber, cached where Peggy's daily inspections failed to find all that had been hidden.

Should she tell Bramwell?

No. What was the sense of that? He probably already knew. After all, who else would have commissioned Peggy to do her daily searches? What a good man Bramwell was, to be so kind to his aunt, who doubtless had no idea her nephew had discovered her admiring tendencies.

Sophie's gentle heart swelled at the thought of the duke of Selbourne's affection for his aunt, the difficulties he must endure finding ways to replace the snuffboxes and other trinkets his aunt must surely pilfer wherever she went. For Lady Gwendolyn probably indulged herself whenever something took her fancy, just as Giuseppe often fancied shiny things, crackly things (like the paper upon which the infamous wager had been penned), pretty little things that made the palms itch to hold them.

Well, at least Bramwell didn't have to know about Isadora's brooch. She'd save him that embarrassment. It would be easy enough for Sophie to return the thing herself, saying she'd found it lying on the carpet in the drawing room, or stuffed down a cushion somewhere. Isadora wouldn't question her. Why should she? The clasp on the brooch might very easily have slipped open, allowing the piece to fall and become temporarily misplaced.

Yes, that's what she'd do. And then she'd have a little talk with Peggy about Lady Gwendolyn's shoe cupboard, and the paperweight stuffed behind a pair of half boots. She didn't know where it belonged, but its owner must miss it.

"Did you find the earbobs, Sophie?" Lady Gwendolyn asked, having poured and then drunk a second glass of wine while Sophie was arguing with herself.

"Indeed I did find them, Aunt Gwendolyn," Sophie said, returning to her chair and placing the jewelry on the table that sat between them. "But do you know what? We never did look through that mass of jewelry I brought with me, did we? We'll have to do that tomorrow, yes? I think I owe you a garnet brooch."

Lady Gwendolyn frowned. "A garnet brooch? Do you know, Sophie, I think I might just have gotten one of those." She sighed, obviously content, her belly warm with wine. "But a woman can never have too much jewelry, can she, Sophie?"

"Never, Aunt Gwendolyn," Sophie agreed, pouring herself a second glass of wine, for her own nerves were still a bit unsteady. "Especially when a woman is preparing to dazzle a man such as the estimable Sir Wilford, yes?"

"Pshaw!" Lady Gwendolyn said, blushing to the roots of her gray hair even as she fought a yawn, so that Sophie began to think the lady would be snoring in her bed long before the curtain rose at the theater that night. "Oh, Sophie, how glad I am you're here. Don't go away, please. Don't ever go away. Because you're so right. We're here to be happy, aren't we? Ah," she ended, closing her eyes as Sophie bent to push a footstool close, for her ladyship's feet, "there is nothing more to desire of the world than to be happy."

Sophie located a shawl at the bottom of Lady Gwendolyn's bed and gently tucked it across the woman's shoulders before tiptoeing out into the hallway, leaving the lady to her nap—and herself with Isadora's garnet brooch tucked up in the pocket of her dressing gown.

Sophie went looking for Bramwell before dinner but could not seem to run him to ground, even when she'd dared to look for him in his own chambers—not that Sophie really thought such things to be daring. She had, however, then spent a few fruitless minutes attempting to hold a conversation with his grace's valet, Reese.

As she walked down the staircase, on her way to the drawing room, she still wondered how one man could possibly be so nervous. She'd been watching Reese off and on since her arrival in Portland Square, as he had such queer ways about him. Amusing. Although, or so it seemed, not to him. Starting at shadows. Always knocking three times before entering a room, always entering that room slowly, peeking behind the door as he entered, as if some bogeyman might be hiding there to jump out at him. Strange man, Reese. Perhaps if she spent some time with him, talking to him, she could discover a way to make him less tense. She would, that is, the moment he seemed more comfortable around her, and not as if he'd just seen a ghost.

Sophie walked into the drawing room, still on the lookout for His Grace, but found only Mrs. Farraday. The woman would knit forever, for Heaven only knew what purpose, and be happy as a clam dug deep in the sand.

"Good evening, Mrs. Farraday!" Sophie called out loudly, then stepped right up to the lady and waved a hand in front of her face, just to make sure she had the woman's attention.

Edith Farraday looked up at her ward, her smile tentative, her eyebrows climbing on her forehead as if this maneuver, that tended to make her look permanently startled, would help open up her ears. "Miss Sophie," she shouted, laying her needles in her lap, "is it time for dinner, then? I'm hoping for a standing rib tonight, I must confess."

Mrs. Farraday didn't have to confess to anything, Sophie knew, because the woman's appetite was quite obvious to anyone who had ever shared the table with her. For a thin woman, a very thin woman, she could probably eat an entire cow at every sitting, with room left over for two slices of pie. "I think Cook said something about veal tonight, I'm afraid," she answered, trying to keep her own voice somewhere below a bellow, as Mrs. Farraday spoke seldom, but always with enough force to command an army to charge, probably so that she could hear herself speak.

The already arched brows climbed higher. "You're afraid the cook steals?" she asked in a near shout. She shook her head, clucking her tongue in time with each sad shake. "Well, then, that puts paid to my standing rib, don't it, Miss Sophie?"

Sophie bent and hugged the old lady, kissing her cheek. What a dear she was. The shoemaker's penniless widow probably still didn't have the faintest idea why she and Desiree had rescued her from the local poorhouse and set her up as Sophie's guardian. And she didn't care, either. She had just stood still for fittings for her new gowns, sat when she was told, gone where she was told to go and, as long as she had her knitting, never asked more of life than a clean bed to sleep in and a good standing rib at least once a week.

"Ah, how touching," Bramwell drawled from the doorway, and Sophie straightened, turning to go meet him halfway as he walked into the room. "The guardian and the grateful ward," he whispered. "Strange, it seems more like the dear, oblivious lady is a beloved pet, rather like Giuseppe and Ignatius. Lord knows you treat her like one, almost as if your roles were reversed. Is that why you're so grateful, Sophie? Because Mrs. Farraday may be your guardian but, in reality, it is you who guards her?"

Sophie grinned. "No need to whisper, Bramwell," she said, deciding to be as informal as he, since it seemed that they had cried friends the other night at Almack's—not that he had gone out of his way to be in her presence these past days. Perhaps he didn't enjoy being part of a crowd? "Mrs. Farraday couldn't hear you from here if you were to cup your hands around your mouth and shout until the chandelier shook."

Bramwell eyed both the distance and Mrs. Farraday owlishly as that woman went back to her endless knitting. "You're jesting."

"No, I'm not. Go ahead," she encouraged him, an imp of mischief invading her, hopefully invading him as well. "Go on. Try it."

His Grace stood for a moment, his head tilted to one side as if considering what he should do, then he called out in his robust baritone: "Mrs. Farraday—run! The room is on fire!"

Three alarmed footmen raced in from the foyer, eyes wide and frightened, reluctantly ready to battle the blaze.

Bramwell immediately looked abashed.

Sophie collapsed in giggles into a nearby chair.

And Edith Farraday just kept on knitting.

"My turn," Sophie said, as a rather red-faced Bramwell apologized, then shooed the footmen back to their posts. She got up and walked closer to Mrs. Farraday. "His Grace has just offered to set me up as his mistress, Mrs. Farraday!" she said loudly, but not too loudly—for the footmen had already heard more than enough, hadn't they? "He says he longs to ravish me tonight until my eyes roll up in my head!"

Edith Farraday lifted *her* head and smiled vacantly at the duke. "No, no, Your Grace," she bellowed. "Don't be distressed. My eyes are quite fine, thank you. I always knit in this light."

Sophie grinned triumphantly even as Bramwell unsuccessfully tried to bite back a laugh, then told her that she was poking fun at a poor, innocent old lady who could not help that she couldn't hear anything below a violent clap of thunder.

"Oh, no, no!" Sophie protested as she gently helped Mrs. Farraday to her feet. She then gathered up the woman's knitting and the bag she kept with her at all times, all the while pantomiming the sound of the first dinner gong going, so that the old woman knew it was time to go upstairs and prepare for the evening meal.

As Sophie watched her guardian leave, a spring in the old woman's step as she contemplated swallowing down whatever the thieving cook had left them to eat, she explained: "I would *never* make fun of Mrs. Farraday. She's the sweetest thing, and I consider myself lucky to have her as my guardian. And, as she didn't hear me, there was no harm done, now was there? I was only proving my point to you, Bramwell. And perhaps funning with *you* a little, yes? At least you're smiling now. You weren't when you came in, you know. In fact, you still seem rather on edge. Shall I pour you a glass of wine?"

She watched as his expression cooled, and he opened his mouth to freeze her with an automatic refusal. But he stopped himself, smiled, and agreed that she could fetch him a glass, and one for herself while she was at it, so they could sit and have a comfortable coze.

Phrases such as "comfortable coze" did not trip lightly from the duke's tongue, so it was probably those words that alerted Sophie that all was not well. Was very much less than well. She'd never be quite sure exactly what had warned her. But one thing was obvious: Bramwell was not a happy man. Therefore, she immediately set out to make him happy again, for his own sake as well as hers. Mostly for hers, if she wanted to be strictly honest about the thing.

As she poured the wine and carried the glasses and sat down on the couch and motioned for him to join her—all the time smiling openly while secretly measuring the depth of his unhappiness, his discomfort—she chattered nineteen to the dozen about the afternoon just past.

She told him of her various suitors. She gave a wonderfully visual recreation of Giuseppe's antics, including the tug-o-war that had resulted when one of her callers had refused to give up his poem to the monkey. She informed him that he must be prepared for an onslaught of suitors asking for permission to court his aunt.

And Bramwell never laughed. He never smiled. Not once. He didn't even pick up his glass. He just sat there, very politely, looking at her, and making her feel as if he were waiting until she ran down, until she had no more silly stories to tell—and then he was going to say something dreadful. Something awful. Something Sophie was certain she did not wish to hear.

It had to have been the kiss. That's what had done it. He hadn't wanted to kiss her; she knew that. She also knew he'd wanted to kiss her again since. A woman, she'd decided, just knew these things. And, probably, he wanted to do more than kiss her. That's what men did. That's what, as she'd come to determine from her readings of her *maman*'s journals, from Desiree's lessons, men thought women were put on this earth for in the first place—to accommodate men and their need for kisses—for more, always for more.

The duke must be going out of his mind with wanting her. Wanting her as his father had wanted her mother. Except that Bramwell Seaton, Ninth Duke of Selbourne, was *not* his father. What his father had done had shamed him, and he'd probably rather face a firing squad at dawn than believe himself capable of repeating what he saw as his father's weakness.

How could her mother have believed it wonderful to be desired? It was terrible; terrifying! Even more terrifying was to desire in return, for Sophie could not deny that she was attracted to Bramwell. Attracted to him as a man of intelligence, of compassion, even of a rather delicious humor—when he forgot to hide it.

Panic seized her. Sophie didn't want to leave Portland Square. She didn't want to leave Aunt Gwendolyn and all the other wonderful people she'd met since coming to London. But to leave Bramwell?

The romantic heart she'd always sworn she did not possess began to ache inside her breast. Her ears rang; she felt dizzy. Fear slid its tentacles around her, gripping her, hurting her, stealing her breath. All the pain she'd vowed never to feel slammed into her at once, robbing her of everything she'd yet to possess.

Was this how her mother had felt when the uncles had

said their good-byes? Hollow? Frightened past all reason?
Lonely, once again to be alone? Love did not exist. Sophie
knew that, believed that. She didn't love Bramwell Seaton.
She couldn't. But, oh, how she very much did like him.
How very much she did, God help her, desire him. Yearn
for his touch, his kiss.

"Sophie, there's something I must say to you, tell you,"
Bramwell said at last, when she'd subsided into nervous silence, when they both had been silent for endless moments, nerve-snapping moments. He took her hand in his,
took both her hands in his, and she closed her eyes against
another wave of desire, another unexpected, rending slash
of that knife called physical longing.

Don't touch me, don't touch me, she cried silently, closing her eyes against the strange, unreadable expression in
his. *Even your fingers against my hand melt me into a puddle of longing.* Maman*'s journals spoke of desire as delicious, wonderful, exciting. How could she have been so
mistaken, or so lucky? This is lust that I feel now, just as
Desiree warned of, joked about. But it's not enjoyable.
There will be no looking back at this moment in fond memory. This is wrong. This hurts. And now, with only a few
words, it's going to be over.*

So unfair, so unfair! He was going to send her packing.
Sophie was convinced of it. And it wasn't just because of
that stupid, impulsive kiss, or because he might want her,
long to have her in his bed. Why, he might not want her at
all! As her mother's daughter, and while also being judged
on her own merits and faults, she might disgust him rather
than ignite his passions.

Yes! That was it! She had been too much of a bother to

him from the very beginning, as much as she had tried to be a help. Giuseppe had pilfered His Grace's favorite stickpin, or something, and Ignatius had probably been squawking out naughty ditties again. The duke was tired of having gentlemen clogging up his drawing room. She'd thrown that stupid brandy snifter when she'd been angry enough, idiotic enough, careless enough, to let him see her dreadful temper. There had to be something. Something. She had embarrassed him somehow.

A million thoughts, none of them good, crowded Sophie's mind and, for once, no solutions presented themselves. But, then, she had never before been so frightened, had so much to lose. She was devoid of a single thought that could provide her with some wiggle room, a way to charm, to tease, to divert, to please. To make Bramwell happy so that she, too, could be happy. No clouds. No rain. She wanted sunshine, she craved it. But all she saw were clouds, and a storm about to arrive at any moment. *Oh, Maman,* she thought sadly, *how did you stand it?*

"Yes, Bram?" she prompted when the silence dragged and dragged, when he didn't say anything else. "You have something to tell me, you said? But you aren't saying anything, are you? Even Uncle Cesse, that most talkative man, had his silent moments. Well, it can wait, I'm sure, if you want to dress now for the theater. We are still going, aren't we? Oh, dear, we aren't, are we? Is that why you're so solemn, yes? I promise, I won't be disappointed if you've made other plans. Truly. Or, if you'd rather—"

He squeezed her fingers. "Sophie, I'd consider it a considerable blessing if you'd just shut up now and listen to me," he said, a small, sad smile robbing his words of any sting, yet frightening her even more. "We have to talk about the other night. About Almack's. About—well, about balconies."

Balconies? Of all the things she had thought of, feared, this was the one thing she'd not considered. He was upset because of that unfortunate incident at Almack's? But surely it had only been a few gentlemen, poking a little bit of fun, teasing Bramwell that he might be thinking of setting her up as his mistress or some such thing. Was this really enough to have him send her packing? Or was this just the excuse he had chosen?

She tilted her head, looking at him quizzically, measuringly. "Balconies?" she repeated, attempting to pull her hands free of his. He wouldn't let her go. "Going out onto the balcony isn't the same as proposing marriage, is it? I thought as much at the time, Bramwell, and Desiree's reaction when I mentioned it to her convinced me of it. That man, those people—they were alluding to something entirely different, weren't they? Something about my mother, and the fact that she was mistress to your father, yes? Mistress to men other than your father. It's all right, Bram. I knew there would be some gossip if I were to go into Society, and I prepared myself for it. But now that they've had their bit of fun, they'll soon stop. I'm convinced of it."

"You'd find a way to see some good in the Devil himself, wouldn't you, Sophie?" Bramwell asked, shaking his head. "Or a way to dazzle him into forgetting he enjoyed being evil. But, even if I believed you to be correct, and that the talk will stop now, I can't take that chance. For your sake."

"I—I see." Sophie lifted her head and looked across the

room, seeing nothing. Nothing but a world devoid of one Bramwell Seaton, Ninth Duke of Selbourne. Damn him for having become so important to her, when she had sworn she would never let someone else dictate her happiness. And so quickly! How had he come to be so important so quickly? How great a fool was she? "You—you're sending me back to Wimbledon?"

"If you had asked me that a few days ago, Sophie, I would have had your coach packed and waiting at the door in a heartbeat," he admitted with endearing honesty. "But no, not now. Now, you'd just be seen as running away. You don't deserve that and, frankly, I don't think your mother or my father deserve it either, as they both wanted you to have this Season."

He took a deep breath, exhaling slowly. "I stared them all down, Sophie, that first year. You may go about the thing differently, choosing to dazzle rascals rather than glare at them. But I still think you can pull it off. Make them forget. Make them see *you,* Sophie, and not an old scandal. But only if you know it all, and aren't, as you obviously were the other evening, forced to sail into battle without being fully armed with the knowledge you need."

She was looking at him closely now, curiously. Seeing compassion in his eyes. Not anger. Not defeat. Not desire. Compassion. He felt sorry for her. She didn't want him to feel sorry for her, didn't want anyone ever to feel sorry for her.

But she also was aware of a wave of sweet relief rolling over her, one unfortunately mixed with disappointment. Relief that he wasn't sending her away. Disappointment that she'd been wrong; he wasn't so overcome with desire

for her, lust for her, that he'd decided to get her out of his
house, out of his sight, out of his life.

Wait just a moment! He *didn't* want her? And she was
disappointed? No! This was much more than disappointment. Irrational anger gripped her for a moment, then dis-
sipated as quickly as it had come. Was she mad, insane?
Had she come to London only to lose her senses? Why
should she be angry? After all, she didn't *want* him to desire her, did she? She most certainly didn't want to desire
him.

So many conflicting emotions! She'd have to go off by
herself, soon, and think them all through. But, first, she'd
have to concentrate on what Bramwell was saying. There
was something she didn't know? Something he wanted to
tell her? What could that be?

"I know *Maman* and Uncle Cesse were lovers for nearly
four years, Bram, that they delighted in scandalizing Society with their very open association, their silly, romantic
exploits. I know that they even died together. I came to
London prepared to deal with all of that, with the whispers,
the giggles, the arch looks. What else is there to know?"

It seemed to be Bramwell's turn to stare off across the
room, and she bit her lip as she waited for him to collect
his own thoughts, waited for him to look at her again,
speak to her. Tell her what he obviously felt she needed to
know.

"Three of your *uncles* are coming to see you tomorrow,"
he said at last, turning back to her, but still not looking into
her eyes, still holding tight to her hands. "Sir Tyler, Lords
Buxley and Upchurch. They asked my permission this af-

ternoon. It seems they want to see how their little Sophie grew up, and help to launch you if they can."

Another time, Sophie would have been overjoyed with such news. Another time. But she wasn't a stupid young woman, and she knew the duke wouldn't have been this distressed if a visit from her uncles was the only thing he had to tell her. "I'll be so happy to see them again."

Bramwell cleared his throat. "Yes, well, I thought that might please you. But about Uncle Willy—Lord Buxley, that is? The man's known for his plain speech, you understand. And he might say something, think you know something you don't fully—"

"Oh, for heaven's sake, Bramwell—tell me!" Sophie exploded, at last succeeding in freeing her hands. "If you have something terrible to say, just say it. I don't think I can stand this suspense anymore, truly I don't."

He looked at her then. Looked at her searchingly, deeply, as if gauging her strength, visually measuring the density of her backbone. "First tell me something, all right, Sophie? Tell me how you think your mother and my father died. I want to have it clear in my head."

"Tell you—" she broke off, shaking her head. This conversation was more than maddening. "Why? You must know as well as I, as well as anyone. They were traveling together, which I know was what delighted the gossips no end. In fact, if I remember correctly, they were on their way to a country house party, which could also be considered scandalous. There was something about a curricle race, two young idiots feathering around a corner in the road, riding neck and neck, unable to see Uncle Cesse's carriage approaching from the other direction until it was too late."

She twisted her hands in her lap. "The coachman tried to avoid a collision, but one wheel of the coach slid over the edge of the road, into a ditch, and the carriage overturned. The doors came open somehow, and both Uncle Cesse and *Maman* were thrown into the ditch, the coach tumbling down straight on top of them."

She looked up at him, her eyes swimming with tears as she remembered her grief, the devastating sense of loss she'd felt, recalled the long, horrible months after the funeral. "Desiree swore to me that the person bringing the news told her they'd died instantly. They didn't suffer. It— it was my one consolation."

"I see. I'd thought it might be something like that. A heartbroken child, a comforting web of lies," Bramwell said bluntly, quickly. "Sophie, listen to me. Difficult as this is going to be, listen to me. Your mother and my father didn't die in a carriage accident, although I can understand why your woman, this Desiree, never told you the truth."

"I—I don't understand," Sophie said, stubbornly refusing to believe him, refusing to consider the sincerity in his expression, his tone. "They—they died in a carriage accident, Bram. Desiree told me so. And now you're saying Desiree lied to me, that what she told me wasn't true?"

"No, Sophie, it wasn't true, although I wish to God it were."

"But why? Why would Desiree lie to me? What possible reason—" Sophie bit her bottom lip, willing herself to silence, willing herself to listen, to understand.

"Let's get this over quickly, all right? Our parents died together, Sophie. That much is true. They were cavorting, stark naked, on a balcony outside one of Lord Buxley's guest chambers during a house party. Probably on the railing of the balcony. Your mother and my father. Your mother hadn't been invited to Buxley's, of course, but somehow found her way to my father's chamber—I know how, but the how of it doesn't matter. It was one of their larks, their mad starts. Reese, all unknowing, opened the doors to the balcony on them. Off-balance, our parents tumbled two stories to the ground, landing on the flagstones outside the music room where the rest of the guests had been gathered."

He took another breath, then added, "Those guests dined out on the story for nearly a year."

Sophie sat frozen for some moments, trying to collect her shattered thoughts, to dismiss the horrendous mental image Bramwell's words had formed in her mind, behind her tightly shut eyes. Her mother, her lovely *maman*. Sprawled naked on Lord Buxley's flagstones, her body the object of all those curious, undoubtedly scandalized but delighted eyes. Her dearest *maman,* an object of ridicule, a thing; a scandal and not a woman, not her mother, her dearest, dearest *maman* anymore. *Oh God, oh God, oh God, no!*

"I see," Sophie said at last as she stood up, her chin high, her hands now at her sides. She ignored Bramwell's outstretched hand as he also rose to his feet, to tower over her protectively. "That, I would suppose, explains Reese's reluctance to open doors, yes? How—how very droll, Your Grace."

"Sophie—"

She took a deep breath. Smiled even as a part of her

died. "Well, thank you, Bramwell. You were right. I did need to know this, yes? And now, if you'll excuse me, I think I heard the second dinner gong. You will understand if I choose to dine in my room, and beg permission to be excused from accompanying you and Miss Waverley to the theater?"

"Oh, Christ, Sophie, don't. *Cry,* Sophie. Scream. Throw something. Here—take this glass and smash it against the fireplace. For the love of God, Sophie, do *something!* Don't be so damned brave," Bramwell said, putting down the glass he'd offered her and taking hold of her shoulders, pulling her stiff, resisting body against his chest. "And don't hate them, Sophie. Don't hate our parents for being who they were, for leaving us to clean up after them, to live with the results of their folly. God knows I've wasted enough years hating them for you. It serves no purpose."

She stood very still, allowing him to hold her, to press kisses against the top of her head, her temple, her nearly numb cheek, the curve of her throat. But she was not so lost within her pain not to notice when his caresses turned from being comforting to being more of an exploration of uncharted territory, his hands sliding along her back, spanning her waist, pulling her closer, closer. Her heart burned, melted, turning traitor at this most inopportune time, and she once again knew herself to be very much her mother's child. For her sins.

But she was also Desiree's pupil, and she had learned her lessons well. She'd only forgotten them for a little while, that's all, forgot that she was to be the dazzler, and not allow herself to be dazzled.

"Don't carry on so, Bramwell," she scolded, pushing

herself back from his embrace and smiling up at him. Oh, could he know how that smile cost her, pained her? She reached up to touch his face, deliberately tracing her fingertips along his cheek, across his taut jawline. "I imagine that, although their deaths came prematurely, *Maman* and Uncle Cesse were rather pleased with how it all turned out. They always could see the humor in shocking the world, couldn't they? And Heaven knows, they'll always be remembered, won't they? Actually, when I think about it, the whole thing is rather delicious, yes?"

And then she frowned, thrusting out her bottom lip, turning cold as ice, cold as a three-year-old grave. "What is not delicious is having you paw me, Bramwell, as if bent upon repeating our parents' history."

Her words obviously stung, as she had meant them to, and he immediately released her, presenting her with his back as he stared toward the windows. "I was only trying to comfort you, Sophie. I'm an engaged man, a sober one, without the least interest in becoming a laughingstock, the latest fodder for the gossips. The last, the very last thing I'd ever do would be to take you for my mistress."

"*Maman* was never *taken*, Bramwell," Sophie said quietly, made strong by her new insight, insight gained with much pain. "She *gave*. There is a difference. And, at last, thanks to you, I think I'm truly beginning to understand her life. And why she cried. Good night to you, Your Grace. And thank you. This has been a most edifying interlude, informative in many ways. Oh, and one thing more. You're right. I would never leave London now, now that I know the whole of what I'm facing, the full reason behind the jokes, the stares. I wouldn't give the world that satisfaction. I'll best them, you'll see. I'll best them all. Even you."

She was just closing the drawing room doors behind her, too defeated, too exhausted to slam them, when she heard the sound of very good crystal shattering against the marble fireplace.

Book Two

Never Say "Never"?

*It would be superfluous in me to point out
to your lordship that this is war.*

—Charles Francis Adams

Chapter Nine

"Monseigneur? A moment of your time, *s'il vous plâit?"*

Bramwell turned slowly, leading with his eyes, his head, as Reese struggled to complete folding His Grace's neckcloth into the Waterfall. He blinked once, to be sure he was seeing what he thought he was seeing. He was. Sophie's maid—Desiree, was it?—was standing in his private dressing room as Reese was making him ready for the day. Amazing. Truly amazing.

"Leave us, Reese, if you please," he said, still eyeing the woman as he slid from the high stool he'd been half-reclining against as the valet fussed over him. She was fifty if she was a day—unnaturally blond, realistically plump, and rather matronly. But with eyes much older than a half century, as old as the oldest profession, and with an air to her that said she was no stranger to gentlemen's dressing rooms, or the sight of those gentlemen in less than a complete state of dress. Amazing, yes. And interesting.

"But, Your Grace?" Reese snatched up Bramwell's coat, holding it by the shoulders. "We are not done, Your Grace."

"Reese, the day I can't put my coat on by myself is the day I shoot myself," Bramwell said, "not that I wouldn't mind a little help with my boots. But later, Reese. For now, I have company."

The valet bit his bottom lip as he looked from his employer to the female intruder. He whimpered a time or two as he shifted his weight from one foot to the other, thrust the coat into Bramwell's hands, then fled the room.

"So, he is the one, *monseigneur*? This Reese person? It was he who tipped your father and my dear Constance over the edge? Until Sophie told me the details last night, I had wondered precisely how it had happened. The balcony I already knew, the Reese I did not. Such a nervous little rabbit, to have caused so much trouble, *oui*? I could have him on a spit, you understand, should I wish it."

"Yes, I can believe that. I'd thought of it a time or two myself, actually."

Desiree's shrug was one of eloquent dismissal as she relieved Bramwell of his coat, holding it out for him, effortlessly taking on the role of valet. "Ah, *monseigneur,* but as you and I know, this is all in the past. There is no sense now in weeping over spilt dukes, *oui*?"

Bramwell felt the corners of his mouth twitching in mild amusement at this expression of Gallic practicality as he turned his back and slid his arms into the coat sleeves. "Perhaps you also do boots, *mademoiselle*?" he suggested amicably as he smoothed down his collar and shot his cuffs, turning to face the maid once more. "I feel slightly at a disadvantage without my boots, you understand."

Desiree made playful shooing motions with her hands, directing Bramwell to the chair in the corner of the room, where his freshly polished Hessians waited. He obediently sat down. She then knelt in front of him, her grin close to coquettish, giving him a glimpse of how she had been when young, and how much she had enjoyed being what she had been.

As if to confirm his suspicions, she said, "Ah, how long it is since I have helped a man on with his boots. Not as long since I have helped one *off* with them, *monseigneur,* if you take my meaning."

"I do," Bramwell told her as Desiree slid one boot after the other over his feet, then laid her weight behind pulling them on snugly, never making so much as a single smudge on the pristine leather. "And have you taught Sophie how to do this? Along with everything else you've taught her?"

Desiree levered herself to her feet, making companionable use of Bramwell's knee when the effort nearly unbalanced her. "You are the true son of your father, *monseigneur.* In looks, in wit—in appetite. How long you will run from these truths is all that remains to be seen, *oui?*"

Bramwell got to his feet, walking over to the tall dressing table, unsurprised to see the tight white line around his mouth as he glared at his own reflection in the mirror, his father's reflection. He pushed down the mirror, attached to the dressing-table top by a hinge, wood meeting wood with a sharp slam of anger. Damn it, they were discussing his father, Sophie's mother. They were not, would not discuss him—his looks, his wit. Or his appetites.

"You knew all along, didn't you? How my father died,

that is, how Constance Winstead died. It was you who fed her the lie about a carriage accident. I can understand why you did it, at first, for she was still little more than a child three years ago. But when she started talking about a Season? In God's name, woman, why didn't you tell her the truth then?" he asked, wheeling to face the maid.

The maid? Oh, no. Oh no, no, no. A talented courtesan. A woman who enjoyed men—knew how to use them, how to manipulate them, how to *dazzle* them, all while not respecting them any more than she would a dog bringing her a freshly killed pheasant. She was all of this. But never a maid. "How could you have let her come here," he ended bitterly, "let her dream of a debut, a marriage?"

"You seem to have trouble saying her name, but we speak now of Sophie, *oui*? You speak of debuts, of marriage. She doesn't deserve either? Is that what you're saying, *monseigneur,* even as you agreed to sponsor her? I confess, I had hoped for more from you."

"Hell and damnation." Bramwell groaned, pushing his fingers through his hair, totally disrupting all of Reese's good work. "Of course she deserves a Season. She wasn't the one scandalizing all of England. But sometimes, regrettable and unjust as it is, the sins of the mother—"

"And the father, *monseigneur*?" Desiree interrupted archly.

"Yes, damn it all, the father," Bramwell went on, then stopped, unable to finish whatever in blazes he had been trying to say. He was sure it had something to do with a quiet debut in Bath or somewhere, a small round of even smaller parties, a mere brush with the fringes of Society, and then a marriage, if possible, or a retreat back to Wimbledon and a future spent raising cats or some such nonsense.

But was that what he had done? No, it was not. He had marched straight into Society the moment the mandatory mourning period had expired, his title to protect him, his own consequence to buoy him, and dared anyone to snicker, to giggle behind a fan, to embarrass him with innuendo or snide jokes.

But he had a title. He was a man. He was not without defenses.

Sophie had nothing. Nothing but her innocence, her grand love of life, her dreams of a Season that had been fostered by her mother, encouraged by her maid. She had just that, and her sincere belief in her ability to dazzle.

And now, thanks to the threat of exposure by the *ton* gossips, she also had the whole truth, which had been nearly enough to crush him when he'd heard it.

"How is she?" Bramwell asked, subsiding once more against the high stool.

"Then you do care, *monseigneur*? At least, as much as any man can care? I had thought as much, hoped as much, which is why I am here." Desiree sat down in the chair Bramwell had vacated, lifting one foot onto her other knee, rubbing at a sore instep.

"But, then," she went on brightly, "how could you help it? She is a lovable scrap, my small Sophie. I raised her, you know. Oh, Constance loved her, loved her dearly. But, from the time she was a small child, it was I who raised her, *monseigneur*. Ah, but you asked how she is, how she feels after you told her what she needed to know. She wept, of course. Wept for nearly half the night, as if her tender heart would break, until she at last fell asleep in my arms. But she will weather this latest storm, as she has weathered all the others. However, as I saw it then, and as I see it now, *monseigneur,* it would be easier, *oui,* if she had help?"

"Meaning me, I imagine. Which, if I might hazard another guess, is *also* why you're here now, scandalizing my valet," Bramwell said, longing to kill anyone who could make the sunny, smiling Sophie cry, even himself. "You've been counting on me since the beginning, haven't you? Since the thought of Sophie having a Season first occurred to you. Otherwise, you would never have allowed Sophie to come within ten miles of me, not if you could help it. Am I correct?"

Desiree's smile was brilliant, turning her, for an instant, into the girl she had been. "Perhaps smarter than your father, *oui?* I do not much like men, *monseigneur.* I have enjoyed them, I'll not lie and say I have not. You men are amusing, at least for a space. And women, too, have appetites. But I am no fool, *monseigneur.* Men use and discard. This I have always remembered. Ah, but Constance? *Mon Dieu,* how she could never see this, and how she did love them! How blind she was to their faults, their failings. Sophie is a little of both of us, *monseigneur.* A hard head, but still, alas, with the soft heart. And, for me, much too high an opinion of her fellow creatures. But you won't hurt her, I begin to hope. I begin to hope for many things, which proves me a female with a foolish, wishful heart after all, no matter how hard I try to be like you men. That, perhaps, or I grow old and foolish. You said the *oncles* were coming today, *oui?"*

"Yes, they are. And this worries you? Why?" Bramwell

looked at Desiree closely, trying to penetrate the woman's speech, see into her mind. The more he learned about Desiree, he felt sure, the more he would understand Sophie. "Are you thinking they might try to hurt her?"

"Think, *monseigneur.* Men use and discard. It has always been so. And they don't like looking behind them, to see if their discards still follow, if you take my meaning. Upchurch? He is simple enough, a fool of a man. The other two worry me, *monseigneur.* If you care at all for my Sophie, and I begin to think you do, they should perhaps worry you a little as well."

She stood, walked to the door, then turned to him, one hand resting on the latch. "So this, *monseigneur,* is why I came to visit today. To warn you of the *oncles, oui.* For that, and to see for myself this gentleman who has made my Sophie so happy, so sad. You are a formidable enemy to all of my teachings, I believe. I have told Sophie no man knows how to love, but only how to want. It would please me very much, *monseigneur,* if you were to prove me wrong. *Bon jour.* You may call the rabbit back now, for I am gone."

But Bramwell didn't call Reese back into the dressing room. Instead, he sat on the chair in the corner for a long time, thinking, wrestling with his thoughts.

The French mentor-cum-maid, Bramwell decided a few hours later, had been worrying for nothing. Watching Sophie with her *oncles* was rather like watching a farce in which only one of the characters knew her lines, with the others forced to look hopefully to each other for clues as to what to do, what to say next.

They had come bearing presents, as all good uncles should, and Sophie, showing no outward signs of her un-happy night, had responded with *oohs* and *aahs,* tearing into each package like a favorite niece on Christmas morn-ing. She held up ivory-sticked fans and silver-filigree nosegay holders and lace-edged handkerchiefs, then be-stowed kisses on each of her uncles' cheeks—all while keeping up a running monologue on how handsome the uncles were, how well she remembered them, how none of them had changed a bit. Not a bit.

Giuseppe had been paraded front and center, tipping his hat, then reaching into Lord Upchurch's waistcoat pocket to find the sugary treat waiting for him there, just as if it hadn't been a few more than a half dozen years since last the two had met. "He remembers me!" His Lordship had shouted, beaming, and then frowned in almost comical ap-prehension. "You don't take him into society, do you, So-phie, child? I don't think that would be good, you know."

Ignatius had also been presented, the paisley shawl lifted from the cage so that the bird blinked itself awake, protested at being disturbed, then surveyed the company. When the parrot's eyes lit on Sir Tyler, it said, in a near-perfect imitation of the man's voice: "Demned coachie! *Squawk!* Quick! My flask! Secrets to tell! *Squawk! Squawk!* Demned coachie! Secrets to sell! Quick, my flask! *Squawk!*"

"Now that's funny. Sounds just like you, you know," Lord Upchurch commented, looking to Sir Tyler.

"Demned bird!" Sir Tyler had returned quickly, hotly, nearly squawking himself before he manfully calmed him-self, laughed. "As if Constance would ever tell anyone about us. What say you, Buxley? Would our Constance ever do that?"

Lord Buxley vehemently shook his head. "Sell our secrets? Not Connie. Had more than enough money to go on with. Some of it ours, too. A good bit of it ours, now that I think on it. Money, land, trinkets. But all of it given freely," he ended, looking to Bramwell.

"I'm sure it was," Bramwell answered, wondering how much of the Selbourne fortune now resided in Constance Winstead's daughter's pockets, and finding that he didn't begrudge her a penny of it.

And then Sophie was off again, gently teasing her uncles with remembered stories of their visits to Wimbledon and the fun they'd all had in their turn, leaving Bramwell to consider what he'd heard. Sir Tyler hadn't looked pleased to hear the parrot mimicking him. Lord Buxley had perhaps protested too much about the unimportance of the money that had changed hands with the woman who had also changed important, prominent bed partners so many times.

Did they see Sophie as just the young girl they recalled from their visits to Wimbledon? Or did they look at the daughter and remember the mother? Did they dread exposure as Constance Winstead's previous paramours? Did they worry that Constance had whispered secrets to her daughter, tales of incidents, of failings, of foibles, that they feared she might use as a lever against them someday? And, furthermore, did Sir Tyler have to keep staring at Sophie, his expression caught somewhere between avuncular sympathy and an admiring leer?

"Selbourne here giving you a ball, Sophie?" Lord Upchurch asked, the sound of his own name snapping

Bramwell back to attention. "You should have one, you know. Or a small party, at the very least. Balls are expensive. All that bunting looped to the rafters, you know, and candles, and musicians, and extra servants. M'wife near but broke me, popping off our daughters, you know." He looked to his two companions. "Maybe if we all anted up?"

"Dickie, you've the brains of a flea," Lord Buxley snapped, giving the man a swift backhanded slap across the top of the head. "Why not just hire a crier to go around the city, telling all the world and his wife—all the world and *our wives*—we had our turns riding Connie to hounds?"

"Discretion, Willy, remember? Discretion," Sir Tyler whispered, but loudly enough for Bramwell to hear.

"Oh, my goodness!" Sophie cried out, her hands flying to her quite attractively burning cheeks as she looked to her uncles in turn. "You're *embarrassed*, aren't you? Poor uncles! How could I not have seen it? You've been so kind, so very kind. But I'm an embarrassment to you, yes? Perhaps you're even *afraid* of me, of what I might say if I were to meet your wives? Oh, you poor, sweet dears!"

She hopped to her feet, beginning to pace the carpet, her winsome brown eyes bright with sympathy and unshed tears, her tumbling curls and rather childish pink gown—had it been a deliberate choice? Of course it had—making her look so young, so beautiful, so defenseless. So—well, so not very intelligent, or sharp, or in the least bit venal.

Bramwell had been ready to defend her, protect her—toss the uncles out on their collective rumps if they so much as hinted at an insult. But now he sat back, crossed one leg over the other, and contented himself in watching a master work.

"You *are* all frightened of me, yes?" Sophie went on, wringing her hands as she sat down again with a small thump, as if collapsing in despair of being so badly thought of, so misjudged by her beloved uncles. "You think I might mean to harm you, to embarrass you. My own beloved Uncle Dickie, Uncle Willy, Uncle Tye." A single tear slid down her cheek, caressing its perfection, making even the knowing Bramwell feel an absolute, unmitigated cad, just because he was one of the world's most lowly creatures, a man.

She spread her hands, giving an eloquently apologetic shrug. "But what can I say? What can I do? How can I convince you that I mean no harm? It's not possible. I must leave London, yes? I must give up any hope of a Season, of a marriage, of—of children of my own." She lifted her chin; brave, resolute, the perfect martyr, even as her bottom lip wobbled heartbreakingly. "And so I shall! For you, for my beloved uncles!"

Bramwell fought the urge to applaud. What a daring, masterful game of cards the girl played. She'd called them, called them all, and he was willing to wager they'd all fold. He looked to Lord Upchurch, sure he would be the first to go down to defeat.

Lord Upchurch pulled a handkerchief from his pocket and knelt in front of Sophie, offering it to her even as he glared at Buxley and Sir Tyler, the fire of fatherly protection blazing in his eyes. "Are you happy now, gentlemen, eh? Pleased with yourselves? Just see what you've done!"

As Lord Buxley ran a finger around his collar, looking ready to bolt at this display of feminine tears and maidenly sacrifice, Lord Upchurch took up Sophie's hand, awkwardly patting it. "There, there, sweet little Sophie. Don't cry. You're not going anywhere. *Is* she?" he said warningly, shooting his companions another dark look.

Lord Buxley found his tongue, and his feet, standing up quickly as he concurred with Lord Upchurch. "It's like I said all along. A fox can't help being a fox. Ain't the chit's fault," he said, glaring at Sir Tyler Shipley.

"Gentlemen, gentlemen," Sir Tyler purred smoothly, smiling at Bramwell. "The child's overset, and rightly so. Perhaps she's right, to a point. We *are* worried that she might say something—in all innocence, of course—that could, um, get us into some trouble at home, as it were. That is what brought us together, brought us here, am I right? But surely, as I now feel, we have nothing to fear from dearest little Sophie. Her mother was always discreet—until Selbourne, of course," he added, looking at Bramwell, his expression one of pity, so that Bramwell longed to punch him. "Have your Season Sophie. I think we can leave here today secure in the knowledge that we're safe, that our secrets are safe."

"Oh, Uncle Tye, thank you!" Sophie exclaimed, jumping up to kiss his cheek, then Buxley's, before throwing herself into Lord Upchurch's arms. "I'm so happy now! You are all just as I remember you! And I'll make you proud of me, you'll see. I'd never do anything to hurt my dearest uncles, yes?"

Bramwell sighed. It was a dazzling performance. Simply dazzling.

Sophie felt the welcome warmth on her cheeks as the sun at last broke through the clouds of a gray London afternoon. Delighted to have the excuse, she immediately opened her parasol, pressing its gilded stem against her right shoulder as she tilted it coquettishly above her head. Twirling the thing lazily, so that the tassels tied to the spines were set to dancing, she smiled at the duke of Selbourne, awaiting his compliment on her fine choice.

Not that this was her only parasol. Oh, no. She had a dozen of the things—or perhaps two dozen. She couldn't recall. She only knew that she had bullied Lady Gwendolyn into having a very nice young man come to Portland Square with a selection of the things for the pair of them, then fairly well told him to leave them all, as she and Lady Gwendolyn couldn't possibly pick and choose among so many pretty contraptions.

"I'm beginning to know how to interpret those smiles of yours, you know, Sophie. And you'd like nothing more at the moment than to beat me into flinders with that thing. Not that you *ever* become angry, right?" Bramwell asked, indicating the parasol.

So much for compliments. Well, she'd try again. Sophie popped her quizzing glass out of the parasol handle on a hidden hinge, then held it to her eye, looking at him in genteel surprise. "Me? Beat at you? Don't be ridiculous, Bramwell. I'm quite in charity with you, as a matter of fact. It was above all things considerate of you to invite me for this lovely drive in the Park. Even if you haven't spoken above two words to me in the past quarter hour."

"Oh, yes," he said, shaking his head and smiling as she replaced the quizzing glass. "Beat me, pour hot oil down over my head, plaster me with chicken feathers, and then have me rolled out of town and into the nearest deep pit. In fact, if you were being any more pleasant to me, Sophie,

I'd say you might just be planning to murder me. Which is why, even though I definitely wanted to speak with you privately after your visit with the gentlemen yesterday, I decided to do so in this very public place. Being, at heart, a prudent man, I considered it safer."

Sophie turned to her right, the parasol moving along with her, pretending to look at a passing curricle in order to hide her pain. Because Bramwell was right. She did want to murder him. Murder everyone in London. Everyone who had known what she had not. Everyone who had snickered, and giggled, and made horrible, snide jokes about the circumstances surrounding her mother's death.

In fact, it had taken everything that was in her yesterday, employing all her lessons learned over the years from Desiree in the art of concealing how she really felt, what she really thought, that had gotten her through that ridiculous interlude with the uncles. Having Bramwell there as well, as if guarding her from those three clearly selfish and frightened old men, had only heaped insult on her emotional injuries.

Because they knew. They all knew. Her uncles, Bramwell, the whole condemning world. Her mother had fallen to her death in the midst of a romantic liaison. Naked. Lying on the ground, her limbs entwined with the equally naked eighth duke of Selbourne. What a sight they must have made! Poor *Maman,* poor Uncle Cesse!

Poor Sophie!

She squeezed her eyes shut. Yes, that was it. Poor Sophie. She didn't really feel all that sorry for her mother and the late duke. They had lived well, they had died unfortunately—but probably had been greatly happy until their second to last moment. She had already mourned their passing, mourned it deeply. In the three years since their deaths, she slowly had come to grips with those deaths, and begun to think of her mother and the duke with affection, with the fondness of wonderful memories, happy memories.

Now she was stinging with her own pain, her own embarrassment. That was the reason she had spent most of the night crying into Desiree's plump bosom, at least half of last night pacing her floor, unable to sleep. And she loathed herself for feeling this way, was so deeply ashamed. It was as if she, like the rest of the world, like this man sitting up beside her, was now condemning those two reckless, beautiful people.

"Sophie," Bramwell said when she didn't answer him, didn't look at him. "You have to remember that your mother wanted you to have a Season. You won't back down now, will you? Run away?"

"Never!" she said with some violence, snapping the parasol shut as she turned to look at Selbourne. And then she smiled, remembered to dazzle. "Did you really think I meant to tuck my tail between my legs like some whipped dog and slink back to Wimbledon? Because of what I said to the uncles? Oh, Bramwell, and I thought you'd listened when I'd warned you about me. I only thought it easier if the uncles thought it was *their* idea that I remain in London. You must admit that they went away happily enough. It is a gift, yes?"

"Yes, I know. A gift. From Desiree, I imagine. Interesting woman, your *maid.*"

Sophie frowned in real confusion. "Desiree? You've spoken with her?"

"Enough to see where you learned your lessons," he admitted, shaking his head. "It's all of a single piece, isn't it? Desiree has, through her own experiences, formed certain notions about life, about people. Gentlemen in particular. You've been raised by her—trained by her, actually—to think as she does, to make those around you happy as a way of protecting yourself. You sensed what was needed to make the uncles, as you call them, happy, and you set out to make them happy, at the same time protecting yourself. But what makes *you* happy, Sophie? Or do you believe that Desiree knows the secrets to your happiness as well as her own? Will you always be so willing to accept her view of life, of people—and never be tempted to do a little looking of your own? Either at your fellow creatures, or within your own heart?"

She tilted up her chin. "I don't think I like this conversation," she said, her brain still foggy from her second nearly sleepless night. The effort to divert the duke's questions, to dissemble, to gauge her responses in relationship to how best to please him and protect herself, was simply too much for her.

"No, I doubt that you do, Sophie," Bramwell responded, carefully maneuvering the curricle past a stopped landau. "But, then again, I find that I don't much like realizing that your maid raised you to believe in nothing more than the perfidy of men. That she taught you that there is no such thing as love, as honest emotion. In fact, I'm rather disappointed in you."

"Disappointed in me? Oh, really?" Sophie countered,

angry once more. Honestly, the man had introduced her to anger in a way she'd never known before, never experienced. And if he thought anger was a wonderful emotion, then he had not lived as she had, grown up as she had, surrounded by pleasantry, by laughter. And her mother's tears.

But, as Desiree had pointed out, those tears had been *Maman*'s own fault, and completely unnecessary. "You would rather then that I would believe as my mother did, that a woman can find her only happiness in the happiness of some heartless, fickle man? You would have me a willing slave to a man's perfidy? But I say oh no, Your Grace. Much better to give everyone what they think they want, even what they cannot see they might need, and be left free to go your own way, yes?"

"And if you find someone who loves you?"

Sophie was getting herself back under control. "But I *do* have many people who love me, Bramwell. Desiree, Aunt Gwendolyn. Many people. And *I* love them. Yes, I try to please them, but that doesn't mean that I don't love them, care for them very much. And you know it, too, or you wouldn't allow me within a continent of your aunt, for one."

"Yes, Sophie, I know that you would never hurt my aunt, or Isadora, or any of those you've charmed since coming to London—including Lorrie and Wally, who see you as a delightful cross between a beloved younger sister and an untouchable goddess. In a way, I envy you your easy ability to draw people to you, to make them feel at their ease. But that's not what I'm talking about, and you know it. What will you do, Sophie, the day that a man loves you, loves you not as a friend, but in the way a man loves a woman?"

Sophie couldn't resist. "You mean, Bram, the way you love Miss Waverley?"

He hesitated, only for a moment, but it was enough for Sophie. Enough to give her pause, to give her hope. But hope for what? She wouldn't think about that now, because her head ached, and she was still waiting for him to answer her question. "Yes, of course," he then said. "The way I love Miss Waverley."

"I see." Sophie smoothed the fingers of her gloves, keeping her eyes averted from Bramwell's. "I hadn't thought of you and Miss Waverley in that light, to be honest with you." She smiled up at him. "Forgive me. You do remember that I occasionally suffer these dreadful bouts of honesty, yes?"

"I do remember, Sophie," he countered, heading the matched bays toward the nearest exit from the Park. "I also remember that you're extremely proficient at steering the conversation away from any subject that might be unpleasant to you. Muddy up your happy waters, as it were. Now answer me, Sophie, please. What will you do when a man tells you he loves you, loves you as a man loves a woman?"

"I won't believe him, of course," she answered frankly. "There are all sorts of love, you know, Bram. Love of country. Love for your parents. The love of good friendship. Love of even your pets, like Giuseppe and Ignatius. A love of good food, fine drink. But a man's love for a woman? No," she said, shaking her head. "That doesn't exist. Or, if it does, it doesn't last. And I didn't learn that from Desiree. Not entirely. I learned that, Bramwell, from the uncles. Mostly," she ended, knowing she was about to shock him down to his toes, "I believe in lust. Desiree says it is the most common of emotions, both in its frequency and in its depth, its short life. But I do think it nice that you say you love Miss Waverley. As I believe she loves you—rather in the way I love Giuseppe, yes? Now, shall we go back to Portland Square, or do you want to speak with me privately some more?"

Bramwell's posture had grown more and more stiff, rigid, with each word she'd spoken, so that Sophie did her best not to flinch, knowing she had pricked and gored him several ways and that he would not allow her to escape from him unscathed once it was his turn to speak again.

But luck—good or bad she couldn't know—intervened before Bramwell could say a word. Because a man was calling the duke's name, loudly, shrilly, in a way that could not be ignored. Bramwell pulled the horses to a stop just outside the Park and waited for the man to approach from across the wide street.

Sophie watched in fascination as the man progressed toward the curricle. He stepped in horse offal, twice—once with each boot. His curly-brimmed beaver took a nip in the brim from a passing coach, and toppled into a puddle. He whirled about to rescue the hat, and his cane smacked a rather starchy-looking matron flat on the buttocks, eliciting a very ungenteel squeal of shock and protest.

Bowing to the woman in apology, the man's cane nearly impaled another gentleman making his way across the street. This second gentleman looked quite angry, and ready to retaliate, then suddenly stopped, his eyes wide as he looked to the first man, and he quickly scuttled away, seeming happy to make good his escape.

And the man, the poor, poor man, was still only halfway across the street.

"That would be Sad Samuel Seaton, I imagine," Sophie said, trying not to giggle as the very tall, painfully thin man, now all but bent double, looked to his right and then to his left, then quickly raced toward the curricle—only to jump back at the last moment as a high-perch phaeton came whizzing by, its off wheel catching the man across the toe of his left boot. "Oh, the poor dear thing!"

"No!" Bramwell warned feelingly. "Don't do it, Sophie. I forbid it!"

"You forbid what, Bram?" Sophie asked, already fishing in her reticule for a handkerchief, for Mr. Seaton would definitely need one to wipe the mud from his face. Heaven only knew how the mud had gotten there, but, then, Sophie had also already decided that it probably would be best not to inquire, for the sad man might just tell her.

"I forbid you to be nice to Sad Sam—er, to Samuel. To be nice to him, to smile at him, to *dazzle* him. If he were to take a liking to you, he'd want to be in my drawing room all day long, and I don't think the mansion could stand up under the strain. The last time he was in Portland Square he set fire to the drapes."

Now Sophie did giggle, at the sight of Bramwell Seaton, ninth duke of Selbourne, all but quavering in his boots because of a poor unfortunate and obviously helpless soul like his cousin—well, she just hadn't expected ever to see such a sight, that's all.

"But on the other hand," Bramwell was saying as the

congested flagway became much like a deserted island, as other pedestrians had spied out Sad Samuel and were making good their escapes as best they could, "this might just prove interesting. You say, Sophie, that you were born and raised to please. To make people happy. That you do it effortlessly. All right, then. Do it," he ended challengingly. "Make a giddy silk purse out of that sad sow's ear. I dare you."

"Hullo there, Selbourne!" Samuel Seaton said, frowning as he beat at his curly-brimmed beaver in an effort to push it back into shape even as he approached Sophie's side of the curricle. He was a man, Sophie quickly deduced, who had difficulty doing one thing at a time. Frowning, brushing, *and* walking were obviously two things too many. She watched, greatly intrigued but not at all surprised, as he tripped over the curbing and fell to his knees.

"A walking, talking disaster," Bramwell said quietly, and Sophie tended to agree.

"Thought that was you, Selbourne," Mr. Seaton continued once he'd clambered to his feet and brushed off the knees of his ruined pantaloons. "Someone said you'd sailed off to Jamaica. Your butler, I think it was. Last week. He must've had that wrong. Servants are like that. Can't keep a good one m'self. I'd come to tell you about my hip, in hopes you'd know what to do. Couldn't walk straight for days. Don't know why. Started off heading in one direction, ended up somewhere else entirely. But it's better now. Of course," he ended, looking much like a whipped puppy, "the other one hurts now. I'm thinking of letting the leeches at me, being bled, but wanted your opinion."

"Samuel," the duke said, his lips moving although his jaw, Sophie noticed, remained firmly clenched, "allow me to introduce you to Miss Sophie Winstead. Miss Winstead, my cousin, Mr. Samuel Seaton. Make your bow, Samuel— and try not to spook the horses while you're about it, all right? There's a good fellow."

"Mr. Seaton, hello!" Sophie trilled, as the man unbent himself from a most awkward bow. "I've heard *so* much about you from His Grace. I'm delighted to make your acquaintance. Truly. But, oh, your poor face. Here, let me wipe that spot from your cheek."

Samuel looked to Bramwell, his watery blue eyes all but bugging out of his head, and said, "Winstead, you say? The Widow Winstead's daughter? Think I heard something about her being in Town. Oh, it is, it is! I can see that now. Looks just like her. Except maybe for the hair. Don't remember all those curls. Well, if that don't beat the Dutch! Why, look at the both of you! It's the Winstead and your papa all over again, stap me if it ain't! And in public, too, just like them. I say, Selbourne, does Miss Waverley know?"

Sophie touched a corner of her handkerchief to her tongue and leaned over, gently dabbing at Mr. Seaton's cheek, even as she itched to slap that same hangdog face. Not that she would, for Samuel Seaton wasn't being deliberately mean. She didn't think he possessed the brainpower to be deliberately mean. "Don't be naughty, sir," she warned with a smile. "There, that's better. Now, as it's coming on to mizzle again—dreadful weather, yes?—and we can't keep the horses standing, may I ask you to dine in

Portland Square tomorrow evening? I'm sure His Grace was just about to ask you."

She straightened up on the seat once more, and knew her eyes were dancing as she looked at Bramwell. "Weren't you, Your Grace?"

As she saw it, Bramwell had more than one option open to him. He could continue to sit there like a beached fish, his mouth hanging open, all but gasping for air. He could bellow out a resounding "No!" and look like even more of a fool in her eyes. He could sail for Jamaica on the next tide. Or he could invite Mr. Samuel Seaton to dinner.

"Don't look back, Sophie," Bramwell said a few moments later, as they drove off, "but the fool is still back there, bowing his thanks to the both of us. You know, of course, that I haven't had that man's knees under my dinner table since my first week in London, three years ago. He knocked over the salt cellar, spilled his wine, and Aunt Gwendolyn had to flee the table when he started telling us, in some detail, of the purges he'd taken to help with his recurrent dyspepsia."

"Poor man," Sophie said, then coughed into her fist. "But you did dare me, Bramwell. I suppose you already know you shouldn't have done that, yes? However, I'd much rather we made the thing into a wager. We should make it much like the wager you and your friends entered into concerning me. A forfeit of some kind, yes? If I cannot make Sad Samuel happy, I shall—what?" She looked at him searchingly, knowing they were both remembering their conversation before the arrival of Mr. Seaton, and knowing that hers was to be a two-edged question. "What *do* you want from me, Bram?"

She watched as a small tic began in his cheek, and knew that he understood all the layers of her question. He was silent for some moments, very tense moments on Sophie's part, much as she hated to admit it, even to herself. "All right, Sophie. A wager it is. If you lose, you'll promise to stop deliberately setting out to *dazzle* people. You'll promise, for two weeks, simply to be Sophie. No pouring of wine, or fetching of footstools, or—or of spending your days reacting to what you believe someone else wants from you. I simply want you to be Sophie. Not Desiree's notion of who you should be. Just yourself, just Sophie. If you have any idea of who you really are."

How dare he! He didn't think she was *real*! He thought she was some sort of toy Desiree wound with a key, as she used to do with a mechanical rabbit she'd owned as a child, then set off to hop about, to amuse and delight. Sophie's bottom lip began to tremble, which she hated, because she knew she should be laughing at his silliness, teasing and coaxing him into thinking anything save what he was thinking. And yet, all she wanted to do was cry. She was in pain, had been in terrible pain since the moment he'd told her about her *maman,* her Uncle Cesse. Because, much as she didn't want to believe it, the actions of others *did* have the power to hurt her, and there were some things she couldn't change, some problems her grins and shrugs and agile tongue couldn't make go away.

She rallied, not without having to call on years of experience in believing—oh, please, *believing*—that she could never be hurt by what others thought, what others did. Because she, as Desiree had always told her, would remain heartwhole. What Bramwell had said the other day had hurt her, even as he'd tried to comfort her. When he'd held her, she'd nearly been destroyed. Now, knowing that he held such a low opinion of her—when she was becoming almost painfully aware of how much she liked him—was devastating to her. Simply devastating.

Not that he'd ever know!

"I still believe you're deluding yourself, Your Grace," she said at last, as he turned the curricle into Portland Square. "However, a wager is a wager. And *when* you lose, you will spend two weeks doing what *I* say. Going where I want you to go. Doing what I want you to do."

He looked at her, one eyebrow raised, as he swung her down from the seat and onto the flagway. "Even for you, Sophie, I don't believe I can agree to go to Hell."

"Hell?" She lifted her gloved hand to his cheek. It was a studied movement, a practiced one, and she knew now that he probably hated it. "Actually, Bramwell, I was thinking more along the lines of Bartholomew Fair. You see, I don't think you're being the real Bramwell Seaton, yes? I think the *real* Bramwell Seaton likes to laugh, to enjoy himself."

She dropped her hand, and her smile as well, becoming serious. "We're very much alike, Your Grace, if what you think about me is true, and what I see in you is likewise true. We both give the world what it wants to see, what we believe it needs to see. I believe I'd like to see the *real* Bramwell Seaton. Now, excuse me, please, while I go roust out Aunt Gwendolyn, for I have a mission to accomplish before Mr. Seaton arrives for dinner tomorrow night, and must make plans."

She brushed past Bramwell, stopping at the top of the marble steps to turn back and smile at him, even though it

drained nearly every last drop of her composure to do so.
"Oh, and Bram? Tell Reese to leave a little of the starch out
of your cravat, please, will you? That way, you'll be much
more comfortable at the Fair."

You look rather rash my dear
your colors don't quite match your face.
                                    —Daisy Ashford

Chapter Ten

Bramwell was just leaving his ground-floor study when he heard the knocker go, and he stepped back, out of sight, to wait for Bobbit to see who was requesting entrance. He felt ashamed of himself, but if his cousin had arrived early, well, he just might have to return to his study for another bracing glass of wine before facing the man.

"Bobbit, my good man! Where is she?" Sir Wallace Merritt boomed, stepping into the foyer, tossing his hat, cane, and gloves at the butler, who expertly snagged them out of the air and placed them on the table. "Where is the little darling? I'm here to worship at her feet."

"Wonderful news, sir! I'll straightaway tell Miss Winstead that you're here," Bobbit said, and Bramwell watched as the butler stood his ground, smiled, and held out his hand, palm up.

"What?" Sir Wallace asked, then grinned sheepishly. "Oh, of course. Put it on my tab, would you, old man? I'll get you before I leave. Probably owe you another small fortune by then anyway, eh? There's a good fellow. Now, take me to her, if you please."

Bramwell stepped out of the shadows. "Wally, what are you doing here?" he asked, clapping an arm around his friend's shoulders and guiding him back down the hallway. "Surely you don't want to beg a free dinner, as I've already told you Sad Samuel is going to be in attendance."

"Sad Samuel? Here? Gad, I'd forgotten." Sir Wallace shivered in either real or very well feigned horror and all but broke into a run, heading for the relative safety of Bramwell's study. "Been good all the day long, Bram. But, damn, that calls for a drink!"

Bramwell watched him go, then turned to Bobbit. "I do supply two suits of clothes a year for you, don't I?" he asked. "And yet—" he broke off, motioning to the butler's attire, which mimicked the Selbourne livery, but was definitely not cut from the usual cloth.

Bobbit flushed an embarrassed pink all the way to his eyebrows. "What you provide is fine, Your Grace, if a bit lacking in its cut and fabric. I've found a tailor more to my liking in Threadneedle Street, Your Grace," he said, bowing. Then he straightened, beaming, a hand to his coat. "Would you like to see the lining, Your Grace? It's satin. Red satin. All the crack this Season, I understand."

"Never mind, Bobbit," Bramwell said with a wave of his hands. "But if you'd apprise Miss Winstead of Sir Wallace's arrival, as I believe it is she whom he wishes to see? If, that is, your heavy pockets don't inhibit your ability to climb stairs?"

"At once, Your Grace," Bobbit said, bowing again and again, even as he backed toward the stairs.

Bramwell turned away, unable to keep a smile from his face, a smile he definitely didn't want his butler to see, and returned to the study. Sir Wallace was sitting at his ease, a glass of wine dangling from his fingertips.

"You're looking chipper, Wally, much like a very contented cat," Bramwell said, taking up the facing chair. "Actually, I think I even see a few canary feathers sticking out of the corner of your mouth. What's happened?"

Sir Wallace sat forward and grinned at his friend. "They're tossing me out!" he exclaimed, then sat back again, wriggling against the soft burgundy leather as if too excited to remain still. "Called me in, sat me down, and told me that I'm more than thirty now, and it's past time I got my sponging, ungrateful self out from under my long-suffering mama's roof. Can you believe it, Bram? I'm *free!*"

Bramwell propped his elbows on the arms of the chair and pressed two fingers of each hand against his lips, tapping them, tapping them, as he looked at the grinning Sir Wallace. The man's wineglass was still half-full. Ordinarily, the glass would be emptied by now, at least twice, and his friend would be heading for the decanter on the drinks table to refill it. "Throwing you out, you say," he ventured carefully. "And you think you owe this new freedom of yours to Miss Winstead?"

"Hell's bells, yes, Bram!" Sir Wallace returned cheerfully. "Don't you?"

"And you're happy about this? Happy that your mother, your aunt, have most probably entered into intimate, clandestine relationships with servants you've handpicked for them? That, with you out of the house, these two good women will doubtless spend their nights cavorting with these same servants, doing heaven only knows what and which I, for one, refuse to imagine?"

"Well, hell, yes, I'm proud. Tickled straight down to my toes." Sir Wallace frowned. "You think I'm an unnatural son?"

Bramwell rubbed a palm across his mouth, wondering if he was the only one in the room with a strangely perverted sense of the ridiculous, the only one who could even *see* the humor in the thing. Now, if Sophie were here? She'd see the deliciousness, the laughable absurdity of it all. Ah, but he shouldn't think that way, should he? "I don't know, Wally," he said at last. "To tell you the truth, I'm caught between being shocked, and wanting to toast your new freedom with you. Where will you go?"

Now Sir Wallace did down the remainder of his wine. "I asked Lorrie if I could move in with him for a few weeks, but he turned me down. Bram, do you think you could see your way free to—"

"No!" Bramwell stated firmly, quickly cutting off his friend in mid-appeal. "I don't think so, Wally. But perhaps you can look to Miss Winstead for assistance? I'm sure she'd enjoy helping you find suitable lodgings. As she says, she's never happier than when helping to make someone else—happy."

Sir Wallace hopped to his feet. "Sterling idea, Bram. Sterling! I'll do just that. God's teeth, how I adore that girl!"

Bobbit had entered the room and was smiling broadly at Sir Wallace, so that Bramwell could tell that the man was already contemplating an increase in this evening's profits. "Miss Winstead is indisposed at the moment, Sir Wallace, dressing for dinner, and sends her regrets. She did, however, ask that you call for her tomorrow at one, at which time she will accompany you as you both inspect the list of properties she has already deemed worthy of your habitation," he said, his hands cupped into loose fists as he scratched at his itchy palms.

"How—how did she *know*—" Sir Wallace stuttered, then shook his head. "How about that, Bram? She already knew the plan would work. Sharp as a tack, that one, sharp as a tack. Gad, but I adore her."

Bobbit smiled, a bit too avariciously Bramwell thought. The butler then cleared his throat, turned to his employer, and continued importantly: "However, Mr. Samuel Seaton *has* arrived, Your Grace, and I've put him in the drawing room. And Miss Waverley's carriage is just drawing up outside. I've instructed one of the footmen to immediately bring her here to your study. Unless you're ready to join Mr. Seaton? But I fear that before you decide, Your Grace, I must first inform you that Mr. Seaton has already broken your late mother's prized Dresden shepherdess, and is even now dropped down on all fours, attempting to pick up the sharp pieces. Remembering your cousin from previous encounters, I've taken it upon myself to send a footman for salve and bandages. And your cousin smells mightily of camphor, if I might be so bold as to say so, Your Grace. I believe he has come to dine with a restorative plaster stuck to his chest."

"Well, I'm gone!" Sir Wallace exclaimed, jumping to his feet almost before Bobbit was finished speaking. "I've never been here. Probably sailed for France early this morning, as a matter of fact. Why, I'll wager I'm already halfway to Calais. Don't know when I'll be back. You'll tell him that, Bram, won't you? There's a good fellow. Miss Waverley, your servant and all that. Got to go, got to go."

"Coward," Bramwell called after him teasingly as his friend barreled toward the doorway to the foyer, Bobbit in hot pursuit, his hand still out, his palm still empty. "I'll be sending round a white feather in the morning, damme if I won't."

"Selbourne? *Profanity?*" Isadora Waverley asked questioningly as she drew back against the doorjamb to allow the fleeing Sir Wallace and the butler to scurry past her. "Lud, such a sad lack of manners! Whatever is going on?"

"Sir Wallace just remembered an important appointment, my dear," Bramwell said, bending over Isadora's hand, then drawing her into the room, careful to leave the door open, as his fiancée was a stickler for propriety. Lord only knew what she thought he'd do to her if the door was closed. Ravish her? He bit his bottom lip for a moment, realizing that Isadora had nothing to fear on that head. As a matter of fact, other than their betrothal kiss, which landed somewhere on her left cheek, as she'd turned her head at the last moment, he couldn't remember a single romantic interlude with the woman who was soon to be his wife. It was a sobering thought, even for a sober man.

"Well, this worked out well, Selbourne," Isadora said, settling herself into the chair Sir Wallace had so recently and abruptly vacated. "Lud, how could you have known that I'd want a private audience with you?"

"Private audience? I'm not the Archbishop of Canter-
bury, Isadora," Bramwell said, heading for the drinks table
and pouring a little unsobering wine for himself and a glass
of ratafia for his fiancée. "I'm your affianced, remember?"

Isadora shrugged her modestly draped shoulders, the
movement bringing attention to the fact that she had fine,
fine, aristocratic bones—and very little flesh. "Lud, Selbourne, you're prickly tonight, aren't you? It's Miss Winstead, isn't it? Her presence is dredging up old memories,
old hurts. Lud, I imagine the gossip is simply shredding
you into pieces."

"The gossip, Isadora?" he repeated, handing her the
glass of ratafia. Ratafia. Horrid drink. Sophie, he knew, had
a much more sophisticated palate, a greater appreciation
for fine wines. Which had nothing to do with the point at
hand, he reminded himself. "I've heard no gossip, Isadora.
But perhaps your ear is closer to the ground, and more
finely attuned to such things?"

She looked shocked, as if he had just slapped her—or,
worse, told her that her grandmother had been conceived
on the wrong side of the blanket. He immediately apologized, knowing his nerves were overstretched, and had
been for several days. "I don't know why I said that, my
dear. Forgive me."

"Lud, Selbourne, think nothing of it," Isadora said, looking up at him with pity in her eyes. "Of course your nerves
are overstretched. I vow I don't know how you go on, truly
I don't. If my father had behaved as yours did? That business about the balcony? Yes, I knew that. But the *other* stories? The very public nature of their liaison?" She spread

her hands in an expression of hopelessness. "Lud, I think I should have died. Simply died, Selbourne."

He scratched at the side of his neck, thinking over what Isadora had said. "The *ton* is dredging it all up again, I imagine? And you're hearing it all, aren't you, Isadora? Did anyone tell you about the time Lord Byron all but tripped over them in the back aisles of Hatchard's? Scribbled a few rather incisive lines of poetry about that episode that were never meant for general publication, I can tell you. Or the story, never proved, that the Widow Winstead and my late father had traveled with Gypsies for a few weeks one summer, telling fortunes and stealing chickens as they wended their way through the countryside, living life in the raw? That one seemed to titillate more than a few people, especially when my father took to wearing a red kerchief in public for a while."

Isadora clapped her hands to her ears. "Oh, stop, Selbourne, stop! I can't bear it! I thought I could, but I can't, I can't!" She took her hands down from her ears and wove her fingers together in her lap, taking a deep breath to steady herself. "Forgive me, Selbourne. I was overcome for a moment. But, if there were just a way, *some* way we could . . ."

"Get rid of Sophie?" he prompted when her voice trailed off.

"Oh, lud, Selbourne, *yes!* I hate myself, truly *loathe* myself for saying such a thing—for thinking such a thing. She's a dear, truly. So sweet, so biddable, so entirely conscious that she has not the slightest notion of how to go on in Society. I could weep for her, Selbourne, truly I could."

She sighed. "But I don't know how long I can continue to ignore the whispers, the hands raised to smiling mouths, the remarks, the innuendo. We are not yet married, and already I've been cast into comparison with your poor betrayed mother. I have not, you see, any familiarity with being—well, with being ridiculed."

She looked at him searchingly. "Did I do anything, Selbourne, to become the butt of so many tawdry jokes? I didn't, did I?"

"I'm so sorry, Isadora," Bramwell said, meaning every word. He should have realized that Isadora would be drawn into whatever gossip might be winging its way through the *ton*. "But it's all a nine days wonder, I'm sure. Once Society comes to know Miss Winstead as you do, as my aunt does, the gossip will die a natural death."

She gave a dismissing wave of one hand as she dabbed at the corners of her eyes with the small lace handkerchief held in the other. "Yes, yes, I know. Lud, there's already talk about Lord Stanley and his mother's lady's maid eloping to Gretna. Scandals are thick on the ground every moment during the Season. But . . . but . . . lud! How do I say this, Selbourne? I—I'm worried. Concerned. Oh, you were only funning me, I know, but the other night? When you said something about the father and the son resembling each other?"

"Like father, like son?" Bramwell said helpfully, beginning to believe he could sense where this conversation was heading.

"Yes! That was it, like father, like son. Well, lud, Selbourne—are you? I mean, you've shown no tendency toward reckless behavior. Impulsive action and the like. But what if it's in the blood? What if it's a family trait that doesn't appear until the later years? I worry, Selbourne. I can't help it."

Bramwell drained his glass and set it on the table. "Yes, I can see where that might be a worry to you," he said reasonably, even as a tic began to work in his left cheek. "One never knows, does one, when someone else, someone who had heretofore looked so ordinary, so unexceptional, might take a notion to strip to his unmentionables at Almack's and swing upside down from a chandelier."

Isadora smiled weakly, looking very beautiful, very aristocratic, and as close to human as Bramwell believed he'd ever seen her. "Oh, poor Selbourne. I've hurt you, haven't I? I never meant—never intended . . ." She sighed once more, a deep, heartfelt sigh. "I think we should postpone the wedding, Selbourne. My papa wrote again, saying his gout precludes any visit to London before the Season ends, which is the same as to say the wedding must be delayed in any case. We'll use that as our excuse, not that anyone will believe us. I do want to marry you, Selbourne. I would make you a fine duchess. But, lud, first we must settle Miss Winstead and get her packed off somewhere. She cannot be in attendance at our wedding. I won't have our nuptials become nothing more than another reason for Society to giggle and make suppositions. You can see that, can't you?"

Bramwell fought the feeling that he was a drowning man who'd just been thrown a handy rope. He remained silent for a few moments, contemplating the ticking clock on the mantel across the room, caught between knowing he'd been insulted in some way—he'd figure out the finer points of that later—and wanting to hop onto the windowsill and crow like a rooster. "I'll send a notice to the papers tomorrow, Isadora. Due to your father's continued ill health, our wedding must be postponed until the Little Season, as I know you still wish the ceremony to be here, in London. Will that suffice?"

"Oh, yes, Selbourne, yes!" Isadora exclaimed happily. "This way we can avoid more gossip, and have dear little Miss Winstead settled and gone from everyone's memories. You're so good, Selbourne, so kind. And so very understanding."

"Yes, I am, aren't I?" he said, then bent down, impulsively kissing Isadora straight on the mouth.

"Selbourne?" Isadora's lovely blue eyes looked ready to pop out of her skull.

"Forgive me, my dear," he said, straightening once more. "I found myself so impressed by your tact in the midst of your own concerns, so very touched by your worries for Miss Winstead, that I—well, I just thought I'd see if I could understand why my father put so much store in impulsive acts. Do you mind?"

"Mind? Lud, I don't know. I never saw you in this light before, Selbourne," Isadora said, rising to her own feet. "It's, it's—"

Bramwell couldn't resist. "Impulsive, yet enjoyable? Different? Exciting? Perhaps even amusing?"

"No . . . it's rather . . . *disconcerting,* actually," Isadora informed him slowly, drawing out the words, and frowning as she examined her reaction. "And, as I've already said, I've never before seen you in this light, Selbourne. Or myself, for that matter," she ended, looking at him as if she'd just realized that marriage meant becoming not only a duchess, but a bed partner as well. She swallowed hard, so that Bramwell could see the muscles in her throat working convulsively. "Shall we adjourn to the drawing room? I believe the others are probably already waiting for us."

"Of course, Isadora," Bramwell said, bowing to her and, with a sweep of his arm, indicating that she should precede him from the room. He smiled at her departing back, feeling very much in charity with his betrothed, but not having the faintest idea as to why, with Sad Samuel awaiting him upstairs, he was smiling as if he suddenly didn't have a care in the world.

Sophie entered the drawing room a full ten minutes after the last gong had been rung, Giuseppe draped around her shoulders. Ignatius was already in residence near the fireplace, sitting on his perch, preening himself. Mrs. Farraday was in a far corner, nodding over her knitting. Lady Gwendolyn sat in her usual chair, a glass of wine in one hand, her other hand straying dangerously close, covetously close, to the small china rose on the table beside her.

The duke of Selbourne was propping up the mantel with his shoulder, a rather faraway expression in his eyes. Isadora Waverley, looking as usually beautiful but unusually pale this evening, was sitting on the edge of one of the couches, staring, openmouthed, as Sad Samuel Seaton showed her the bulb of garlic he had hung around his neck.

"Supposed to keep away head mucous, stuffiness, and the like," Sad Samuel was saying. "And it has. Now, I fear, all my troubles are in my chest. But the plaster should take care of that, don't you think, Miss Waverley?"

Isadora, always the lady, smiled as she brought a scented handkerchief to her nose and breathed deep.

Sophie also smiled, feeling wonderfully content, and more than a little excited at the prospect of a stunning success—and Bramwell's defeat. The stage was set, as she had asked Bobbit to set it just before she dived into her yellow, watered-silk gown after an afternoon spent hunting down precisely the perfect answer to Sad Samuel Seaton's unhappiness. The fact that part of that perfect answer had been so rude as to piddle on her new shoes was only of passing concern, and only to Desiree, the cleaning of the shoes being a part of her self-imposed "maidly" duties.

"Oh, forgive me, everybody," she said as she sailed toward the center of the room. "Have I kept everyone waiting? Mr. Seaton, don't you look just fine. How very good to see you again!" She dropped into a most graceful curtsy for someone who wore a living shawl, then looked at his right hand, which was wrapped in a cloth bandage. "Goodness! Whatever has happened? Have you cut yourself?"

As conversation starters go, Sophie had stumbled into the mother lode, as her inquiry set Samuel Seaton off on a near orgy of explanation, demonstration, and lamentation—ending with a wide sweep of his left arm that succeeded in knocking over two small portraits that stood on the table behind the couch. "My fault. I'll get those!" he exclaimed, turning and climbing over the back of the couch before Bramwell could utter more than a desperate "Good God, Samuel, *no!*"

Twenty minutes later, the table righted, the new debris swept up, Sad Samuel's additional wounds attended to, and as Isadora smiled gamely while holding a cold wet cloth to her abused cheek—Mr. Seaton's knee having come into fleeting contact with her face as he'd catapulted over the back of the couch—it was decided that dinner could be delayed no longer.

More than an hour later, and with the cook being informed by a desperate duke that they could very nicely live without two of the planned courses—and, for God's sake, no flaming desserts!—the small party was back in the drawing room.

Sophie looked around the room once more as Lady Gwendolyn struggled to find some topic of conversation that could not eventually be led back to either bodily functions or the imminent threat of plague to the unwary.

Deciding that she had found the perfect time to make a small announcement—a time when no one would be of a mind to delve too deeply into her account of what she was about to tell them—Sophie slapped her hands to her cheeks and gave out with a surprised, "Oh, dear, I forgot!" She called Giuseppe to her side, ordered him to lift his little red hat, and everyone watched as the monkey fished in it for a moment, coming up with Isadora's garnet brooch.

"My brooch!" Isadora exclaimed, grabbing at the piece of jewelry, so that Giuseppe bared his teeth and screeched, then headed directly for the chair, the mantel and, lastly, the chandelier, the brooch still clutched in his paw. "I thought it was gone forever. Miss Winstead, wherever did you find it? And how will we ever get it back?"

Sophie stood beneath the chandelier and held out her arms, so that Giuseppe, after chattering a refusal or three, could hop safely down to her. "Much as I am ashamed to admit it, Miss Waverley," she said as she returned the brooch, "Giuseppe is a thief. However, in this case, I believe the fastening on your brooch may be defective, so that you lost the piece somewhere in the house, and Giuseppe merely found it. In any case, I recognized it immediately when he brought it to me. You're happy to have it back, yes?"

Isadora was ecstatic to have it back, yes. So ecstatic that she didn't seem angry with Giuseppe, or the least bit prone to question Sophie's story. Bramwell, however, was another matter, and Sophie shot him a quick look from beneath her lashes. He, in his turn, was looking at his aunt, who was busying herself in turning an emerald ring round and round her finger, a puzzled frown on her face.

"I lost something once," Sad Samuel said as Isadora slipped the brooch into her reticule. "My coach."

"Excuse me, Samuel," Bramwell broke in. "I couldn't have heard you correctly. Did you say you lost your *coach*?"

Sad Samuel nodded morosely. "I did do that, yes. Took it to Bath when I went there for the waters. Horrid, sulfury stuff, and did my phlegm no good, no good at all, in case any of you are thinking to try the waters for yourselves. Had to post home. I took a chill that first night, damp sheets at the posting inn most like. Never did find the coach. Or the horses. Strange, isn't it?"

"I don't know, Mr. Seaton," Isadora said, always polite, even as she turned to look at Sophie helplessly. "Lud, I imagine such a thing could happen to anyone."

Sophie did her best to ignore Bramwell's strangled chuckle as she sucked in her bottom lip and nodded agreement with Sad Samuel's assessment of the strangeness of having mislaid a coach and four. "And the coachie, Mr. Seaton?" she asked when she could trust her voice. "Did you ever find him?"

"Demned coachie!" Ignatius called out, definitely in Sir Tyler Shipley's voice, so that Sophie had to hide a cringe at her silly mistake. "*Squawk!* Quick! My flask! Secrets to tell! *Squawk! Squawk!* Demned coachie! Secrets to sell! Quick, my flask! *Squawk!*"

"I know that voice!" Sad Samuel exclaimed, hopping to his feet, not without incident, as his quick action had caused a collision between his shin and the leg of the low table placed in front of the couch. He limped over to where Ignatius sat on his perch, obviously about to prompt the parrot into speaking again. "Selbourne, help me out. Who *is* that?"

Sophie swiftly stepped into the breech. "Oh, Mr. Seaton, Ignatius always prattles on like that. The voice you heard was that of my mother's uncle. Uncle James. Do you really think you knew him? He was a seafaring man before he went into seclusion." She sighed theatrically. "Poor, darling Uncle James. He contracted some strange tropical illness, in the South Seas, I believe. Last time we saw him, when he gave us Ignatius, his nose had just dropped off. Did you ever hear of such a thing?"

Sad Samuel scuttled back toward the couch so quickly he nearly came to grief as he tripped over Mrs. Farraday's knitting bag. "I—I must have been mistaken," he gulped out, putting fingers to his wrist to monitor his pulse.

Bramwell walked past Sophie's chair on his way to the drinks table and bent down to whisper in her ear. "Well, that made him happy, all right. Do you know any other parlor tricks, or are you willing to cede victory to me?"

Sophie merely smiled, snapping her fingers so that Giuseppe came to her, once more draping himself around her neck.

"Mr. Seaton?" she ventured after a few moments, once the man seemed to believe he might not be on the verge of expiring from fright. "You will forgive a little boldness and plain speech, I'm sure, as I am country-raised, and don't hold much patience with pretense and pretty words meant merely to flatter."

Bramwell, just passing behind her chair again, made a rather rude sound low in his throat.

"I realize you and I have only just recently met," Sophie continued, undaunted, "but I was taken with you from the first moment."

"You were?" Sad Samuel squeaked, his eyes going all round and shocked.

"Oh, yes, indeed, sir," Sophie continued earnestly.

"Why?" Sad Samuel asked.

She smiled sweetly, her shrug, she believed, one of her best. "How can I say this? I suppose I was caught by . . . by an air of *sadness* about you, Mr. Seaton."

"Yes," he said, nodding in agreement. "I've not had an easy life, you know. Sickly, and all that. And then there's this tendency I have to, well, to bump into things. You may have noticed? It's my nerves, you understand. They're easily overset. Why, I remember the time—"

"Exactly!" Sophie broke in as Bramwell took up a position directly behind her chair, probably the better to be able to whisper "Aha! I've got you!" into her ear when she, as he supposed, failed miserably in her attempt to make Sad Samuel Seaton happy.

Foolish man. Did he think her a rank amateur?

"And yet, for all of your trials, Mr. Seaton," she pressed on, "you are truly a most likable man. But, I fear, a lonely one as well. Being lonely is a terrible thing, and can quite easily lead to oversets of the nerves, even to a concentrated concern over one's health, and even to a certain physical clumsiness, yes? So I thought, and I thought—you don't mind that I thought and I thought, yes? Because I do so like it when those around me are happy."

"She does, you know," Lady Gwendolyn put in loudly from halfway across the room. She hadn't come within ten feet of Sad Samuel the whole evening long, having already informed Sophie that she might be a charitable soul, but she'd be twigged if she'd turn herself into a martyr to Sad Samuel's clumsy ways.

"Thank you, Aunt Gwendolyn," Sophie said, biting at the inside of her cheek so as not to giggle aloud. Then she turned back to Sad Samuel. "As you can see, I hope, I am a fairly happy person. And do you know why?" She waited for him to shake his head in the negative, then said, "It's because of Giuseppe. And Ignatius. My little animal friends. They have been *such* solace to me in my loneliness after my mother's death. And they must be cared for, loved in return, so that it is impossible to be too sad or too concerned for oneself, not for long, yes? Aunt Gwendolyn? Will you please ask Desiree to come in now, and show Mr. Seaton what I've bought for him?"

"Of course, my dear," Lady Gwendolyn said, already heading for the double doors that led to the hallway.

"What you've *bought* for me?" Sad Samuel said, swiveling in his seat, the better to watch the doorway.

"What you've *bought* for him?" Isadora exclaimed, then smiled. "Oh, Miss Winstead, how kind of you. But nothing too personal, I hope. Because, lud, that wouldn't do. That wouldn't do at all."

"What you've *bought* for him?" Bramwell ground out from between clenched teeth as he leaned over the back of the chair, making it easier for him to breathe fire into her ear. "You've bought Samuel a *friend*?"

"Yes, Bramwell, oh, ye of the infinitesimal faith in my abilities," she said, turning slightly in her chair, the better to whisper at the man—and the better to see his face as he realized he'd lost their wager. "I bought him a friend. A friend he can count on never to leave him, always to love him, completely and unconditionally. A friend to care about, so that he doesn't have so much time to worry about himself. A friend to take out in public, where others can see, and admire, and enjoy—and begin to realize that Sad Samuel is not quite the nemesis everyone seems to believe him to be. In short, Your Grace, I've bought your cousin a *dog*."

"And you think that will work?" Bramwell whispered back at her. He gestured with his chin, urging her to look in Sad Samuel's direction. The man was still waiting for Lady Gwendolyn's return, occupying himself in prodigiously blowing his nose, then holding up his handkerchief to inspect his success. "It will take more than a dog to fix *that*."

"Yes, I know," Sophie said happily, rising to greet Lady Gwendolyn as she came back into the room, Desiree behind her, doing her best to hold onto a pair of wriggling, yipping, wonderfully adorable coal black poodle puppies. "That's why I bought *two.*"

Bramwell walked back into the mansion after handing Isadora and her abigail up into the coach, eager to speak privately with Sophie before she could escape to her bedchamber. He caught her just placing her foot on the first step, called her back into the drawing room, then closed the doors behind them, surreptitiously locking them.

"I could have waited until morning to listen to your concession speech, Your Grace," she said, dipping down slightly so that Ignatius could step off her shoulder and back onto his perch. "I'm very good at what I do, yes?"

"A single swallow doesn't make a summer, Sophie," he told her, going over to the drinks table and pouring them each a glass of wine. "Sad, er, my cousin may have become embarrassingly adoring and almost adorable when he saw those two dogs—"

"Poodles, Bramwell," Sophie interrupted. "Romeo and Juliet, to be even more precise. I wonder, does your cousin have the faintest idea what it means to have both a Romeo and a Juliet?"

Bramwell smiled. "In another six months or so, everywhere he looks, there will be a Capulet?"

Sophie returned his smile, accepting the glass of wine. "Ladies simply adore puppies. And Mr. Seaton has already assured me he intends to take the little darlings with him everywhere he goes. Just like Poodle Byng, he told me, and Heaven knows that man has made good use of his dogs. Why, Mr. Seaton says he's already planning to have a special high seat fashioned for them up behind his horses, so that they can better see and be seen when he takes them driving in the Park. And did you notice? He didn't trip over a single thing as he was carefully carrying them out of the drawing room."

"And it has been known to snow in June," Bramwell shot back, knowing he wasn't being exactly graceful in defeat. "Oddities do occur."

Sophie giggled. "Oh, give over, Bram. Your cousin took his first steps this evening in finding that something exists outside his nervous disposition and his—pardon me, please—his phlegm. I've won, and you know it."

She sat down on the couch, resting her back comfortably against the cushions Lady Gwendolyn insisted were necessary to bodily comfort. "So? What day would be best for you to escort me to Bartholomew Fair? I can't tomorrow, I'm afraid, as I'm already promised to Sir Wallace early in the day, and Miss Waverley and I do want to drop in at Hatchard's later in the afternoon, so that I might possibly locate a book I've recommended to her. Besides, I understand that the dear, widowed Lord Charles Anston brings his daughters to Hatchard's quite often, believing good literature to be quite edifying to young minds."

Bramwell felt his stomach muscles tighten unexpectedly. "You've set your sights on Anston?"

He watched as Sophie dipped a finger in her wine, then sucked the glistening liquid from her skin. God, she was driving him mad! All of Desiree's lessons, and executed with all the innocence of a young woman who hadn't the faintest idea what her actions really meant, what they invited, what the consequences to that invitation would be for her, for him. "Set my sights on him? Well, yes," she said, smiling so that her adorable nose wrinkled. "I suppose you could say that. At the very least, I am exploring—options."

She took a sip of wine and changed the subject. "The evening went well, yes? But I will admit to an anxious moment or two, thanks to my carelessness in saying the word," she shot a quick glance in Ignatius's direction, "c-o-a-c-h-i-e. Now I understand why Uncle Tye—Sir Tyler—was so worried."

Bramwell sat down beside her, feeling in charity with her once more. How could he not? She was maddening, infuriating, more beautiful than anyone could imagine, had a heart large enough to care about people such as Sad Samuel, and she spoke to him as if he were her very best friend in all of the world.

And she'd probably kill him if she knew how much he wanted to kiss away her every last stitch of clothing, reveal her in all her perfection, touch her, worship her, love her with his mouth, his hands . . .

"My cousin's reaction gave me a bad moment or two as well, Sophie," he said as companionably as possible while cursing himself for a lusting, rutting boar. "And yet, your veiled reference to leprosy, I admit, bordered on the brilliant. But should I be making a list? I mean, does the bird imitate anyone else?"

"Say *Connie*," Sophie told him, leaning close, to whisper the suggestion in his ear, her breath wine-sweet and inviting. Driving him mad. "Ignatius is Uncle Cesse to the life. Honestly."

Bramwell's smile froze in place, his lust momentarily

forgotten. "I don't believe it," he said, a considerable amount of his good feeling, the hail-fellow-well-met ca- maraderie that a moment before had been growing be- tween Sophie and himself also draining away. "He can sound like my father?"

She nodded, watching him closely, as if her admission was a test, to see if he really was an unnatural son, a per- son who could dislike his father even beyond the grave.

"Connie," he said, loud enough for the parrot to hear.

"Connie!" Ignatius responded at once, the bird's voice so close to Bramwell's father's that he was hard-pressed not to jump to his feet, and say, "Yes, sir!" the way he had done as a child. "Kiss me, Connie! *Squawk!* Pucker up! Pucker up!"

"Good God," Bramwell said on a groan, shaking his head. "Somebody ought to strangle that bird."

"As she told me her grandfather owned a parrot himself, Miss Waverley likes him well enough. Ignatius," Sophie said more loudly, as if to make the bird less obnoxious in Bramwell's eyes, "you like Miss Waverley, don't you?"

Ignatius, upon hearing Isadora's name, immediately began bobbing his bright yellow head up and down, show- ing off what he'd learned since coming to Portland Square: *"Squawk!* Lud, no, Selbourne! Lud! Lud! *Squawk!"*

"Oh, dear, I didn't know he did that!" Sophie choked out, jumping to her feet. "Come on, Ignatius. It's past time all naughty parrots were in bed."

Bramwell had risen at the same time, partly in shock at hearing his betrothed's voice coming out of the parrot's mouth, partly because Sophie had stood up and he, as a gentleman, was bound to do so as well—and partly because he really didn't want Sophie to leave. Not just yet. Perhaps not ever.

"Tell me about the brooch first, please," he said, for the question had laid heavy on his mind all evening. "Did Giuseppe really find it?"

Sophie lied well, he remembered, and she looked ready to give fibbing her best effort now. Strangely, she opened her mouth, then hesitated. She seemed to be having some difficulty in looking straight into his eyes, almost as if her considerable talent for well-intended deception had unexpectedly deserted her. Did that mean anything? Was she softening toward him, so that she found herself unable to lie to him quite so easily anymore? Or was he simply reading too much into her reaction, being hopeful when he really didn't care if she told him the truth or smiled openly while she lied?

But he did care, damn it! He cared very much! He wanted her to tell him the truth, to trust him enough to be honest with him. To trust him as a friend, as a man. On every level.

"Sophie?" he prompted. "I'm waiting. Did Giuseppe really steal the brooch?"

"Well, of all the silly questions, Bramwell! Of course he did," she said at last, her voice bright even as she still averted her eyes. "Giuseppe is always finding things and bringing them to me. I immediately recognized the brooch as belonging to Miss Waverley." She looked at him appealingly. "You won't punish Giuseppe, will you? He means no harm."

"Neither does my aunt, Sophie. But, then, you know that, don't you? You know it, and you're protecting her, just the way I've been doing."

"Your aunt? Why, Bramwell, I really don't have the faintest idea what you're—oh, I give up," she said, her gloriously perfect shoulders collapsing in a defeated slump that was almost laughable. "I admit it. I found the brooch in with Aunt Gwendolyn's jewelry. She means no—oh, I've already said that, haven't I? Very well then, *neither* of them means any harm."

"No, I'm sure they don't. And I'm pleased you didn't give the poor old dear away. However, Miss Waverley already knows about my aunt's, er, proclivity for picking up the stray item or two. The brooch, unfortunately, is not the first of her possessions I've *discovered* here in Portland Square over the past months and had to return to her. In fact, she's already mentioned the potential for embarrassment if Aunt Gwendolyn should be found out, and has suggested she be sent away."

"Sent away? Locked up?" Sophie asked, looking immediately incensed, and ready to do battle.

"No, Sophie," he answered, a part of his brain wondering why it always smelled like spring whenever she was close by. It was odd. Even now, while in the midst of a fairly uncomfortable conversation, Sophie's mere presence made him feel lighter, younger, more aware of himself as a man, of her as a woman. She was constantly soothing to him, yet constantly exciting. In short, he supposed he simply felt *alive* whenever she was near. It was very strange, for he'd thought he'd been alive all along. Had he only recently begun to live?

He took a steadying breath, then went on: "Miss Waverley merely suggested Aunt Gwendolyn be sent to the country, to Selbourne Hall, where she couldn't end up being branded a thief or, worse, a woman who has misplaced her mind. Miss Waverley meant it only for the best, I'm sure, to protect my aunt from herself."

Sophie nodded, considering his words. "I see. That's all right then. Of course Miss Waverley would think she was doing Aunt Gwendolyn a kindness, although it would never occur to her to just go on as you've been doing—simply returning whatever Aunt Gwendolyn has admired. Miss Waverley would have chosen the safest way, the most proper way, to solve the problem. Well," she ended, smiling, "I'm certainly glad she didn't want you to have Aunt Gwendolyn locked up. Because otherwise I would have had to put my mind to hurting her, yes?"

Bramwell laughed out loud. "And you would, wouldn't you? For a young woman who vows to remain heartwhole, you show a great interest in protecting those around you. But, before you protest, I understand now, Sophie, really I do. My aunt is a totally lovable, harmless creature and would never think to hurt you, so you gave your own heart willingly in return. It's only the male of the species you hide from, are afraid of, see as heartless predators wanting more from you than you feel it safe to give."

She gazed up at him for a long time, time during which he once again realized how alone they were, how closely they were standing to each other, how loudly the clock on the mantel behind him ticked off the time. Time to feel their easy camaraderie shift, change, re-form itself once more into lust, as Sophie would call it. To lust. To desire. To, God help him, love.

"I—I . . . yes," she said at last, both sounding and looking confused, unsure of herself, as if something she once felt to be clear in her mind was now becoming muzzy, more difficult to understand. "Men are cruel . . . the uncles . . . even Uncle Cesse. I'll love, yes, but I'll never fall in love. Not me. I won't . . . won't allow it. Besides, it doesn't really exist. Not in the way *Maman* believed in it. The word love is so pretty, filling the gullible with silly dreams. The real word is lust, and I'll never let myself forget that. Unlike my *maman,* I will live my life heart free, and on my own terms."

Bramwell had to stop her. Stop her from saying what she believed, what he had often believed himself, but did no longer. He stepped even closer to her, their faces now only inches apart. "Isadora has postponed the wedding until the fall, saying her father is too unwell for the ceremony to go forward now," he said before he could measure his words. "In truth, I believe she's simply trying to distance herself from me slowly, one small, proper step at a time. I doubt we'll ever marry."

Sophie tilted her head to one side, looking at him quizzically. "Oh, poor Bramwell. It's all the old gossip coming back, isn't it? Because I've come to London, yes? Miss Waverley isn't accustomed to having her good name being spoken of in whispers. You must be suffering horribly, and it's all my fault." When he didn't respond, she prompted him again. "You are unhappy, yes?"

Was that relief he'd heard in her voice, coloring her sympathetic words with hopes of her own, or had he simply heard what he'd wanted to hear, needed to hear? "I don't know . . ." he said, hearing his own voice trailing away into nothingness. He lowered his head another fraction, until his lips were only a whisper, a heartbeat from hers. "God, Sophie, I don't know . . ."

"Bram, I don't think this is—"

"Don't think, Sophie," he said, nearly moaned.

He watched her eyelids flutter closed as he tentatively touched his lips to hers. Her warm lips, soft, and tasting of wine. Their bodies weren't touching, not at all. Except for their mouths. And yet he still somehow felt himself being drawn inside of her, felt her falling into him. The heat between them was intense, almost to the point of discomfort, the quick rush of desire nearly causing him to stagger where he stood.

And the sweetness. Oh, God, the nearly unbearable sweetness of her.

This was her first real kiss. He wouldn't consider the other time, his foolish, impulsive action that night in his study. Because this, for them both, was the first time. For all the practiced coquettishness, all the feminine wiles, the knowing smiles, the extensive education in the more bawdy aspects of life, all that she thought she knew, she remained an innocent. Incredibly innocent. Untutored. Nearly unaware.

He felt that same innocence, that same awakening inside himself that she must be feeling. It was as if he'd never kissed before, never lived before.

Sophie's lips trembled beneath his, then tightened together, as if returning his kiss meant that she should apply pressure in return to the pressure she felt coming from him. He knew she had no idea that he wanted her mouth open, that he longed to run his tongue over her teeth and tongue, feel the warmth and the moisture, stake his claim more fully. He sensed that her arms had begun to flutter at her sides as she decided if it would be all right to touch him, to put her arms around him.

He also knew, somewhere in the remaining yet now infinitesimally small, sane, sober part of his brain, that if she did touch him, if she did open her mouth to him, they would both be damned. Because he was feeling a sudden urge to dance across rooftops. He longed to make long, leisurely love to Sophie in an open meadow planted in wildflowers, to ride wildly through the streets with this maddening, laughing beauty at his side—to do all the wonderfully silly things he could think of, that his father had ever thought of, and more.

And knowing this, knowing all of this, he touched her just the same.

Perfection met his fingers as he cupped them around her breasts, slid them along the bodice of her gown, dipped them inside to lift, to free, to mold, to feel the burn of her soft, firm flesh against his palms.

Her mouth opened slightly as she moaned in what he prayed was ecstasy, leaned more fully against him in what he told himself had to be surrender. He took full advantage of this small victory. He deepened their kiss for as long as she allowed it, then eased his head back slightly, ending the kiss. He looked at her as she stood before him, her expression unreadable, her mouth warm and trembling.

Somehow he'd never know quite how, his fumbling, worshiping fingers found the buttons holding her gown closed. Opened them. The fabric whispered now as it slid easily from her shoulders, puddled on the floor at her feet, and Sophie stood before him naked to her waist, open to his gaze. She looked at him in return. Waiting. Silent. Condemning.

No woman had ever been more alluring, more physically perfect—compelling in her beauty, irresistible. She was every sin he'd ever imagined, every gift he'd ever dreamed, everything man had been damned to want since the dawn of time. Desire flared in him; lust raged through his body. He wanted her. He had to have her.

He loved her.

And so he withdrew from her, from the sweetest temptation he'd ever known. The pain of that withdrawal began killing him with each inch he moved, the sudden loss of a wild abandon only dreamt of and never realized cutting at him, ripping at him, leaving him bereft. Old, tired. Sober.

He turned his back and walked a good ten feet away as she stooped to retrieve her gown, to slip the front-closing buttons back into their moorings.

"Bastard," she said quietly, so quietly he barely heard her.

He whirled around to face her, knowing why she'd said what she'd said. "No, Sophie," he told her, taking a single step forward, reaching out a hand, then letting his arm drop to his side, remaining where he stood. "Yes," he corrected in a raw, tortured whisper. "Yes. I'm a bastard. I am, if you believe that I'm like the uncles. Do you really believe that?"

She shook her head, her curls tumbling around her face. "No, I don't believe that, Bram. I believe you're *worse* than the uncles. A thousand times worse. Why, you're probably going to tell me you love me now, aren't you? Go

ahead, admit it! You're about to say you love me. And you
don't. You *want* me. But you'll call it anything you want,
just to *get* anything you want. Did you like what I gave
you, Bramwell? Did it give you *pleasure?*"

"Yes! *No!*" He stabbed his fingers through his hair,
knowing himself to be on the very edge of losing all control. "Sweet Jesus, Sophie—you're such a child! A child
who'd allow herself to be stripped just to prove a man to
be the most base creature in nature. A child whose mind is
filled with knowledge but no experience, with misconcep-
tions taken as gospel from a whore."

"Which whore, Bramwell?" she shouted at him even as
he cursed his own tongue, cursed his unforgivable out-
burst. "Desiree? Or *Maman? Which* whore? The one who
sees life as it is, men as they are? Or the woman who
wouldn't listen, who insisted on believing in love?"

"Sophie—" he began, trying desperately to assemble
something resembling coherent speech in his mind.
"There's lust, yes. There's desire. But there's also love. To
love a woman is to desire her, to want to kiss her, hold her,
make love to her. You can't separate the two, it's impossible. You've just got to learn to trust yourself, trust your
heart. Trust the person you love to love you in return. Believe me, please believe me."

"Believe you? *Believe you?*" She whirled about, spying
a candy dish on the table, lifting it, aiming it straight at his
head. He didn't take evasive action, deciding he'd merited
any punishment, even if he were to be knocked uncon-
scious by the heavy dish. Hell, he deserved it—that, and a
lot more. A second later the dish shattered against the wall,
having missed him by a good three feet.

"Damn you, stand still!" she cried out, picking up the teapot that had been brought into the room earlier, throwing that at him as well, missing him yet again.

She'd picked up the sugar server before he reached her, grabbed hold of her forearm, forced her to hand the server over to him, then pulled her close against his chest. "Tell me, Sophie," he whispered against her ear even as she struggled to be free. "Tell me what you felt when we kissed, when I touched you, when I looked at your body. Desire? Lust? Love? Could you separate the feelings? Did you even want to? Or is it impossible to separate them? Are they all part and parcel of each other? Is the answer to disbelieve everything—or to learn to trust your own heart?"

He felt the tip of her slipper make sharp contact with his shin and released her in reaction. She moved a few feet away from him, glaring at him across the distance of those few feet, a chasm of more than a thousand miles. "Damn you, Bramwell Seaton! Don't confuse me!" she nearly screamed.

His shin would be black-and-blue for a month. He'd probably limp for a week. Bramwell summoned a smile from deep inside the hell he'd dropped into, knowing the pain in his shin was nothing compared to that in his heart. "Oh, God, no. Don't confuse the girl," he said bitterly. "Raise her to drive a man wild, let her know—hell, *teach her*—how to inflame a man past all sanity, then tell her all a man can feel is lust. Tell her that's all we're capable of, raw, uncivilized bastards that we are. Don't give a man a drop of credit, don't believe a word that comes out of his mouth. And, most of all, don't believe in your *own* feelings, Sophie. Just lump yourself and *your* wants, *your* needs, in with those of the men you've been taught to despise. Or are you going to tell me you don't want me as much as I want you?"

She looked at him, gave a small anguished cry, turned, and ran to the doors, only to find them locked. "Bastard!" she flung at him again, her eyes wild with pain. "Let me out of here. Let me out of here now!"

Bramwell removed the key from his pocket, seeing the obstinate child, the hurt orphan, the desirable woman—all the many parts of Sophie Winstead come together before his eyes for the first time. "Well, hasn't this been enlightening, if somewhat loud and expensive—that was a very good teapot, you know, and it's probably now dented beyond repair. But look what we've learned. You're not perfect, Sophie. You'd like to be, you've been raised to be, trained to be—but you're not. And you know what else I've learned? I like you better imperfect. I like you willful, even throwing things. And I still want you. I'm not sure, but I may even love you. But you don't believe me, do you? You can't, not yet. You still don't understand a word I'm trying to say."

"*I* don't understand?" she spat back at him. "No, Bramwell—it's *you* who doesn't understand. You say you like me better imperfect. Well, of course you do. But you like me best for who I am, the Widow Winstead's daughter. The daughter of a whore. How comforting it must be for you to desire me—to lust after me—knowing that Society wouldn't so much as blink if you were to take me as your mistress."

"Not just a child, but an ignorant child! Is that all our kiss meant to you—all you think it meant to me?"

Bramwell replaced the key in his pocket, grabbing on to Sophie's arm and dragging her back toward the couch, all but pushing her down onto the cushions. "Now sit here, young lady, and shut up. Listen to me. You're a person in your own right, much as you refuse to see yourself as more than a reflection of your mother, as Desiree's perfect little creation. And it's damn well time you began to value yourself."

"Oh, would you just look who's giving out advice? Are you going to be presenting me with clay tablets soon, brought down from your mountaintop?" she spat, hopping to her feet once more, glaring at him. "And who are *you*, Bramwell Seaton? Do you know? Can you tell me? Do you value who *you* are? Making yourself into the opposite of your father in every way you can doesn't make you anything less of a *creation*, any more real."

Bramwell looked at her for a long moment, saw her stripped of all her studiously crafted artifice, all the charm she'd learned, the lessons she'd absorbed. And he saw the hurt there, the tears, the fears she usually hid behind a smile but now tried to disguise with her temper, with harsh words, unpalatable truths. Hiding, always hiding. But not from him. Not anymore. "You've got quite a way with a sharp knife, don't you, Sophie?" he asked gently. "And much better aim than you have with crockery."

Her eyes clouded for a moment, then flashed with new fire. "It—it was meant to, Bramwell," she declared, lifting her chin.

"Why? So that you can protect yourself?" he asked, cupping that defiant chin in his fingers. "Are you that afraid of me? That afraid of what you feel for me, what I feel for you?"

"I—I have to go now. Please," she said, her voice breaking as she let the fullness of her pain show at last, that pain slicing his own heart to ribbons.

He watched as she fled the room, ran up the staircase, her hands pressed to her mouth.

Bramwell closed the doors once more and leaned against them. "Ah, Sophie," he said as he then walked aimlessly about the room, picking up bits and pieces of the evidence of Sophie's explosive temper, the "flaw" she tried so desperately to hide, the flaw he loved so well, that made her real to him at last. "Ah, Sophie, Sophie, what can you be thinking?"

"Sophie loves you!" Ignatius screeched in a very good imitation of his mistress's voice. *"Squawk! Squawk!* Sophie loves you!"

Bramwell picked up the cushion lying closest to him on the couch, meaning to toss it at the mocking, laughing bird, then sat down, the pillow still in his hand, and smiled.

It wasn't until later that he began to kick himself mentally, realizing he might have been too rash, might have made more mistakes than he had progress in his attempt to understand Sophie . . . and himself.

If there were dreams to sell,
What would you buy?
  —Thomas Lovell Beddoes

Chapter Eleven

"Why didn't you tell me?"

"Tell you? Tell you what, *chérie*?" Desiree asked idly as she took a freshly pressed night rail from a drawer. She straightened, one hand to the small of her aching back, for she had fallen asleep in a chair, waiting for her charge to come to bed. "Ah," she said after a moment, nodding her head. "He has kissed you, *oui*? The so sober duke has unbent his starchy self, and he has kissed you. And don't bother to lie, *ma petite*. I am Desiree, and I know. I have a sense about these things. The tear stains on your cheeks, the confusion, that glow from within that shines from your eyes. I have seen your *maman* looking thus, too many times to count."

Sophie remained in the middle of the bed, sitting cross-legged atop the satin coverlet, still fully dressed, her skirts billowing around her. She'd been sitting thus for a full ten minutes, composing herself, watching Desiree sleep, listening to the woman snore. Now she grabbed her bent knees, rocking back and forth, refusing to give in to impulse and run to the nearest mirror, to see if she really looked different, if Bramwell's kiss, his touch, had actually changed her outside as he had melted her insides.

"He kissed me, yes," Sophie answered, knowing a fib told in the face of her dearest friend would be as effective as employing a feather to topple a mountain. "Once. Just the once. And he—he touched me. Nothing more than that. But it was . . . it wasn't at all like I'd thought. It was beautiful, Desiree, outstripping anything I'd ever imagined, even as I wanted to hate what he was doing. It was sweet, yet mysterious, exciting. It was—"

"It was a mistake," Desiree ended for her firmly as she came to sit down on the edge of the bed, the night rail becoming wrinkled as she clutched it tightly with both hands. "*His* mistake, *chérie*, and one he doubtless does not plan to repeat. Until the next time, and the next, and the next. Until he is drunk with desire for you, mad with wanting you. Then, *chérie*, he will ask you to become his mistress, his true love, the one true love of his life. He will make promises he has no intention of keeping. He will ask you to love him, to trust him, and to stand back, watching, as he weds that stick of a Waverley and sires his heirs on her. And then, after you have given him your heart, your love, your youth? Ah, then, *chérie*, he will leave."

Sophie had heard all of this before, all through her childhood years, had it all explained to her by Desiree each time she had sat in her bed in Wimbledon, listening to her *maman* sobbing in the beautiful gold-and-white satin chamber down the hallway. Her *maman* would weep as if her heart were breaking, because it was. Her silly, trusting heart. Broken again and again, trampled on by men who had promised so much, taken so much, and then gone away.

Even Uncle Cesse would have disappeared, Desiree had warned Sophie, for she had caught out her good friend Constance with red-rimmed eyes only a week before Sophie's *maman* had run off to meet with her beloved Cesse, to die with her beloved Cesse. Constance had not said that the duke was throwing her over. In fact, she had flatly denied it, said she was crying because she was happy, because she had a wonderful secret she couldn't yet share, even with her very dearest friend. As if Desiree had believed that pack of nonsense! No, Constance had been on the verge, the very brink, of having her heart broken yet again.

And so Desiree had informed Sophie.

But this was different. Sophie was sure of it. She was not her *maman*, and Bramwell wasn't his father, or one of the uncles. He wasn't Caesar, turning away from his wife and to the charms of a doomed Cleopatra. He wasn't Napoléon, giving Josephine her *congé*. He wasn't Henry VIII, willy-nilly lopping off heads to leave him free to bed yet another woman he lusted after. He wasn't any of the hundreds, thousands of men who made vows, made promises to wives, to young maids, to lovers—never meaning to keep either the vows or the women. He wasn't!

"You're wrong, Desiree," Sophie said earnestly. "Bramwell isn't like *Maman*'s gentlemen. He told me he and Miss Waverley will probably never marry."

"He said that? Oh, *chérie*, now I should kill him," Desiree ground out from between clenched teeth. "I should sneak into his chamber this very night, and I should kill him. You believed this drivel, this *canard*? They all live between their legs, even dukes! Sophie? *Think*, my dear, befuddled darling. Think! When did the duke kiss you? Before he told you he and Miss Waverley would probably not marry? Or after?"

"It was, it was *after*." Sophie pulled her bottom lip between her teeth, considering the scene, replaying all the words and actions in her head. She took what she knew, combined it with everything Desiree had taught her, and felt an icy coldness invade her every blood cell.

"What a fool I am!" she exclaimed, taking hold of Desiree's outstretched hands. "He made me feel sorry for him, gave me reason to believe that *I* was the cause of everything—and yet not an unhappy cause. He warned me not to think, and I didn't! I let him kiss me, confuse me, make a fool of me, make me want to believe—ah, Desiree. Thank God I had the good sense to finally run away, yes?"

Desiree squeezed her hands. "And why, *chérie*? Why did you run away?"

Sophie looked down at her hands, seeing that her knuckles were white as they held tight to Desiree's fingers. "I don't know," she said quietly, honestly. "I didn't want to, not really. I—I suppose I was frightened? Yes, I was frightened. Frightened that I wanted so much for him to kiss me again, touch me more and more. Make love to me, I suppose. So I threw the teapot at him." She shook her head. "Perhaps a few other things as well? I can't remember. And—and I kicked him."

She peered up at Desiree. "I was horrid, Desiree, as horrid as I've ever been in my entire life. And he said he liked me that way. That he might even *love* me that way. It was all so confusing, but wonderful in some crazy, inexplicable way."

"Oh, this is a smooth one, my love," Desiree told her, gathering her close. "And yet, not without possibilities, if you were your *maman*, willing to risk her heart again and again. But you are not, *chérie*. Remember that. You are *not* your *maman*. I raised you for more than diamonds, and trinkets, and fleeting moments of happiness bound to be crushed under the weight of tears. I pray, yes, that there is such a thing as true, lasting love, even though I have never myself seen such a thing. I pray that you will be one of the lucky ones who finds it. You deserve a real, lasting love. But I raised you to use your head, *chérie*. Losing your heart to a man betrothed to another is not using your head. It is entirely another part of your anatomy that comes into play at such times. And the timing, it must be impeccable, *oui*?"

"The timing?" Sophie didn't understand, and said as much.

Desiree kissed her on both cheeks. "I've said too much for so late in the evening. Leave that to me, *chérie*. Have I ever turned your steps in the wrong direction? Just leave everything to Desiree, and keep smiling, keep dazzling, continue to be your most lovable self. Pretend, when you see His Grace, that this evening never happened, *oui*? I want, just this once, to be proven wrong, *chérie*. Just this one time before I die. Nothing is impossible, *oui*?"

"Desiree? Are you saying that it might be possible? That there is such a thing as true love outside of poetry? Are you

saying that what I'm feeling for Bramwell could be love—
and that he could be falling in love with me?"

"I'm saying, *ma petite*, that, for now, you should keep
your eyes open and your legs closed. I cannot be any more
plain than that, can I?"

Sophie blushed as she hid her face against Desiree's
ample bosom. She'd read her mother's very frank, de-
scriptive journals without really understanding much of
them, but while still learning much more than an innocent
young girl probably should know. She'd listened to Desiree's explanations of lust, of desire, of this mysterious attraction between men and women that had caused endless
trouble and heartache since the beginnings of time.

Empires had toppled, armies had been launched, murder
had been done, good names ruined, lives destroyed—all
for this thing women called love and men knew as desire.
Lust. But, whatever its name, this most basic of communi-
cation between the sexes was dangerous. History had
proven it. Her *maman* had suffered its consequences. And
Sophie had grown up wanting no part of it.

And yet? And yet?

She heard Desiree telling her to climb down from the
bed before her gown was ruined, and she complied. She allowed herself to be stripped of her garments, her hose, her
evening slippers. She lifted her arms and let the night rail
fall over her curiously aware body. She dutifully splashed
water on her face and watched herself in the small mirror
above the washstand as she scrubbed at her teeth, spat into
the basin. She ascended the small steps to her bed once
more and accepted Desiree's kisses on her cheeks as the

woman tucked the covers around her, clucking like a hen over her one chick.

And then, at last, she was alone. Alone with her thoughts, her memories, her questions.

With only her bedside candle and the soft glow from a small, banked fire to light the room, she lay with her eyes open, staring up at the canopy above her head. She relived those strange, enlightening, frighteningly wonderful moments in the drawing room. She touched her fingertips to her mouth, feeling her lips grow rigid, begin to tremble.

She slid her hands under the coverlet and skimmed them over her body, fleetingly touching the breasts Bramwell had touched, brought to life. She ran her hands lightly down over her belly, stopping just before she arrived at the place that had become warm and fluid the first moment Bramwell had looked deeply into her eyes and told her not to think.

So, this was desire? Desiree had hinted at all of it, while saying next to nothing Sophie had understood at the time she'd listened to her lessons. Now she understood why she hadn't been able to understand.

Because the words were not the feelings. Understanding the method was not the same as experiencing the desire firsthand. Learning how to entice, to interest, to dazzle, had absolutely nothing to do with protecting her heart from becoming enticed, interested, and dazzled in return.

So, yes, this was desire. And the longings, Sophie knew now, were far more powerful than the years of warnings.

This was what had toppled all those governments, taken the heads from so many queens, led to all those intrigues, been the downfall of so many, including her own *maman*.

It was powerful stuff.

But it wasn't love. Not according to Desiree.

It wasn't forever. Not according to the uncles.

And it didn't come without its costs. Lust, desire, love—no matter what name it was given, it was never given freely. There was always a price to pay. Always the fear of an ending.

Sophie knew she had to remember that. She had to remember that Bramwell was betrothed, no matter what he hinted to the contrary, no matter that he had kissed her, held her, said that he might love her. Desire her or not, the Bramwell Seaton she believed she knew would never willingly open himself up to the gossip, the ridicule that would most certainly come if he were to actually marry the Widow Winstead's daughter, the daughter of the woman his father had set up as his mistress.

If he were to *marry* her? Was she mad? Did it take no more than a few fleeting moments of passion to stand all of her common sense on its head?

Oh, and how her head did ache. How her heart ached as well.

It had all seemed so simple at the beginning. She would come to London. She would have a most delightful Season. She would meet interesting people and make friends with the world. She would marry for convenience, as most everyone did, have the children she longed for, and begin a life of laughter, of gaiety, of enjoyment. There would be a lovely house in the country, a mansion in London. Parties. The theater. Dancing. If she felt desire, which she doubted she ever would, she would indulge that feeling, keeping her heart safe as she did so. Never to be hurt. Never to cry.

And there was nothing wrong with any of that. Men did it. They did it all the time, probably since the very *beginning* of time. But, then, men didn't love, did they? They didn't gaze into a woman's eyes, pledge undying love and devotion, and really mean it. Not according to history, or the uncles, or her *maman*'s journals or, most especially, Desiree.

Tonight Bramwell had contradicted everything Sophie believed, everything she'd been taught. Why? Because he loved her? Or because he needed her to believe in love so that he could take what he wanted? Could she believe what he said, after so many years of believing the opposite? Could she trust him? Could she trust herself?

She had to keep remembering, keep reminding herself. Only fools believed in love. Fools, and poets, and young, silly, romantic females.

And yet, and yet . . . even Desiree, that most practical of women, had just tonight hinted that she still longed to believe in the promise, the miracle, of real love.

And so do I, Sophie thought sadly, turning her head into the pillow and willing herself to sleep as the bedside candle sputtered and died. *Oh, so do I.*

Bobbit, lightly stroking his new watch fob, entered the study and announced that Baron Lorimar had come to call.

"Tell him I've died," Bramwell said without raising his eyes from the empty glass he was studying. "It was a putrid fever. Terrible, but mercifully swift. Tell him the ser-

vices were extremely moving, but that he missed the funeral."

"Pity. I would have enjoyed speaking the eulogy," Baron
Lorimar drawled, sliding his long frame into the leather
chair across from the desk. "Odd. I just passed Wally in the
foyer, and he was sober as I've ever seen him, while you
look to be doing your best to drown yourself in wine before noon. He seemed happy; you look sadder than your
cousin Samuel. Wally's going off for an afternoon with the
most delicious morsel in all of London; you're sitting here,
alone. I don't suppose you'd care to explain any of that?"

"I had a single glass of wine, Lorrie. One. Only an idiot
bent on self-destruction would drink water in this city."

"Don't interrupt, please," Lorimar said, smiling. "I think
I'm unraveling a conundrum. And the answer to this puzzle is—Miss Sophie Winstead. Am I correct?"

Bramwell glared at his friend, briefly considering the
pleasure he might take in leaping across the desk and hitting him. Hitting someone. Hitting something. "I may have
made an idiot out of myself with her last night," he said,
deciding hitting someone wouldn't do him much good.
Unless he could kick himself.

"You did? Well, good for you," Lorimar shot back,
crossing his legs at the ankle as he slouched in the chair.
"About time you figured you weren't cut out for a life of
starched collars and full conformity. Was this a private or
a public idiocy? You score two more points if you made an
idiot of yourself in public, you know."

Bramwell felt a smile beginning to tickle at the corners
of his mouth. He and Lorimar understood each other so
well. There was no need for long explanations with Lori-

mar, for sordid confessions. The Baron knew he had kissed Sophie, or done something similarly reckless. And he knew that Bramwell was caught somewhere between hating himself for what he'd done and wanting to shout what he'd done from the highest rooftops in the city. "No, not in public, Lorrie. But I'm giving it some serious consideration. If she'll have me."

"If she'll have you? Well, good for you all over again, and doubled! I'd begun to wonder if blood still flowed through your veins, you'd resisted for so long. I doubt Bobbit has yet to make a single groat on you—although you probably owe him a king's ransom this morning. But wait a moment. This would also mean you'd have *two* young ladies in your life, Bram. I don't think that's allowed. Unless," he continued, his voice taking on a sharp edge, "you're sitting here thinking of marrying the Waverley and keeping The Winstead on the side? I certainly hope not, my friend. Because I couldn't allow that. I really couldn't."

"And you think I could?" Bramwell felt his blood growing hot, fueling his temper once more. "My God, Lorrie, how far must I go to prove that I'm not my father?"

"You never were, Bram," the Baron said evenly. "In fact, you were very much your own man all of your life—up until the moment your father executed that none-too-graceful leap from Buxley's balcony and straight into legend. It was only then that you lost your way, Bram, trying to be what you were not. Taking up the title with both hands and a heavy, sober heart, turning your back on any hint of nonsense, bracketing yourself to a woman you would never have taken a second look at before your father's death and your humiliation? No, you would have done none of that if you'd come into the dukedom in the usual way. Is your family's good name worth such sacrifice? The sacrifice of your own happiness? Of Miss Waverley's chance for happiness?"

He pushed himself to his feet. "I'd drink another glass of that wine if I were you, Bram, really I would. Maybe the whole bottle, and another one as well. Get yourself very, very drunk, then take a good look at yourself. Look at your life before the balcony scene, your life since that day—your life as it stretches in front of you now. Examine the choices that are yours and yours alone. You'll end up with a bruiser of a headache, but I think you might also end up the wiser for the pain."

Bramwell ran a hand through his hair as he looked up at his friend. "How long were you going to let me continue to make a bloody fool of myself, Lorrie?" he asked. "If Sophie hadn't unexpectedly come into my life—how long would it have been before you tapped me ungently on my brick-stupid head and waked me up to what I was doing?"

"I had considered that, if my first idea didn't show promise." Lorimar smiled, his usually unreadable gray eyes twinkling. "You know, Bram, for an intelligent man . . ." he said, his voice drifting off into suggestive nothingness before he ended, "well, let's just say it might be time you had a long talk with Sophie's maid, my friend, *n'est-ce pas?*"

Man was born imperfect. He lived and he died, still flawed, still imperfect. But, by damn, he should bloody well learn *something* along the way!

That was the conclusion a few hours of thought and a bottle of very good wine had brought to Bramwell Seaton, Ninth Duke of Selbourne.

He had been born into one of England's finest families, one of its premier titles, one of its largest fortunes. All of that hadn't given him what he really wanted. He had never felt his mother's love, known his father's pride.

But he'd grown up, grown into a man, begun to travel his own road. He'd found friends, his own life, his own happiness.

Or so he'd thought.

All it had taken to change that life had been his father's disgrace. The ridicule his father had brought to the family name. If Bramwell hadn't had loving parents, he'd at least always had his heritage to cling to, to make him feel, if not loved, at least respected. Cecil Seaton had destroyed all of that. His usually more discreet mother, the late duchess, very indiscreetly succumbing to a plateful of bad fish while in the company of her latest lover, had finished what his father had started.

And Bramwell, now cursing himself for being stupid, stupid, *stupid*, had let his life be changed.

Why?

Because he had been happy, if still relatively young and a bit of a rascal, had he suddenly believed himself cursed with what he began to see as a Seaton family failing? Was enjoying life a sin?

Conversely, was striving these past three years to rebuild his family's name a sin?

"Anything, if taken to excess, is a sin," Bramwell said as he mounted the stairs to Sophie's bedchamber. "At least I think that's how it goes. But somewhere, by God, there has to be a *happy* medium."

He turned down the hallway, a fresh bottle and two glasses in his hands, following the sound of Desiree's voice raised in song. The woman sounded carefree, without a worry in the world.

Well, that wouldn't last for long!

He stopped just in the doorway of Sophie's bedchamber and leaned a shoulder against the doorjamb, his hands crossed against his chest—the bottle dangling from one hand, the glasses from the other—his pose purposely relaxed. "*Mademoiselle?* A moment of your time, *s'il vous plaît?*" he drawled in imitation of the day the maid had cornered him in his own dressing room.

Desiree seemed to freeze in the act of placing a tapestry pillow in the center of the freshly made-up bed. "*Monseigneur?*" she said, slowly turning to watch with gimlet eyes as Bramwell strolled fully into the large guest chamber, set down his burdens of bottle and glasses, and took up a seat on a pink-and-white striped chaise longue. "There is something wrong, *oui*? Or, perhaps, something to celebrate?"

Bramwell knew his grin bordered on evil. "That would depend, Desiree," he said, pulling a cheroot out of his pocket and sticking it, unlit, into the corner of his mouth. His smile widened as the maid raced to find a striking match before dumping hairpins from a small china plate, probably thinking to use it to hold the ashes. "It would depend, you see, on how truthful you are in the next, oh, five minutes?"

"Truthful, *monseigneur?*" Desiree repeated, swallowing down hard as she pulled a small table close beside the chaise longue and placed the china dish on its surface. She leaned forward to light his cheroot. "In what way?"

Bramwell puffed several times on the cheroot, drawing the smoke into his lungs. "In every way, *mademoiselle*," he purred, exhaling a ribbon of fragrant blue smoke, "but I think we should perhaps begin with the Baron Marshall Lorimar's visit to Wimbledon. That would have been some months ago, *oui*?"

Desiree, a woman Bramwell already knew was not the sort to stand on ceremony in any case, immediately plopped her voluptuous frame down beside him on the chaise longue, staring at him goggle-eyed. "*Mon Dieu!* I am undone!"

Bramwell couldn't help himself. He deliberately smiled around the cheroot still clamped between his teeth, deliberately wrinkled up his nose as he did so. God, but he felt alive! More alive than he had in—when? Three years? He was Bram Seaton again. Naval officer, gentleman, and a man who knew pleasure and laughter and the occasional bout of ridiculousness—and damn well enjoyed them. "Yes, you could say that, couldn't you?"

Desiree quickly recovered her composure. "It was the baron, of course. He gave it away." She shook her head. "I should have known better than to trust a man, *oui*? They are always the downfall of desperate, trusting women. What did he tell you?"

In truth, Lorimar had told Bramwell next to nothing, but he wasn't about to admit that to this clever woman. "He told me his side of the story, of course, men being end-lessly perfidious. But I thought it only fair to allow you to tell me *your* side of things before I had you tossed out on your ambitious ear."

"And Sophie along with me? Oh, no, *monseigneur*, you wouldn't do that," Desiree said, visibly relaxing. "But," she went on, gifting him with an eloquent Gallic shrug, "I suppose it is time for some small truths, *oui*?"

"Small, middle-sized, large. Complete and total, as a matter of fact." Bramwell pulled the cheroot from his mouth and rose to his feet, beginning to pace. "Did I mention that I'm not by nature a patient man?"

"I could make you more impatient than you have ever known. Were I younger, not so devoted to pastries. Were your interests not already involved elsewhere," Desiree said, shrugging once more. "Ah, well, that time is past for me, and unlamented. And, since I have gotten what I want—you would not have troubled to come to me if I hadn't—I suppose the truth is owed, *oui*?" She looked at him intently. "You do love her, *monseigneur*. She would not have come back to this bed last night still a virgin, did you not love her."

Bramwell crushed out the cheroot in the china dish, leaning toward Desiree as he did so. "We're here for your confession, *mademoiselle*, not mine," he reminded her coldly.

Desiree laughed in sheer delight, which was surprising to Bramwell, for he had thought he'd just leveled the woman with his most fierce scowl, his most threatening voice. "I have lived long enough to see a miracle, *monseigneur*. God is indeed good, *oui*? The Baron Lorimar, he was right. All the heart of your father, *monseigneur*, all the heat, the fire, the delicious nonsense. Hidden for years, but

always there, always ready, waiting. But with a steadfast-
ness never seen in the father. You are perfect for my little
Sophie. Perfect!"

"And betrothed to marry another," Bramwell put in
facetiously, rising and going to the table, picking up the already uncorked bottle, pouring each of them a glass of
wine.

"Bah! That is nothing, *monseigneur*," Desiree said, accepting a glass. "A mere *bagatelle*, a nuisance soon forgotten. Trust Sophie in this, *monseigneur*. In her zeal to
make everyone happy, the little minx is already well on
the way to most comfortably settling *Mademoiselle* Waverley, unaware that she is also helping herself to her own
happiness. Life is so interesting when one is in Society,
oui? The dance, the whirl, the excitement. My Sophie
was born for all of it—to be the happy, laughing queen of
all of it!"

Bramwell's head was beginning to spin, and he knew it
had little to do with no breakfast and a bellyful of wine. "I
prefer to let the subject of my soon-to-be-broken engagement to Miss Waverley lie for the moment, *mademoiselle*.
We were discussing Baron Lorimar, I believe? That is why
I'm here, remember?"

Desiree took a deep drink of the wine, then nodded her
head as she swallowed. "Of course, of course. *Certaine-
ment*. We will discuss the Baron Lorimar. He came to me
in Wimbledon early last winter, entirely unexpected, and
with a sad tale to tell. His good friend, he said, was in danger of losing himself to dullness. He needed to be awak-
ened, brought to realize that life was more than playing a
role he believed was his duty. He needed some fun, some

excitement, some *joie de vivre*. There was a daughter of Constance Winstead, *oui*? The Baron had thought he was right in believing this, remembering this. And he had an idea. What had brought joy to the father . . ."

As Desiree's voice trailed off, to be followed by a wink that was surely meant to imply what she had not bothered to explain, Bramwell found himself sitting down beside the maid once more. It was much more respectable than falling down. "Go on, please. He met Sophie, and then— what?" he said, noticing that his lips had gone numb.

"He met Sophie? Then you do not know anything, do you?" Desiree questioned him, her tone no longer happy, but disdainful, condemning. "You think that Sophie has known from the beginning, that she knows now, *oui*?"

Bramwell rubbed a hand across his mouth. "I'm an idiot, aren't I, Desiree? But I did think it, if only for a moment. This was your plan, yours and Lorrie's. Not Sophie's. Please, go on. Finish it."

Desiree gave a small, delighted chuckle. "Ah, yes. A miracle. I am looking into the face of real love. For you were not angry when you thought—for just that moment that you thought it—that Sophie may have been in on our little scheme. You were crushed, brokenhearted. There is yet hope for this sad old world, if true love between a man and a woman is still possible, *oui*?"

She stood up, poured both of them another glass of wine, and began pacing the same small carpet Bramwell had trod moments earlier. "Let me see. How did it grow from there? Oh, yes, I remember. I was to get Sophie to London. But how, *monseigneur*? How was I to get her there? And not just in London, but smack into the middle of Society, into your orbit. Better yet, under your roof?"

Bramwell was beginning to understand. It was either the wine, or he was waking up, becoming more and more himself again. "You had the letter from my father," he said. "Which, I do believe, means your considerable talents extend to that of forgery?"

Desiree pointed straight at him. "Now, *that*, *monseigneur*, Sophie does know. I could not keep it from her. Not when that fool of a solicitor insisted upon spending the night, then wandering out of my chamber the next morning still tucking his shirt into his breeches." She shrugged, winking in delight. "I am still quite good, *monseigneur*, and the solicitor, he was happy to do anything I asked. Signature, seals, anything! And that was that," she said with a snap of her fingers. "You had no choice but to take Sophie in, as your father had promised, and you, *monseigneur*, are an honorable man, *oui*?"

Bramwell rose and replenished his glass yet another time, eyeing the level in the bottle as he sat down once more. "So Lorrie did see Sophie for the first time *after* she was installed here in Portland Square. That's obvious enough, for even Lorrie isn't that good an actor. He was genuinely bowled over by her, which serves him right, now that I think about it. The wager, the paper listing the wager, however, was all planned out beforehand, as a part of the scheme you and Lorrie hatched between you."

He eyed the maid curiously. "And *you* picked up that paper, not Giuseppe. The monkey only was told to give it to Sophie, so as to stir the waters more, make us more aware of each other. Am I correct?"

"You're very, very good, *monseigneur*," Desiree told him, giggling. She was now on her third small glass of wine, and the bottle was empty. "But I had more of a plan that just those silly wagers of the baron's. I instructed Sophie to tell you immediately that she was irresistible, and that you should not fall in love with her. She was sure I had done this so as to have you take her in dislike, make her safe from your advances if you should have thought to make her your mistress, but—"

"But you really did it so that I'd be sure to be interested," Bramwell finished for her. Desiree, he believed, would have made an admirable general—and an even better tactician.

"*Oui*. I thought to hasten matters. Gentlemen are sure to come forward the moment one tells them to please, please, back away. But no one can dislike Sophie. She is totally lovable, *oui*? She couldn't know how she had immediately become attractive to you. She has learned my tricks, *monseigneur*, but she has not yet learned them all. And still, even last night, when she came to me with her face glowing with love for you, I continued to warn her away."

Bramwell drained his glass. "You're holding out for marriage," he said flatly, realizing that he had somehow come to find himself in the unique position of possibly having to apply to his beloved's maid for permission to marry. This entire scene was ludicrous. Laughable. And he hadn't enjoyed an interview this much in years. "Once Sophie, that is, all unknowing of what she is doing, neatly removes the single obstacle remaining in our path."

"Not the only obstacle, *monseigneur*," Desiree told him, suddenly serious as she crossed to the small chest beside the bed and opened the top drawer. "My only fear of bringing Sophie to London was in having her within the same orbit as the uncles. Society miss or duke's wife, they may not want her here. Because of these," she ended, holding up what looked to be about a half dozen slim, leather-bound journals. "I've been waiting for the correct time to show them to you."

Bramwell was suddenly quite sober. "Those belonged to Constance, I'll assume," he said quietly, watching as Desiree held the journals between her hands, preparing to replace them in the drawer.

"*Oui*," Desiree said absently, reaching into the drawer, running her hand over its interior. "They are very dear to Sophie, much as I pleaded with her to burn them, burn them all. Constance wrote down everything, you see. She had a separate journal for each of the uncles, along with much gossip of a more silly nature. And that, *monseigneur*, is what worries me. The gentlemen, they must all know of the journals, *oui*? Constance was always fond of saying she had no secrets from the world."

"If they do indeed know about the journals, and remember their existence, I imagine the uncles are feeling much the same way now about their own secrets," Bramwell said, frowning. "There are what—about a half dozen of them?"

"*Oui, monseigneur*, six. Constance did not begin her journals until Sophie was, oh, seven or eight years of age,

I suppose. One man is dead, the uncle of your friend, Sir Wallace Merritt. From the pages of her mother's journal, Sophie learned how to make Sir Wallace happy. She saw it as providential, *oui*? Another is in Scotland, and of no worry to me. There is, of course, your father. And the three uncles. Six men, six journals."

Bramwell watched as Desiree dropped to her knees and pulled the drawer clear of the chest, frantically looking into the cavity. "But there are only five now. One is not stuck in here," she said, her voice rising in alarm as she looked to Bramwell. "I had hoped. But, oh, *monseigneur*, it is not here. Which one is missing?"

Bramwell waited as Desiree opened one journal after the other, quickly scanning the first page, then throwing it onto the bed. "Lord Buxley's," she said at last, looking up at him, her expression one of near panic. "Of all of them, why one of the London uncles. *Mon dieu, monseigneur!* What are we to do? Lord Buxley's journal is gone!"

Bramwell sat very still for a long time, then slowly got to his feet. "As Giuseppe can't read—he can't, can he?—I believe I will make a small visit to my aunt's chambers," he said finally. "If I find the journal there, one question will remain, a question I must ask my aunt."

"What would that question be, *monseigneur*?"

His smile was tight, and not at all amused. "Well, Desiree, I'll tell you. As my aunt is an inveterate lover of gossip, I must first assume that Sophie told her about the existence of these journals, not realizing the temptation she had unwittingly put in the dear, light-fingered old lady's way. I'm willing to make that leap in logic, as I believe you might have already done. Which begs the question, dear woman—did my aunt just now borrow the one, or has she been treating the journals as a sort of lending library for some time now, then going out into Society, fully armed with her newly discovered knowledge?"

"*Mon Dieu!*" Desiree breathed out, collapsing her rump onto the floor. "The *oncles* won't like this, *oui*?"

"Exactly," Bramwell said, already on his way out of the room.

A chapter of accidents.
—Earl of Chesterfield

Chapter Twelve

Sophie lingered at a table of books that concerned gardening, field drainage, and the proper composition of compost, pretending an interest as she kept one eye trained on the doorway. What was taking Sir Wallace so long? Honestly, give the man one simple assignment . . .

The afternoon had gone wonderfully well, thanks to Bobbit's discreet inquiries at a local pub frequented by house servants that had led to a list of several promising lodgings to be inspected. In fact, Sophie and Sir Wallace had quickly located very likely the most ideal bachelor quarters in all of Mayfair, the entire project taking less than two hours. A Mr. Forester, late of Hampshire and now in an extreme rush to return there after a brief, expensive sojourn to London's raciest gaming hells, had been more than delighted to turn his furnished accommodations over to Sir Wallace, and to include his small staff as well in the bargain.

Which had left more than enough time for a visit to Hatchard's, and a bit of matchmaking. Again thanks to Bobbit's network of talkative house servants, Sophie already knew that Lord Charles Anston and his four daughters would be there at precisely three o'clock—just another reason his lordship would be so right for Miss Waverley, being such a punctual, dependable, responsible sort of fellow.

Sir Wallace, as per Sophie's earlier arrangement, would leave Sophie safely browsing at Hatchard's while he drove over to escort Miss Waverley to meet with her, another arrangement the well-prepared Sophie had already made. Once Bramwell's betrothed was present, Sophie would bring Lord Anston and Miss Waverley together. Sir Wallace would then, keeping strictly to the script Sophie had furnished for him, remember a most pressing engagement elsewhere and beg Lord Anston to be so kind as to see to getting the ladies home.

It was a brilliant plan. Simple. Direct. But with no room for error. The timing had to be perfect.

And Sir Wallace was late. A good twenty minutes late as a matter of fact. And Lord Anston was showing signs of being ready to gather up his daughters and depart.

But, then, Sophie told herself, he hadn't as yet seen her here, had he?

Giving her curls a toss, and pinning a bright smile to her face, she stepped out from behind the table and headed straight for the eldest Anston daughter, brushing a shoulder against her as she moved past, then quickly stopping to offer her apologies for being so clumsy.

"My goodness, what a beauty you are!" Sophie then exclaimed as the two bent to retrieve the small pile of books that had fallen from the girl's arms, to scatter on the floor. "You have the look of Lord Anston about you, don't you? Those lovely blue eyes, that small cleft in your chin. Oh, goodness, yes, the resemblance is remarkable! I'm Sophie, by the way. Sophie Winstead. Your papa was kind enough as to call on me the other day, in Portland Square. I'm staying there with the duke of Selbourne's aunt, in case you are wondering if it is permissible to speak with me, and Lady Gwendolyn makes me absolutely acceptable, yes? Is your papa here, then? I just arrived, and have not seen him. He is such a doting papa, isn't he, so proud of his beautiful daughters. Now I see why. If anything, he has not said enough about your beauty. You'll have a Season soon, yes?"

Shock, flattery, a tumble of breathless words, a few smiles that held nothing but artless female talk—all of these combined to gain the immediate confidence of Miss Sarah Anston. Within moments she had dragged Sophie over to where her obviously bored father stood bracing up one of the many bookcases that littered Hatchard's nearly from floor to high ceiling. At Sophie's sunny greeting, he snapped to attention at once.

All four Anston daughters were soon gathered up and introduced, and Sophie gushed over and flattered each of them in their turn. They were lovely girls, really, and very well behaved, very eager to talk. By the time Sir Wallace finally showed himself, fairly dragging Miss Isadora Waverley along with him through the aisles, Sophie was able to introduce them all to each other, telling Miss Waverley about Sarah's love of reading, Ruth Ann's wish to witness the new King's Coronation, Lucy's adoration of her puppy, Fluff, and little Mary's tumble from a beech tree just before their trip to London, which explained why her left arm was strapped up in a sling.

"You may not know this, girls," she told them, lowering her voice just a trifle, as if imparting knowledge that definitely would impress them, "but Miss Waverley here is an *expert* on the London Season. I cannot tell you how much she has helped me, a silly country miss with more hair than wit, how many pitfalls she has saved me from in only the short time I have been in Mayfair. Lord Anston?" she then asked, looking at him directly. "Don't you agree? Miss Waverley is absolutely the most *perfect* person one could ever think to have about when one is launching a Season, yes?"

Miss Waverley colored prettily to the roots of her hair— probably the first time color had ever invaded those lovely, porcelain cheeks. "Lud, Miss Winstead, you embarrass me. I did nothing. It is the same with you as it would be with these four dear young ladies. The beauty, the sweetness— all the materials are there. It is just that I can help to mold, to shape, to instruct. And it has been delightful. Truly delightful. Lud, can there be anything more satisfying than to see another lovely young girl properly launched?"

"Really, Miss Waverley?" Lord Anston asked, looking at her thoughtfully. "So many women would run, screaming, from the prospect of, say, popping off four motherless daughters over the next decade."

"Then the more fools them, my lord," Miss Waverley stated firmly, reaching down to tuck an errant curl behind little Mary's ear. "That's better, dear. Now stand up straight, so that everyone can see your wonderful posture and marvel at what a well-brought-up child you are. Lud, how I tremble as I remember my long days spent wearing a horrid back board, until I'd learned my lesson about posture."

"You know, Miss Waverley," Lord Anston began, still looking at her rather intently ("measuringly" might be too strong a word for a gentleman Sophie hoped to see tumbling into love in the middle of Hatchard's). "You might not remember, as I was nearly trampled in the crowd of eager gentlemen seeking your kind attention during your first Season, but I was one of your most devoted admirers before you became betrothed to Lord Coulbeg, may he rest in peace. But I felt my status as a recent widower, lined up against the dashing earl, put me sadly out of the running, if I might be so bold as to speak freely."

There was that blush again, Sophie noticed, realizing that pink cheeks made Isadora Waverley much more humanly beautiful than did the icy coolness with which the young woman accepted Bramwell's equally cool kiss on her hand. She doubted that either Lord Anston or Miss Waverley would ever fall madly, deeply, passionately in love—as she was beginning to see the emotion—but they were definitely suited to each other. Definitely. And they'd be happy with each other. Content. She sighed, feeling quite content herself.

"But I *do* remember you, Lord Anston," Miss Waverley was protesting prettily even as Sophie was congratulating herself. "Very well, indeed. Lud, I believe you were called back to your estate just as we were getting to know one another. Why, I had all but fallen in love with your tales of your estate, as I do so love the countryside as you described it. Anston Manor, isn't it?"

"Yes," he said, smiling and nodding. "Ruth Ann here broke out in spots, and Sarah right after her, so that I had to return there. To Anston Manor, that is."

"Oh, *Papa!*" Miss Anston exclaimed in youthful high dudgeon, turning to Miss Waverley. "Papa just doesn't understand that he shouldn't speak of such things as *spots.*"

"Papas are like that," Miss Waverley said, nodding in agreement. "Lud, I remember the time, one evening during a small dinner party, when mine was about to tell the vicar about my—well, lud, never mind what it was. Mama stopped him before I could perish of embarrassment, thankfully."

"Mamas do that," Ruth Ann said sadly. "Except we don't have one anymore. Not in ever so long, since little Mary was born."

"Oh, you dear, sweet thing!" Miss Waverley exclaimed, giving the child an impulsive hug as she looked to Lord Anston. "Lud, my lord, but I can see that you need some lessons in the sensibilities of gently nurtured young girls like your sweet daughters."

Lord, but it was simple, this making people happy. Almost laughably so. And so very satisfying. Sophie gave Sir Wallace a sly nudge in the ribs with her elbow and then took his arm as if wandering off to inspect another table of books—this one dedicated to naval tactics. "Where were you?" she asked in a whisper. "I had about given you up, you know."

"Miss Waverley insisted I take tea with her before we came here. Never ate so fast in m'life, I swear it. Now, what the devil are we doing? Something's havey-cavey here, I can feel it. You're up to something, aren't you? All this business about leaving you and Miss Waverley here and loping off like some Johnny Raw who doesn't know gentlemen don't ask ladies to Hatchard's, then abandon them there. I like you, Miss Winstead, I truly, truly do. But sometimes you make me want to start carrying a flask about with me again, I swear you do."

"Oh, you dear, sweet thing!" Sophie said in imitation of Miss Waverley as she patted his cheek, then winked at him. "As things are going even better than I had dared to hope, let's see if this helps to give you some idea of what I'm about, all right? Here's a hint. Do you care to wager on just how long it will be before Lord Anston comes up to us and offers to escort Miss Waverley home? I'll give him ten minutes."

"What? Is *that* what this is about? Oh, it is, it is! I've seen matchmaking before, and this is just the sort of thing matchmaking people do. You're throwing Miss Waverley at Anston's head, aren't you? Straight at it—*wham*! And you stuck me smack in the middle of it, too. Why, of all the sneaky, devious"—he looked over his shoulder at a smiling Lord Anston—"five's more likely, I'll wager," he then ended confidently, shaking his head as he grinned at her. "Yes, five minutes, no more. Do you think he knows Miss Waverley is Bram's intended?"

"Do you really think he cares?" Sophie countered, picking up a thick tome having to do with Nelson's strategies at Trafalgar. "Or that Miss Waverley cares?"

Sir Wallace turned so sharply, throwing another look toward the place where Lord Anston and Isadora Waverley were now deep in conversation, that Sophie had to pull on his neckcloth to bring him back to attention. "Never be obvious, Sir Wallace," she warned. "Now, as it probably isn't in the least ladylike of me to wager anyway, I should consider it a kindness if you were to step on my hem as I move away. Aim for the lowest ruffle, just here, on my left side, if you please. I'm never without a second plan, you understand, in case the first should prove unwieldy."

"But—but I'll rip your gown," he protested, clearly still not understanding what she was about. Which was quite all right. He was a man, and not accustomed to subtlety. Personally, she believed Nelson might have survived Trafalgar, had he a woman on board to assist with tactics.

"Yes, you will, won't you. It's already held in place by little more than a single thread, Desiree being quite good with a needle, so that you won't have to step all that hard. And then I'll have to go straight back to Portland Square, leaving Lord Anston either to say good-bye to a woman he is just beginning to most happily know, or offer to take her up with him when he leaves, yes? You see, I've decided I should totally leave her orbit for the remainder of the afternoon. Miss Sarah Anston already likes me entirely too much, and I believe I want her concentrating quite solely on Miss Waverley's much-more-deserving charms."

Sir Wallace took out his handkerchief and mopped at his suddenly perspiring brow. "I don't know, Miss Winstead. Bram might not like this, even it if does seem a good idea. Never could see him and Miss *Lud* making a match of it. Lorimar, neither. Gave her that name, Lorimar did. But this is rather underhanded, ain't it?"

"Oh, most definitely underhanded, Sir Wallace. But with all of the best intentions. For His Grace. For Miss Waverley's happiness. Now, are you up to the game, or not?"

He gave one last, quick look over his shoulder, then sighed. "You haven't been wrong yet, Miss Winstead, I'll say that for you."

"How true," she said, smiling. "And, please, call me Sophie."

"Sophie it is," he agreed, then screwed up his courage, closed his eyes, and stepped down hard on her hem.

Sophie was holding up a length of ripped flounce as she stood in the foyer, thanking Bobbit for all his help in settling Sir Wallace, among his other courtesies to her, when she felt a hand close around her arm just above the elbow.

"Come with me, Miss Winstead," Bramwell ground out behind her from between clenched teeth, unceremoniously pulling her about and all but dragging her down the hallway toward his private study.

She raised her eyebrows questioningly to Bobbit as she looked over her shoulder at the butler, but he just spread his arms and shook his head.

She allowed herself to be very nearly flung into a leather wing chair as Bramwell swung around to give the door a hard shove closed with his outstretched arm, then plop himself down on the desk, glaring at her.

Goodness, but he was being masterful, although Sophie was fairly certain he hadn't dragged her in here in order to kiss her again, more was the pity. Because she really very much would like to have him kiss her again, tell her again how he might, just might, be in love with her. She remembered Desiree's warning to behave herself, sighed once in regret, then succumbed to an urge to tease Bramwell anyway. "I suppose asking if you'd like me to pour you a glass of wine would be the height of folly, yes? And a kiss, I'm nearly convinced, is totally out of the question?"

"Don't be dazzling, Sophie, if you don't mind," Bramwell warned tightly even as he looked at her with what she assured herself was more than a smidgen of longing. She watched, smiling, as he ran a hand through his hair, mussing it quite adorably even as he bit out, "We've got bigger problems at the moment."

"Bigger than the fact that you, a betrothed man, kissed me last night? Really, Bramwell? And I had thought—" She broke off, shrugging, feeling very much in command of this situation, which was a pleasant change from their interlude the previous evening. "Then last night meant nothing to you, yes? *I* mean nothing to you?"

"Ah, you mean something to me, Sophie," he responded, his expression fairly bleak, and yet curiously amused—a very confusing mix. And doubly adorable. "You mean that I haven't had a comfortable night's sleep since I first learned of your existence. You mean that I have drunk more wine in these last days than I have in the past six months. You mean that I'm looking at my life and learning things about it and my friends that both enlighten and infuriate me. You mean that I have found myself in the position of being both the happiest and most hopeful of men while at the same time believing I might have been better off to have drowned when my second-to-last ship went down off the coast of Spain. But that isn't why we're here."

He was happy? Hopeful? Happiness and hope flared in Sophie as well. Hearing Bramwell so close to incoherent gave her confidence yet another small boost, and she settled herself more comfortably into the chair. Maybe, as she was beginning to believe, as he had told her last night, there was such a thing as true love. And maybe, just maybe, it wasn't entirely confined to the female of the species—perhaps the odd gentleman or two were capable of the emotion. Like Bramwell Seaton. "Then you're glad you kissed me?" she asked, unable to keep the womanly satisfaction out of her voice.

"It has always amazed me how a woman will push and push at a man when the man obviously doesn't want to discuss something. Glad, Sophie? How could I be glad about it? I'm not *glad* about it, no," he answered flatly. "It was the wrong thing to do. Definitely."

"Oh," Sophie said quietly, her new confidence not quite up to surviving such a deflating statement. "I see."

"No, damn it, you *don't* see! I wanted to kiss you. I wanted to throw you onto the carpet in front of the fire and make love to you all the night long. I wanted it more than I would have believed I could ever want anything!" Bramwell all but shouted. "I still do, God help me. But I was stupid, wrongheaded. I put the cart before the horse."

"Really?" Sophie considered this for a moment, even as she fought a sudden impulse to leap to her feet and break into song—or spread her wings and fly about the room several times. As she was exquisitely aware, as Desiree had told her, timing was everything. He'd had the kiss right, he'd just had the timing wrong. That was what he was saying, wasn't it?

Happy tears pricked behind Sophie's eyes as she gave up all the teachings of a lifetime, turned her back on them joyfully and walked away—and figuratively stepped forward into the arms of trust, of love. She loved Bramwell Seaton. She'd probably loved him forever, even before she'd set foot in Portland Square. And she trusted him to love her back.

Which didn't mean she could entirely forgive him for saying she wasn't perfect. It was true. She wasn't. But a man in love really shouldn't say such things, should he?

She decided another small bit of teasing was in order. "And which am I, then, Bram? The cart, or the horse? I imagine I'd be the cart, yes? Miss Waverley would be the horse. I don't think that's flattering to either of us, to be truthful about the thing. Perhaps, if you think hard on it, you could find another way to say what you mean?"

He put his palms on the desk on either side of him and leaned toward her as she grinned up at him, even went so far as to waggle her eyebrows at him. "You'd try the patience of saint, Sophie. You know that, don't you?"

How wonderful this was! To feel so free to be herself, to know that she was loved, to know that she loved. How happy she and Bramwell would be, for all of their lives. "Yes, Bram," she agreed, feeling rather full of herself, this new power, this dizzying confidence. "I do know. Do you want to kiss me again? You might have placed too much importance on the ones we shared last night. And I might have a few reservations of my own, yes? Perhaps if you kissed me again . . ." She raised her chin another fraction, pursed her lips, and closed her eyes.

"Oh, for God's sake!" He pushed himself away from the

desk and began to pace as Sophie bit her bottom lip to hold back a giggle.

"Tell me more about love, Bram, please. I may not have listened all that well last night, what with objects flying around the room."

That stopped him mid-pace. "What?" He pressed a hand against his forehead. "How did this happen? I bring her in here to tell her something, something crucially important, and now we're talking about *love*? Last night she doesn't want to hear a word about it—today, she's asking for a seminar on the subject! I'm being dazzled, that's what. I'll probably spend the rest of my life not knowing if I'm on my head or on my heels. I should throw her out of here on her head right now, that's what I should do."

Sophie stood up, went to the drinks table, poured him a glass of wine. Poor dear thing, he looked so harassed. She knew how he felt. This hadn't been an easy night and day for her, either. Coming to life-altering revelations seldom was. "I understand, Bram. You have other things on your mind. But I do want to talk about this. I think we must. So I'll begin, yes? I'll tell you what I think, all right? Love between a man and a woman doesn't exist, I said. Only desire, even lust. I want to be happy, and believing oneself to be in love is the simplest, straightest route to unhappiness. I've said all of that, believed all of that. Definitely. But now I'm beginning to have some few second thoughts on the subject."

"You're beginning to have—" He threw up his hands. "Why am I repeating everything the girl says? God's death, Sophie, you certainly do pick your times, don't you? A man would be a bloody fool to even *mention* the word love around you. I certainly learned that last night, while I was dodging teapots. After all, it was you who told me that a man only speaks of love in order to get what he wants, and then leaves. That men only believe in lust, in desire. And now you're saying—oh, no. No! We're not going to get into this now. Not right now."

"But you were telling the truth last night, yes? You *do* believe in love, don't you, Bram? You don't want to, but you do. You want me to believe in it, too," she said, handing him the glass, which he took. "Except that I very much think you still believe it makes fools of men. It's even probably why you betrothed yourself to dear Isadora, and why you can't look me in the eye today."

"I'm very fond of Isadora!" he pronounced in a fairly impressive bellow.

"Yes, Bram," Sophie said reasonably. "And that's terribly sad. For you, for Isadora. Only think of what you both are missing. Much more intelligent to look for real love, even if it makes fools of us, yes?"

"As in your mother and my father, I suppose? Skyrocketing stark naked from a balcony isn't exactly a sign of intelligence, Sophie," he pointed out sarcastically. "Divorcing your wife to marry your paramour isn't—"

"What did you say?"

"You didn't know that either?" He looked away from her for a moment, muttering something under his breath, then took a deep breath and looked at her. "I found the documents in my father's personal belongings. He had everything ready to go, just a week before he died. His solicitors had been hard at work, the wording of the petition was in place. The only reason he'd agreed to go to Buxley's was in order to line up allies who would help him. Otherwise, and for probably every day of their marriage after I was conceived, my parents were only in the same place at the same time by unhappy accident. So, yes, Sophie, my father was on his way to very publicly divorcing his wife, obviously so that he could marry your mother. Just another Seaton scandal."

"I—I think perhaps I should sit down now," Sophie said quietly, marveling at the way the room had begun to spin. He took hold of her arm and helped her to a chair as she swayed where she stood. "But he was going to leave her," she went on, speaking out loud, but really only talking to herself. "Desiree said she found *Maman* crying, which proved Uncle Cesse was about to leave her, just as they all had left, all the uncles, all those times. *Maman* said Desiree was wrong, that she was happy, that she had a secret. He was going to marry her? He wasn't going to leave?" She looked up at Bram, her eyes swimming with happy tears. "Oh, Bram, don't you see? This just makes it all even more clear to me, to both of us!"

"How?"

It was a simple question, but Sophie didn't have a simple answer. What did it change—learning that Uncle Cesse had really, really loved her mother, had been willing to stand up to the scandal of seeking out what would be a difficult, hard-won divorce from his marriage of social convenience in order to wed his one true love? Well, for one thing, it definitely fell into the category of being the miracle of love Desiree had admitted even she still hoped to believe in even after her cynical lessons.

But Bramwell obviously had seen his father's intentions as just more proof that love made fools of men, that it was better to form a comfortable yet loveless alliance between social peers than to risk his heart—or lose his mind, which was probably what he thought love demanded from a man.

She was beginning to believe she understood love. She was beginning to believe in love with as much conviction as her mother had done, and damn the consequences. She wanted love, desired love above all things, now, and forever. Bramwell's love. Only his. In or outside of wedlock. Because that didn't matter. It simply didn't matter, not when she loved him so much.

But, while she had been about to throw caution to the winds, take Bramwell anyway he wanted to take her—Lord! She *was* her mother's child—he was still caught between wanting her and his convictions of these past years, convictions built on his family's disgrace, his father's hey-go-mad life, that man's scandalous death.

Last night she had weakly joked that she and Bramwell were fools. How right she had been!

To Bram, love still meant making a fool of himself, because love made fools of men. And, possibly, quite probably—definitely—of women as well. It certainly had almost made a fool of her, for she'd foolishly been about to declare her love for him, offer herself to him. Just as last night he had nearly been foolish enough to admit his love for her.

A pair of fools seemed rather fun, as her mother and Uncle Cesse had been. But to be a fool on her own? No, that didn't sound the least bit appealing. Not to her, and obviously not to Bramwell.

She had learned so much. They both still had so much to learn.

So, how did one go about building a pair of happy fools? That was certainly something to think about, wasn't it? Because she was not about to cry craven at the first hurdle and slink away. Not now. Not when she loved. . . .

"Sophie?" Bramwell prompted, bending down to put a finger under her chin, lift her head so that she had to meet his eyes. "Are you all right?"

She shot him her sunniest smile, the one that crinkled up her nose and made her eyes shine. "Oh, yes," she said with considerable gusto. "I'm simply fine, Bram. For a moment I was sad, thinking of how things might have been for *Maman* and Uncle Cesse. But they were happy, yes?" She patted his hand, reminding him that he still held her chin, and he let go, straightening once more and looking at her searchingly.

"Now," she said, taking a deep breath and letting it out slowly, "I think you said there was some sort of problem? Something more important than our discussion of love?"

"Not more important, Sophie," he said, still looking at her strangely. She really, really wished he wouldn't look at her that way. Hungrily. Yet sadly. As if he longed to touch her, but knew he wasn't free to do so. Yes, he still had so much to learn, poor darling. But that was all right. He loved her. He really did. Now that she understood that, she'd help him get through any remaining problems. Sophie would fix everything, just as she always did. And, if she was very lucky, they'd both have a lot of fun along the way.

"It's not more important?" she prompted, wondering

what he'd do if she lifted up her hand, ran her fingers through his hair. No. Better not. The fellow was hanging by a frayed thread as it was.

"No, it's not. It's just—different. This problem is about your mother's journals."

"Her—you know about *Maman*'s journals? How?" Sophie was suddenly all attention, thoughts of love and fools and happily-ever-afters flying from her mind.

She could sense that he wasn't going to tell her the whole truth, even before he opened his mouth. But that didn't matter for long, not when he began speaking.

"Peggy has been commissioned to bring me anything, um, *unusual* she might find in Aunt Gwen's rooms," he said, taking up his wineglass, and his pacing, once again. "When she brought me Lord Buxley's journal, I confronted my aunt."

"Oh, dear," Sophie said, her shoulders slumping. "I never should have mentioned them to her. She does possess a prodigious love of gossip, doesn't she, Bram? It must have been much like hanging a sugar treat in front of a baby. Lord Buxley's journal, did you say? Well, that was innocuous enough, I suppose. Unless Aunt Gwendolyn wanted to learn more about the first time his lordship cornered a fox on his own. That," she ended quietly, "and how he liked to chase *Maman* about the room while she wore nothing but a fox cape he'd given her, with him calling out 'Yoicks! Away!' "

"I know. I've read the journal. But there were also several mentions of many personages in the *ton*, many of them not exactly flattering if anyone were to go about in Society, quoting them," Bramwell said, one side of his mouth lifting in a smile. "I've read four of the journals so far, as a matter of fact. I now understand where you got the idea that led to Wally's freedom. Very inventive, your mother."

"You've read—did you say four of them? I thought Peggy only brought you the one."

"And I only intended to read the one," he told her earnestly, and she believed him. "However, after speaking with my aunt, and learning that she had already read them all? Well, you can see the problem, can't you?"

He had read four of them? But, obviously, not the one about Uncle Cesse. No, he wouldn't have done that. Stubborn, stubborn man! Sophie turned toward the window but closed her eyes, able to see the pages of the journals page by damning page. "Uncle Tye's brushes with the cent-per-cents. Uncle Dickie's dabbling in cheating during his years at Oxford. Angus McLeish's sympathies with the French. Horace Autley's by-blow, set up as a footman at his father's own country estate. And all the rest. All those little bits of gossip they'd told *Maman* over the years. About Lady Jersey, Lord Byron, *two* prime ministers, even that business about the Prince Regent, back when he was the Prince Regent, and—"

"Yes, for all the gossip about our new and still-uncrowned king, that one retained the power to startle," Bramwell cut in. "And now Aunt Gwen knows it. She knows it all, Sophie. And, unfortunately, she's already nattered a time or two with some of her friends about one or two of the less, shall we say, *incriminating* tidbits?"

"This isn't good," Sophie said, knowing she was understating the enormity of what had happened, and by a long chalk.

"Oh, but it gets better, Sophie. Much better," Bramwell told her as she watched him, her bottom lip stuck between her teeth. "After I sent my aunt and Mrs. Farraday off to Bond Street—buying a new bonnet seems to hold a most miraculous power to cheer my aunt no end, even when she knows she's been very naughty—I had Peggy help me search her rooms. And we came up with this, sitting right out in the open, on her dresser, so that we know it's a new addition to her *collection.*"

She took the small object Bramwell held out in his hand, recognizing it as a snuffbox. It was a lovely piece, all gold and polished enamel, with initials engraved on the top lid. She turned it over and over in her hands, then opened it. "She's done this before, poor dear," she said. "And you've returned things like this before, with no one the wiser. I know you have because you've already hinted at it, and Peggy told me the rest. You can do it again, yes? The cover is initialed, like so many of them are. Do you know who it belongs to? I imagine you do. Or is there something I'm not seeing? There is, isn't there? You wouldn't be looking quite so stern if there weren't."

"Oh, I know who it belongs to, Sophie. And, yes, there is something you're not seeing. Here, let me show you," he said. "You already know so many secrets, one more shouldn't make any difference." He took the snuffbox from her nervous fingers and, pressing on a nearly invisible button on its lid, opened a secret compartment and pulled out a small scrap of paper, carefully unfolding it before reading its contents aloud. " '16 Aug. St. P F. Troops ready, per my order. S.' "

"Well, that's certainly clear," Sophie said, genuinely confused. "But I suppose it means something to you, yes?"

"Let me refresh your memory, all right? The sixteenth of August of last year marks the day of Peterloo, the massacre of innocent men, women and children in Manchester, at a place called St. Peter's Fields. It has been said, ever since, that Lord Sidmouth may have planned the whole thing, turning what was meant to be a peaceful protest assembly into an excuse to set government troops on the citizens. Sidmouth, of course, denies this. He also must have never needed to pass the note, and likewise forgot he'd left it in his snuffbox."

"And he might *still* not remember the note, unless losing the snuffbox jostles his memory. But if he does remember? Bram, that note—if he thought Aunt Gwendolyn had taken the snuffbox, and if you were to personally return the snuff-box, pretending to have found it, and if Lord Sidmouth believed you had discovered the note . . ." She gave a small shiver. "Lord Sidmouth isn't a nice man, if I remember *Maman*'s journals correctly."

"Exactly. There are a great many 'ifs' in all of what you say, Sophie—except that business about Sidmouth's bull-dog disposition—and none of them appeal. So, as I see it, we have two problems in front of us right now. The first, my aunt's gossiping, which may have already prompted at least one of your uncles to wishing you out of London, or underground. We'll consider that tomorrow, as I already believe I can settle that whole business successfully. And secondly, the return of Sidmouth's snuffbox. That, I'm afraid, we'll have to deal with tonight."

"Can't we simply throw the thing away? Connecting its disappearance to Aunt Gwendolyn is possible, but far-fetched, yes? We could be worrying about nothing. He'll most probably just think he's lost it, and that will be the end of things."

"It would, if my aunt hadn't been one of a *very* small party of ladies to take tea with Lady Sidmouth yesterday afternoon. I've already returned one of Lady Sidmouth's fans to her, last Season, telling her Aunt Gwen picked it up by mistake, and a silver teaspoon this Season, explaining how it had somehow fallen into my aunt's reticule. I don't think she believed me either time, but she didn't say anything, and just accepted the return of the articles."

"Oh, Bram," Sophie said on a groan. "The spoon fell into her reticule? Couldn't you have done better than that? I could think of a half dozen reasons more believable than that obvious farradiddle, without even applying myself to the task."

"And you're proud of that, I suppose?" Bramwell asked, softening his voice with a smile. "However, if Sidmouth has realized his snuffbox has gone missing, and if he re-members that he might have a note inside its secret com-partment—it doesn't much matter what the note contains, just that one might be there—and if Lady Sidmouth puts fan and spoon together, coming up with one lovable but light-fingered Lady Gwendolyn? Well, I really don't want to think about that, do you?"

"No. I don't suppose I do."

Bramwell took a deep breath. "Now," he said, releasing

that breath slowly, almost reluctantly, "as much as I didn't want to tell you any of this, I have been able to think of one way, only one way, to return the snuffbox *without* anyone from this household crossing Sidmouth's threshold before he discovers the thing among his belongings. Unfortunately, my plan includes Giuseppe which, doubly unfortunately, includes you, as he listens to you. I tried earlier to have him obey me, but I might as well have been speaking to the fireplace poker."

Sophie looked up at Bramwell, saw the concern in his eyes, his seriousness—and something else. He looked eager, alive, adorably young, ready for adventure. Lovable. So wonderfully lovable. She leaned forward, her every sense quivering with excitement. "Go on, Bram. Tell me your plan. I'm listening . . ."

On such an occasion as this,
All time and nonsense scorning,
Nothing shall come amiss,
And we won't go home till morning.
                              —J. B. Buckstone

Chapter Thirteen

Bramwell sat on the edge of the bed, having dismissed Reese after that man had all but wept over his employer's choice of late-evening attire. The journal, the journal concerning his father's time with Constance Winstead, burned his hands as he held it, stared at it, but steadfastly refused to open it.

He'd begun to forgive his father. Had remembered the love he'd borne the man, even when it wasn't returned. He'd begun to feel some compassion for his sire, not to mention an astonishing degree of empathy, and he didn't want to muddy the waters of his memories now with the truth. A lie he could live with, a comforting lie based on his father's problems and the man's apparent inability to love his child born of a woman he'd despised. But the truth? Ah, did he really want to face the truth?

He pushed his tongue around inside his dry mouth, trying to moisten it, slowly drew in a deep breath, and opened the journal.

There was a lot he didn't bother to read, although he did find himself chuckling over those first pages and Constance Winstead's hilarious reminiscences of the evening she and his father had first met, and she had believed his eloquent father to be somewhat slow. For he'd barely spoken a word to her, and then only in "stammers and terse proclamations." Hadn't he been much the same, when first he'd discovered Sophie Winstead standing in his foyer?

For all their differences, it appeared the Seaton men had equal failings when it came to their initial encounters with the perfect Winstead beauty. And, as time had gone on— not much time, no more than a week—his father had seen Constance Winstead as more than a perfect beauty, but as someone he could love.

As Bramwell loved Sophie.

He would leave Constance and her Cesse their privacy, he'd decided as he'd quickly paged through some of the more personal pages, those recounting their blossoming love affair in all its glory, its passion—and its considerable foolishness. Constance had been a rambling sort of journalist, her sentences long, and faintly garbled. But then, since she was writing the journal for herself, he supposed it was enough that she understood what she was writing. Still, it was difficult going. In fact, after he had skimmed over nearly half of the journal, he'd been about to close it and put it away—until he'd seen his name written in Constance's lazy, looping scrawl.

Cesse came to me tonight, so happy! Bramwell was mentioned in dispatches again, with some feat of derring-do or another. He was about to burst, Cesse was, telling me yet again how proud he is of his son, his brilliant, stubborn, wonderful son who would put himself into danger, make a hero of himself just to spite his papa. I remember how unhappy he used to be when he spoke of Bramwell. I remember the first time Cesse told me what a sad failure he had been as a father. Ah, men, they are such fragile creatures.

Bramwell blinked, finding it difficult to believe what he was reading. Then, eagerly, he turned the page.

But it is not too late, I told him then. It is never too late to go to the boy, to tell him what a sad muddle those years had been, and to beg forgiveness. To take the boy in his arms, to begin again. How easy it is to make others happy, and how rewarding for someone like me to see my dearest Cesse smile and say that, yes, yes, I can do this! I love now, I know love now, and I can do this. I can risk everything, make a fool of myself if he spurns my apology. But I will have gone to him, clasped him tightly to me, and said the words. I will have taken that step so long untaken.

But the eighth duke of Selbourne had never taken that step. He had died before Bramwell's return to England. And the son had never known. Bram blinked several times, for his eyes stung. He turned the next page with trembling fingers, and read on.

Ah, since that day, the day my Cesse wept, and lamented, and finally forgave himself—how happy he has been, we have been. We plot Bramwell's course, sticking pins in a map my clever Cesse has drawn, charting each battle, saving the newspapers that tell of the events of this terrible war. There is little but storms at sea to threaten Bramwell now, so that Cesse is content to wait, knowing his son is safe, will soon be home.

Indeed, at times I tire of this talking of this paragon of a Bramwell, of the recounting of letters Cesse had from his deans, telling of the boy's brilliance at school. Of course he is brilliant! He is my beloved Cesse's son. But still we laugh, and Cesse tugs on Sophie's curls, teases her, and tells her he knows of a handsome young man—ah! the dreams my Cesse dreams! Only last night, he awoke laughing, saying he had dreamed we were at a masquerade ball together. He was dressed as a satyr, complete with tail, he told me, and I was an innocent young maid in white. Forever young and beautiful and innocent, and rather dangerously coy and flirtatious. I liked that. And then, being Cesse, he reached for me, smiling so wonderfully, so silly in his pretending to be evil, and we began to kiss, and kiss. He even nipped at my neck, like a stallion about to cover a mare, silly man, before he . . .

Bramwell closed the journal without reading on, wondering what Sophie had thought of such intimate details as she had read the journals. For an innocent, she'd had quite an education. Which, he thought, smiling in a bit of a satyric way himself, might not be all that terrible.

Then he opened the journal again, found the passage concerning himself again, and reread the entry.

* * *

"You read the journal, yes? The one *Maman* kept while she was with Uncle Cesse? I can see it in your eyes."

Bramwell lifted the hood of the black-velvet cloak Sophie wore and gently pulled it over her head. "I read it, yes. Why didn't you tell me?"

She adjusted the hood more closely over her curls. "You weren't ready to hear whatever I would have said, I suppose," she mumbled, trying not to look into his eyes. In truth, she'd wanted him to come to some sort of peace about his father on his own. Only then would it mean something for him to read her *maman*'s journal. And she had been right. Bramwell had always loved his father, and had finally admitted it to himself. She'd sensed that days ago, and been glad. Now, knowing his father had loved him in return completed the circle.

She kept her eyes averted, knowing that if she dared to look again and see what she'd believed she'd glimpsed in Bramwell's eyes a moment ago, she might just have to put her arms around him and hug him. The boy and the man, at last united; whole, complete. At last at peace with the past. Not that this idea of holding him, hugging him close, didn't have its appeal. But then she'd probably cry, and get all silly and sentimental. They had other things to do right now. Important things. Silly things. "Giuseppe!" she called out quietly but firmly. "Come here, now."

"You don't mind creeping out this side door, like a pair of thieves?" Bramwell asked as the small monkey lightly climbed down from the row of wooden pegs holding the servants' cloaks, bounded across the small hallway and into Sophie's arms. "I really should have thought of a better plan. Skulking around Mayfair in the middle of the night—it borders on the ridiculous."

"Yes, it does, doesn't it?" Sophie replied happily. "And it's only a little more than an hour past midnight, with lots more time for being even more ridiculous before dawn if we want, yes? Do you like my gown? I had to borrow one, as I own no black, being a good little debutante. It's one of Peggy's, but without the apron. Desiree had to turn up the hem a full eight inches, and still it drags a bit." She pushed back the edges of the cloak, to better show off her costume. "And, here, in the bosom, it's tight, yes?"

Biting her bottom lip to hold back a giggle was becoming an enjoyable habit, she decided as she watched Bramwell's reaction to seeing her breasts straining against the heavy black material. Lord, but she was becoming daring! But, oh, how much fun she was having. No wonder her mother had so often gone dancing about their house in Wimbledon, singing.

And didn't Bramwell look handsome! She was accustomed to seeing him in black, but not in unremitting black. "And where did you get your clothing, Bram?" she asked as he unceremoniously pulled the edges of her cloak together for her. "Reese certainly wouldn't allow anything like that in his wardrobe, and Bobbit and you aren't really of a size, are you?"

"I was in the Royal Navy, Sophie, remember? I have no end of rough-and-ready clothing, more's the pity," Bramwell grumbled as he opened the door to the small side garden and cautiously poked his head outside, as if expecting a half dozen members of the Watch to be waiting to pounce on them and drag them off to the nearest guardhouse. "And, in case you're wondering, this wool itches like the very devil at my throat, and I remember these trousers as being a good bit looser. Now, come on. It's safe to move. Sidmouth's town house is only a few blocks from here, so we can go on foot—if you can keep that damn monkey quiet."

Sophie dutifully admonished Giuseppe to stop his chattering—obviously the animal did not take kindly to being stuffed beneath her cloak—and followed Bramwell into the darkness, giving him a quick, impulsive pat-pat on his rather delightfully interesting backside as she did so. She really did like the way his trousers fit him, even if he didn't.

"Tell me more about Lord Sidmouth," she said, as they made their way toward the mews, and the alleyways that connected Portland Square with those behind Sidmouth's residence. She'd already transferred Giuseppe to her shoulder, as he refused to remain hidden beneath her cloak, and he was draped about her neck like a living shawl. "Is he really as dismally awful as *Maman* wrote in her journals?"

Bramwell took her hand to keep her from stumbling over loose cobblestones, and answered her—probably so that he could keep her from asking more questions about what he'd thought of her mother's journals. "Viscount Sidmouth is Home Secretary, Sophie," he told her, keeping his voice to a low whisper as a horse whinnied inside a nearby stable. "He's immensely unpopular, a bully, and ruthless as all—well, he's ruthless. The best one could say about him is that he's a sincere and dedicated Tory, and believe me, Sophie, that isn't much of a compliment."

"So," Sophie commented as Bramwell unexpectedly flattened her against a high wooden fence, pressing his body against hers to conceal her presence as a sleepy coachman steered his equally weary horses through the alleyway, "if he catches us out, he probably wouldn't see the humor in any of this, yes? Still, you're being terribly solemn about something that could turn out to be a most wonderful adventure. Would you like to kiss me?"

Their bodies were stuck together from knee to chest, Sophie tinglingly aware of every inch of their closeness. Which was why she had asked her question. She believed, the knowledge dawning on her slowly, but pleasurably, that she just might have the makings of being a one-man wanton, and she thought Bramwell might like to know that.

His head was mere inches from hers as he gave out a low curse, then caught her mouth with his own, the fierceness of his kiss nearly melting her dark, heavy hose to the soles of her tingling feet.

"Now, shut up," he breathed into her mouth a moment later, as her heart, temporarily stopped, began to beat again, tripping along with all the rushing speed of a galloping stallion. "What the devil was I thinking? I knew I shouldn't have brought you along."

"Oh, you might say that, Bram. But you know you wanted to," she all but purred, stroking his cheek. Giuseppe, obviously feeling a bit jealous (and perhaps a mite crushed), began loudly chattering nineteen to the dozen—which caused Bramwell to grab the animal by the throat, pull him close, and glare into his little monkey face. Giuseppe lifted a hand to his small red cap, tipped it jauntily, then puckered up his monkey lips as if offering

Bramwell a kiss. And Sophie bent in half where she stood, still holding on to Bramwell to help keep her balance, and laughed until her sides ached.

All in all, it was an enjoyable few blocks' walk to Lord Sidmouth's residence. In fact, although Bramwell grumbled about juvenile overenthusiasm and addle-headed females in general, Sophie skipped for the entire length of the last block.

He should be home. In bed. Alone. He should not have cried off from Isadora's plans to go to Lady Buxley's soiree, and been sitting in a hot, stuffy room right now, listening to some ten-thumbed creature saw away on a violin, or fracture a perfectly good tune on a piano. He should be out on the town with Lorrie and Wally, drinking too much, talking nonsense, and perhaps turning a card or two.

He should, in short, be anywhere but here, outside Lord Sidmouth's town house, skulking around in the dark and looking for an open, second-story window through which he intended to push a flea-bitten, yellow-toothed, light-fingered, less than aromatically appealing, faintly amorous monkey.

And yet . . . and yet . . . damn, but it was good to feel alive! And young. And adventurous. Breaking the rules, enjoying breaking the rules. And feeling not in the least bit betrothed, although very much in love. Although he had considered strangling Sophie more than once in the past twenty minutes. But she probably knew that. Sophie was a good girl, and a good sport. And he wanted this silliness over soon, so that he could kiss her senseless, and lose his own senses as well.

"I don't see one," Sophie whispered, treading lightly on

his right foot as she leaned in front of him, to get a better look at the darkened upper stories of the town house. "Oops, I'm sorry, Bram. You know, I just now thought of something we might have wanted to consider before this. You don't suppose Lord Sidmouth is one of those who believes the night air dangerous to one's health, do you? Because that would be unfortunate, yes?"

"It wouldn't help matters. Does Giuseppe know how to open windows? And, Sophie? I'd consider it a kindness if you'd tell him to climb down off my back. He keeps trying to pull my hair."

"Oh, don't worry about that, Bram. Giuseppe's just looking for nits," Sophie explained, holding out her arms to entice the small monkey into them.

"He's doing *what*?" Bramwell asked, much too loudly, he knew. "He's doing what?" he repeated, whispering this time, as he rubbed at the back of his head, which suddenly itched.

"Looking for nits, silly. You know. Itty-bitty baby lice eggs. Or is that louse eggs?" She shook her head, dismissing her own question. "Monkeys do that, you know. Groom each other. It's a sign of affection, I think. But don't worry, Bram. I'm sure you don't have any nits. Or louses." She looked up at him, grinning so that her nose wrinkled adorably. "Lices?"

He looked down at her dispassionately for a few moments, then declared, "I think I'll go out into the center of the Square now, and start jumping up and down and shouting. If I'm lucky, one of the Watch will come and take me away to someplace safe, like a gaol cell."

"A gaol cell? Better take Giuseppe with you then, Bram," Sophie teased. "Bound to be louses there, yes?"

Bramwell knew when he'd had enough, and he was just about there. Grabbing Sophie's hand, he daringly pulled her around to the front of Sidmouth's town house, hoping against hope that there would be one, just one, window open overlooking the Square. "Aha!" he exclaimed a moment later. "Success! Here," he said, reaching into his pocket and pulling out the snuffbox. "Give Giuseppe his climbing orders, all right?"

"Certainly," Sophie said. "Giuseppe," she went on, looking intently into the monkey's face, so that he tilted his head and returned her gaze. "I want you to take this. That's a good boy. Now, put it under your hat. Wonderful! What a good little Giuseppe you are. Now, what I want you to do next is climb up that drainpipe over there—straight up that drainpipe, yes, and then climb inside the house through that window. See the window, Giuseppe? Good! Then I want you to *put* the snuffbox on a table and come straight back to me."

The monkey made a very monkeyish face and scratched his head.

"Oh, dear," Sophie said worriedly. "I think we have a problem. He doesn't understand. Giuseppe *takes*, he doesn't *give*. How can I make him understand? Bram—quick! What's the opposite of *fetch*?"

"Newgate Prison," Bramwell drawled dryly, shaking his head. It wasn't, but that's where they'd all soon be, if Giuseppe didn't perform as hoped. The Square was quiet, totally deserted, everyone who could be out and about already gone—Lord Sidmouth, he knew, among them—and those who'd remained at home already in bed. Still, time was slipping away from them, and he couldn't be sure they wouldn't soon be spied out by someone returning home early or sneaking away from a dull party being hosted in one of the houses here in the Square.

"Very funny, Bram," Sophie said, then snapped her fingers. "I've got it!" She knelt beside Giuseppe, who was now sitting quite at his ease on the flagway, picking at his toes, and said, "Take the snuffbox into the house, Giuseppe—and bring Sophie something pretty. Something pretty for Sophie, Giuseppe, yes? Now—*go!*"

"Oh, good," Bramwell commented, seeing a fortnight or more of nights spent looking for open windows in Sidmouth's town house as Giuseppe scampered off, climbing the drainpipe as if it were a great iron tree. "But I do have one small question for you, Sophie. What do we do when he comes tripping back down here clutching Sidmouth's plans to overthrow the new king?"

"Bram! He plans to overthrow the new king? You said he wasn't a nice man, but he really plans to—" Sophie asked, wide-eyed, then slapped at Bramwell's arm. "Don't *do* that!" she commanded. "I thought you were serious."

Bramwell began to laugh, quietly, but his laughter faded away to nothing as a coach pulled into the Square, passing by the flambeaux outside one of the other houses, casting light on Viscount Sidmouth's coat of arms as it was painted on the door of the coach.

With a quick look to the open window, knowing Giuseppe was still inside the town house, he then grabbed Sophie by the upper arms and pushed her into the wrought-iron fenced stairwell leading to a belowground doorway in front of the Home Secretary's town house. She went quickly and quietly enough, bless her, and didn't even protest when he laid her flat on her back against the damp cobblestones in the small space at the bottom of the stairs. He lay down on top of her, hoping to shield her with his body.

"Not a word, Sophie," he whispered into her ear as the coach drew closer, the jingle of harness and the rattle of wheels against the cobblestones growing louder, then coming to a halt not twenty feet from where the two housebreakers lay quietly, barely breathing.

She did, however, pull on both his ears, bringing his face down to within a hairbreadth of her own as she whispered fiercely, "Giuseppe's still in there!"

"I know," he whispered back, pulling himself slightly away from her once more, hoping to hear better what he couldn't see taking place on the street level.

Still hanging on to his ears, she pulled him right back, her eyes wide-open, her expression intense, as if she longed to scream at him, but knew she couldn't. "He might even be in Sidmouth's bedchamber."

"Then I suppose we should hope Lady Sidmouth either is inside that coach, or she prefers to sleep alone," he shot back at her, trying to move away again, because he was sure he was all but smothering her. "Although, knowing Sidmouth, she might view Giuseppe as an improvement."

There was another sharp pull on his earlobes—she seemed to be unable to release them—and his head was brought back down to within an inch of hers once more. *"What?"* he demanded, beginning to tire of having his ears tugged.

"That *wasn't* funny," she gritted out from between clenched teeth. "You might think it was, but it wasn't. I just thought you should know that. And I think my left hip is broken. I hesitate to mention it, and I'm not complaining, really. But it might hamper our chances of flight, should we be discovered down here."

Bramwell slid a hand between them, automatically running his hand over her hip as he would an injured man under his command aboard ship, searching for broken bones. What he found was the small pistol he'd tucked into his pocket—just in case, he'd told himself at the time. The pistol was jammed between them, pushing into Sophie's leg.

"Sorry," he said, removing the pistol, then rubbing at her sore hipbone before drawing back his hand as he finally realized what he'd been doing. And how good it felt. How good *she* felt.

"Sophie?" he asked as he felt her body begin to shake beneath his. "I didn't mean to be so—well, so personal. I'm sorry."

"You—you're *lying* on top of me, Bram," she whispered. "What could possibly be *more* personal?" Then she buried her head against his chest, trying to snuffle the sound of her giggles. God bless the woman—she was one in a million. Perhaps one in a hundred million!

All the time they'd been lying there, and it really had only been little more than a minute, doors had been opening above them, light had spilled onto the flagway, servants had been rushing to the assistance of their master and mistress, horses had been neighing—and Lord Sidmouth had been talking. The man was a prodigious talker, Bramwell knew, but he wished the fellow would take himself, and his conversation, inside. Or maybe he didn't. Because there was still no sign of Giuseppe.

"Damnedest dull squeeze I've ever seen," Sidmouth was saying—shouting, actually—as he stood on the flagway not five feet away from the wrought-iron-enclosed stairwell. "What was Buxley's wife thinking? As if a party isn't a success if you aren't jammed in together so closely you learn more about the fellow standing behind you than anyone of any decency cares to know. Halton's either hung like a stallion, or he stuffs himself. Last time you'll get me to one of those sad crushes you favor, woman, you remember that!"

"Yes, dear," Lady Sidmouth replied much more quietly, but still close enough for Bramwell to hear the disgust in her voice. "Why don't you go directly upstairs, dear, and I'll have Ryland here bring you some warmed brandy?"

"You do that, if you can get the damned lazy lout to move above a crawl," Sidmouth said, and Bramwell, who was now struggling under much the same urge not to giggle as Sophie had been a moment earlier, listened as the sounds of His Lordship's footsteps—followed by those of at least two hovering footmen—disappeared into the bowels of the town house.

"Ryland?" Lady Sidmouth said, her voice growing louder as she climbed the portico, heading for the foyer.

"Yes, milady?"

"I wonder. Have you ever considered murdering Lord Sidmouth in his sleep?"

"Any number of times, milady."

"You're a good man, Ryland," her ladyship declared on

a sigh, her voice slowly fading as the door closed on the Square. "A good man."

Luckily for Bramwell and Sophie, who couldn't possibly have been faulted for being unable to contain their mirth, the coach loudly moved away then, heading for the mews.

"You can get off me now," Sophie said after a moment, at the same time her arms were snaking around Bramwell's back, pulling him closer.

"Yes, I know," he answered, adjusting his body slightly, moving it more comfortably against hers. "And I'll do just that," he went on, pressing his mouth against the side of her throat, her cheek, her chin. "Anytime now, I'll do just that."

Sophie ran one hand up and over his shoulder, sliding her fingers into his hair. "*Maman* and Uncle Cesse once—well, you know—behind the Horse Guards."

"I'm not my father," Bramwell said, kissing her lips lightly, once, twice, a third time. "Not that I condemn him."

"I'm not my mother," Sophie answered rather breathlessly, cupping his cheeks between her hands. "But I am curious."

"Reading isn't knowing, Sophie," he told her.

"Talking isn't showing, Bram," she replied.

Bram felt his blood running hot, even as his common sense told him Sophie had no idea as to what came next. Oh, she might *think* she did, but she didn't. Not really. And he'd be damned if he'd show her here, stuck in this damp stairwell. "This is crazy."

"I know," she admitted, sighing. "And poor Giuseppe is still inside the house."

Giuseppe! How on earth had he forgotten the monkey? Bramwell looked down at Sophie, realized his right hand had somehow come to be cupping her slim waist, and knew the answer to that question. He pulled her to her feet, then motioned for her to remain where she was until he climbed the stairs far enough to be able to peer through the wrought-iron railings, make sure the Square was empty once more.

He'd gotten to the third step from the top, Sophie close behind him, when a door opened across the Square, cutting a wedge of yellow light onto the flagway. He squinted into the distance. "Isadora?" he breathed incredulously as his fiancée appeared. Wasn't she supposed to have been at Lady Buxley's? What was she doing here? He watched as his betrothed's almost invisible maid stepped down the flagway toward a waiting coach that had somehow come into the Square without his noticing it. Isadora, however, lingered on the top step leading into the town house, talking to someone as that someone held both her hands in his.

"Lord Anston," Sophie whispered, and Bram looked down to see Sophie standing with her hands clutching two of the wrought-iron bars, the hood of her cloak thrown back to reveal her distinctive curls, her face stuck up against them. "I didn't know he lived here," she said, turning her head to smile up at Bramwell.

"Then it's the only thing you didn't know," he answered with new insight as he remembered Desiree's declaration that Sophie would take care of the "mere *bagatelle*" of his

betrothal—not because she was a scheming
benefit herself, but simply because she wanted Isado.
happy.

He looked at Sophie for another long moment as she
grinned most happily herself, obviously more than a little
pleased with what she was seeing. Then he turned his gaze
back to Isadora once more. She looked positively beautiful, animated, even from this distance. As she listened to
something Lord Anston was saying, a young girl with curling blond hair joined them on the portico and Isadora
laughed—actually appeared to be laughing out loud and
quite genuinely—then reached down and kissed the girl's
cheek.

He honestly couldn't remember ever seeing Isadora so
happy.

"Well, I'll be damned," he said, smiling—and then hit
his forehead against the metal railing as a fuzzy ball of fur
unexpectedly landed on his back with a fair degree of
force.

"Giuseppe, you're back!" Sophie squealed, grabbing the
monkey and hugging it to her. "Oh, Giuseppe, I was so
worried about you!"

"Yes," Bramwell drawled, rubbing at his sore forehead.
"We were both near to tears with fear for him, the rat-faced
little monster. In fact, I would most probably have gone
into a sad decline had he not shown up this very moment.
Does he still have the snuffbox?"

"Giuseppe," Sophie prompted. "What's in your hat?"

Bramwell held his breath as the monkey took off his little red cap, reached inside it, and pulled out, "a *pearl necklace*? Oh, my God, it is. It's a bloody pearl necklace!"

... is already safely returned. But I'd be
of that necklace for you, Your

... made jarring contact with the wrought-
... second time at the sound of the voice coming
... darkness. How hadn't he noticed that the door to
... town house had opened once more, spilling revealing,
condemning light onto the flagway, and onto both him and
Sophie? Well, he knew how. He'd been too distracted,
watching his fiancée giggling with Lord Anston, that's
how. And thinking he'd never seen anything quite so
charming, so edifying, so *freeing*.

"You'd be Ryland, wouldn't you?" Sophie asked as she
climbed all the way to the stop of the stairs, then leaned
down to rub sympathetically at Bram's abused forehead as
he remained rooted to the third step from the flagway.
"Bobbit told me about you. You're cousins, yes? Why, you
know, even in this half-light I believe I can see the family
resemblance. Something about the very fine shape of your
chins."

I'll kill her, Bramwell thought as the full import of what
had happened, what was happening, was brought home to
him. There had been no need for either of them to have
been skulking about all evening, playing at housebreakers.
A thoroughly dazzled Bobbit was firmly in Sophie's irresistible thrall, Sophie held the butler equally firmly in her
affection—and Bobbit knew Ryland. Was bloody related to
the Sidmouth butler! It would have been a simple matter
for Bobbit to hand the snuffbox to Ryland, and for Ryland
to replace it.

But it wouldn't have been half the fun.

He deposited the double strand of pearls in the butler's outstretched hand, following it with a gold coin he pulled from his pocket. "You have my thanks, Ryland," he said as the butler bowed, accepting both.

Bramwell then grabbed Sophie's elbow and began dragging her back toward the shadows . . . just as he heard a loud slamming sound above them . . . and just as Isadora's coachman turned the horses around the small Square in order to exit it, and he caught a glimpse of his betrothed sitting, wide-eyed and openmouthed, seemingly gawking at the pair of them.

After all, we're living under the same roof.
Getting me alone, day or night—anytime at all—
could hardly be more convenient, yes?
                                      —Sophie Winstead

Chapter Fourteen

It was nearly three o'clock in the morning before Sophie
had bathed, pulled an open-fronted ivory-silk dressing
gown over her creamed and powdered nakedness, and allowed Desiree to brush her hair dry as they sat together before the fireplace.

Desiree had prepared her charge for her wedding night,
and no ceremony had been performed. No promises made,
no vows spoken. Nor, Sophie felt with all her heart, were
any needed. She belonged to Bram, and he to her. They
both knew it. The words would come later, all the sweet,
loving words, the promises of forever. But she would give
him her love now, because it was her choice, and her love
was hers to give. She knew how.

Sophie wandered about the candlelit bedchamber, picking
up the odd ornament and putting it down again, stopping to
peer into a mirror and marvel yet again at the faintly dreamy
expression she couldn't seem to remove from her face.

She finally settled herself on the deep window seat that looked out over Portland Square and watched as Desiree did some last-moment fussing, poking pillows into greater fluffiness on the bed, smoothing the covers, sprinkling a scattering of rose petals on the sheets. The moon that had so considerately hidden itself behind clouds earlier in the evening now shone down brightly, turning the Square into a fairyland, the room behind her into a softly lit bower of silk and satin. The air in the room was scented from the night-soft breeze, the rose petals, the many freshly cut flowers that sat in their vases.

Sophie had gone over the events of the evening with Desiree, the two of them giggling like schoolgirls about Giuseppe's escapades, Lord Sidmouth's inopportune arrival, poor Bramwell's seeming inability to keep his head clear of the wrought-iron railing, Ryland's providential appearance to save them at the last possible moment.

It was only now, as she nervously told Desiree about Isadora Waverley's unexpected presence on the scene that Sophie turned solemn, questioning. "It's probably all for the best, Desiree," she ended consideringly. "I've known since the very beginning that she and Bram weren't suited to each other. But now I wonder. Did I throw her at Lord Anston's head to help her, or to help *me*? Because she's sure to cry off from the betrothal tomorrow."

"Ah, *chérie*," Desiree told her as she came to stand beside her charge, pushing the mass of tangled curls away from Sophie's face. "They would never have wed happily in any case. From the moment I first saw the duke watching you, I knew this. Just by being alive, by breathing, you doomed that mismatched pair to finding their own, deeper happiness. This is no sin, *oui*? This *Mademoiselle* Waverley, she would have been crushed to have the duke reject her. But now? Now he can allow her to go to her happiness, as he goes to his. You have done a good thing, Sophie. Your heart, your intentions, were pure."

"Perhaps," Sophie answered, feeling guilty heat rushing into her cheeks. "But I might also have been thinking of myself—just a little, yes?"

Desiree gave one of her most eloquent, Gallic shrugs. "This is life, *oui*? And it ends happily, even for me. It makes the heart light, to believe in love again. I did once before, you know. In Paris. *Bah!* That was long ago, and this is no night for ancient stories. It is your turn now, *chérie*. Your *maman*, she was right. I was wrong. It is the men who were wrong. Ah, but to find the right one? She did, at last, I know that now and thank *le bon Dieu* for it. And now, *ma petite*, so have you found this right man. In the end, nothing else matters, *oui*?"

Sophie sighed, pulling her knees up to her chin and hugging her legs, so that her bare feet stuck out from beneath the hem of her dressing gown. "You always know just what to say, don't you, Desiree? But I am selfish. I want him so much, love him so much. I never thought—I never knew. It's like magic, yes?"

Desiree dropped a kiss on her hair. *Oui, ma petite*, it is like magic. The only magic."

"Never to be alone. Never to be lonely. This is why I was born, Desiree. Why I'm living. To love Bram, to have him love me." She sighed again, and smiled, and laid her cheek against her knees. "I must have done something right in my life, Desiree, yes? To be so lucky?"

"It is he who is lucky, *chérie*. He had only to stop, to lift his eyes up to the skies, and the brightest star fell into his hands. The sun, the moon. Be happy, *chérie*, be very happy."

He was bathed, shaved, and dressed only in fresh hose, gray-green trousers, and a flowing white shirt, sans neck-cloth. He had done without the services of Reese, not only because he was able, but because the less the nervous valet knew, the better it would be for him. Clandestine affairs made the man nervous, and not, Bramwell knew, without good reason.

He traveled the darkened corridors on stockinged feet, turned the last corner that led to Sophie's guest chamber, and laid a hand on the door latch.

And then he stopped, reflected on what he was about to do.

Technically, he was betrothed, all but married in the eyes of the English courts, if not God. Technically, what he was about to do was to enter a virginal bedchamber and lay claim to a young woman without benefit of clergy, without promises of love, without so much as a hint of perma-nence. Technically, he was about to make—he believed, hoped, prayed—a willing Sophie Winstead his lover.

She said she'd begun to believe in love, even after all she'd seen of her mother's unhappiness. She'd even teased him unmercifully with her new opinions on love, hinting that she loved him, that she knew he loved her. She said she'd realized that not all men were like the uncles, who had broken her mother's heart, who had said they believed in love but only wished to indulge their own lust. She'd cried in happiness when she'd learned that his father had really loved her mother, had planned to spend the rest of his life with her.

And he'd been right in his own assumptions. Love *did* make fools of men. What he hadn't understood was that, with the right woman, a man could be a most willing fool, and content to be foolishly happy and well loved every day and night for as long as he lived. It had taken Sophie, silly, wise, wonderful Sophie, to teach him that.

Oh, yes. There would be tears. Perhaps even moments of anger. Ha! With Sophie's temper, how could there not be? But, beneath it all, the love would be there. The memories of laughter, the hope that the sun would shine again, the willingness to be with that one special woman, in the good times, through the sad times—for all time.

And if that one special, perfect woman came to him with a too-talkative parrot, a larcenous monkey, and a conniving maid—well, what of it? He'd take Sophie Winstead rich, poor, sick, well, dressed in diamonds or lying on damp cobblestones, pulling on his ears.

"So, the reason you're standing here, outside her bedchamber instead of being inside it with her, would be . . ." he asked himself out loud.

He depressed the latch and stepped inside, his nostrils quickly picking up the scent of flowers as well as the special light, lemon scent that he'd grown to associate with Sophie. His gut tightened. As his eyes grew accustomed to the faint light of several candles, he cast his gaze toward the windows, seeing the shafts of moonlight streaming across the carpet, the empty, turned-down bed.

Desiree, it would appear, knew her job well, as well as

she knew him. She'd known he'd come to Sophie tonight, in the ways only women probably would ever know such things. Because this was a scene purposely set for love.

And then he saw Sophie, all tucked up into herself in the deep window embrasure, her cheek resting on her knees as she looked at him. Smiled at him. Sweetly. And with a hint of mischief shining in her eyes. A world of welcome. An unabashed eagerness that slammed into his most willingly dazzled brain with the force of a cannonball.

I'm the luckiest man in the universe, Bramwell thought, moving across the room toward her as she gracefully uncoiled her body, stood in front of the window embrasure, the moonlight highlighting the curves of her body through the nearly transparent material of her wonder of a dressing gown. *So lucky to love her, to have her love me in return.*

He took her hands as she offered them to him, offered herself to him, this slight touch of skin against skin having more power to hold him than being lashed to the mast in the midst of a summer storm. She smiled again, and any fears he might have had that this was wrong, too soon, too impulsive, fled his mind in that instant, blown away on the wind of that storm that now raged inside of him.

"I don't know who you are," he said to her, his voice little more than a hoarse whisper. "You're a dream, a wish, a prayer. You're everything I didn't know I needed, yet everything I'll ever want. Every time I look at you I'm caught unawares, shaken out of what I believed to be my well-ordered life as I see the promise in your eyes. You're a dozen different women, Sophie Winstead, and I can't live without a single one of you. This is surrender, Sophie. Complete and unconditional."

"Yours, Bram?" she asked, stepping closer. "Or mine?"

"Ours," he said, lifting her hands along with his as he reached for the satin bow that held her gown in place just above the rise of her breasts. "Tell me, Sophie. Tell me we're not dreaming."

She helped him with the ribbons that seemed to have turned to knots beneath his suddenly trembling fingers, then shrugged the gown from her shoulders to stand before him, naked and glowing in the moonlight. Her tumbling curls lit with a golden glow from the streetlamp outside, her skin turned to silver as it was kissed by moonlight. "But we are dreaming, Bram, yes? A dream that will last a lifetime, beginning tonight."

Bram's gaze swept Sophie, from her soft, living curls to her small, bare feet. He took in the physical beauty of her, the stunning perfection he'd dreamed of, glimpsed before only briefly, guiltily, had been longing to possess ever since he'd first wondered how her kiss would feel.

"I love your body, Sophie," he told her, skimming his fingers across her shoulders, closing his eyes as he moved them to her breasts, felt them come alive for him, tauten, respond. "I love your hair, your face, your smile. But only because they are all a part of you. I want to make love to your body because I want, need, to make love to *you*. To make you mine. Now, forever. Do you understand, Sophie? Do you understand that this is the fullness of love? The desire, the love, they're intertwined, making a beautiful whole."

She raised her hands to the buttons of his shirt, loosing them one by one. "You talk too much," she said, smiling up at him. "You worry too much more. I understand, Bram,

I promise you. I understand. And I'm not afraid, I promise. Don't you be afraid, either. I'm a virgin, yes, but not in my mind. I read *Maman*'s journals as a child, without understanding, but now they are all clear to me. In my mind, Bram, I have made love to you so many times, and you have made sweet love to me."

She pressed a kiss against his bared chest, nipped at his skin with her teeth. "Take me to bed now, Bram. Because the time has passed for these nebulous things called dreams, yes? Dreams we cannot touch, cannot really feel? Now it is time to live them."

The candles had all guttered in their holders, but that didn't matter. The moon still shone softly into the room, spilling over the rumpled covers, the two bodies lying close together on the bed, locked in each other's arms.

"You were so brave," Bramwell said, kissing the top of her head, burying his mouth against her soft curls.

"I was so *eager*," Sophie responded with delightful honesty. "Very possibly shameless, yes?"

His low, easy chuckle rumbled deep inside his bare chest. Had he ever felt this free, this willingly chained? Had he ever been so happy? "And all without a word of love," he then said, suddenly sober once more.

"You spoke your love eloquently, Bram, without having to say a word." She pushed against his chest, raising her head to look into his face. "But you could say a few now, yes?"

"God, I love you, Sophie Winstead!" he declared, taking her cheeks in his hands and pressing his forehead against hers. "I love you, I love you, I love you. I'll tell you so every day, every hour, every minute, for the rest of our lives."

She wrinkled up her nose, as if considering his words. "So often? That should most probably be sufficient. And I'll tell you, too. I love you, Bramwell Seaton, Ninth Duke of Selbourne. I love you, I love you, I love you."

"And you'll marry me?"

Sophie smiled. "So gallant, Bram. But I think perhaps you're forgetting Miss Waverley, yes?"

Bramwell grinned wickedly, remembering Desiree's words. "Isadora? That problem is no more than a mere *bagatelle*, my darling, thanks to you and your burning desire to make all of those around you happy. Although I believe you may have had some help this time. Isadora was beginning to have second thoughts about bracketing herself to a notorious, indiscreet Seaton even before she saw us tonight. I plan to go to her first thing tomorrow morning—unless we decide to stay here in bed until noon—and graciously allow her to break my heart so that she can pursue her own happiness."

"I'm in love with such a good, kind man," Sophie said most facetiously, playfully nipping at his earlobe with her perfect white teeth.

"Yes, I am, aren't I?" he teased, running his hand along her rib cage, heading slowly, determinedly toward her perfect breasts even as she boldly, marvelously, drew her fingertips down his chest and his muscles began to ripple beneath her touch. "Sophie? Tonight was your first time. Are you sure you really want to be doing that? That we should be doing this again so soon?"

"Doing what? This?" she asked, sliding down his body

so that her head was against his chest again and she could press kisses on his rapidly heating skin, skate the tip of her tongue over his nipple. She ran her tongue down the center of his chest, dipped it into his navel, traced a small hot, moist circle on his lower belly—then suddenly withdrew, collapsing on her back beside him on the bed. "But, if you don't think we should . . ." she said sadly before shrieking in delight as he growled, then turned to cover her with his own body.

They had come together so quickly the first time, their first touch feeding fires already burning. He had kissed her, kissed her deeply, passionately, hungrily, and then lifted her high in his arms and carried her to the bed. The two of them had tumbled down onto the covers in a tangle of arms and legs and a combined, firm determination to rid Bram of his restrictive clothing as quickly as possible.

His hands had skimmed her, learned her quickly, as her perfection had already been indelibly branded into his brain. He had felt her tremble under his touch even as she had touched him in return, holding him to her almost feverishly, telling him with her hands, her mouth, that this was no time for long seductions. They had been seducing each other since that first day, that first mind-shattering meeting of their eyes.

Only as he had moved to enter her, easing her legs open so that he could bury himself in her, fill her, had he been at all gentle. And even then the gentleness had not lasted for a moment longer than it had taken for his mind to understand that she was ready for him. She had been wonderfully moist and gloriously hot; magnificently tight, and yet pushing herself against him, lifting herself to him, silently urging him on to what had been a shattering explosion of passion that had left them both shaking, silent, amazed.

But now, ah, but now there was time for more. Time for long, leisurely lovemaking. Time to begin teaching her more of what she'd thought she'd known, what she'd read about in her mother's amazingly frank journals, but had never experienced. Time to savor, to enjoy, to worship this woman he loved with his body, his mind, his entire being.

He moved his mouth against hers, teaching her the many mysteries of the kiss. She was an avid pupil. "This is love," he told her between long, drugging kisses. "This is desire so intense it shatters me, humbles me. This is all I am, all I can give to you, want from you. Your closeness, your kiss, your love."

"This is love," she whispered, holding him tightly, as if she would never let him go. "This is desire born of love. There's nothing else I'll ever want, ever need."

He smiled against her mouth, all at once rather happily evil. Oh, how much she supposed, his darling Sophie. How little she still knew.

He wanted to kiss her, kiss her everywhere. He didn't know where to start. At the top of her warm, living mass of curls, or at the soles of her small feet. He wanted to say what could never be said in words, not even by the most eloquent man ever born. He wanted to love her, cherish her, adore her, drive her wild with the ultimate carnal splendor that, he now knew, could only be reached in the arms of true love.

Because this was not lust. This was not a temporary indulgence of need, a selfish taking. This was giving, as he'd never before known he could want to give. He would worship her with his body, even as he loved her with his heart, his mind.

He began moving down the length of her. Leisurely— each move excruciatingly slow, intense, adoring. He savored her sweet perfection. So deceivingly slim, so small. And yet so voluptuous. The fullness of her breasts. The soft mound of her belly. The luxuriant sweep of her hips. Everything about her was soft, womanly. Lush. She was a woman born to love, born to be loved.

He could have wept, so intense was his love, his need to show that love. He would go anywhere, dare anything, just to be near her, just to hear the sound of his name on her lips. To see her smile. To watch as she teased, as she played, as she opened her heart to the world and spread her unique joy, wove her special magic. Dazzled.

She was silk. She was fire. She was his everything.

He found the heart of her sexuality. Claimed it. Worshiped her with his fingers, his tongue, his teeth, his mouth. So sweet. So sweet.

Her voice came to him through the swirling mist of his intense desire. "Bram?" she whispered softly. "Before . . . I thought that before . . . that at last I knew. Understood. But *this* . . . this is so different. I feel so . . . so—oh, Bram!"

He knew what she meant. Before . . . the first time . . . she had been pleasured. But now she was at last beginning to feel the full measure of desire. Her hips rose from the bed as he ministered to her, educated her, brought her to the brink, took her over, held her as she shattered. She flowed into him, moved against him, free and uninhibited, her trust in him so complete he was awed by it. Humbled.

And when she reached for him, her beautiful face glowing with love, with new understanding, with a desire that matched his own, he went to her willingly, eagerly, and marveled as she shyly, then boldly, demonstrated all that she had just learned.

A man's body was quite an interesting construction of nature. Hard where hers was soft. Flat where hers was rounded. There were ropes of muscle across the shoulders, running down the arms, repeated in the long, straight legs. A soft, tickling brush of hair on the firm but yet still welcoming expanse of chest Sophie had claimed as her own personal pillow.

Bramwell's heart beat so slowly, almost leisurely in his sleep. But she had heard it race, gallop along at a furious pace. She had pressed kisses against his pulse points, smiling against his skin as she'd known that she had a lot to do with his rapid heartbeat, his shallow breathing, the sheen of perspiration that had made his skin slick, almost feverish beneath her boldly investigating hands.

Sophie snuggled more closely against this man she loved, her body deliciously aware even as she could not ignore the slight soreness between her thighs. Even that *petite* pain was pleasurable.

She shouldn't disturb him, although the rising sun had replaced the moon, and the house around them was coming awake. Desiree would keep the household at bay—the maid who would want to clear the grate, the footman who daily brought her hot water for her bath. . . .

Her bath? Sophie smiled. She'd like to bathe with Bramwell. Yes, that would be lovely. But not here, not in some small tub. In the countryside. A small, rippling stream, with the sun filtering down on them through a canopy of trees. Birdsong all around them. The scent of wildflowers coming to them on the breeze as, with their bodies cooled by the water, heated with desire, he could place her on the grassy bank and . . .

"Bram?" she whispered, threading her fingers into the curls on his chest.

He sighed in his sleep, pulling her more closely against him, his eyes still closed.

"Oh . . . Bram-*ammm* . . ." she repeated, turning slightly so that she could run her tongue over his nipple, feel it harden, come to attention. She slid her hand down over his flat stomach, then lower, to run her fingertips teasingly across the top of his thighs. She felt the ripple as his muscles tensed in response.

"You want to kill me, don't you?" he asked, still not opening his eyes.

Sophie giggled, then levered herself upward so that she could all but fling herself on top of him, sliding her hands around his upper back as she showered his face with a dozen light kisses. "I love you, I love you, I love you!" she exclaimed happily—then blew into his ear, nipped his earlobe, slid her tongue down the side of his throat, to the pulse point that now pounded there with all the fury of a galloping stallion.

"You were right last night, Sophie. You're shameless!" he told her, levering her over onto her back, tickling her mercilessly, until she dissolved in helpless giggles.

"I am, I am. I admit it. I'm utterly shameless," she told him, wriggling to get away from his hands. "I'll admit to anything, if you just stop that. I *hate* being tickled!"

His hands stilled at either side of her waist, still touching her sensitive skin, as if to warn that he could begin tickling her again at any moment. "Ah," he said, grinning down at her, his eyes burning with mischief. "So now we have it. Sophie Winstead is shameless. She's also a flirt and a tease, yes?"

Sophie hesitated for only a moment, but it was long enough for Bramwell to flick a single finger against her skin, starting off another ripple of sensitivity. "Yes, I confess. I'm a shameless flirt and a most dreadful tease."

"And not necessarily always honest," he pressed on, looking entirely adorable as his hair tumbled onto his forehead. She reached up to run her fingers over the darkened stubble on his chin. Part man, part boy, completely adorable.

"I was honest enough to warn you not to believe yourself to be in love with me," she pointed out, then frowned. "Thank heavens you had the good sense not to listen to me."

"I couldn't listen to you, Sophie. I was much too occupied with falling in love with you, and hating you because I couldn't help making a fool of myself."

"Poor darling," Sophie said commiseratingly, stroking his beard-roughened cheek. "And do you still feel so foolish?"

His smile was positively evil. "I suppose I'll become accustomed to the feeling, eventually," he said, then kissed her. "And you'll become accustomed to the notion that I'll still love you most foolishly fifty years after I'm dead? You'll believe that?"

Sophie's bottom lip began to tremble. Not because she knew a beautiful woman's tears had the power to dazzle, but because she loved this man so much that her heart ached with that love. "What a pair of fools we are, Bram," she said, then took a deep breath, steadying herself. "No. That's not true! The only fools are those who refuse to believe in love, yes? I feel so sorry for them, knowing they must be so unhappy. I do so hate to see anyone sad."

Bramwell rolled his eyes comically, then twisted himself over onto his back, so that Sophie was lying on him from chest to knee. "You're going to try to make everyone else happy, aren't you? Everyone in the whole, sad world. Don't bother to deny it, Sophie, because I think I can see through your inventive twists and diversions now. In this short time, you've made Aunt Gwen happy, Wally, Sad Samuel, Isadora, me. Who else? Come on, Sophie, tell me the truth."

"The truth? About what?" Sophie was enjoying this game. "But, darling, I'm nearly always truthful. I've certainly always been truthful with you. And—and honest. Truly!"

"Really," he said, his lips twitching as he did his best to look stern—which was probably quite a difficult feat, seeing as how she had begun to move her lower body against his, and could feel how quickly his attention was turning from thoughts of confession to those of seduction. "And I suppose you consider forging my late father's name to some official-looking document meant to have me take you under my roof and help you to have a Season to be *honest*?"

She sat up abruptly, still spanning his body, and he winced in his unexpected discomfort. "You *know* about that?" she asked, truly shocked. "You *know*, and yet you still love me?"

"Yes, I know. I knew. And I still love you. I've told you so, haven't I? I love you even more because you're not quite as perfect as I'd believed—although I'll admit you're as close to perfect as I could have dreamed. But, Sophie? I'd love you even more if you'd move your left leg just slightly to the left—ah, that's better. I mean, you do want us to have children someday, don't you?"

Sophie shifted her weight on him, feeling herself begin to blush as he raised up his hands and cupped her perfect breasts in his palms. She slapped his hands away. "Don't distract me!" she ordered, looking down at him intently. "When did you know that Desiree had made that silly letter up out of whole cloth?"

"When were you going to tell me that she did?" he asked in return.

Her smile began slowly, grew wide. "When we were both very, very old? When you were positively ancient, and perhaps as deaf as Mrs. Farraday, and I could whisper it so that you couldn't hear? Never? After all, I'm going to be a duchess now, and very proper and circumspect. The past, at least bits of it, should rest in the past. A woman, even a duchess, should have *some* secrets, yes?"

"Then you really weren't ever going to tell me?"

Sophie took in a long breath, let it out slowly. "To be honest, Bram? No, I wasn't going to tell you. At first, because I was afraid, and now because it simply doesn't matter, does it? There was no reason to make you unhappy."

He pushed himself up on his elbows and motioned for her to move away from him. "Find a dressing gown, Sophie—one I can't see through, please—and put it on," he said as he sat up. "We need to talk, and I think we'd better both have clothes on while we're about it. All right?"

She did as he asked, locating a more modest dressing gown in the cupboard, and slipped her arms into the sleeves. She ran her fingers through her hair, pushing the riot of curls out of her face, and looked at Bramwell as he stepped into his trousers, buttoned them.

"Would you like a glass of water?" she asked, starting toward the pitcher on the dressing table. "It's warm, from last night, but—"

"Sophie—*sit!*" Bramwell commanded, coming around the bed, taking hold of her shoulders. He steered her backward until the backs of her knees came into contact with the chaise longue, at which point he pushed her down, then sat beside her, taking her hands in his. "Sophie, listen to me. I don't want a drink of water. I don't want a glass of wine, or for you to fetch me a footstool, or try to anticipate my every need. I don't want you to light my cheroot—unless you really want to. I don't want you to do *anything* you don't truly, honestly, sincerely want to do. Not to please me. Do you understand that?"

"But, *Maman* always said—"

"I *know* what *Maman* always said," he interrupted. "God knows I've already *read* enough of what your *maman* thought was the way to interest, please, and hold a man—that was what she was writing about, Sophie. You do know

that, don't you? How to flirt, how to tease, how to ingratiate yourself, how to *dazzle*?"

"Well, yes, but—"

"No interruptions right now, Sophie, please. I love you.
We've established that, I think."

She nodded, beginning to understand what he was trying
to say, and loving him all the more for how difficult he was
finding his explanation.

"All right. Trying to make me happy, make the world
happy, falls into the same harebrained category. You are
not responsible for the world's happiness. Yes, you might
like to see those around you happy. That's commendable,
truly. But it's not your *responsibility*. And if you think
that telling me about the letter Desiree concocted, or that
you bought a dozen bonnets when one would have done
as well, or that you think my new jacket is a truly putrid
shade of green or anything at all unpleasant is something
to be avoided, then you'd be wrong. I want to marry you,
Sophie, have you with me always and forever. Not to
cushion my life, but to fill it, complete it. I won't go away
if you don't please me every moment of every day. Your
mother might have thought that, about the uncles, but it
isn't true. They left because they'd never intended to
stay."

"But you're staying?"

"Try to get rid of me, Sophie," he said, drawing her
against his shoulder. "I promise you, you won't succeed."

She pushed back her head, looking up into his face.
"Even if I still get angry sometimes, and shrewish, and
throw things? You still wouldn't leave me?"

"Only if your aim improves, darling."

"Oh. My aim is terrible when I'm angry, I know," she said, grimacing. "I can barely hit a wall with a book. It's a failing, yes?"

"Idiot that I am, Sophie, I find it to be a fairly adorable failing," he said, kissing the tip of her nose.

She snuggled against his shoulder. "All right, Bram," she said, yawning into her hand. "I think I understand now. In fact, I know I do. I will please you when I want to, and won't when I don't, yes? I will be honest, even when being honest couldn't possibly make you happy, and I will not be—*am* not—responsible for making the whole world happy. Now, if that's all settled—are you hungry, darling?"

"Well, yes, thank you. As a matter of fact I am," he answered, kissing the top of her head before she slid out of his arms and stood up, looking down at him.

He'd begun to believe he knew everything about her. But it seemed that he'd missed the flash of mischief in her eyes just now, just before she turned away from him.

"Well, then, Your Grace," she said, skipping over to bounce herself up and onto the bed, "why don't you just pick yourself up, take yourself over to the bell pull, and summon someone to bring your breakfast? Lord knows you must remember how."

"Minx!" he charged, his voice full of laughter as he leapt to his feet and followed her to the bed. "Never listen to me again, Sophie—promise me," he said, turning her onto her back as his hand found its way inside the opening of her dressing gown. "Now, come here, woman, and *dazzle* me."

Upon hearing her beloved Sophie's delighted giggles, Desiree, who had been standing guard just outside the bedchamber for the past hour, shook her head and gently shooed away a young maid heading down the hallway toward the room. "You're too young for this, *petite*," she warned kindly, then closed her eyes and smiled.

My dear, my dear, you never know when
any beautiful young lady may not
blossom into a Duchess!
    —Maria, Marchioness of Ailesbury

Chapter Fifteen

Bramwell walked into the drawing room and planted a kiss on his aunt's cheek on his way to the drinks table, offering to pour her a glass of wine.

"I don't really imbibe this early in the day—is that the correct word, dear? Imbibe? But I will say that you look rather happy. No, more than happy. You're positively glowing."

Bram frowned. "Well, that's not good, is it?" he asked, winking at Lady Gwendolyn. "I think I should be looking guilty, and quite sad."

His aunt put down Mrs. Farraday's yarn—the ball of soft yellow wool she had been about to stuff up her sleeve—and turned to look at her nephew. "I don't understand. Why should you be looking guilty? I was the one who read the journals, and then told Amelia Crossley that business abut that MacLeish person and Constance Winstead. But that's all I said, I promise you that! I've racked my brain, and racked it again, and I'm sure that's all I said." She spread her hands, as if loosing a captured pigeon to the skies. "And the rest of it I've ordered to simply *fly* out of my mind!"

"I can't tell you how that gratifies me, Aunt," Bramwell said, sipping from his glass. "However, if you don't want to have to forget something else, you might want to find something to do in the morning room or elsewhere for a while. Isadora wrote in her note that she'd be here now, saving me a trip to Mount Street, and her coach just drew up out front. I think our conversation should remain private."

Lady Gwendolyn nodded. "Yes, dear. Desiree already told me. You're going to let her toss you over even though you really want to throw her away." Both hands flew up to cover her mouth as her eyes grew wide and panicked. "Did I say that? I didn't mean to say that. That is, I mean that I didn't mean for you to know that I knew that, and that I knew that I shouldn't say . . . well, *that*. Not that I know *that*. Or should. I mean. That is. Um. Oh, what *do* I mean? Bramwell, don't just stand there, laughing at me—*help* me!"

Bramwell helped his aunt to her feet, figuring that was as good a place to start as any. "It's all right. I know just what you mean, Aunt," he said soothingly, all the time guiding her toward the door. "But we will have to have a few more conversations on the subject of discretion, I believe."

"Oh, my goodness, yes! I really think we should. Definitely." The knocker went, and Lady Gwendolyn all but up jumped out of her skin as she picked up her skirts and headed for the staircase leading to the bedchambers. "I'm gone, I'm gone! Bobbit—" she called out, leaning over the railing in order to see down into the foyer, "don't you dare move one step toward that door until I'm gone!" Then she paused on the first step, her hand on the newel post, and turned to Bramwell. "I like your smile, Nephew. It's good to see it."

"Thank you, Aunt Gwen," he told her departing back, then started toward the door to the drawing room, motioning for Bobbit, standing below in the foyer, to answer the knock.

He counted to twenty, then stepped out into the hallway once more, just as Isadora was climbing the last stair to the first floor, her abigail left behind in the foyer. Obviously this was going to be a very brief visit.

"Selbourne," Isadora said, her voice more clipped than usual. She inclined her head slightly as he bowed over her hand, his lips missing her gloved fingers by a good inch or more. "We must talk."

"I know," he answered, leading her toward the nearest couch, then sitting down beside her. "I had wanted to come to you, but I had other business to attend to first, I'm afraid. However, before we begin, I have to tell you that it was entirely my fault. Sophie had absolutely nothing to do with anything. It was—"

"Sophie? Selbourne, stop, you're confusing me. What does Miss Winstead have to do with anything? And you really shouldn't be so informal, referring to her by her Christian name."

Isadora stripped off her gloves, a precise pull on each of her fingertips, one after the other, accomplishing the feat with admirable grace. "Lud, I don't know when I've been this nervous, upset. Charles wanted to come here with me, but I refused, of course. This is my burden, I told him, and I must carry it alone. It's the Waverley way."

She laid her gloves in her lap and looked at Bramwell, her eyes eloquent with a message he was damned if he could read. "Selbourne, I have done you a great disservice, and I cannot, therefore, in good conscience marry you. There! I've said it. Lud, that was difficult!"

Bramwell's mind was all but stumbling over itself in its rush to understand what in the devil Isadora was saying. *She* had done *him* a great disservice? "Isadora, I'm sorry," he said, seeing that her usually alabaster cheeks were chalk white, that her bottom lip had begun to tremble. Not that she would cry. Lord, no. Waverleys didn't cry. "You're obviously overset, Isadora. It's I who owe you my deepest apologies."

But she wouldn't let him speak, seemed determined not to let him speak. "Lud, Selbourne! *You*, apologize to *me*? When I felt my heart leap in my breast when I'd learned you wanted to cry off from Lady Buxley's party last night, leave me with my evening free to make . . . to make . . . lud! To make a fool of you, Selbourne. There is no way to dress this up in clean linen. I *betrayed* you, Selbourne. Lud, I'm such a wretched, wretched woman!"

Bramwell opened his mouth to correct her, to say that it was he, not she, who should be begging forgiveness. But then it dawned on him. All at once a blinding flash of lightning lit up the entire world, and he saw, he understood. Isadora had decided how this interview would go, and he would be a cad not to allow it, even if he didn't understand it.

"How did you betray me last night, Isadora?" he asked quietly, fishing in his pocket for his handkerchief. For he'd been wrong. Waverleys did cry. At least this one did.

Isadora wiped at her eyes, blew her nose, then went to return the handkerchief, which Bramwell smilingly refused to accept. "I—I had been having second—second thoughts. For *days*. Horrible thoughts. Unworthy of a duchess, of your duchess. I was ashamed, Selbourne. If I had loved you—if you had meant the world and all to me, I should have survived it. The gossip, the old scandal that reached out to touch me wherever I turned."

She needed to resort to the handkerchief again, as her nose had begun to run in earnest now. It was rather wonderful, though, seeing Isadora as a real woman, and not just as the perfect wife for a duke, which was how he'd previously seen her. She leaned toward him, looking at him earnestly. "Do you love me, Selbourne? I don't think you do."

He leaned forward and kissed her damp cheek. "You're right, Isadora. I don't love you. But I'm finding that I *like* you much more than I would have believed a week ago. But you love someone, don't you? Do you want to tell me about him? I believe you mentioned someone named Charles?"

For the following ten minutes Bramwell's only function was to serve as a willing pair of ears while Isadora spoke of Lord Charles Anston and his daughters, Sarah, Mary, Lucy, and Ruth something-or-other. How kind Charles was, how she'd remembered him so fondly from years ago, how they'd met unexpectedly after she'd seen him come to visit Miss Winstead, and how their friendship had blossomed again almost immediately. How wonderfully polite and pretty the daughters were, how very much she was needed by them, would find her utmost happiness as their friend, their mentor, their mother.

It was all settled. She and Charles—and the girls, of course—would drive down to meet with Isadora's father. They were leaving London that very afternoon, in less than an hour. They would then be wed in the family chapel before retiring to Lord Anston's estate in the country until next Season, when Sarah—or was it Lucy? Bramwell was having trouble keeping the four names and various ages straight—would come to London to be presented. Everything was wonderful. Everything was settled.

Except that Isadora was still betrothed to Bramwell.

That part was still presenting just a smidgen of a problem. . . .

"Then, Isadora," Bramwell ventured at last, wondering why he felt it necessary to ask, "you didn't see me out and about last night?"

"See you?" she repeated, her frown warning him to silence. "I don't know to what you are referring. See you *where*, Selbourne? I told you. I was visiting with Charles and the girls. It was very proper, but very private. I didn't see anybody, barely another soul all evening. Everyone was at Lady Buxley's you know. I've already heard it was a sad crush—extremely successful. But, now that you mention it, I did see something very strange as I was being driven away from Charles's town house."

It was all a game. They were playing a game Isadora had devised for some reason he'd probably have to have Sophie explain to him, and it was his turn to move a piece. "What did you see, Isadora?"

"Well, lud," she supplied quickly, "it was the strangest thing. The coachman turned through the Square, the better to exit it, I suppose, as Charles's town house is quite near the entrance. And, while he was driving around the Square, directly as we were passing by Lord Sidmouth's residence—well, lud, Selbourne, you just won't believe it, that's all."

Bramwell's smile was stuck to his face; he couldn't unstick it even if he tried. "I won't?"

Isadora lowered her voice to a whisper. "It was Lord Sidmouth himself. Standing directly in front of one of the upstairs windows—and without a stitch of clothing on! He was standing there, and then he slammed down the window. Very angrily, I'd say, as if he wasn't pleased to have found it open. I imagine one of his servants must have done it against his orders, or some such thing. Now, don't you think that strange?"

"That he'd be naked, Isadora, or that he'd close his own window?" Bramwell asked, relaxing as he remembered that there had been a loud sound from somewhere above him just as he'd dragged Sophie into the shadows.

"Lud, Selbourne—that's *so* funny!" Isadora exclaimed, giving him a playful rap on the wrist with her gloves as she stood, clearly relieved that their interview had gone so well, that he had been so cooperative. She reached into her reticule and handed him the Seaton family ring, a most imposing ruby. "Here, Selbourne. I was honored to wear this, but I find that I will be even more happy being Lady Anston than I could ever have been as the duchess of Selbourne. Lud—that was rather insulting, wasn't it? I didn't mean it that way, truly. I don't know if I'm on my head or my heels since I found my dear Charles again. We just talked and talked—for hours! Oh, please, forgive me. Forgive me for everything. And say good-bye to Sophie for me, please. I owe her so much."

"You do?" Bramwell asked, slipping the ring into his pocket, knowing that it would not be the one he'd give to Sophie. Sophie should have diamonds. And sapphires. And emeralds. And, perhaps, rubies. He'd have this particular one made into a necklace. Yes, that would suit her. He shook himself back to attention, believing that Isadora had just given him a clue to the reason behind her generous action. "What do you owe Sophie, Isadora?"

"My thanks, Selbourne, my deepest, most heartfelt thanks. Poor Selbourne, you don't understand, do you? But I do, and Sophie will, and that's enough."

Bramwell nodded his agreement to forward Isadora's thanks to Sophie, then snapped to attention as his now-former fiancée pulled on her gloves once more, saying briskly, "You'll allow my father to handle the notice in the newspapers, of course, and graciously accept all blame for the termination of our engagement. Papa will be as vague as he can possibly be, but the *ton* will all know why I've rejected our marriage. Or at least they'll think they do. They'll blame it on your father, and Miss Winstead's mother. They'll say I was appalled by the gossip and such. That's unfortunate, but unavoidable. And then, as I'll be married shortly, there will be the rumors that I had actually jilted you for another. But it can't be helped, can it? You're a good man, Selbourne, and I can only ask you to be brave. For your sake, for Sophie's. I'm eternally in her debt. Be brave for her."

"I'll do my best to help Sophie weather the storm, Isadora." Bramwell bowed over her hand, feeling as if he should have a medal hanging from his chest after being given such a bracing round of congratulations for having excelled in a battle he'd yet to fight. Isadora would have made a fine general. And he would wager she'd make a finer, if somewhat stern, mother. Little Ruth something-or-other and her sisters had better learn to step sprightly.

"I'll walk you to your coach," he said, not seeing, but still sensing that Sophie was somewhere above their heads, hanging over the second-floor railing, hearing every word.

"No need, Selbourne," Isadora said. She surprised him down to his toes by leaning forward and kissing him on the cheek, then holding on to his shoulders, remaining close. "She's up there, Selbourne, so don't look," she whispered into his ear. "I want you to know that I wish you both as much happiness as I've found with Charles. Lud, you're so well suited to each other. She'll make a fine, if rather original duchess. And I'll be a good mother, I really will. Just please allow me to be first to the altar? Oh, and someday you must tell me what the two of you were doing at Lord Sidmouth's. But not now. Good-bye—Bramwell."

"Good-bye, Isadora," he said, his admiration for the women in his world growing by leaps and bounds. "And thank you."

Bobbit ushered Lord Upchurch into the drawing room directly after dinner, the man brushing past him almost before he could be announced.

"I've got terrible news!" Lord Upchurch exclaimed, going directly to Bramwell, who had been amusing himself by kissing Sophie's fingertips, one after the other, as Sophie giggled and his aunt looked on in a delicious mixture of shock and pleasure at seeing her nephew so happy.

"So do I, Upchurch," Bramwell said affably. "I know you have a mole shaped much like Lord Sheridan's profile stuck to your—"

"Bram!" Sophie protested, jumping up to take Lord Upchurch's arm and lead him to a nearby chair. "You just sit down now, my lord, and allow me to pour you some brandy. You look wretched."

"Well, I *am* wretched, you know. Can't remember when I've been this wretched. Except perhaps for that time I was cold and wet after being caught out in a rainstorm, and backed up too close to the fire to warm m'self and—no, no! I can't think of that now. It's Sir Tyler, Selbourne. The journal wasn't enough for him."

"It wasn't?" Sophie turned from the drinks table, the snifter of brandy in her hand. "But His Grace met with you all this afternoon, showed you the journals *Maman* had kept on each of you, and then you all threw them into the fire, yes? You have His Grace's word, my word—the past is gone, burned up and forgotten. I must say, my lord, that I'm sadly disappointed if you're intimating that the duke of Selbourne's word in the matter cannot be taken as gospel."

There. She'd sounded quite duchesslike. Sophie was rather proud of herself, and Aunt Gwendolyn was smiling at her, as if she, too, was pleased. This being a duchess couldn't be all that difficult. A "Your Grace" here, another "Your Grace" there. Sprinkle a few "the duke feels," or "the duke says" into the conversation, and keep your chin high as you did it. Nothing could be more simple. She'd learned a lot from Isadora, more than she had realized. And she was going to do just fine. It was all a matter of dazzling others, this time with what was soon to be her most impressive title.

"But it's not *me* saying it, Sophie . . . er . . . Miss Winstead," Lord Upchurch protested. It was obvious that, even in his agitation, he had noticed her new air of superiority, of consequence. "I'm quite content with the way things worked out. Satisfied, you know. But it's just as I said. Tye—Sir Tyler? He's up to mischief."

Sophie looked to Bramwell, who was eyeing Lord Upchurch carefully. "Sir Tyler," he said. "Yes, you did say that, didn't you? Not Lord Buxley, and not you. Just him?"

"Exactly! Oh, Your Grace, he's impossible to calm. He wanted Buxley and me in with him, but we won't go that route. Discussed it between ourselves, you know, and decided against it. But I thought I should warn you."

"This is all my fault, Bramwell," Lady Gwendolyn lamented, wringing her hands. "If I hadn't said anything to Amelia—"

"Hush, Aunt Gwendolyn," Sophie said soothingly, dropping to her knees beside the older woman, patting her hands. "Lord Upchurch can't be the least interested in that right now," she went on quietly, hoping the woman took her meaning. The journals had been burned. Buxley and Upchurch seemed satisfied. But, if they knew Lady Gwendolyn had read them? Well, they'd be all for tossing her into the fire along with the journals then, wouldn't they?

Bramwell must have been thinking much the same thing, as he quickly said, "Thank you, Upchurch, for coming to me so quickly, being so honest. Did Sir Tyler share his plans with you, or are you only aware that he intends some sort of retribution?"

Lord Upchurch looked confused for a moment, as if he was trying to sift all the words through his brain, sort them out into smaller ones he might better understand. "Oh!" he said at last. "You want to know what Tye plans to do, don't you?"

"No, Upchurch, I don't, actually," Bramwell said, something in his tone alerting Sophie to the fact that nothing Lord Upchurch had said had come as a surprise to him. "But, out of idle curiosity, I'll ask anyway. Do you or Lord Buxley know what Sir Tyler Shipley has planned?"

The older man shook his head and sighed. "Haven't the faintest idea. He asked us, we said no, and he went off. Madder than fire, you know. Always was a bit of a hot-head." He looked to Sophie. "But I felt I should warn you. Always liked your mama, you know. Wouldn't want to see anything bad happen to the daughter."

Bramwell removed the snifter from Upchurch's nerve-less fingers even as he laid an arm across the man's shoulders and maneuvered him toward the hallway. "Assure yourself, Upchurch, that you have my most sincere appreciation for having come here tonight. But I believe I can take it from here, all right?"

Lord Upchurch looked back over his shoulder, to Lady Gwendolyn, who was waving good-bye to him, to Sophie, who smiled and gave him one of her very best shrugs. "Well, if you think so, Selbourne—Your Grace. But, I—"

"Bobbit," Bramwell broke in. "His Lordship was just leaving. Has Baron Lorimar arrived as yet?"

"Just now, Your Grace," the butler answered. "He and Sir Wallace await you in your study."

Bramwell gave Lord Upchurch a last bracing pat on the back, then stepped back into the drawing room. "Sophie? If you'd join us . . ."

"What's happening, Sophie?" Lady Gwendolyn asked, grabbing on to Sophie's forearm, detaining her. "Something is going on, isn't it?" She released her grip. "But, no, no. I shouldn't ask. If I don't ask, I won't know. And if I don't know, I can't tell. It will be better that way, I believe. Much better. You just run along, dear. I'll sit here and yell to Mrs. Farraday, ask her opinion on the weather. And then she'll tell me all about her new heather-colored yarn. Again."

Sophie dropped a kiss on Lady Gwendolyn's hair, then quickly followed after Bramwell, taking his arm as he assisted her down the stairs. "You've done something, haven't you, Bram? What have you done? You told me that taking the journals to the uncles this afternoon would fix everything, and it did—for two of them. But not Uncle Tye, yes? So what did you do? And why haven't you told me about it?"

"I was a trifle busy, darling," he answered, as they turned the corner at the bottom of the stairs and headed toward his private study. "Making love, losing a fiancée, gaining another, burning books—it made for a full afternoon. And I barely slept last night, you know. Why, I'm surprised I didn't fall facedown in the pudding at dinner."

"You're a mean, mean man, Bramwell Seaton," Sophie

declared, glaring at him through slitted eyes. "You were simply protecting me. Admit it!"

"Protecting *you*?" Bramwell threw back his head and laughed out loud. "Protecting the woman who thinks it her responsibility to fix everything, to make everyone happy, to solve all the problems of the world? Hardly, darling. I was protecting *myself*. Now, let's see what Wally and Lorrie have been able to find out, all right?"

"Lorrie and—oh, never mind," Sophie said, sighing. "*Maman* always said we women must sometimes allow our men to be masterful."

"God bless her," Bramwell responded, then gave her a quick kiss on the cheek before opening the door to his study. "Gentlemen!" he called out happily enough. "How went the hunt? Was I right? Please tell me I was right. I'd enjoy appearing brilliant in front of my darling, soon-to-be-wife."

"Probably owe Bobbit a packet for that one," Sir Wallace commented. "That, and you have to become Sad Samuel's bosom chum for—what was it, Lorrie? A month?"

"Why, Sir Wallace," Sophie trilled, batting her eyelashes at him. "Whatever do you mean? It almost sounds as if you've made some sort of *wager* among yourselves, yes?"

Sir Wallace slapped his forehead so hard he winced. "I'm a dead man! Lorrie, shoot me. Make it quick. Painless."

"Relax, Wally," Bramwell said, escorting Sophie to a chair, then taking up his place behind the desk. "She knows. She has known from the beginning. And, now that I think about it, you might want to shoot Lorrie. Thanks to him and his schemes, you're probably the poorer by several hundred pounds."

"Later, Wally, later," the baron said as Sir Wallace turned to him questioningly. "For now, I think I should answer Bram's question. Yes, my friend. You were right. Straight down the line. And Shipley has seen the advantages in accepting your conditions with all the civility with which a man fairly foaming at the mouth is capable."

"So it's over then, before it could even begin. Good, as the whole notion of what he must have been planning was fairly ridiculous. You both have my thanks. Would you two care for a drink?"

"Over? What's over? What was Sir Tyler planning to do?" Sophie had spent the last moments looking from Bramwell, to the baron, to Sir Wallace, back to Bramwell—and she didn't understand anything she'd heard, seen. "Bram, I think I really must insist—"

"We'll have that drink later, Bram," Baron Lorimar said, winking at Sophie. "I think you two should have some time alone. Wally? Stand up, we're leaving."

"But—but we just got here, Lorrie! We haven't even said our best wishes to Sophie here, or Bram. We really ought to do that, you know. Only polite. Condolences first, to Bram, for having been tossed over, then congratulations, for getting Sophie here to say she'll marry him. It's only right."

"Wally," Bramwell said threateningly.

"Come here, sit down. Say three words, stand up. Leave." Sir Wallace threw up his hands and got to his feet. "All right, Bram, I'm going. Don't have a dashed idea why, but I'm going. Good evening, Sophie. Are you sure you want to marry Bram, here? You'll have the devil of a time understanding him, stap me if you won't!"

Sophie jumped up to kiss both the two departing gentlemen, not sure what they had done for her, but convinced they had just made her future brighter. Then, once they were gone, she turned on the man she would share that future with, and said, "You have five minutes, Bram. Then I may simply have to strangle the truth out of you."

"What, no offer to light my cheroot?" Bramwell replied smoothly. "You aren't about to pour me a glass of wine, fetch me a footstool, rub my weary brow? Isn't that the way to get what you want from a man? Well, I'm disappointed, I must say so."

"Bramwell . . ." Sophie ground out from between clenched teeth, doing her best to look threatening, then gave it up as a bad job and ran around the desk to all but throw herself in his lap. "What did you do, darling? What brilliant, wonderful thing did you do?"

"Marvelous," he said, kissing her cheeks, her nose, her mouth. "Brilliant, wonderful, *and* marvelous. You forgot that one."

She gave an exasperated cry and began to tickle him unmercifully, until he caught her hands in his and surrendered.

"All right, all right, I'll tell you, I'll tell you all of it," he said, laughing. "Shipley wasn't content with the mere burning of the journals because there was still someone who could talk, who couldn't be bound by his word of honor."

"Aunt Gwendolyn? He meant to hurt Aunt Gwendolyn?"

"No. Shipley's an idiot, but not that much of an idiot. It's *Ignatius*, darling. Shipley plotted to shut one of us up, definitely—but it was that damned parrot."

Sophie leaned back against the desk, her hands clasping the edge. "Ignatius? But—but what possible damage could Ignatius do to Uncle Tye?"

To answer her, he lifted her onto the desk, so that she watched while he went to the corner of the room and pulled the shawl from the parrot's cage. "Coachie, Ignatius," he said. "Coachie."

Ignatius dipped his head a time or two, fluttered his clipped wings and, in a near-perfect imitation of Sir Tyler Shipley, called out: "Demmed coachie! *Squawk!* Quick! My flask! Secrets to tell! *Squawk! Squawk!* Demmed coachie! Secrets to sell! Quick, my flask! *Squawk!*"

Sophie still didn't understand, and said so.

"Neither did I, darling," Bramwell admitted, lifting the cage from the table. "Until I remembered that Ignatius did his little trick in Shipley's presence. Something in his reaction jostled a memory somewhere in the back of my brain. There was nothing about Ignatius in your mother's journals, which confused me at first, until that jostled memory became clearer. After that, it was a fairly simple matter to ask Lorrie to do some checking for me."

He walked back to the desk and took Sophie's hand in his as he walked fiancée and parrot toward the door. "Secrets to tell, Sophie. Secrets to sell. Demned coachie."

Sophie concentrated on the words, but didn't feel in the least enlightened. "No, I still don't understand. I want to, but I'm totally at sea. Bram, would you please just tell me?"

"It had to be about nine or ten years ago, I imagine," he said as they walked down the hallway to the foyer. "Before he gave you the parrot, and during my single Season in Town. Shipley's coachman was beaten into a jelly, nearly killed, right here in the city, inside Shipley's own stables. I remembered it because it caused quite a stir, with all of Mayfair checking under their beds, sure that murderers were everywhere."

"Go on, please," Sophie said, nodding to Bobbit before starting up the staircase.

"Think about it, Sophie. We were at war. Shipley worked in His Majesty's government. He may have been selling secrets, he may not have been. At this late date, I don't suppose it matters. Then again, it may have been the coachie who had secrets to sell, such as where he was driving Shipley. I think that more likely, to tell you the truth."

"Where he drove him? To Wimbledon, you mean, don't you—to see *Maman*, yes?"

"As Shipley was and is married to a very rich, very jealous woman, yes, I do mean Wimbledon. Sir Tyler has a fairly prodigious temper, and he was always good with his fives. I think his coachman was blackmailing him, frankly, threatening him—and that Shipley took umbrage with that idea."

"And beat his own coachman," Sophie said, shivering. "Is the coachman dead? I mean, did he beat him to death? Because, if he did, we certainly cannot allow him—"

"The man lived, Sophie, although he chose to depart for a less violent climate somewhere in Wales. Still, Ignatius must have heard Shipley, absorbed those few words the man spoke in anger, and now he trots them out anytime someone says—" he hesitated, looking down at Ignatius. "Well, you know the word, Sophie. So dear Uncle Tye gave Ignatius to you, to hide the evidence as it were, and now you've brought Ignatius with you to London, where he immediately performed his most dangerous party trick. You can see how that might unnerve Shipley, make him want to turn your beloved parrot into parrot soup."

"Into parrot—*well*!"

Bramwell put a finger to his lips, warning her to silence as they walked past the entrance to the drawing room, where Lady Gwendolyn and Mrs. Farraday were holding a somewhat loud conversation about the straw-bonnet-wilting properties of a thick London fog, and pulled her toward the flight of stairs that led to the bedchambers.

"Yes, darling," he said as they climbed the flight, "Shipley wanted Ignatius dead. Strangled, plucked, and boiled, I imagine. And Lord Upchurch wasn't the first to come to me. Lord Buxley didn't even let me get as far as the street this afternoon after we'd had our small journal-burning ceremony, before he chased after me, warning me that Shipley wasn't satisfied with my solution. That he wanted the bird destroyed. I had thought Shipley might want *you* strangled, darling, but it seems he believed you when you said you'd never breathe a word of anything you know."

"That's because I dazzled him, Bram," Sophie said with a nose-crinkling grin. "And you said dazzling didn't work. Ha!"

"I never said it didn't work, darling," he corrected as he left go of her hand and opened the door to his bedchamber, motioning for her to precede him into the room. "I just said you shouldn't do it. I've had second thoughts about that since this morning, by the way. Dazzle to your heart's content, Sophie, as long as you *love* me."

She watched as he set Ignatius's cage on a low table, amazed at how comfortable she felt in this chamber. Not at all naughty. Just comfortable, because she belonged here. She always would. But when Bramwell came toward her, his intention clear in his smile, she held him off, saying, "But why is Uncle Tye—Sir Tyler—no longer a threat to us, er, I mean, to Ignatius?"

He put his hands on her elbows as she reached out to touch his waist. "Now you're going to have to be brave, darling. I couldn't have Lorrie promise something we couldn't in all good conscience promise, now could I? Couldn't have him say we'd train Ignatius never to say what he says if *that* word came up in conversation. So," he said, looking at her closely, "I'm sending Ignatius to the country, to Selbourne Hall. I've got quite an aviary on my estate, and he'll be comfortable there even when we aren't in residence. In other words, darling, Ignatius has had his last Season." He bent his knees, the better to see into her eyes, and asked, "Do you hate me? I did it for the best."

"You'll march him off in chains, I suppose?" Sophie tried to be stern, but Bramwell looked so apprehensive that she couldn't let him suffer for another moment in the belief that she might hate him for sending Ignatius into a very comfortable exile. "Oh, Bram, don't worry," she said, smiling. "It was the only solution that was fair to everyone. Especially," she continued, her voice dropping to a whisper, "when I consider what happens when he hears anyone say the word *spurs*."

"Spurs?" Bramwell repeated, also whispering. "What does he say?"

She motioned for him to bend his head even closer, and whispered the words into his ear.

"You're kidding!" he exclaimed, looking toward Ignatius, who was grooming himself, oblivious to their hushed conversation. "My God, Sophie—whose voice does he use to say *that*?"

"Well," Sophie told him as she took his hands and began backing toward the bed. "Let's just say that the duke of Wellington probably will be quite pleased to learn that Ignatius will be permanently rusticating on your estate."

"The duke of—Lord, Sophie, I love you!" Bramwell exclaimed, tumbling her onto the bed and following her down.

"Sophie loves you! Sophie loves you!" Ignatius called out in an excellent imitation of his mistress's voice. "Sophie loves you! *Squawk!*"

"You know, I'm going to miss that bird," Bramwell said, smiling, before Sophie took hold of his ears and pulled him down for her kiss.

Epilogue

I know this balcony, love . . .

Give me a thousand kisses, then a hundred, then another thousand, then a second hundred, then yet another thousand, then a hundred.

—Catullus

Kiss till the cow comes home.
—Francis Beaumont

Epilogue

Bramwell stood at the bottom of the stairs, looking up at his wife as she hesitated for a moment before putting out one satin-slipper-clad foot and beginning her descent toward him.

She was perfect. She shimmered in pale green silk, from the knot of material that covered her full breasts, to the sweeping hem that floated down the stairs behind her. Her shoulders were bare, her arms covered in softest white kid to just above the elbows. A magnificent necklace of diamonds and emeralds was put to shame by her shining eyes.

She wore her hair severely pulled back from her face tonight, caught up in some sort of curling cluster at the top of her head, a circlet of diamonds and braided silk holding it in place. Her eyes, wide and faintly tilted, her magnificent cheekbones, her long, delicate neck—all were perfect. There had to be other words, more eloquent definitions, but none suited Sophie better than that single, simple word. Perfect.

And then she smiled at him, and she became more than perfect. She became his Sophie. His Sophie of the crinkled-up nose, playing at duchess, and asking him to join her in the enjoyment of their private joke—because, for as regal and duchesslike as she might appear now, only an hour earlier she had been a shameless wanton, all flash and fire in his arms.

Dear God, how he loved her!

"She becomes more beautiful every day, Bram," Baron Lorimar said, coming up behind him just as Sophie arrived at the bottom of the stairs, then passing him by to offer his arm to his friend's wife. "Your Grace," he drawled, as Sophie slipped her arm through his, "you will send every other woman present at Lady Upchurch's ball weeping into the night the moment you walk through the door."

"How you do flatter me, Lorimar," Sophie said, smiling up at him, dazzling him as Bramwell watched approvingly. "I'm sorry to be so late, but Desiree had the worst time with my hair. It became sadly tangled somehow. Has Bram offered you a glass of wine before we go?"

"Lady Gwendolyn did the honors, actually," the baron told her as they walked into the drawing room, Bramwell trailing behind, shaking his head. "And then she and Sir Wilford took themselves off into a corner, their heads all but pressed together as they fell into some deep conversation or other. You've been giving her lessons, haven't you?"

"Only a few," Sophie admitted, winking at him. "Aunt Gwendolyn found him to be most charming when he came to pay a morning call on me when I first arrived in London, but I think he went away much more interested in her. In fact, Sir Wilford has become nearly a permanent guest in the house of late, isn't that right, Bram?"

"The poor fellow doesn't stand a chance, Lorrie," Bramwell declared with all good humor, touching a hand to the slight bulge in his waistcoat and wondering how he was going to manage slipping Sir Wilford's snuffbox back in his pocket after Peggy had found it in his aunt's clothespress that morning. "Hello, Wally, you're looking fit. Did you and my cousin have a good day?"

Sir Wallace leapt to his feet in order to bow over Sophie's hand. "Better than good, Bram," he said, lifting his glass of lemonade in a toast to the world in general. "Attract the ladies like bees to honey, those dogs of his do. No better place to be these days than riding through the park in Samuel's carriage. I'm thinking of getting myself a couple of hounds of my own as a matter of fact, seeing what they did for Sad Samuel. Well," he then said, looking around the room, "if we're all ready? I want to speak to Bobbit a moment before we go. He's promised to tell me about a most sterling new shop that specializes in custom-fitted gloves."

"He *owns* that shop, Wally," Bramwell told him as Sophie giggled. "And you probably paid for most of it. You, Lorrie, and me. Definitely me."

Sir Wallace looked to each of his friends in turn, colored hotly, and said, "Oh." Then he shrugged, as if accepting of the news. "I still need new gloves, you know, so I suppose that's all right. Isn't it? Shall we go?"

It was nearly three in the morning before the duke and duchess returned to Portland Square, to mount the flights

to their chamber, their arms linked, both of them still bask-
ing in the glow of a most successful evening.

And neither of them quite ready for bed.

"Help me with these fastenings, please, darling," Sophie
said, turning her back to her husband.

"Gladly," he answered, coming over to her and pressing
a kiss against the nape of her neck as he began working at
the closings of her gown. "Hmmm, you taste good."

She turned in his arms as the gown loosened, holding it
to her breasts as she smiled up into his face. "Surely you
aren't still *hungry*, darling?"

"Famished," he admitted as she stepped away from him,
allowing the gown to fall into a puddle at her feet, leaving
her in only the merest of undergarments, a pair of silky
stockings. "And becoming more hungry by the minute."

She held out her arms to him. "Oh, poor darling Bram.
Come here to me. Sophie will fix that. Sophie will fix
everything."

"I can't imagine why I ever wanted you to think you
shouldn't. God, Sophie, but you look lovely, standing there
in the moonlight shining through the windows."

And that's when Bramwell got an idea. A most wonderful, delicious idea. With more haste than care, he stripped
himself out of his jacket, his shirt, his shoes. "Stay right
there!" he ordered as he went over to the bed, ripping the
coverlet from it. He opened the doors to the balcony that
overlooked the darkened Square as Sophie watched, giggling, and spread the coverlet on the narrow landing that
was enclosed by a highly decorative, secluding balustrade.

Satisfied with what he'd done, he then came back into

the room, swept his wife up in his arms, and carried her toward the balcony.

"Bram?" she asked as he gently deposited her on the coverlet and knelt down, preparing to join her.

"You think I'm insane, don't you?" he asked. "That this is insane. We could be seen from the Square, if anyone really looked. We could make utter fools of ourselves. And you want me to take you back inside."

"No, darling," she said, stroking the length of his thigh, so that his mind, which he already considered fairly well lost, spun off into the night, to be replaced by desire. "I just want you to lock those doors behind you. I'm convinced Reese would appreciate that, yes?"